This book is dedicated to my daughter, Thea Kearney, and my friend and Literary Executor, Angelina Oberdan, and to all women who wish to fulfill their creative urges, unencumbered by restrictions put upon them by preconceptions of their gender. It bespeaks the predicament of women artists whose lives were, or are, dominated by patriarchal constructs.

Acknowledgements

The title-page photo of Emily Dickinson is the poet at about age thirty years, or so the author believes. It appears in the back of Richard B. Sewell's biography, *The Life of Emily Dickinson*, (published by Farrar, Straus and Giroux by arrangement with Harvard University Press, 1974, 1980, paperback edition.) It was used by permission of Mr. Herman Abramson, since deceased, who bought it years ago from a bookseller in Greenwich Village, New York City. The name and date in handwriting on the back read: "Emily Dickinson, 1860." See "Selected Bibliography" and "Notes to the Reader" for further explanation herein.

The title page photo of William Smith Clark is included in *William Smith Clark, A Yankee in Hokkaido*, by John M. Maki, published by Hokkaido U. Press, Sapporo, Japan, 1996. Both biographies mentioned here, the Maki and Sewell, are highly recommended reading. Colonel Clark was the founder of The University of Massachusetts at Amherst as an agricultural college. He was a Civil War hero of his region as Maki describes in his biography. The Clark letters come from the aforementioned Maki text, and were published in newspapers now in pubic domain, or are reprinted by permission of Hokkaido U. Press, Japan for this not-for-profit venture.

Dickinson's texts included herein are early, published versions of ED's verses and letters, now in public domain. Every effort was made to insure that all texts used come from public domain editions, edited by Mabel Loomis Todd and Thomas Wentworth Higginson, or Martha Dickinson Bianchi. Any discrepancy will be gladly rectified and is the responsibility of the author, not her publisher. Write to the author daniela@garden.net

The non-fiction *Afterword; Emily Dickinson: Lover of Science and Scientist in Dark Days of the Republic* first appeared in Chelsea Literary Review, Number 81, Spring, 2007. Grateful acknowledgement is due to Chelsea and its editor/publisher, Alfredo de Palchi for permission to reprint the essay herein. © 2007 and 2010 by Daniela Gioseffi.

Wild Nights! Wild Nights!

The Story of Emily Dickinson's "Master," Neighbor and Friend and Bridegroom

A Biographical Novel by

Daniela Gioseffi

With a Non-fiction Afterword

"Lover of Science and Scientist
In Dark Days of the Republic"

Plain View Press
P.O. 42255
Austin, TX 78704

plainviewpress.net
sb@plainviewpress.net
512-441-2452

ISBN: 978-1-935514-44-2
Library of Congress Number: 2009943157

Cover design by Susan Bright.
Cover photograph by Simon Camp,
"Pelham Hills" photo: www.thousandhillsphotography.com

Contents

Afterword By the Author

Notes To the Reader

Acknowledgement is due to Ruth Owen Jones, Amherst historian and guide at the Emily Dickinson Museum, for her article in *The Emily Dickinson Journal*, Vol.XI, No. 2, 2002. Her article aroused my interest in her thesis regarding the true "Master" of Emily Dickinson's texts and helped to inspire this book and its essay/afterword. [See bibliography following *Afterword.*]

I wish to acknowledge Wellspring House, a retreat for writers and artists, in Ashfield, Massachusetts, where parts of this book were written. Ashfield is the birthplace of William Smith Clark, a leading character in the novel. Clark's childhood home still stands in the town. I'm grateful for the quiet hours spent in the Emily Dickinson Room at Wellspring House with its kindly directors, Preston and Ann Browning. The retreat is near Amherst where I visited the Dickinson Museum many times. I acknowledge the guides there who gave interesting tours of both The Homestead and The Evergreens. I acknowledge The Jones Library Special Collections in Amherst, where I enjoyed many hours of reading as I researched this book. I want to note the cordiality of its librarians, particularly, Tevis Kimball, Curator.

I'm indebted to friend, poet, and literary scholar, Angelina Oberdan, for her astute suggestions. I thank Harry Bernstein, author, for his thoughts on an earlier draft. I acknowledge Alfredo de Palchi, editor/poet, for his publication of the afterword in *The Chelsea Review of Literature*, New York: Spring 2007. That publication acquired for me encouraging comments from several writers and poets, i.e. Galway Kinnell, Robert Hass, Alice Quinn, Grace Paley, Pat Falk, Fran Castan, Nina Cassian, and Maurice Edwards. I acknowledge my deceased husband of many years, Dr. Lionel B. Luttinger, for his encouragement. He, too, was a lover of Emily Dickinson's poetry.

The title page photo — which I believe is Emily Dickinson at about thirty years of age — appeared in the back of Richard B. Sewell's biography of *The Life of Emily Dickinson*, (Harvard University Press, 1974), where it was used by permission of Mr. Herman Abramson, since deceased, who had purchased it from a bookseller in Greenwich Village, New York City. The name and date in handwriting on the back of the photo state: "Emily Dickinson, 1860," though the second "i" in the surname is not clearly dotted, a common misspelling of the poet's last name. Opinions vary as to whether it's a portrait of the poet, but Charles Sweetser, a relative of E.D., and Elizabeth Holland, one of E.D.'s closet friends and correspondents, had New York City addresses. It's possible the photo was sent to one of them, or to another correspondent, and ended up acquired by a New York City book dealer.

The hair arrangement, expression, clothing style, and features of the 1860 photo image match those of the well-known youthful daguerreotype of E.D. except that the cheeks are fuller. One feels Richard Sewell would not have included it in his eminent biography, if he did not feel it might very possibly be a photograph of the poet. I sized this photograph of a womanly character in the same dimensions as the well-known girlish daguerreotype, then printed them both on tissue paper in exactly equal dimensions, and placed them over a light making one show through the other. The features match exactly in their spacing, i.e. space between eyes and eyebrows, size of eyes, nose, lips, earlobes. The only discernable difference is that the cheeks are fuller in the mature image marked 1860. It must be remembered that E.D. was ill prior to the making of the famed daguerreotype taken when she was seventeen. That ubiquitous daguerreotype has too thoroughly characterized her as a thin, sickly, somewhat morose girl, despite the fact that it's the poet as a mere teenager of seventeen just arisen from some weeks in a sickbed.

E.D.'s sister, Lavinia, and Mrs. Mabel Loomis Todd, first editor of the poet's work and intimate of the poet's brother, Austin, found the youthful daguerreotype inadequate as a portrayal of the mature poet. E.D.'s face would have become fuller at thirty years of age than it was when she was seventeen and sickly.

Despite the controversy surrounding this photograph, it is included here, because the author feels it represents the mature poet, and her own pronouncement that she had "a gypsy face." One might feel strongly that this is the attractive portrait of a soulful and womanly E.D. The reader can decide. It better matches the character of a fully erotic woman as portrayed, herein — a poet who led a social life — not the reclusive, spinster who has been perpetually mythologized in the American mind. Indeed, the purpose of this biographical novel, and its essay afterword, is to honestly portray the woman who wrote the poetry the world so admires. The book seeks to offer a more accurate reading of E.D.'s texts as a result of knowing her very possible life story as hinted at in her texts and in the factual afterword of this book.

Dickinson's texts, included herein, are early, published versions of her verses and letters, now in public domain. Every effort was made to insure that all texts used come from public domain editions, edited by Mabel Loomis Todd and Thomas Wentworth Higginson or Martha Dickinson Bianchi. Though we E.D. scholars debate a great deal over punctuation, i.e. dashes, periods, commas, or alternatively elocution marks, in the poet's texts — and worry over a choice of word here or there in the original, holographic drafts which gave alternative choices by the poet — these scholarly concerns do not effect the general reader who might find them somewhat pedantic. Many believe that the verses retain their vibrancy in these public domain versions. The labors of Thomas Wentworth Higginson, the poet's first publisher, and Mabel Loomis Todd, her earliest editor, deserve a good deal of respect. They worked from handwritten drafts, many unfinished and of difficult script, before the age of typewriters or computers. One might feel they did a great justice to Dickinson's work in bringing it to the light of publication with conventional punctuation, more easily acceptable at the time she first blossomed into print and found an appreciative audience that helped to preserve her poetic legacy.

Elocution marks, or commas, dashes, or periods offer similar pauses of breath in the reading of a poem. Punctuation, after all, was derived from pauses in the spoken word similar to elocution marks. Elocution was a more important study in Dickinson's day, especially for women, than was written rhetoric. School exams were most often given orally. Dickinson did seem to use conventional punctuation in the few texts that she allowed published anonymously during her lifetime, even if she was, on occasion, unhappy with the publication's editorial liberties. I believe, as do other E.D. scholars, that the dashes in the poet's manuscripts were elocution marks — indications of how the poems should be spoken aloud — but punctuation serves much the same purpose and originated from pauses of human breath that create intelligible speech.

Use of the public domain texts for the purposes of this novel is justified and makes little difference to the general reader. Indeed, many of the poems or verses included in the most recently complete poems of E.D. were never finished and remain elliptical and opaque for that reason. One can easily imagine that E.D. might have been appalled to have every unfinished note or scribble for a poem published as a finished piece. Poet Susan Howe addresses this problem of E.D.'s enigmatic verses in her book, *My Emily Dickinson*. (See bib. following *Afterword*.)

For editions of the poet's texts that are slightly different and brought back to what R.W. Franklin feels were the poet's intent, one can look to his edition of *The Poems of Emily Dickinson*, 1999. One respects Franklin's monumental labors, but who can know for sure the poet's intent? The "Master Letters" herein are not the originals, but are inventions that capture their basic flavor. The actual three "Master Letters," are copyrighted, until 2030, by Harvard University Press and can be secured from bookstores and libraries.

This book was five years in the making and is offered as a not-for-profit venture on the part of the author. Any discrepancies regarding copyrights should be addressed directly to the author at daniela@ garden.net or c/o Plain View Press.

I thank editor, Susan Bright, of Plain View Press for her belief in the vitality of this book as well as for her commitment to women's writing and feminist ideals. I thank Pam Knight for her help with production. Thanks is owed to Galway Kinnell, much admired Pulitzer and National Book Award winning poet; to Robert Hass, former Poet Laureate of the USA; to Alice Quinn, Executive Director of the Poetry Society of America for reading the afterword upon which this biographical novel is based and for encouraging remarks they wrote to me — especially Galway Kinnell who read the essay/ afterword and said: "It should be a book." Though I think he meant for me to write a scholarly biography, I've chosen, as a playwright and poet, to dramatize the facts included in my non-fiction afterword: *Lover of Science and Scientist in Dark Days of the Republic*. E.D. scholars might wish to read the *Afterword*, first.

Daniela Gioseffi, New York, 2010.

Part 1
To Be Alive Is Power

Nature Is What We See....

I climb the "Hill of Science"
I "view the Landscape o'er"
> *Such transcendental prospect*
> *I ne'er beheld before!*

—Emily Dickinson, *The Indicator*
Amherst College: 1852

Summer 1857: "Come Slowly Eden"

Awakened from sleep, Lavinia heard a murmur, then a groan, coming from the dark stairwell out in the hall. For a moment, she thought she was dreaming. She arose from her bed and tiptoed into the hall. The moon beaming in the window made a streak of light across the floor to the back stairwell. She thought she heard skirts rustling down in the darkness. She went to the top of the servants' staircase, a passageway to the scullery with an entrance hall at bottom, an area that had five exits to various parts of the mansion. Lavinia's sister, Emily, had taken to calling it her "Northwest Passage."

Lavinia thought she smelled a faint aroma of meadow grass and muddy boots. She peered down into the dark well and was startled to hear a deep groan, a rustling of cloth, a moan that sounded like Emily's. She thought she heard a man's voice whisper: " I love to hold you in my lap like this, Little Daisy—sweet as the berry wine you give me."

Lavinia listening, thought she heard her sister, Emily, sigh, then a constant breathing, growing deeper. A little frightened, she called softly down the dark stairwell. "Emily, is that you?" She perceived a rustling of crinoline skirts, followed by a tap of boot heels going toward the back of the house. She heard the back door open as someone hurried into the night, and she thought she heard Emily whisper: "Goodnight, Master!"

As Lavinia's eyes grew accustomed to the dark, she saw the shadow of Emily appear climbing upward in her indigo gown with white lace collar. Emily's moonlit hair in disarray made a reddish aura of curls around her pale face. In her hand was a bouquet of daisies.

"It's only me, Vinnie Dear." Emily came breathlessly up the stairs, holding her white crinoline and blue satin skirts high. "Why aren't you asleep?"

"I *was* asleep, Em. Noises woke me!" Lavinia yawned in a whisper. "I thought you were still at Austin's and Sue's."

"I was at Sue's soiree, Sister Dear. I stayed quite late. The guests were as fascinating as ever. Do go back to sleep, now. I'll tell you all about it in the morning. I'm on my way to bed with a bit too much berry wine in my head!" Emily didn't want to wake her ailing mother asleep down the hall. It was Lavinia's turn to stay at home with their sick mother. Their statesman father was, as often, away in Worcester at a convention of his Whig Party.

"Goodnight, Vinnie!" Emily hurried into her bedroom, across from her sister's. "Sleep well." She quietly shut her door, then sighed with exasperation. Once safely inside, she placed her handful of daisies in the pitcher of her washstand, lit the oil lamp, always ready on her writing table, and sat down in front of the window facing Amherst's Main Street. She drew a piece of paper, pen, and inkwell from a drawer in the front of her small table. After a long and thoughtful pause, she began to write:

> *Come slowly, Eden!*
> *lips unused to thee,*
> *Bashful, sip thy jasmines,*
> *As the fainting bee,*
>
> *Reaching late his flower,*
> *Round her chamber hums,*
> *Counts his nectars—enters,*
> *And is lost in balms!*

Summer 1847: Ten Years Earlier

Austin, come quickly, Father's beating the horse to death!

Austin Dickinson, mounted on his stallion, came galloping up the drive. Chickens scattered and his sister Lavinia's many house cats fled from his horse's hooves. He reared his horse to a halt in front of the carriage barn where he found Lavinia, waving her arms frantically.

"Austin, come quickly! Father's beating the horse to death! Emily's come down out of her sick bed and crying at the top of her voice. He ignores her pleas."

"Damn! Why is he beating Romeo?" Austin dismounted in consternation.

"Heaven knows? Perhaps he didn't look humble enough!" Lavinia mocked.

"Will Clark says *never* beat a horse if you want it to obey! Why can't he learn? Everything has to be his stubborn, old way!" Austin muttered angrily, but changed his tone to suit his father as he, with Lavinia, ran into the barn.

Austin found his sister, Emily, weeping and fallen to her knees on the stable floor, trembling and coughing as she implored. "Father, please! The beast meant no harm. Why make him suffer?

Austin quickly intervened. "Father, let me handle the new horse for you! Why upset yourself? You know that Clark used the John Solomon Rarey method to break him in. Romeo doesn't understand whipping!" Austin took the whip from his father's hand as he continued to distract him. "You need to bond with the animal, Father, and he'll be the best horse you've ever had. I'll bring Clark around to show you himself. He's trained perfectly obedient horses for Hitchcock, Tyler, and Williston, too. Calm down, Father. Such rages aren't good for you!"

Austin hoped invoking the names of professors and trustees of Amherst College would make his father listen. He secured the whip from him and turned to his sisters, "Emily, you're trembling like a babbling brook. Vinnie, please take Em upstairs to bed.

"There now, Romeo." Austin gently petted the horse's neck, soothing the welts he found there. "That's a good boy." The horse stopped rearing and whinnying.

Emily, wearing only her thin, white nightdress, allowed herself to be pulled to standing and led away by Vinnie who threw a shawl around her older sister's shoulders. Her auburn hair in loose disarray, Emily coughed as she stumbled toward the house, tears drenching her face. "Thank God, you're home, Austin!" She whispered as Vinnie, the younger and more robust of the two sisters, half carried her into the house.

"Emily, it's only a *beast* after all!" Edward felt a measure of guilt as he addressed his oldest daughter. "Back to bed with you now!"

Austin whispered to the horse his friend Clark had named and advised him to buy. There's a good boy, Romeo!"

"*Romeo*, indeed!" Edward with contempt for the horse's name, voiced not a word of regret for his fit of rage. He threw the carriage harness to the floor. "Tie the stubborn beast to the carriage yourself, Austin!" Squire Dickinson, maintaining his dignity as best he could, picked up his briefcase, brushed the sleeves of his black jacket, and limped from the barn. "I'll ride your horse to my client in Montague instead. See if *Romeo* steps on your boot as he did mine when you harness him! I hope he's not broken my toes. I'll return by evening. Take *Romeo* to your classes at the college."

"Don't heel my horse too hard, Father, please! Ariel flies easily with a touch of the reigns!" Austin called after Edward, a noted lawyer of his rural region who was off to deal with one of his clients in the neighboring hamlet of Montague.

"*Ariel*, indeed!" murmured Edward, again disapproving of Austin's Shakespearean names for their horses. Ignoring his son's directive, he mounted and heeled the horse hard, lurching too quickly forward in a sudden cloud of dust. "Damn!" muttered Edward as he grabbed his hat down tighter, rearing the horse to a slower gallop.

"Ease the reins, Father!" Austin, called after as Edward galloped away. Though he enjoyed the spectacle of his dignified father off in a cloud of dust, cursing and nearly losing his hat, he worried Romeo might have injured his hard working father's foot.

Austin returned to tending Romeo according to the latest Rarey methods—so anti-Puritanical in lack of punitive measures. He reasoned his stern father enjoyed privately mocking the less worldly men of the provincial town, and would eventually—out of necessity—take to modern ways of horse handling. Both of them admired fine horses, so important to the industries of their ancestral village. "I'll have to be absent when father mounts or harnesses after he has a lesson from Master Clark. He'll be embarrassed if I see him being affectionate with the horses." Austin told himself.

Mrs. Dickinson, as usual in her black mourning dress, waited at the kitchen door ringing her hands in her white apron. "Now, Emily, back to bed, Dear! You mustn't defy your Father," she softly reprimanded. She gave only gentle words and an offer of food, but no comforting hug to her daughter. Affectionate display was scarce in Edward's household. "I'll bring a hearty bowl of soup and Chamomile tea as soon as you wash your face. Vinnie will tend you abed."

Though truly concerned about her seventeen year old daughter, Emily Norcross Dickinson spoke with timid resignation. As she, herself, had been, Emily was sick, coughing off and on through the winter and into early spring. Mrs. Dickinson had known much loss to death and dared not feel too deeply. Her parents and two of her brothers died of typhoid, cholera, pneumonia, and consumption. Resigned to "God's ways," she dealt with anxiety by being an obedient housewife, living dutifully as a Calvinist Christian, and offering quiescent kindness with good food and garden flowers wherever she could.

"Father wants us all to sit for our daguerreotypes soon, Emily, before you go off to Mount Holyoke in autumn. He wants us to keep well to have healthy portraits to remember each other by while parted." She spoke softly up the stairwell to her girls, hoping to divert their attention from their father's horsewhipping. "I do not always agree with your father, but I never defy him. It's no use. He'll have his way." Returning to tend to her soup she thought: "Thank Goodness, Edward's gone until evening. God forgive me, but we have peace in the house. I'll cheer Emily with a nosegay from my garden on her tray."

With the heavy duties of her household, and her husband's constant entertaining of trustees, professors, seminarians, and students, from Amherst College, plus his clients coming and going, and his law apprentices boarding with the family, Mrs. Dickinson had no time or patience for the books her daughter, Emily, loved to read and ponder. Lavinia, her hardiest daughter, helped with housekeeping, while Emily often hid in her room reading and resting from wayward rambles in the woods hunting wildflowers. Emily, when not ill, helped with gardening and baking to which she'd taken quite well, ultimately outdoing her mother's prowess at baking Indian-rye and ginger breads.

Summer 1847: After Church a Dull Tea

The flowers of the field are mine…

Squire Edward Dickinson stood in the first-row pew of the Congregational church, with his wife, son, and two daughters, neatly arrayed beside him. The family of five wore their understated, Sabbath attire. They returned their hymnals to the rack and kept their well-thumbed *King James Bibles* in hand to carry home with them.

The most distinguished families of Amherst always waited behind the assemblage to exit last from the Meeting House of the First Church of Christ. At the corner of South Pleasant Street and Northampton Road, the brick, meetinghouse in Classic Revival style, with its large Ionic columns and white New England steeple, had stood at that corner since 1829 in the village of Edward 's birth.

A prominent lawyer, trustee, and treasurer of Amherst Seminary, Mr. Dickinson stood stiffly erect directing his family in a whisper: "Emily, children, no moving ahead. Mind your manners better than others. I want to invite Reverend Colton to tea now after service," he explained softly as he ushered them ahead of him from the pew. The church was the very one his father Samuel Fowler Dickinson had attended when he'd built the brick mansion across from the church, now beyond his means and lost to his family. "Be sure to tell Reverend Colton how excellent his sermon was, as I wish to talk with him about the railroad and acquire his approval for the station site. Perhaps, he'll mention what a fine enterprise it will be for the village in next Sabbath's sermon, and stock will be easier to distribute."

He turned to Emily Norcross to continue whispering his commands: "It's best, My Dear Wife, that *you* invite the Reverend most cordially to tea, and to stay for lunch, as it's all of your labor. Say how well you enjoyed his sermon. Austin, you second the invitation with enthusiasm. Emily and Lavinia, you repeat your mother's cordiality with a sweet curtsy. Be patient as the exit greetings are almost complete."

Emily and Lavinia Dickinson, arm in arm, followed their parents and brother, Austin, down the aisle. "Oh, Vinnie, now we shall have to attend Father's tea, and the whole of this lovely day will be taken with his railroad promotion!" Emily Dickinson—petite and doe-eyed with her thick hair pulled tightly into an auburn bun at the back of her head under her brown, straw bonnet—surreptitiously whispered into her younger sister's ear. The girls were a year and a half apart in age and shared adjacent rooms in their white, Victorian, frame house on North Pleasant Street not far from the church center and adjacent to the village graveyard.

"Emily Elizabeth, please, you know it peeves Father when you whisper after he speaks."

"Yes, Mother, we apologize," answered Lavina, always outwardly agreeable and inwardly rebellious.

Emily Norcross, a petite woman, was an older version of her namesake. She was dressed as usual in a dark Puritan gown with an ivory brooch held by a ribbon at her throat, and straw bonnet tied beneath her chin. She mildly scolded her daughter. "Emily, you've left the new sun umbrella Father brought you from Boston in our pew. Fetch it, please, quickly.

"Yes, Mother." Emily hurried back to her pew where she found the handsome junior seminarian, William Smith Clark, starting down the aisle. "Ah, Miss Dickinson, you forgot your parasol! I was bringing it to you." His cheerful and intense gaze stung her with shyness as he turned the handle of her sun shield toward her and bowed slightly from the waist, keeping his intense blue eyes directly peering into her large brown ones.

"Thank you kindly, Mr. Clark." She said, trying to look him in the face, but finding she hardly could.

"Such a lovely summer's day. Please call me *Will* if you *will!*" He smiled intently. Shall I walk you home as I did from the meadow last week when I found you picking daisies? What a splendid chat we had! I liked when you said; 'I hope you love birds, too. It is economical. It saves going to Heaven.' I was also pleased to see you know much about wildflowers. Most Amherst ladies only know the cultivated plants of their gardens."

Emily was astounded at the handsome senior student's invitation and his exact recitation of her words. She had met Will Clark crossing the meadow on her way home from Amherst College bringing her father, the college treasurer, his lunch basket a few days earlier. As she paused to fill the emptied basket with wild daisies from the Dickinson meadow on Main Street, Will Clark greeted her and walked her home to North Pleasant Street.

There was an awkward silence as Emily smiled back, and then she found herself saying: "I've walked a good deal in the woods hunting wild botanicals."

Will Clark eyed Emily Dickinson closely as she spoke. He'd been thinking much about her since they'd met in the meadow. "She's not beautiful, yet attractive. Her eyes are a bright, chestnut. Her hair's a rich auburn. Her teeth and skin are fine. She's demure and brightens if she relaxes. She's shy, and I enjoy penetrating a woman's shyness. She's exquisitely neat in her dress like my mother, and loves to have flowers about her. She's witty and articulate, and of good family. I'll court her by teasing." He thought.

"Weren't you afraid that snakes and goblins would get you, Miss Emily?" he goaded.

Emily read his thoughts, but as she felt a tinge of condescension in his question, she answered with spunk. "When much in the woods as a little girl, I was told that the snake would bite me, that I might pick a poisonous flower, or goblins kidnap me, Sir, but I went along and met no one but Angels—who were far shyer of me than I could be of them—so I haven't that confidence in fraud, Sir!"

Emily knew that Will Clark, an acquaintance of her brother's at school, was among the top science students at Amherst Seminary, to be graduated at next year's commencement with the class of 1848. She knew Clark loved to ramble in the woods, up hills and into caves looking for gemstones, beryl, and rare botanical specimens. Indeed, she knew he put himself through college with such labors, selling valuable finds he'd located around the countryside. "How exciting it would be to hike with him in search of nature's rarities!" She mused silently.

Will Clark was well aware that Emily's grandfather, Samuel Fowler Dickinson, had founded Amherst Seminary. He decided that Emily—daughter of the college treasurer, a leading citizen, and the most respected lawyer of Amherst—would make an excellent catch for a wife. A small wren of a girl less than five-feet tall and slender, Emily Dickinson resembled her gracious if shy mother whom he knew kept a good and frugal home. He'd enjoyed sumptuous, student meals at Mrs. Dickinson's hearth. He was ambitious to find himself a proper wife who would insure his societal ambition to escape the poverty of his father. Dr. Atherton Clark, a very Christian country doctor doled out medicine to poor rural folk—giving his ministrations far too inexpensively for his own family's good.

Emily felt the attraction between herself and Will Clark. As was the custom, for Amherst students to dine, upon occasion, with villagers, William Smith Clark had sat at table with Emily, her brother Austin, and her father on a few occasions, and she had met him, too, at social teas held by the college President, Professor Hitchcock. Young ladies of the village were invited to socialize in polite company with students of the seminary.

"I'd enjoy your company, Will…" She began, but Vinnie, seeing Emily was delayed against their father's command, and always curious about young men of the college, hurried up the aisle and took her older sister's arm, surreptitiously poking her in the ribs.

"Emily, Father's waiting!" Vinnie smiled demurely at Mr. Clark—whom she knew as a charming acquaintance of her brother. The village was small and the congregation intimate enough that all in some degree knew each other—especially those associated with Amherst Seminary so central to the town. Will Clark was three years older than Austin. As an upper classman, particularly admired for his prowess at science and entertaining oratory, he commanded respect from Austin and his friends. Wherever Clark went, villagers flocked around him to hear his new ideas. Emily and Lavinia had often seen Will Clark, surrounded by attentive listeners on the corner of Main and Pleasant Streets, or on the village commons or lawns of the college, telling adventurous stories of his search for beryl in the hills, his discovery of fossils, gemstone or rare flowers, his new ideas for their agricultural society. With bravado, he told of his plans to study in Europe or go West in search of gold.

"Good Sabbath to you, Mr. Clark! Forgive me, but Mother awaits Emily's attention."

Mr. Clark, bowed his head to the Dickinson sisters. "A very good Sabbath day then, Miss Lavinia, Miss Emily."

Emily glared ever so briefly at her sister. "As I was about to say, Will, I would enjoy your company, but Father has duller plans for me to take tea with Reverend Colson regarding railroad ventures. Will you forgive me? Perhaps, we can soon walk homeward another day."

"I most certainly understand your father's ventures *always* come first, Miss Emily. That's a fact of the village. Perhaps, another day then, *and soon?*"

Emily, gaining courage smiled directly into his eyes to demonstrate her sincerity, "Yes, another day if the goblins and snakes of the woods don't get me." She allowed herself to be led away by her sister.

Will Clark enjoying her retort called softly after her: "Or if those shy angels of the wood you speak of do not tempt you away with them."

Emily hid her thrill at his words, at the fact that he had accurately remembered hers and responded with wit—just as her brother Austin, whom she so adored, would have. Lavina, on the other hand, giggled helplessly if softly enough to be undetected by her mother.

Their mother demurely addressed their father as they were about to exit the church.

"I shall invite the reverend most cordially to tea and lunch, Edward, since that's your wish, though there's so much work for me and the girls to accomplish before the commencement celebration coming soon."

"I shall take the Reverend for a ride in our new carriage, after lunch, My Dear, to show him the chosen railroad site. Thus you and the girls can get on with your planning for commencement festivities."

"Very well, My Dear." Mrs. Dickinson complied unquestioningly, as usual, with her husband's wishes. Edward Dickinson exited the front portal of the Puritan church leading his family forth to greet Reverend Colton who was offering salutations to each departing family as they went off into the summer sun.

"Good Sabbath to you, Squire Dickinson, Mrs. Dickinson, Miss Emily Elizabeth, Miss Lavinia Norcross. William Austin, My Good Fellow!" The Reverend quickly acknowledged each member of the family by name, proud of his prowess at knowing all individually, but paused at Austin—feeling it his duty to particularly befriend all up and coming young men of the village. "Ah, Austin, I hear you may already be among the few to make our Alpha Chapter of Phi Beta Kappa when we bring it to our seminary! Your freshman studies are going well. Master Clark, who will be graduated next year, is the only other student doing so well. The trustees, particularly Mr. Williston, will be offering Mr. Clark a professorship, and an induction into Phi Beta Kappa, retroactively, should he decide to return to our beloved valley from Germany where he intends to acquire a Ph.D. Perhaps, he shall be our *first* Ph.D. professor—and I hope you shall be among our next when you finish your studies hence, Austin. Thanks to your father, the future of Amherst College grows rosier every day!"

"We'll see, Reverend. Young men are finding opportunities in the West." Austin replied.

"Ah, but I understand that you're going to teach in North Boston for a bit when you've done at Amherst. You'll manage to civilize those immigrant Irishmen to our New England manners. No small triumph, My Boy! We're most happy to have you with us studying at your Grandfather's own fine seminary after your spell at Williston Academy."

"Yes, Reverend, and I'll be off to Cambridgeport and Harvard when I finish my studies at Amherst—though I should like to go to Germany as Clark will. Father believes an education in Boston is every bit as good as one in Europe, I'm afraid."

"Well he is absolutely correct, My Good Boy! Our American universities are coming up in the world, and we Yankee patriots must support them. Why should you have to go to Germany? Yale was good enough for me and made a fine lawyer of your father."

"I prefer Harvard Law School. It has a more modern attitude, and my uncle Joel Norcross is in Cambridge. I will have family there."

"Ah, My Dear Austin, I fear you shall find many Transcendentalists at Harvard to corrupt your good Calvinist upbringing! Beware of losing your Salvation, but Harvard is a good school for law as I understand. I'm pleased you'll study here in Massachusetts." Reverend Colton, with his beatific gaze, white hair, and neat beard always seemed most sincere, if not vibrant, in what he conveyed. "We need your venerable Dickinson stock here in our Pioneer Valley, Sir. I hope you will never consider going Westward in vain search of gold as so many young fools who have come to naught."

"Susan and Martha Gilbert's brothers are doing very well in Michigan," answered Austin. "With all due respect, Reverend, I do hear of great riches to be had in the West with its long growing season and rich farmland."

"Perhaps so, but what a pity that the Gilbert brothers left their orphaned sisters and went West. A good Puritan's duty is first to his family and his own community. Isn't it so, Edward? And, poor Susan Gilbert has had to go off to Utica New York to live with her aunt, while Martha and Harriet stay here working in Mr. Cutler's store, day and night! Miss Susan plans to teach, I hear. A pity for a woman to have to work outside the home where her truest duty is, I say."

"Indeed, Reverend, exactly my sentiments." Edward Dickinson agreed.

Reverend Colton—intimate with his congregation—was helping Edward persuade Austin of his future course.

Edward offered the silent prompting of a glance at his wife and at his unspoken command she uttered sweetly, "Dear Reverend Colton, won't you please have tea with us and stay for lunch, too, if you please. We'd be so honored by your presence—after that splendid sermon on frugality of the soul—a subject I was so glad to have the children hear."

Austin enjoined with feigned enthusiasm: "Indeed, a fine sermon it was Reverend—on the importance of saving *both* the spirit and the purse for a rainy day."

"It's a pity your Grandfather Samuel, a good and well intended man, did not have your appreciation for such prudence of the purse, though no man on earth could question his generosity of soul or Godliness. Your father and I have spoken often of your grandfather's silent suffering. A pity your father had to sell his noble family home to assume your grandfather's debts." Again, Reverend Colton is helping Edward to teach Austin not to fall into the trap of his grandfather, Samuel Fowler Dickinson, who bankrupted the college and himself in his service to Christian education.

Edward had found his only son and heir to the family fortunes, Austin, a bit too spendthrift with his allowance, buying fancy clothes and books full of new, liberal, ideas. Edward had asked Reverend Colton to preach on the issues of frugality of spirit and pocketbook to warn Austin to be prudent.

As the family, with their pastor in tow, began their walk toward home, Reverend Colton nodded toward the large brick Federal style mansion across Main Street. "I pray one day, for your father's sake, you shall again take your rightful place in that fine home."

Though he knew the Godly man well intended, Edward was embarrassed by the reference to his Father Samuel's financial ruin. "My father's duty to the village academy and the seminary went too far for his own good. As I've often told Austin, it's important to keep one's feet on the shore as one pulls the boat in. Some day, God willing, we shall possess the Dickinson homestead again. But for now, Mr. and Mrs. Mack are most happy there, Reverend, and we are glad for their comfort—despite their alien Transcendental ways! My family is perfectly content in our comfortable home on North Pleasant Street. I was born on that street, and it's like being home as when a boy. Therefore, Good Reverend, save the strength of your prayers for the more needy among our village. My wife's made a fine home on North Pleasant Street."

"Indeed. None in the village has such a spirit for improving our whole lot as you do, Edward. Your industry benefits all. Amherst has its truest Patriot in you. I understand you succeeded in venturing to bring the railroad to our doors!"

"Yes, but it may still take years to have the tracks come this way from Springfield and onto Belchertown. I must raise more capital with stock ventures. I started some time ago to plan for it. The sooner the locomotive makes her stop here, the easier it will be to expand the student body of our seminary. The sooner we expand the student body, the more teachers we can employ to teach our Christian virtues for the Glory of All Mighty God."

Lavinia whispered into Emily's bonnet. "And the sooner more handsome young men will come to Amherst for our gleaning, Em?" The sisters laughed softly as they strolled behind their father, brother, and the reverend through the muddy road, lifting the hems of their petticoats and dresses to the ankles of their high-button boots to avoid puddles. The unpaved roads of Amhest were full of deep carriage ruts and hoove prints.

"That's if they don't all go West after being graduated!" Emily whispered back.

"Hush, girls, Father's speaking." Mrs. Dickinson walked behind her husband with the girls to keep them in check. "You know he dislikes whispering when he speaks," she reprimanded softly. Then added with a wink: "He can't bear not knowing what you're saying!"

Austin, wearing his new summer suit from a Boston shop, walked tall beside his father pretending to be intent on the conversation. Actually, he was watching the young ladies, with their sun bonnets, ribbons, and flowing Sunday gowns, parade down the street after church. He caught sight of Martha Gilbert walking with the Cutlers on the opposite side of the road toward their general store in the village and offered a gentlemanly tip of his hat. Austin fancied Martha for her sweet shyness, so like his mother's.

Emily noticed Will Clark rambling ahead down Main Street with other young ladies and gentleman, entertaining them with his talk. They were all laughing roundly at what he was saying. His hands gestured freely. There was such a sense of freedom in his swagger and bravado. Emily envied his poise and assurance. She walked obediently with her sister and mother, behind her father and brother, wishing she could be with Clark and his company of revelers. As her family with Reverend Colton approached North Pleasant Street and turned off from Main, Clark and his youthful entourage went south toward the college. Emily's spirit enviously followed Clark as the Reverend droned on.

"With the railroad come to Amherst, Edward, more villagers will be in need of a lawyer who can settle land deeds and administer their contractual affairs. Our industry grows so that we shall have the largest factory for straw hats and baskets in the region. I see your wife and daughters have their summer bonnets from Amherst's own industry?"

"Of course, Reverend! The factory does well. I met with the board of directors this week. They're ready to offer more shares. The factory buys all of my rowan, and everyone else's, too. There are many Irish workers coming here to till our land and work in the factory. The village has grown to nearly 3,000 this year. If we can sell enough stock in it, the government in Washington will grant us a supplement to bring the railroad here and make the village more attractive for graduating students to remain and put the outlying lands to good agricultural use."

"Our rocky land full of stumps and boulders fetches smaller price these days. Our short growing season tempts more and more young men of the valley Westward to take advantage of The Louisiana Purchase." Reverend Colton went on. "But, we have found fossils and meteorites, and precious stones in our valley. Young Will Clark's discoveries of valuable beryl and gemstones here have encouraged young men toward geological pursuits. Professor Shepard says The Smithsonian Institute at Harvard wishes to buy one of his specimens. All nonsense compared to the values of the study of scripture, I say, but it's a sign of the times. More's the pity! Young men are turning from the study of the Bible to science everyday. But, we need to keep scholars who can improve our bounty here and learn modern science in our penitent valley! Mr. Clark, bright as he is, has afforded to stay among us as a seminarian because of his rock hunting expeditions. He could not have managed the tuition otherwise."

Edward nodded agreeably. "Indeed, I know, Reverend. We're planning on expanding our studies at the seminary to chemistry, agriculture, animal husbandry, botany, geology and other sciences 'in service to the glory of God!' as President Hitchcock is fond of saying. We must have more young Yankees willing to stay in our valley for the sake of our simple Christian virtues, even if it unfortunately means more science and less Bible study."

"Dickinsons have been in this valley for more than a hundred years, Austin—even before our founding fathers declared our Great Union and our Freedom from The Crown! We need more young men of fine families like yours to stay in our Pioneer Valley. Amherst needs you! You come of venerable Yankee stock, Dear Boy, as I'm sure your father's told you!"

"Indeed, Reverend, father *has* told me such many times." Austin turned to wink at Emily and Vinnie who knew their father's constant litany.

"Indeed enough times to fill the bucket of the moon." Emily whispered into Vinnie's hat, and their mother ignored it smiling, too. Mrs. Dickinson had heard the stories of Dickinson venerability too often. Edward Dickinson, fairly modest in most ways, was greatly proud of his New England stock, his village, and its seminary founded by his father.

The Reverend followed Edward into the front door of his large house. He gestured Reverend Colton into the parlor where the preacher knew he would soon be given a fine lunch at the hands of Mrs. Dickinson. The reverend settled into the comfort of a red velvet, chair across from Squire Dickinson's. Mrs. Dickinson gave each of the three men a crystal goblet of homemade berry-wine on a silver tray. The Reverend sipping his comfortably in his cordial surroundings felt the need to compliment his host.

"You've done a splendid job as treasurer, Edward. All the trustees are so confident in your abilities. Amherst College is becoming the best seminary in the region. Your father—Samuel, the most devout man I ever heard of in the entire Connecticut River Valley—would be proud to know that you're redeeming his vision. You, and Trustee Williston, and President Hitchcock have retrieved his blessed seminary from ruin and turned it into a reputable college. We're full of gratitude for your labors."

Emily and Vinnie went into the scullery to doff their bonnets and don their aprons in order to help their mother serve lunch.

In the front parlor, Reverend Colton took a long sip of berry wine and muttered on. "You are always in our prayers, Edward, for so many here depend on your abilities to expand our good industries, and now you bring us a railroad. Bless you! We shall bring more souls from the cities to be redeemed here in our penitent valley—away from the vain temptations so readily found in Springfield, and Boston!"

"Your prayers are appreciated by all of us, Reverend. After lunch, we'll drive in my new carriage to see the spot up Main Street where the station can be located. I'll show you how the train can continue on through Belchertown. We've a fine new horse trained by Mr. Clark at the college. Some new idea of training horses devised by one John Solomon Rarey."

"Splendid! I've heard of his techniques from Will Clark. I shall enjoy an afternoon ride on such a lovely summer's day as this one. Amherst seminary's trustees are all astir about the railroad. My vote on the village council shall surely be with you."

"Dear Reverend, thank you, again for your sermon on frugality," said Mrs. Dickinson as she returned to refill his glass from her crystal decanter. "Edward has taught me the importance of frugality from the very beginning of our marriage. I'd have it no other way, as my father was of a similar spirit. Can I get you a pillow? Is your chair comfortable enough, Reverend?"

"Quite, thank you!" nodded the Reverend.

"Yes, Reverend, thank you for a fine sermon," enjoined Austin, yet again, attempting to fulfill his father's wishes, even as he retrieved the latest copy of the influential *Springfield Republican* from the parlor table. Its news interested him much more than the bellicose pronouncements of his elders. "There's an article here about locomotive travel by the editor, Samuel Bowles, which I shall inspect and inform you about momentarily." He offered the last by way of excuse to bow out of the conversation all too obsequiously filled with compliments to his father.

Emily had returned to serve a tray of *hors d'oeuvres*. Imbued with Will Clark's ebullience, she could barely contain herself.

"Yes, thank you, Reverend, but I'm so glad that God is *not* so frugal in bringing us so *many* lovely flowers this summer! Are not His wild roses beside the road stunning in their aroma? God's honeysuckle bushes and greenery and many plush daisies nod their heads so radiantly in His sunny fields! I am grateful to our beneficent God for the opulent splendors of His summer bounty! I am thrilled by His *generous* and luxurious garden here on our blessed earth!" Emily sighed and curtsied, holding out her tray to the Reverend who regarded her in astonishment. "I'm so grateful for Our Lord's *generosity*. His glorious lack of prudence!"

In Emily's mind, she was fulfilling the ideals of her botany text at Amherst Academy where she'd completed her final year of study. At the same time, she was having a bit of private fun with Austin and Vinnie by stirring the conversation with some *rapture*—an emotion held down by their Puritanical father and the reserved, Calvinist reverend.

Lavinia repressed laughter. Edward Dickinson cleared his throat at his daughter's off-the-point pronouncement. Austin smiled broadly at Emily, sharing the joke while noting his stiff father's discomfort. He imagined his father's assumption that Emily must have been dreaming to go off on such a contradictory tangent.

"Thank you again, Reverend, for your fine sermon on frugality of the soul." Lavinia curtsied handing Reverend Colton another glass of berry wine to cover for her sister. "Emily and I were much impressed."

"You're welcome, Miss Lavinia," answered the reverend, glaring at Emily.

"Ah, well, Reverend." Squire Dickinson quickly interceded. "The young ladies do love their spring flowers, and like to cheer us with bouquets for our table and nosegays for our desk. My dear wife has taught Emily great love of the garden. They're always out there together through spring and summer, tilling flowers and vegetables."

"Master Leonard Humphrey at the Academy tells me that Miss Emily excels in her botany classes—but I hope not to the detriment of her *theological* studies." Reverend Colton warned. "We'd hope with her silver tongue to have her graduate a fine missionary wife from Mistress Lyon's Mount Holyoke one day. She can help to gather in the heathen with her pronouncements."

"Oh, Reverend, we do not wish for our little Emily to travel away from us in foreign lands. Though we'll send her to Mistress Lyon's seminary in South Hadley, it shall be for the purpose of staying in our blessed valley and finding a fine Yankee husband who will make her a good Puritan wife," Edward assured him.

"Mistress Lyon requires high scores in theology and scripture on her entrance examination for admission to Mount Holyoke, and unless Miss Emily's scores in *theology* are as good as those in botany she may not enter." The reverend, feeling he was doing his job, turned to give Emily a reprimanding look which made her shrink back into her collar, and lower her large chestnut eyes like a wren ceasing its song.

"I shall do very well in theology and scripture, Reverend, I promise you." Emily's full lips pouted. "I can recite many passages from scripture by heart. Especially from *Revelations*."

"And you, Master Austin, shall do so well in your law studies that one day you shall take your father's place in the firm and be as much a village patriot as he. Yes?" The reverend smiled at the young man who, startled from his newspaper, pulled himself tall to seem attentive.

"That is my plan for him." Edward said proudly, but refrained from smiling as he rose, sat beside Austin, and gently took the newspaper from his hands to tuck it behind the sofa.

Austin gave a sidelong glance at Emily and she smirked back at him. Their practiced expressions said, "There goes father again, ruling his dynasty without a thought to our dreams."

Summer 1847: "I Hear a Funeral In My Brain"

Upstairs in Emily's bedroom, the sisters rested after lunch. "If father ever condescends to smile at a rose or a robin, I'll faint to see his face crack!" Emily complained to Lavinia as they doffed their gowns and put on their white housedresses to help their mother with the washing up after lunch. Emily flung herself down on her bed and raised her arms to the ceiling, arching her auburn paisley shawl aside with one dramatic gesture. "How can anyone ignore the glory of this summer day, Vinnie, to speak of frugality and railroads? Ah, I could faint from palsy just to breathe the scent of the orchard full of fragrant peaches with one gold cheek and one pink one so soft and inviting—bobbing as the bobolink serenades them."

"Dear Em, I think you are dreaming of Will Clark's face more than peaches. I saw him singing on our fence like a whippor*will* when he walked you home from the meadow the other day, carrying your basket full of daisies." Lavinia was fond of teasing Emily about boys. There were always plenty of young men from Amherst college coming and going to and from their father's house so near the campus. "But, do be careful what you say in front of Father's colleagues. You know he was angry with you last Sabbath for commenting on *photosynthesis* as the sheerest *poetry* of God—from that botany book Master Humphrey lent you—instead of reciting an aphorism from scripture. Be careful, or you'll have us stuck in the house all autumn praying for our ruined souls instead of out hay riding with Austin's handsome college chums!"

"Oh, Lavinia, you and your flirtations with students will get you in trouble with father, too. If he saw you sitting on Mr. Lyman's lap, twisting your long curls around his neck, he'd have horsewhipped you!"

"Oh Em, you know that stern as Father is, he never raises a hand to us."

"But he has his ways of punishing with his silent treatment and his looks that curl our toes. He'll have us baking, cooking, and serving the trustees, mannequin professors, and the students at their commencement to keep us in check! Mother would die of the labors of such a party all by herself. We'll be helping mother serve at his annual commencement tea, and you'll have your fill of students on the lawn then!"

"Yes, Em, we'll be allowed to charm and entertain the worthiest graduates—after a week of hard labors. Churning butter, dusting stairs, beating the parlor rugs, baking breads. Ah, but Em, it will be worth it! Lyman will be there!"

"Vinnie, I'll gather the nuts and berries, and arrange the flowers, if you'll dust the stairs and clean the dining room and parlor with Mother.

"Surely, Em! I'd rather dust and sweep the house than pick among the sticky bushes. It's less hot and thorny and full of bee stings. You have my contract! That is if you promise to be the one to play the piano and sing hymns for Father's guests after tea. My piano playing is not so good as yours."

"Very well, Vinnie, we have a contract, though I'd rather play songs than hymns for Father, but dust makes me sneeze! How I love to wander in the fields now in summer with wildflowers abloom, bees buzzing, and robins singing their morning and evening vespers!"

"Especially when there's the hope of meeting Mr. Clark, your whippor*will* in the meadow!"

"Oh, Vinnie, hush about Clark. What's the use? He'll be off to Williston Academy to teach and then he'll sail to Germany, and I'll be off to Mount Holyoke, and…"

"Does it break your heart to think of it? Will Clark's so handsome, smart, and witty. He's perfect for you. You'd be soul mates rambling through the woods in search of specimens!"

"Father would never consent to Will Clark, even if he should ask for my hand, Vinnie. He's a poor lad, born of a country doctor. Father says, we must marry men of good Calvinist stock and fine means, or not marry at all!"

"Why risk your health in childbirth for a poor man's poor children?" Vinnie imitated their Father's voice precisely to make Emily laugh. Then, she imitated her mother's cadence perfectly. "Father will have his way; no use arguing."

Emily laughed again at Vinnie's skillful mimicry. "Luckily our stash of berry wine is still full from last summer the way that mother doles it out so frugally—unless it be to Father's guests! So we'll have plenty for the commencement celebration. I'll save some of the sweetest berries I pick for you to soothe your throat from the dusting. But, the baking will be wondrously huge this year. We shall need enough teacakes and gingerbread loaves to feed a hefty army. There are more students being graduated this year than ever before. I must help mother make dozens of cream puffs. I'll go to market on Monday for flour and ginger, salt and sugar. The churning will begin on Tuesday. It will be nothing but house labors. Picking wine berries and walnuts will be my only sport this week."

"Says Austin these days: 'Father has helped to develop this town from a tiny village to a thriving hamlet in the shortest time, and we must be proud patriots of her!' " Vinnie mimicked her brother's deeper tone with such accuracy that Emily was regaled with laughter.

"Austin says so many things with such a *hurrah* and a new manly voice now he's come home from Williston Academy, Vinnie. You have his sound exactly! I fear you'll run away and join Booth's Theatre Company the next time it tours Northampton!"

"Austin is feeling his oats! Such manly power as he gallops up the drive! He scares my kittens to death! All the chickens run for their lives, Em! How will we bear it when he's gone to Cambridgeport and doesn't bring his college chums calling in the parlor?"

"He still has three more years to study here, thank goodness. After that, we'll be stuck in the kitchen serving Father's clients and his mannequin professors!" Mother will never intercede for us as Austin does with father. We will be as lost to the scullery as she, obeying father's every wish for cakes, donuts, tea, and sherry—fetching to and fro like innkeepers. I'm so weary of father's meetings in the front parlor. I have to sit in silence until spoken to. "*Ladies should be demure!* says Father, but Austin can talk his head off telling jokes, and father beams."

"Ah, but I noted you didn't mind fetching for Will Clark when he was here at Austin's meeting of the Horticultural Society! He'd make a lovely husband for Ms. Emily Elizabeth Dickinson, Belle of Amherst."

"Well, Master Clark's not a mannequin! He's so gentle and feeling with horses. I find him kind and lively. Unfortunately, he debates too roundly about Transcendentalism and a woman's right to a profession. Father would never consent.

"You must have a man of good means!" says Father.

"Look how he frowned at poor George Gould when he came to dinner with Austin last week. I like George so! Father would never agree to George Gould or Will Clark as my suitors."

Vinnie continued to imitate their father: "These young whippersnappers with their newfangled ideas and empty pockets! Girls beware!"

"Clark believes that Transcendentalism furthers science with its reverence for God's Natural Creation, and I agree. From what I read in an article in the *Springfield Republican*, Ralph Waldo Emerson's ideas are good for women's education, Vinnie. I think I prefer his beliefs to Father's Calvinism."

"Don't talk that way, Emily! Father would be beside himself to hear you, but I must admit that Professor Clark *is* one of God's great *natural* creations, so handsome is he! Oh, Em, it is so unfortunately true that you shall be off to Mount Holyoke, and Master Clark shall be off to Williston Academy and then Germany! Perhaps, you'll find a nice professor at Holyoke, as handsome as Mr. Clark."

"Oh, Vinnie, it is all girls there and all the teachers are women, too. You know that, don't you? There are no masters like Master Humphrey at Amherst Academy. I cannot behave like a boy any longer, and must grow to be a woman and wear long skirts—as much as I regret it. Only girls and women and prayers shall greet me in South Hadley next term. And I shall study Latin and Greek all day and *theology* all night. I'll be so homesick for you and Austin."

"No Em, father says you will study geology, botany, astronomy and philosophy to glorify Our Lord as well. But, sad day, you won't have your favorite head master, Leonard Humphrey, as your botany preceptor to lend you all his texts. I saw they are hidden beneath your bed with a Valentine you are composing, and with Valentine's Day so far off, too.

"Oh Vinnie, that was last year's Valentine. And what were you doing with your nose under my bed?"

"Why dusting of course, Dear Sister, to save you the labor as usually I do, and there were all Mr. Humphrey's botany books—his signature inside the covers, with not a speck of dust on one, all still warm from your hands and heart." Vinnie giggled.

"Well, Father thinks I should be churning butter for Mother or baking his favorite ginger-bread—all day billowing at the oven fire instead of enjoying botany books for fun."

"That's what you get for making such good gingerbread to be Father's favorite, Em!"

"Father is such a contradiction to me, Vinnie. He disparages suffragists who demand that women be allowed to vote, but supports our education for the glory of our supposed future husbands. Yet, he's tyrannical toward us, and Mother, feeling all our learning is only to glorify his home and entertain his guests. Mother cares not a snit for reading or writing, only for her household duties, church committees, and Bible Society—always seconding Father's opinions without a thought of her own."

"But, Mother doesn't seem to mind bending to his will."

"As far as we can see, she doesn't, but I wonder how she really feels. I've had to spend hours in my room preparing for my admittance exam to Holyoke—studying mathematics, ecclesiastical history, geometry. Father is such an ardent believer in the benefit of a girl's boarding school experience, even if it means sending me miles from home in September. I wish I could be sixteen forever and always at home with you and Austin, Vinnie. Why do our youthful days have to end! I'll die of loneliness without you."

Emily stood and gazed sadly past her garden and to the granite headstones of the graveyard beyond her upstairs window. So many of my dearest friends have met the Angel of Death these past winters, Vinnie. It scares me to go away." Emily's face was deeply pensive as she stared from her upstairs window at the graveyard beyond her yard and blooming summer garden. "Perhaps, I'll never return."

"Em, don't say that! Father will be paying a handsome sixty dollars a month to send you to that fine school of Mistress Lyon. A fortune indeed! And, Austin says he'll come and bring you Mother's homemade sweets if you study well. He's a good brother and will do so, and I shall come with Father by coach, and bring the flowers from your garden. Perhaps with mother, to visit, too! Now, don't fret, or you'll be sick again, and you are looking so well today, Emmy!"

"I'll never be as apple-cheeked as you, Dear Vinnie! Your daguerreotype was lovely to look at. I'm an apparition of a sad stick of a girl in mine. You're the true Belle of Amherst, not me! You're becoming so pretty, Lavinia." Emily turned to pensively stroke her sister's thick, dark wavy hair.

"I can't believe how many of our sweet friends are dead already, Vinnie. It's so strange, isn't it, that children die? What sort of God lets so many *children*, who have not begun to live, die in their innocence as Sweet Sophia did last winter? When I look out my window at the graves, I hear a funeral in my brain, the mourners treading, treading…"

"Emily, stop such sad thoughts! You mustn't ask such questions of Our Lord. God's will shall be done. So Mother says. Now, come!"

"Yes, Sister, I'm coming." Emily wistfully followed Vinnie down the stairs—dreaming of how Master Clark, Master Humphrey, and Austin's newest friend, Mr. Gould, would be at the Commencement Tea with exciting ideas for the future. "Dear Vinnie, you always like to be safe on the shore like Mother, while I, as Austin, love the danger of braving the sea," she said as she followed her sister's bouncing, black curls down the stairs to the scullery.

Summer 1847: The Barnyard Some Days Later

Gently does it, indeed!

Emily blushed while she watched Will Clark's hands softly stroke the horse's mane, his voice coaxing and tender—his clear eyes pure with light—as he trained the big beast to loving obedience. "Thank you, Master Clark, for showing father what Austin and I have been trying to persuade him of: Gently does it, indeed!" In front of her father, Clark had insisted on lifting her by the waist to her sidesaddle mount of *Romeo*. Then with reigns in hand, he led the horse in a trot around the barnyard.

"You see, Sir, now you can trust this beast with your littlest girl. He will be gentle as she whispers in his ear. Especially if she pets him, caresses his neck, and gives him a sweet apple after every ride." Will Clark showed his radiant smile. His blue eyes sparkled in the sunlight.

As Edward Dickinson watched William Smith Clark lift his daughter, Emily, into her saddle, he sensed the electricity between the two young people and disliked it. Though Clark was very bright and admired at the college, Edward knew he was the son of a country doctor from Ashfield, now practicing in Easthampton where the family owned nearly no land.

"So, Mr. Clark, you will be heading for Germany for your studies, next term? Professor Shepard of our natural science classes is proud you're accepted to study science abroad. Your discovery of those large beryls at Acworth certainly excited his interest in your rock hunts. He's thrilled Mr. Williston will subsidize you as our first graduate to study abroad for a Ph.D."

"Since Germany has the best advanced science studies in the world today, Professor Shepard has recommended I should study the natural sciences, geology, and perhaps the chemistry of soil and botany, too, for the horticulture and agriculture of our valley. I had thought to be a physician like my father, but..."

Emily interrupted to impress her father with Clark: "Professor Shepard has mentioned Master Clark as the source of a specimen of Arkansite in his article in the *American Journal of Science and the Arts*,

Father. Did you know? Master Clark made quite a stir at Professor Hitchcock's social tea last week. All the students gathered around him to examine his specimens of garnet, tourmaline, tranite, columbite, zircon, too, which he discovered in Connecticut near New Haven on one of his recent rock hunts." Emily turned excitedly to Clark: "How I envy your friend, Mr. Monross, Master Clark, for being able to accompany you on such rock hunting expeditions. Austin says he wishes he could go with you sometime." Then turning back to her father, she implored: "Might I go, too, Father, if Austin were able to go as chaperon? I'd so love to help find such specimens for the college cabinets."

Edward realized that Emily wanted Clark as her suitor. "Rock hunting is not for ladies, Emily Elizabeth! Bible studies, cooking, gardening at home like your mother, suit you best. Scientific exploration is excellent for men like you, Mr. Clark. Perhaps, when you return, you'll take the teaching post Trustee Williston has offered you in return for his patronage. He has much to extend to you, and he's taken quite a liking to your style of lecturing. I understand he's offered you a job as preceptor at Williston Academy so that you can earn for your studies abroad when you've been graduated from our college next year?" Squire Dickinson meant for Clark to understand that Mr. Williston was his best bet for patronage, not himself.

"Oh, you'll be teaching at Easthampton for Williston Academy next year, Master Clark? Austin attended there in 1842!" Emily tried to hide her distress at her father's implications."

"Yes, I knew Austin when I attended Williston. I served as a tutor to the younger boys and taught Austin botany and chemistry."

"I recall he spoke of you often. Austin found your horticulture lectures inspiring. Perhaps, when you return, Father shall buy a fine Morgan horse with advice from a *Philip* such as you!" Emily wanted greatly to encourage what her father discouraged.

"Ah, Miss Emily, I see you remember your Greek for *horse lover*. Yes, a Morgan horse is best for the sidesaddle of a lady. Morgans trot smoothly, high-stepping, without jolting, and help you ladies keep your skirts down." Clark smiled mischievously into Emily's eyes.

Squire Dickinson cleared his throat at Clark's daring mention of ladies' skirts, and Clark led Emily's horse to the other side of the barnyard to whisper, out of her father's hearing. "Though I'm a *Philip*, I hope you realized that I love *women* far more than horses." Clark joked. "I named your new horse "Romeo," especially knowing your fondness for Shakespeare, Miss Emily!"

"Perhaps, I should call you after Shakespeare's *Romeo* instead!" Emily laughed softly. "But, what's in a name when a rose by any other would smell as sweet!"

"What light from yonder window breaks? Tis the East, and Emily is the sun!" Clark answered flirtatiously.

Edward, left behind at the barn door, seeing his daughter's delight from afar, cleared his throat and straightened his collar. "Come Emily!" He called out. "Your mother needs help with the baking." As Clark returned Romeo bearing Emily back to the barn door, Edward was polite. "I'm indebted to you for the lesson, Mr. Clark. Please excuse us. We must get back to our chores. You'll be at our commencement celebration coming soon, won't you?"

"I'll be around another year, Sir, and then teaching at Williston Academy for at least a couple of terms to save for my studies in Germany. Ralph Waldo Emerson of Concord has traveled there recently and is making his lecture circuit now on the ideals of German *pantheism*."

"I consider such beliefs blasphemous, but I suppose Mr. Emerson's lectures are well wrought if he is invited to tour the Lyceum. I consider his rebellion from our Trinitarian ways into the realm of *Unitarianism* as a dangerous example to the young. I do not condone all he has to say against our Calvinism."

"But, Sir, one can be a good Christian, even an Evangelist, as I hope I am, and still find wisdom in Ralph Waldo Emerson's love of nature as God's Blessed Creation. Professor Hitchcock, too, preaches that the study of the natural world is a tribute to Our Lord's Creation."

"In any case, please excuse me as I must return to the office today to prepare an important brief. Also, I must welcome a new apprentice who is arriving to study with us, a Mr. Benjamin Newton, who'll be here next term. Too bad you'll be in Germany, as Mr. Newton's a follower of Mr. Emerson, but he's a good law student. I shall try not to hold it against him."

"How tolerant of you, Sir." Will Clark winked at Emily as her father turned to walk toward the house. He took her by the waist to help her dismount. She could only smile in return as he set her down, lightly in front of him, close enough that she felt his breath on her face. She thrilled from the touch of his warm hands on her waist as he hesitated letting go.

As if he had eyes in the back of his head, Edward added as he strode to the porch for his jacket and brief case: "Emily will be off to Mount Holyoke, Mistress Lyon's Female Seminary for her studies in fall. Good wishes with your preceptor post at Williston Academy, Mr. Clark! And, your studies in Germany beyond that! I trust we'll see you a week hence at the commencement celebration here on the lawn."

"Easthampton is only a horse's ride away," he whispered looking into Emily's eyes. He continued softly. "I shall visit Amherst often while teaching at Williston Academy as I love to ride through the Pelham Hills." As he tied the horse at its post, he knew beyond a doubt that the stern and Calvinist Squire was not encouraging a courtship of his daughter. Clark was disappointed, but, as was his way, undaunted.

"Please forgive my need to take Romeo to my client in Montague now, Mr. Clark. First, I'll go in to bid my wife a good day. Thank you kindly for the lesson in horse handling." Edward Dickinson, though austere, was known for his fine manners.

Emily smiled wistfully hoping to encourage what her father did not. "I'm sure the students at Williston Academy will love your classes best, Master Clark, if you teach them as gently as you do horses. We'll miss you in Amherst."

"Thank you, Squire Dickinson, for passing Mr. Williston's compliments onto me. His opinion means much, as does yours, Miss Dickinson. It gives me confidence to carry the light of learning further, so that when I return to New England, I might be of service, perhaps to Amherst College, chief among our valley's seminaries. All at Amherst College owe gratitude to your father, Samuel, who founded it. Mr. Williston tells me, Sir, that you've above all been instrumental in guiding Amherst toward success." Clark called after Edward who stood on the porch waiting for Emily. He gave one last attempt at ingratiation.

"Thank you, Master Clark, and good day! Emily, there's much butter wants churning, and baking wants billowing. Your mother needs you. I strongly believe that a woman's place is in the home in service to her family. Don't you, Mr. Clark?"

Realizing that it was no use trying to please the unyielding Squire, Clark felt defiant in being snubbed. "I believe a woman has the right to an education, as much as a man, Sir, if you will forgive my saying so in front of your daughter. Mr. Williston's industry in button manufacturing was initiated by his wife's venture into the business with her cottage industry. Mr. Williston believes in women's education for a profession outside the home. His wife is his chief accountant. It's a staunch belief of mine that women should be encouraged to use their minds as teachers, scientists, economists, writers..."

"I see." Edward looked with cold astonishment upon Clark's brash statements as the young student finished saddling Romeo for him. "Well, as I said, Mr. Clark, I'm a great believer that a woman's place is in the home for the good of her family's spiritual health. My good wife agrees. Good day."

"Good day, Squire Dickinson." Clark would grovel no more as he felt disregarded by the eminent Squire. He resolved to have his triumph. "I may be a country lad, but I know an intelligent and witty woman when I see one, Sir. I'm sure you'll be a good scholar, Miss Emily. We all know you're a fine writer. Your brother told me your compositions at Amherst Academy were sorely envied. He read us one at Williston Academy over tea one afternoon. I've never heard better appreciation of our valley's natural attributes." Then he whispered to her with a smile, as he mounted his horse: "Don't let Calvinism get the best of you at Holyoke! I hear Headmistress Lyon can be fierce with God!"

Emily felt her heart skip. She looked into Clark's eyes with a longing so deep that it stirred his spirit. With defiant pride, he turned, his glorious black stallion, Othello—lent him by his wealthy patron, Williston—toward the open gate. Reared her up and rode away at a sudden gallop. He looked back only to tip his hat at Emily. Forlornly, she waved goodbye to Clark.

"Emily, come along now," Squire Dickinson called from the porch. "Mother needs you!"

"Yes, Father. I'm coming." Emily granted softly, still staring after Clark.

Fall 1847: Mistress Lyon's Female Seminary

It is a sweet feeling to know that you are missed,
and that your memory is precious at home.

Emily began to feel homesick as she watched the trees and fields just turning gold and red along the winding country road from the coach window. She felt a pain in her heart as if it were in her stomach, as she listened to the plaintive and continual clip-clop of carriage-horse hooves. Holding a linen handkerchief to her nose to ward away the ample dust of the road and often adjusting her bonnet as the wheels hit a rut and knocked it to one side, she composed lines of verse in her mind:

These are the days when Birds come back,
A very few. a Bird or two,
To take a backward look.

These are the days when skies resume
The old—old sophistries of June—
A blue and gold mistake....

As the coach joggled along the South Hadley Road from Amherst she observed her father in the padded seat across from her. "Oh, look at Father pouring over his client accounts and ignoring this lovely fall day. I wish he'd learn to smile and enjoy life." She remembered how stern he looked in his recent portrait.

"Excuse me, Father. May I ask why didn't you smile for your daguerreotype? You looked so solemn. Was it because I was going away to South Hadley?"

"But, I *was* smiling, Emily Elizabeth. That *is* my smile! I was happy that you were admitted to Miss Lyon's Seminary! Now, we have faces of each other to look at and keep us well while you're away. And, why didn't you smile for *yours*, Emily Elizabeth?"

"But, I *was* smiling father, like you, though I was tired and still reeling from my weeks in bed coughing. I didn't feel good knowing I'd be leaving you and Mother, Vinnie and Austin, and our dear home, and all my dear friends at the Academy: Sue, Martha Gilbert, Abiah Root and Master Humphrey. Who knows if I shall ever see them all well again!"

"Now, now Emily Elizabeth, you shall, God willing, and I will send your brother to see you soon, with your favorite pies and cakes—homemade by your mother. And your mother and sister and Austin and I will visit soon. I'll bring them myself. Vinnie will bring your garden's last flowers. She's promised to take good care of them while you're away. You'll do very well at Mount Holyoke, Emily Elizabeth. Your sweet tongue will charm new friends in no time. None will resist your graces! You grow to look more like your mother did in her youth every day. Why Austin tells me you're a Belle of Amherst, and his friends fancy your wit! Soon a Christian gentleman of means and standing will be asking for your hand when you've finished your studies at the seminary. I shall choose just the proper husband of means and Godly education for your good future."

"But, Father, many young men of the college and our village are planning to go West as Susan Gilbert's brothers have. There are greater opportunities and cheaper, better farmlands for them there. There are fewer men of our station who wish to stay in our valley than ever."

"Never fear, Emily. We'll find you a proper Christian of good Yankee stock. If not, it would be better not to marry as you have a good home with your father. Why should you starve far from home or be deprived of good care? You shall be happy and serve your proper husband well as a fine Puritan wife, just as your mother serves me well. A woman's education enhances her home, and makes her a good wife and mother. All you need worry about for now is doing well at Mistress Lyon's seminary. I know you'll make me proud, as gifted at recitation and composition as you are. Now, I must read this brief."

Emily sank back into her seat. This was the warmest verbal affection her father had ever offered, but his talk of choosing her husband scared her. She began to dream of the coming August commencement party at the college, when she'd see Austin's college mates: Master Clark and George Gould, and Master Humphrey, teacher at Amherst

Academy, whom she liked so well. She had bid a sad goodbye to him as she returned his treasured botany texts. She felt she loved him. She fancied Will Clark and George Gould, too, but neither of them suited her father.

She and Vinnie had clung together weeping that morning as she finished dressing and packing for her trip to South Hadley. She'd hoped she might see Will Clark again before he went off to teach at Williston Academy in Easthampton. He fascinated her with his clever repartee. His staunch egalitarian talk against slavery and the bondage of women, his belief in the study of nature and science as pursuits of the soul, thrilled her—to say nothing of the way his warm hands had caressed her waist as he lifted her from her father's horse, Romeo. His deep blue eyes gazing steadily into hers remained an image in her mind. Four years her senior, Clark was a junior at Amherst. "I'm determined to be home in time for his commencement party next August, no matter what," she resolved.

Austin's witty and philosophical friend, George Gould, seemed an easier catch for her. She sensed how much he liked her company, but she knew her father would never approve his penchant for the new Transcendental teachings that were threatening the Calvinist doctrines of the valley. "Gould's empty pockets vex Father as much as Clark's do. Father finds all the men I prefer to be poor rural rebels, not of the caliber of a Dickinson pioneer," she ruminated. How pretty Lavinia is growing. If only I had her hardiness. I'll miss her motherly ministrations. She looked at the shawl she was wearing and remembered Vinnie's words:

"Emily, here's an extra shawl mother knitted just for you. Do keep well, Dear Emmy, and drink plenty of cool water. Mother worries about your health. So does Father. Promise you'll eat and sleep well, Em, promise!"

"For you, I shall, Vinnie" she'd answered. "For you and Austin, I'll return well. Oh, if only we were children again! I don't know how to grow up. Parting is all we know of Heaven and all we need of Hell."

"Emily, don't talk that way. You say such piercing things! You break my heart. We need nothing of Hell! Father does not like the word uttered in his house. Be careful what you say at Mount Holyoke Seminary. Head Mistress Lyon is very strict with the teaching of scripture, Mother says. She is bent on saving souls, and perhaps, she can save even your unremitting soul, Dear Emmy. Keep well and go with God."

"Oh, Vinnie, I'd rather stay here dusting the stairs and sweeping leaves from the doorway with you and mother, and riding in the woods with Austin and his circle, than go off to South Hadley to be saved without you, Vinnie. I'll be so homesick."

"We'll come to see you very soon, Em. I'll bring your flowers, and Mother will bring her pies and fruits."

"Oh, Vinnie, Sue Gilbert wrote that a novel called *Wuthering Heights*, by Ellis Bell of England, is a thrilling new read. She's managed to buy it at a bookshop in New York, when Mr. Cutler wasn't around. She's sent it to Martha and said I should read it when she's finished. She wrote Martha that I'll be enthralled by it. Do get it from Martha and bring it when you visit. I'll have to hide it under my bloomers at Mount Holyoke! I've sneaked Elizabeth Barrett Browning's poems under my Bible and lexicon in my valise. But, do bring *Wuthering Heights* to me, Vinnie inside a basket of flowers. So father won't know. Do tend my garden! Promise you will bring me the last rose of summer! Vinnie, do visit soon."

"I will, Em. I will," Vinnie promised tearfully. The girls had parted weeping as Emily climbed into the coach with Edward sitting stiffly upright across from his daughter, his ever present briefcase at his side. Austin waved a plaintive goodbye, but none of the family touched their departing Emily, as it was not their custom to embrace. Only Vinnie, when alone in their rooms upstairs away from their father's gaze, had hugged her beloved sister in parting. Squire Dickinson found affectionate displays unseemly and too stirring for Godly good and discipline.

September 1847: Mount Holyoke

We are what we make of ourselves.
—Mistress Lyon

Edward Dickinson, with Emily at his side, entered the Mount Holyoke Female Seminary and took off his hat to greet Head Mistress Mary Lyon. South Hadley was about ten miles from Amherst Village, but the ride took nearly two hours through woodlands and meadows on a winding, deeply rutted road. Emily was weary from the long, rugged, and sad journey, but she dutifully curtsied and stood beside her father.

"Welcome to Mount Holyoke, Squire Dickinson. Miss Emily Elizabeth." Mistress Lyon greeted in somber tone. "God willing your journey was good on this fine September day!"

"I'm pleased you have accepted my daughter at your school, Mistress Lyon. We may make a good Puritan wife of her yet—though I fear she fancies herself a botanist and poet. I know her scores were only middling, but she is excellent at her lexicon and writing."

"Yes, Squire Edwards, but her scores were not of the lowest in theology either. I can see your daughter has fine potential for learning. After all, she is of the Dickinsons of our Great Pioneer Valley, good Puritan stock, and she'll do well for your sake, I'm sure—and for the pride of Christian womanhood in our great state of Massachusetts!"

"Yes, Mistress Lyon, Emily had been quite ill with fever before the exhausting three day examination, so I am grateful that you make allowances for her. She is well again. Praise the Lord."

"Her day will be plotted out with military precision, Squire Dickinson. There will be time for rest scheduled early every night. When the girls are not in classes, they often complete chores. I've given Emily an easy one, to polish and set out and collect the knives in the dining hall. No heavy work—since you told me of her recent illnesses. I met your handsome son Austin when he brought Miss Emily's examination results and entrance papers. A freshman at Amherst Seminary now, yes? You must be very proud of him near the top of his class, I hear! Is he destined for the priesthood?"

"I hope he will take over my law practice in Amherst, thank you, Mistress." Edward replied without a trace of a smile. "Austin and Emily get on well and are alike in temperament. She may miss her brother and sister, but she will get used to your routine and find her studies stimulating, I'm sure. She was a dutiful student at our Amherst Academy."

"Yes, an excellent one. Miss Emily, there will be many fine friends for you here, too. We have the best young ladies of the valley within these portals, studying the ways of our Blessed Lord. Many have become devoted missionaries, carrying Lord Jesus's word forth into the world. We are what we make of ourselves, Miss Emily! You will be happy here I'm sure."

"I'm sure I will be, Mistress Lyon." Emily complied, but in her mind a darkness welled as she looked around at the austere halls of the seminary and noted the drawn, wrinkled pallor, and stern face of its aging head mistress.

"Will you take tea with us, Squire?"

"No thank you kindly, Mistress. Much obliged. I've work at home, many briefs to prepare. My good wife has packed me a basket of fruit, bread, and cheese for my journey homeward to my office." Squire Dickinson donned his hat and departed without demonstration. He did not look back or wave to Emily, though the corners of his eyes watered as he contemplated leaving his favorite daughter to live far from home. He climbed into the coach and was gone in a cloud of dust, as Emily's eyes, averting the gaze of Mistress Lyon, watered fiercely as she set her trembling lips firmly as her father's.

"Come Emily! I shall introduce you to the guardian of your floor. We've placed you on the upper floor, with your cousin, Emily Norcross. You can behold our countryside from there and look homeward toward Amherst. Your mother was a good student here. She loved her teacher Miss Caroline very much. Did you know they were friends until Miss Caroline was taken by the Angel of Death to God's Paradise?"

"Yes, Mistress, I did. Is Cousin Emily Norcross here already, then?"

"She's waiting for you upstairs in the fifth floor dormitory room you shall share."

"Thank goodness she's arrived safely from Monson. I shall be so glad to see her, Mistress! We have not met in some time, since the death of Grandfather Joel Norcross in May last year when we traveled to Monson for his funeral. Thank you for rooming Cousin Emily and me together, Mistress Lyon."

"It will be fine as long as your studies go well. Your cousin is a disciplined girl, but if there is too much chatting after hours, and I see poor grades, there will have to be other arrangements. We tolerate no exceptions from the rules here, or a black mark goes beside your name. Too many of those and your father will be sorely disappointed. Do I make myself clear, Emily Elizabeth Dickinson?" Mistress Lyon called all of her students by their full names in order to set them in her memory. There were many families of the same surname in the Pioneer Valley, and she had to keep their identities clear.

"Perfectly, Mistress Lyon." Emily conceded, lowering her large brown eyes to feign very obedient humility, all the while hoping there might be some mischief she could make. "We are different. That's why we need each other's company." She'd often told Austin, but the thought of him made her homesick. "Thank goodness Emmy Norcross will at least be here with me," she reasoned. "But, she's so religiously obedient and timid like Mother. We shall not have the fun I have with Austin and Vinnie."

Winter 1848: Dear Brother, Austin

The devil is exorcised in frenzy here,
but I remain among The Hopeless.

Attending the weeping conversion of her schoolmates in Ms. Lyon's Christian revival meetings every week made Emily uncomfortable. All the wailing girls who were so ready to be reborn to Jesus seemed to her distraught in their confession of sin.

"I'm not sure what my sins are," she thought to herself, echoing Austin's convictions, "so how can I confess them? I don't feel anything I've done is so wrong, unless it be my love of walking in the woods, looking for wildflowers, or hating to help Mother with the dusting. Cooking and serving Austin and Father all the time, as Vinnie and I do, seems penitence enough!

I wonder what horrible sins make these girls so distressed in their penitent desire to come to Jesus?" Emily puzzled.

Mistress Lyon commanded the assemblage: "Abdicate your selfishness. Give up your avarice, and follow me! Jesus begs you with His scarlet heart pouring beams of light! Come to our Lord Jesus Christ and be born again in your soul! My Girls, be all you dream of being! Give up all fancy and embrace the reality of God. Fancy is the worst leader of souls. There is no place here for imagination when scripture actualizes all thought needed in Divine will." Ms. Lyon's intoned in her deepest rhetorical voice cracking with emotion. She felt that her time would soon be up on this earth. She believed that the more converts she brought to Jesus, the better place she might win for herself in Heaven if Heaven had been ordained for her.

Weary and overworked, unmarried, without children of her own, sexually repressed, and thoroughly frustrated with founding her seminary for young Christian women, she had not been feeling well. Her face showed the strain of pain and exhaustion beyond her years. She clutched her Bible to the black breast of her Puritan dress and wept with beatific joy as she repeated, "Come my wayward children, come to Jesus! Be reborn in your soul!"

The way the weeping girls clutched their breasts and tore at their bodices, clinging to each other, made Emily suspect that some sort of emotion akin to hysteria was really at work in the dark confines of the meeting room. Lit only with candles at the altar as the focus, the whole scene had a hypnotic effect. Mistress Lyon's craggy face glowed pale from her white collar, as darkness enveloped the rest of her body. Only her hands and face shined forth in the candlelight as she held her Bible aloft, weeping with sorrowful joy. "Come forward and fall on your knees to Jesus! Be reborn and have your spirit revive its joy in God and his Holy Son, Our Savior. In the name of the Father and Son and the Holy Ghost! Feel the ecstasy of your prayers!' She whined crossing herself. "Pray, My Dear Girls! Pray to be delivered unto Him who is The Shepherd of all in the Valley of Darkness. Follow Him into the light of your soul!" Miss Lyon's lowered her head and prayed, reciting scripture from the last books of the Bible. "Come to Jesus before the flames envelop us!" She cried. "Give up the Devil, toss him from your spirit, evict him from your body, and come, come, come to Jesus, Our Holy Savior!"

Emily, seated at the back of the assemblage as usual, among the small group designated as "The Hopeless," lowered her head in embarrassment to see Mistress Lyon clutching at her breasts and weeping so profusely. Some of the girls began to faint to the floor, crying out: "Jesus! Take me, Jesus! I want to come to you. Penetrate me with your ecstasy! Excite my soul!"

Watching this infectious display of emotion made Emily want to withdraw all the more for fear any commitment would be coerced rather than sincere. It seemed to her that the soul was a private thing, and if she were to marry her heart to Jesus Christ forever, she had ought to do it in privacy and silence. She thought of how Edward—a devout man—did not allow himself to display emotion in the Amherst church revivals she'd witnessed. She thought of Austin who, like her, kept wondering what his sins were and how to feel remorse for them. She noted, too, that some of the pickiest and meanest girls, who wore large gold or silver crosses around their necks, were often the first to be converted and would dictate to others what behavior should be. Some of them who were the first to grab the food at table, instead of pass it, were the first to declare they were saved. She reasoned that perhaps they did have sins they understood well and were truly in need of it.

She was waiting for real feelings to overwhelm her into conversion, but somehow they did not come from Mistress Lyon's sermons.

In the dim light at the back of the chapel, neither weeping or rejoicing, she took a small pencil she'd hidden up her sleeve and jotted a thought on a scrap of paper that marked Revelations her favorite chapter in her Bible. All were required to carry their *King James Bibles* to Mistress Lyon's revival meetings. Emily marked the passage which read: "…the rest of the men who were not killed by these plagues, yet repented not of the works of their hands that they should not worship devils and idols of gold and silver, and brass, and stone, and of wood: which neither could see, nor hear, nor walk." Then she wrote on the small scrap of paper:

> *I shall know why, when time is over.*
> *And I have ceased to wonder why….*
> *I shall forget the drop of anguish*
> *That scalds me now, that scalds me now.*

Finally, Mistress Lyon walked down the aisle toward Emily's pew with her weeping followers, the new converts clinging to each other and Mistress Lyon's skirts. They would now be led away to the Mistress's private chamber to complete their conversion with special cakes and tea. Emily quickly tucked her pencil stub up her sleeve and closed her Bible. As Mistress Lyon passed frowning towards "The Hopeless," Emily bent her head as if in prayer for her lost soul as she reasoned inwardly:

"I had such peace for awhile, when I thought I'd found my savior. I must admit, I'd not exchange those moments of peace when I thought he heard my prayers, for all the words of doubt in my lexicon, but Jesus let poor Sophia die, and she was the sweetest of friends: kind and gentle. She died no matter how hard I prayed. Jesus let my very meek and devout mother be sick for such awhile after Vinnie was born, no matter how hard I prayed. How can I believe he hears me now? Perhaps, it's the endurance of suffering that saves the soul? I don't believe these others, who are so sure, are really sure, but perhaps only play-acting in the frenzy of the moment to please Mistress Lyon and acquire special cakes and tea in her chambers. I hear she serves sweeter cakes in her private chambers after conversion than in the dining hall. Maybe the saved deserve better reward? Perhaps it's sinfully cynical of me, but Father means what he says, and I don't feel that Mistress Lyon always does, except when she be disciplining us.

If Father and Austin can wait to be saved then I can, too. And if Mother, already saved, suffers more illness and fear of death than he, then how has being saved helped her? True, she's very kind and generous, and never shows a temper, but she seems so squashed by Father's self-assuredness, even as he says she should please herself. She knows he really wants her to please him, and so she does, but I've never seen them kiss or touch as these girls are hugging and holding each other now and clinging to Mistress Lyon's waist and elbows." Emily felt quite alone and apart in her quandary of doubts. "Why does Mistress Lyon fervently hug and kiss each girl upon the mouth as they come up to her to be 'Saved,' why does that grate on me so?"

"I'm not so sure about Mistress Lyon. She does not have gentle kindness in her face as Mother who suffers her Christianity so quietly. Nor does she seem so self-assured as Father who, though he attends church so generously and prays with militant force, will not come on his knees to Jesus to be saved. Perhaps, Father feels no need to be saved as Mistress Lyon does, as I've never seen him fall to his knees with the Passion of Christ. Is it because Father is too proud? I feel Mother is afraid of having another child since giving birth to Vinnie made her ill for so long. She often retires early with a headache, excusing herself from Father. When she gave birth to Vinnie was the only time I heard Mother scream and groan behind her closed door. It frightened me so. I remember it still even as I was merely three-years-old and put to bed in my crib. I'm quite confused and anguished to see my schoolmates tear at their bodices, and fall on their knees with fainting and weeping. Shouldn't 'Salvation' bring the light of peace and a tranquil joy? Somehow, I feel Mistress Lyon is a lady that 'doth protest too much!' If she had a good husband, and children to love her, would she claw at her own bosom so much, and look so wrinkled, stern, and pained? God, forgive me such thoughts—but if He's Almighty God, he's given me these thoughts, all the same."

"Yet, I should remember how hard Mistress Lyon has worked to give young women an education when there were no seminaries for girls at all in New England." Emily coughed as she left the chapel and climbed the many stairs, five flights up, to her cold dormitory room. She'd been ill often during the winter. Homesick, she dreamed of the day she'd watched from her dormitory window with her Norcross cousin as her family approached the portal of the school for their visit. They alighted their coach all dressed in Sabbath finery.

"Oh, Cousin! Come with me to greet them. Mother will have good cakes and pies for us! Vinnie will have brought us flowers from my garden and fruits and nuts from our orchard. It will be grand to see them!" She didn't mention the novel from Sue she hoped to find hidden in the bottom of Vinnie's basket, as Cousin Emily Norcross never read romantic novels and judged them too scandalous for Christian girls.

Austin had come yet again as winter began, bringing sweets and a pie made by her mother which her schoolmates had devoured so quickly, she'd had but one portion in sharing the baked goods with them. Only some apples and nutmeats had been left her for later.

She missed Valentine fun in Amherst, the most joyful holiday of the year in her village, when fervent spirits were loosened a little from Puritan constraints. No Valentines were allowed at her Calvinist seminary. When she sneaked to the post office to deliver some written home by other girls, she was nearly found out and punished. She wrote home to Austin:

My Dearly Missed Brother,

I suppose you've written and received a quantity of Valentines this week. Every night I've searched for Cupid's messenger. Many of my classmates received beautiful ones; and I've not quite done hoping for one. Surely my friend, Thomas, has not lost all his fomer affection for me! I entreat you to tell him I'm pining for a Valentine. I'm sure I shall not very soon forget the joy of last year's Valentine holiday. Monday, Mistress Lyon stood up in the hall and forbade our sending "any of those "foolish notes called Valentines." But those who were here last year, knowing her opinions, were sufficiently cunning to write and give them into the care of Dickinson during the vacation; so that about 150 were dispatched on Valentine morn, before orders should be put down to the contrary effect. Hearing of this act, Miss Whitman, by and with the advice and consent of the other teachers, with frowning brow, sallied over to the Post Office to ascertain, if possible, the number of the valentines, and worse, still, the names of the offenders. Nothing has yet been heard as to the amount of information, but as Dickinson is a good hand to help the girls, and no one has yet received sentence, we begin to think her mission unsuccessful. I have not written one, nor do I intend to. Your injunction to pile on the wood has not been unheeded, for we have been obliged to obey it to keep from freezing up…We cannot have much more cold weather, I am sure, for spring is near…. Dear Austin, please ask Vinnie to send that lovely little hair comb you gave me when we visited with you in Boston.

Your very affectionate sister, Emily

Life was dreary, except when the girls could have a climb up Mount Holyoke for flower picking in spring or early summer. But winter was freezing cold in the dormitory rooms. Her Norcross cousin, though diligent and kind, offered no stimulating conversation or joking as Austin had! Indeed, Emily Norcross was always tired and coughing a good deal. She was pale and drawn and hardly ever laughed. Emily thought she seemed quite ill and always praying, readying to meet her maker.

My Dear Austin,

Aren't we Dickinsons rather different from others? Don't we need to be together to enjoy life? No one is as good at humor as you are, Dear Brother, and it makes me very sad indeed to hear someone trying to tell a joke, if you are not there to enjoy it with me. There's always such fun wherever you are, Austin. My studies go well, but many of the texts are the same as those I've already studied at Amherst Academy. I know that this is an opportunity that I should love, but I feel tired and gloomy. And now I seem to cough a good deal from the cold in our room—just as Cousin Emily Norcross does! Mistress Lyon preaches roundly against the use of fancy and I dare not write such imaginative or original compositions here at Holyoke as I wrote at Amherst Academy. I had such good friendships there, and miss them all so: especially Master Humphrey and Sue Gilbert. They are so very clever! I study chemistry, botany, Latin, history, and natural philosophy, plus plenty of scripture, of course. I do love this seminary, and all the teachers are bound strongly to my heart by ties of affection, yet I am not persuaded to become a Christian and be "born again" to Jesus. As I told cousin Emily Norcross, I've no particular objection to becoming a Christian, and I feel sad when others are called to Christ before me, but I just don't honestly feel it, Austin, as you've said you don't either.

Your affectionate sister, Emily

When Edward heard that Emily had a cough that she was not admitting to him, he sent Austin to bring her home by coach from South Hadley. She resisted leaving, as she felt it the brave thing to do. She wrote later to Abiah Wood, her friend from Amherst Academy:

Dear Abiah, My Dearest Former and Much Missed Schoolmate,

Austin came, sent by Father, to bring me home. I had some recourse to words, and a desperate battle with them was waged, between my sophomore brother and myself. Finding words would not win my will, I resorted to girlish tears. But, my tears also failed. As you might imagine, Austin was victorious, and I was vanquished by his victory! You must not think that I don't love home, as I adore it, but I couldn't bear leaving my teachers and companions before the end of the term, to go home where Father will be dosing me daily with horrible tasting medicines and making me have daily visits from the doctor. I'll be given huge cups of warm drinks and nursed by all the old ladies of Mother's Bible Society. Father is quite handy at giving medicines unwanted by the patient, and I was dosed sans mercy, quite constantly upon my return home to bed. Finally, out of sheer pity, I think my cough disappeared. So, I'll be back at Holyoke to finish the semester until August. I feel a bit like a prisoner, like Jane Eyre in her orphanage, in that moving novel by Currer Bell that I so love, and that father's apprentice, Bowdoin, lent me. But, Oh Abiah, , I know you don't approve such Romantic novels, as my cousin Emily Norcross doesn't, either. You're good Christians, and I'm still not 'saved' and sit at meeting among 'the hopeless' where I remain doomed, it seems, to stay.

Your most affectionate friend, Emily

Emily was so pleased and happy, set free from Mistress Lyon's watch, at home for her two weeks respite in January that it was difficult to return for the remainder of the spring and summer term. She found she missed the protective assurance her father provided, even in his cool sternness. "The memory of home, *that holy place*, full of Austin's laughter, Mother's delicious food, and Vinnie's amiable companionship, glows inside me as I fall asleep each night," she wrote again to Abiah Root.

Many of her Holyoke schoolmates cuddled together in the cold of the dormitories at night, whispering under their blankets, but Cousin Emily Norcross was timidly obedient and very quiet—like her aunt, Emily's mother—and offered no physical affection. Emily missed Vinnie and her friend Sue Gilbert who were not afraid to cuddle secretly with her when she was ill or afraid.

She and Susan had often slept entwined in each other's arms when Sue had visited her in Amherst. She felt an inexplicable thrill in feeling Sue's body so close to hers through the night—only their flannel gowns separating their warm flesh. She wished that Austin would marry Sue so that they might always be intimate sisters, true forever in affection. She resolved to foster a scheme that would keep her "Dear Susie" close forever. Sue was growing into a voluptuous and charming young woman. Emily envied her sparkling wit and curvaceous magnetism, so attractive to the young men of their town. She wrote:

Dearest Susie,

I hope that you'll return to Amherst after your studies at your seminary in Geneva, New York. I hear it is very progressive there. Of all the girls at Amherst Academy, Sue, I've been most fascinated by you and your intelligence. I feel such sorrow for you, Susie, losing your mother and father and now your favorite sister, Mary. I pray for Dear Mary every night. You mustn't be too sad, Susie, Vinnie and I will be your sisters whenever you need us. We admire you so! Mary would want you to be happy and alive with us.

Your admiring friend who grieves with you, Emily

Mary had died in childbirth and the idea of treacherous childbearing was something that, for good reason, profoundly frightened the young women. They'd whispered about their fears of it long into the night when Sue had come to visit and stay with Emily.

When Austin finally came again for Emily in August at the end of her term, Emily had determined to begin bringing Austin and Susie together as her mates in reading and other delights: rambles in the woods, horseback riding, picnicking, hayrides, taffy pulling parties, and other social pleasures. She was petrified that Austin might decide to go West as other young men of the village were doing and as Sue's brothers had. Her hope was that Sue could tempt Austin to stay in Amherst where they could all be a happy family together forever, and she would always have her dear friend Susie at her side. Emily so loved the sights and smells of home. She wrote to Austin to justify her desire to stay there:

I'm not alone, Austin, in leaving my seminary as many of the girls leave after one year's study. I've doubled up on many of my classes and managed to finish nearly two years in one. I don't want to miss the graduation festivities on the lawn of our house which will be attended by Master Humphrey of Amherst Academy whose intelligence in matters of botany and natural science I so admire. I want to see and hear George Gould with his spiritual and philosophical discussions, and others of your wondrous friends, Austin. I love to hear the talk between you and your venerable Yankee fraternity brothers of Alpha Delta Phi! I anticipate that William Smith Clark of the rival, new fraternity, Psi Upsilon, composed of self-made men, will be there, too. Since you and Clark are among the best speakers of Amherst College, a debate between you will be stimulating beyond belief. I long for your lively levity, Austin.

Affectionately, Emily

Emily did not dare mention their manly charms of which she'd become more aware than ever after a year of study in exclusively female company. She'd been used to having the boys of the village about at Amherst Academy. She particularly missed her preceptor there, Master Humphrey, with whom she shared a passion for botany.

August 1848: "Home Is Where the Hearth Is"

"Well, Austin, I have a *wee* cough again, and it will be Father's medicine now for days, whether I wish to take it or not." Emily groaned as she and Austin traveled homeward through the West Hadley dale in the horse drawn coach. He will insist that I rest and open my mouth to his spooning of the nasty taste of what doctor orders. Yet, I shall be so happy to sit and laugh by the hearth with you and Vinnie after Mother's good dinners, when Father retires to his study and his briefs. Bowdoin lent me a marvelous novel, you know, when he visited. What an adventure he had getting past the Mistress and teachers to visit with me in the receiving parlor. He had to hand *Jane Eyre* to me all wrapped up in pink ribbon and say it was a book on Bible study from Mother. Vinnie helped him wrap it for delivery. Calvinist schooling is dismal, indeed, and I'm hopelessly unsaved by it! Though the dinners in Mistress Lyon's dining halls were good with plenty of roasts, vegetables, bread, and butter, I have been coughing too much to eat, of late. Promise not to tell father."

"About your reading *Jane Eyre* or your coughing, Em? I must tell you that it *is* your cough that caused Father to make me come for you. You know how worried he becomes if one of us is sick. The minute one of us gives out a tiny cough, he declares: "Your Dear Mother was able to give me only three offspring and one son, and by God, I shall keep them all alive to carry on this family no matter how much costly medicine it takes!" Austin imitated their father's tone exactly, making Emily smile as Vinnie often did with similar mimicry.

Austin was taking on his father's role as he grew more mature. "Home will be best for you, Em. You don't really need Mount Holyoke Seminary. You can read plenty in the sanctuary of your room. There are my college friends, and the lectures that ladies can audit at Amherst, now, and Father's apprentices, too, like Bowdoin, to educate you. There's a nice new fellow in Father's office, one Benjamin Newton, whom Father is going to appoint to tutor you. Perhaps, you can be 'saved' at our own village church. I'm sorry to say huge revival meetings are planned there this fall!"

"And why should I be 'saved' if you haven't been, *Mr. Transcendentalist*." Emily laughed as she coughed, drying her tears of departure on Austin's linen handkerchief. He'd presented it to her in an exaggerated gesture of gallantry as she wept leaving Mount Holyoke and her schoolmates. "For My Lady's pearly tears!" he said bowing his head, "now that you've become a *lady* and not a Tom Boy! I see you've done up your hair in that comb I bought for you in Boston. You've allowed your curly hair to grow to some length, too, and are in your long womanly skirts now, Little Sister. No more girlish bloomers and pinafores for you, eh?" The coach bounced its passengers over the rutted road as it rattled toward Amherst through the August afternoon.

"Dear Brother, never forget I'm the older of your sisters. You can call Vinnie *Little Sister*, not me! I've learned much at Miss Lyon's school. I simply have not been 'saved' by her."

"Miss Lyon's face would stop a clock from ticking, so I don't see how it can start a soul running! *It's the face that sank a thousand ships!*" Austin laughed satirically.

Emily heartily joined his laughter. "Austin, you're a rascal to be so unkind to poor, old, witch-faced Mistress Lyon! She was once quite a handsome woman, they say, before she founded the seminary and worked too hard for its success. Though it is a wonder how her love of Jesus took all of her comely looks away!"

Austin laughed at his sister's irony. "Now there's a paradox for you. Saved by Jesus to look like the Devil!"

"Oh Austin!" Emily laughed again. Then stunned by the sight of New England's purple asters beginning to bloom in large clumps by the sides of the road as the carriage made its way over hill and through dale, she leaned out of the window to smell the country breeze. "Look, how richly the August countryside is in bloom, now! I could faint of the smell of earth in the air! Who has not found heaven below will fail of it above. God's residence is next to mine. His furniture is love," she crooned to her brother.

"Emily, I fear you suffer the effusions of a poet and Father will have none of it."

"Yes, Austin, Father has pretty much decided it's all about *real* life! Don't dare laugh at my *true* feelings though. Don't you think there's a monumental difference between the silly effusions housewives write and the true emotions great poets like Shakespeare create? It will be so good to be home with you and Vinnie. I've felt a part of my soul was missing! I've tried to put being homesick out of my mind, but to tell the truth, it hasn't worked. I wish I could be as independent as you, Dear Brother."

"Well, you're only a girl, Em!' Austin teased jovially. "You can't gallop astride a horse and keep those long, ladylike skirts down, and go off to Boston to teach Irish ruffians as I shall to earn my tuition for Harvard. What do you expect?"

"I expect that this Thanksgiving, you'll take me with you hunting in the woods, Dear Brother, as before—letting me wear your hat, jacket, and boots, so no one will be the wiser that I'm a lady! I love to explore the woods and fields in the pure white snow as we used to, Aussy. We weren't allowed to do that at Holyoke except in spring. Mistress was afraid we'd catch a chill and she'd have to answer to our parents. I expect to help you bag the biggest wild turkey of the winter woods for Mother's oven! Will you let me borrow your britches? Please, Kind Sir?"

"Well if you promise to follow doctor's orders and rest and get well of that coughing, I promise I'll take you hunting in November and let you wear my old britches and boots. How's that for a contract? But, only when Father is not about."

"Perfect, Dear Brother, we have a gentlemen's agreement! And since busy Father is hardly about, you'll have no trouble fulfilling it." Emily shook hands across the coach with Austin just as their father did with his clients in sealing lawyer's agreements.

As the sun began to set leaving them in a slight chill, Austin threw his jacket over his sister's knees. "There now, Em, rest and enjoy the scenery until we're home for Mother's good supper! I must study in this law book while there is still some light. I've a present for you at home under the piano cover. A new book I've been reading: *Kavanagh* by Henry Wadsworth Longfellow. I know you'll like his mellow treatment of our New England life. It's a charming and cultured read of earnest allusions to European art. There's a modern, cultivated minister, nothing like our dear, bellicose Reverend Colton. And there's an aspiring poet among the characters, one you'll empathize with. I've hidden the book under the piano cover in the parlor where Father won't see it. You can read it when you've a mind to."

"Thank you, Austin, I shall, indeed." Emily felt very grown up sharing secrets with her maturing brother away from their Father's ears. She coughed softly into Austin's gallantly lent handkerchief and rested her head back against the seat cushions. She gazed out at the dusky trees framed in the orange sunset and the purpling Pelham Hills. Their beauty made her eyes water with joy. "Home! What a lovely word is that, Austin. I fancy I smell our hearth in your handkerchief. People say that home is where the heart is, but it's as much where the hearth is."

Words played in her head to the rhythm of the carriage horses' hooves: "The meadows, mine, the mountains, mine, all forests, stintless stars....the motions of the dipping birds, the morning's amber road, for mine to look at when I like…ah, home… home."

August 1848: Edward Dickinson's Annual Tea

From all the jails the boys and girls
Ecstatically leap,
Beloved, only afternoon
That Prison doesn't keep.

They storm the earth and stun the air,
A mob of solid bliss.
Alas! that frowns should lie in wait
For such a foe as this!

Talk and laughter filled the discursive air. Amherst students, commencement celebrants, and professors bustled about the lawn of Emily's home. Glasses of berry wine clinked with merry toasts of congratulations to the graduating students of Amherst College. Ladies teacups rattled on their saucers as they chatted happily.

Emily, in her best indigo gown, with her hair pinned up and an azure ribbon at her throat, wore bright sapphire-colored, button earrings in the latest fashion, newly purchased at the Cutler's General Store and manufactured at the Williston button factory in Easthampton. Her cheeks were ruddy from the August sun and her cough was cured away. Three weeks of rest in her own familiar bedroom, across from Vinnie's, had made her healthy again. It helped too that Cousin Emily Norcross was no longer keeping her awake by convulsively coughing the nights away in a dormitory bed beside hers. It was healing to have her sister and college-going brother to laugh with after supper, her mother's cooking, and her father's stern, but assuring admonitions in support of her health. She was glowing with the happiness of afternoons spent in her own garden among the butterflies and bees. Suddenly, Emily looked up startled from the tray of cream puffs, teacakes, and gingerbread she was passing around to her father's guests.

"Ah, Miss Emily, you look very charming today! If I may say so, you seem more sophisticated then when last I saw you. Was Mount Holyoke good for your spirits?" Graduate William Smith Clark's handsome, big blue-eyed, smiling face, had surprised Emily as she went about her hostess duties. Clark could see the joy in her glowing face, and he found it very attractive. He couldn't help flirting.

The very sight of Clark made Emily weak in her knees. Her tray trembled as he looked upon the cakes she offered. He was sensitive enough to see that he had an effect upon her. "I'll try some of this gingerbread that I hear you make yourself, and your father loves so much. He brags that yours is the best gingerbread in all of Massachusetts. He wants you to enter your rye and Indian bread in competition, too, at the County Fair." Clark deliberately allowed his hand to brush Emily's fingers as she held the tray, and he chose a cake from it. "Ginger is thought to be an *aphrodisiac*, you know, Miss Emily?"

Emily laughed. "Well, if it is an aphrodisiac, Master Clark, it has not seemed to brighten Father's brow with passion for more than his railroad ventures! As you can see, Mother is at one end of the garden with the ladies and their teacups, and Father at the other with his gentlemen associates talking of railroad stocks and drinking berry wine! What of that chemistry?"

"Well, let me try this *gingery* effect upon my own more ready disposition!" He munched his cake with bravado. "You look more charming with each swallow! This delicious ginger makes me want to waltz you around the lawn in your pretty, blue gown. Your father should allow dancing at these commencement gatherings."

"That will be the day, Sir, when Father allows dancing." Emily laughed heartily.

"Come rest your tray on this table, and I'll walk you to the apple orchard down the primrose path with me. Your luscious gingerbread has made me weak with passion!" Clark enjoyed making her blush.

"Will Clark, stop teasing me!" Emily bantered in return. "Or, you shall have no more of my cakes!"

"Miss Emily? Surely you can tell the difference between teasing and flirting, though they're often akin! If only your father didn't frown so at me, I'd be courting you daily. I sense you know that very well."

Emily was thrilled by his words. "Please, don't mind Father, Will. He's just set in his ways. I know he admires your accomplishments as a student, just as Austin does. Professor Shepard of geology and President Hitchcock are always praising your efforts. That beryl you found at Achton is the talk of the seminary. And the zircon, garnets, tourmalines, columbite, and uranite you have added to Professor Shepard's specimen cabinets are immensely important to the reputation of the college."

Clark was impressed that she remembered the minerals and gemstones he had contributed to the college science halls. "You've an excellent memory for my specimens, Miss Emily. What a good geology student you'd be."

Emily put the attention back upon Clark. She wanted him to know that she was fascinated by his work. "You and your friend Manross being published in *The American Journal of Science* for your discoveries of petrified wood and Arkansite have done Amherst proud, Sir. Mr. Williston says you mesmerize the students with your lectures. My brother Austin agrees. I think he's envious of your expertise in science."

"Ah, but can I beguile a fine young lady like yourself? That's the question! I'm not so good at grammatical writing and lexicography as you are, Miss Emily."

"Oh, but your graduation speech on alchemy, Sir, and its pioneering efforts leading mankind into the truer science of chemistry, was so well delivered. Everyone was enthralled. I had not thought about how important alchemy was before the Father of Inductive Philosophy had lived. 'Now, we know that all inquiries into the nature and affinities of material *must* be the subjects of experiments and not of speculation.'"

Clark was thrilled that Emily felt as he did about science and chemistry and quoted his speech accurately. Feeling themselves in heaven, they looked into each other's eyes and began to stroll toward the orchard, only to hear Emily's father call after her from the garden benches as they passed. "Emily, please bring a tray of your splendid ginger cakes here to President and Mrs. Hitchcock! I've been telling them how well you did at Mount Holyoke this past term! They're thinking of sending their daughter soon."

"You see, I don't have a chance to mesmerize Miss Dickinson with her father on guard!" Clark whispered to Emily still on his arm.

"Clark, my dear young man," said Mr. Williston strolling up to them on the lawn. Let me remember you, again, to my daughter, Harriet, whom I'm sure you recall from your days at my academy. Good evening, Miss Dickinson. Do you know my daughter, Koupoulani, as we call her, after the Hawaiian Queen to whom her father was an advisor?"

"Yes, Sir, we've met many times at our mutual cousins, the Sweetsers." Emily answered politely, if abashed by the additional intrusion. "Koupoulani is an exotic, memorable name."

"Harriet was given it by a tribal King and Queen to whom her father became Christian advisor when he was a missionary in Hawaii saving heathen souls."

"Yes, Sir. We all certainly know that," Emily replied hiding her sarcasm in a sweet tone. Harriet, a pretty, if stern-faced girl, a year older than Emily, curtsied politely to Will Clark, keeping her gaze fixed upon him. She was dressed grandly in a pastel-pink, summer frock with a large flower-laden bonnet on her head. The flowery Hawaiian fabric did not at all match her staid manner. The nosegay of wildflowers Emily had fastened at her collar was paled by the garden-laden bonnet of Koupoulani—known as "Cousin Harriet" to Emily through her neighbors, the Sweetsers.

Loquacious in his friendliness, Samuel Williston, a wealthy trustee of the college, and Squire Dickinson's associate on the board, went on proudly reciting what was already known to all. "Harriet's father, Reverend Richards, sent her to be educated here in America, and she has become our dear daughter, a part of the family since she was very young. She has finished her time at Williston Academy and spent a year at Mount Holyoke, too. Perhaps, Miss Emily, you will have memories of your seminary days there to share with Koupoulani?"

Harriet responded with her eyes still fixed on Clark. "But, Father Sam, I was in the class a year ahead of Cousin Emily. We did not meet there, and I was among the *first* to be saved and excused from common meetings often, thereafter, in any case."

Emily caught Harriet's pious innuendo. "I'd be most happy to share my Mount Holyoke experience with Cousin Harriet, Mr. Williston, but if you will excuse me, Father is calling me to his side to tell President Hitchcock of my time at the seminary. Professor Hitchcock is thinking of sending his daughter to Mistress Lyon's school next year, too. I'm bid to bring them some cakes. Excuse me, Cousin Harriet, Mr. Williston, Mr. Clark." Emily curtsied toward Will Clark. Their eyes met and she tried to send him a look of reluctant departure. He penetrated her gaze with his own as he bowed at her departure. He turned to Williston's adopted daughter, Harriet.

"I shall have to call you '*Queen* Koupoulani,' Miss Harriet. Your father has spoken so highly of your virtues. I understand that you teach at Williston Academy since I left there for Amherst College. I'll be lecturing there in Easthampton, now that I've been graduated."

"Yes, I teach theology since I returned from Mount Holyoke." Harriet Williston was clear and precise in all she said and did, but there was no spirit of fun in her. A goody-two-shoes sort, she spoke with flat, passionless diction, devoid of humor. She was a pious child of missionary stock. Samuel Williston, unable to have children of his own with his beloved wife, was a business tycoon of the valley who had amassed a goodly fortune in button manufacturing, a cottage industry begun by his wife, and built by him into a growing factory endeavor that supplied buttons to Philadelphia, Boston, New York and Chicago retailers. He was a devout Christian, and a Calvinist, much respected for his philanthropy and his strong stance against slavery. Mr. Williston was even more admired than Squire Dickinson among the goodly men of the region. Williston had an approachable manner and more wealth to share at large than Emily's austere father.

Emily glanced back in sorrow to see that William Smith Clark offered Harriet Richards Williston his arm. "Would I could take the Queen's place," she thought in sorrowful frustration.

Clark addressed Harriet. "Shall we stroll in the orchard? I wanted to examine Mr. Dickinson's variety of apple trees? Mr. Williston will you join us?

"No, indeed, you two young people have a nice ramble. You don't need me hobbling along on such a lovely summer's evening! I want to talk with Master Humphrey about his curriculum at Amherst Academy. Perhaps, he has some new ideas for my Williston Academy, as I understand he's been a fine headmaster here. Perhaps, I'll invite him to come to Easthampton and give my teachers a talk on his educational philosophy—though your silver tongue will do us well next term, Master Clark. I'm sure you have some ideas for us to reform our science curriculum. Teaching the chemistry of soil for agriculture is an excellent idea you've proposed. Do go on and show Harriet Mr.

Dickinson's orchard trees. It does my heart good to see her on the arm of a fine young man like you. Your Father's the best physician in Easthampton. I'm glad to call him my doctor these days, Will. He's always ready to give medicine to the poor of my growing village. Bless him. It's no wonder he's produced such a fine graduate of a son, and, a good Master teacher. "

Clark realized that if Mr. Dickinson was discouraging his courtship of Miss Emily, Mr. Williston was offering outright encouragement to him to woo his adopted daughter, but Harriet Richards Williston with her bland personality and religiosity did not interest him in the way that Emily Elizabeth Dickinson did. Emily's wit and naturalness, her love of the woods, wildflowers, and birds intrigued him. He sensed no overwrought religiosity in Emily, but a sincerity beyond homely sentiment. Still, Mr. Williston was the wealthiest man in Western Massachusetts, and if Squire Dickinson would have none of him, Mr. Williston was more than happy to be his patron. Though he knew there would be no clever innuendo in Miss Harriet's conversation, he strolled with her toward the orchard. If he won her hand, he'd win a fortune that would not only put Squire Dickinson back in his snobbish place, but finance his dreams of a rosy future. Ever since Will's father Atherton Clark had moved the family to Easthampton and had the good fortune to become Mr. Williston's physician, the Clark family fortunes had changed for the better. "Harriet Richards Williston would be a lovely catch for you, Will," his father had told him.

"Yes, Will," his mother Harriet Smith Clark had seconded her husband, and then later privately implored: "You might eventually launch yourself as a successful statesman, as did my dear departed father, Senator Smith. Oh, My Dear Son, your life would not be so financially arduous as mine has been since I married your dear father. Please think of courting Harriet Richards and having Squire Williston as your patron. What a blessing Williston could be to all your ambitions! You deserve the opportunities that your father, Dear Man, cannot give you."

Emily, as she obediently offered her tray of cakes to the Hitchcocks, looked back to see Will Clark and Harriet Williston stroll away together. Harriet's lavish bonnet bobbed with pink blossoms as they went. Emily's heart sank with a terrible premonition that she could not fathom. The very sight of Clark had sent a thrill through her being. She resented her duty to her father at that moment, as never before, yet she controlled her emotions, as Dickinsons were trained to.

"Good evening, President Hitchcock, Mrs. Hitchcock. Won't you try some ginger cake? I'm afraid that Father brags more about my baking than it deserves. Mother's the real cook. I always use her recipes. These are her good cream puffs. Please try some. Can I serve you some tea, some wine?"

"Emily, please tell President and Mrs. Hitchcock about your time at Holyoke." Edward politely demanded. "They are thinking of sending their daughter there next term."

"Yes, Father. It's a fine school for Christian ladies. The teachers are diligent and affable. I'm happy to be at home again in Amherst, but there is so much to learn from the teachers at Mount Holyoke, too. Now, when I audit lectures here at Amherst, I understand them better. Your commencement address on the glories of our beloved Pioneer Valley was most inspiring, President Hitchcock. I feel just as you do, about the wonders of our landscape, the Pelham Hills at sunset; the brooks babbling through our hemlocks, maples, and oaks; our meadows fresh with the smell of rowan; our dazzling autumn views of Sugarloaf Mountain; the prism of colors caught in the early frosts that blanket our sight with crystalline sunlight. South Hadley had some lovely vistas of our blessed valley from my dormitory windows, too. I'm sure your daughter will find her term at Mount Holyoke Seminary rewarding as I did."

Edward beamed at his daughter's verbal prowess, as Emily's eyes wandered again to Clark and Harriet. As they disappeared beyond the slope of the orchard in the fading summer twilight, she felt intense frustration.

Her father noted the direction of her gaze and was pleased to see Clark stroll off with Harriet Williston. He felt relief in thinking to himself, "Poor as a church mouse, that smart, upstart Clark. I have my own brilliant Austin to finance. No daughter of mine will marry such poverty no matter how astute. Williston can afford Clark. He has no son of his own, and his adopted boy, Lyman, is deluding himself with Unitarian Transcendentalism in rebellion of all he's been taught.

Williston needs Will Clark in his family. I certainly don't." Satisfied with his silent conclusion, he turned to President Hitchcock of Amherst College again:

"Yes, Professor Hitchcock, my Emily's fond of auditing your natural science lectures. She's always singing praises of our Pelham Hills and valleys and very excited about your amazing dinosaur fossils. She's read everything written about them. Your discoveries have put Amherst on the map of the world to the Glory of Almighty God."

As her father went on talking, Emily stared wistfully in the direction of the orchard into which Will and Harriet had disappeared. She saw the fireflies of late summer twinkling after them. She'd hoped one day to accompany Clark on his adventures as an astute natural scientist: hunting beryl and fossils, exploring hidden caves in the hills for gemstone, silver, and rare wildflowers. Her eyes watered with acute disappointment.

Early Autumn 1850: Ben Newton Of Worcester

Wise are ye, O ancient woods! wiser than man.
>—Ralph Waldo Emerson

Emily, was pleased to find Benjamin Newton, her father's law apprentice and her favorite tutor, studying his law book in a rocking chair by the kitchen hearth when she returned early from church. The rest of the family stayed on for the revival meeting held after the regular service. Ben often came from the Dickinson law office a short walk away to study by the hearth and have his tea. He was a Unitarian and did not attend church services in Amherst where no Unitarian Fellowship existed. Mrs. Dickinson, who had long ago been "saved," was often busy in the kitchen overseeing preparations for lunch after services. Emily used the excuse of wanting to help her mother to avoid staying after Sunday services for revival meetings now taking place regularly at the village church.

"Why light a kettle at the office, too, when there is always one hot at home in my wife's kitchen?" Newton's frugal patron, Squire Dickinson, told him. "And, you can help my frail wife to lift her heavy pots and carry out the ashes from the hearth when you are there taking your tea. She'll feed you hearty soups and stews in return. She's a generous woman, always wanting to please guests and visiting students."

Emily often skipped church completely, pretending not to feel well, so she could sit by the hearth with Ben Newton of Worcester and gather his wisdom of the world beyond her village. Like him, she didn't enjoy the passionless sermons delivered by Reverend Colton at her family's Congregational Church. She preferred to read scriptures by herself, especially "Revelations"—so full of fanciful imagery. She was always reading Shakespeare's plays and sonnets, and Elizabeth Barrett Browning's poems, too, whenever she had time alone in her room.

Another of her father's apprentices, Mr. Bowdoin, was often seated near the hearth with Mr. Newton. They both gave Emily books to read as Bowdoin had surreptitiously lent her his copy of *Jane Eyre*, when she was at Holyoke. Emily, so enthralled with the novel, read it many times over, memorizing several passages therein. She dreamed of being as spiritually independent and steadfast as Jane Eyre, as devoted in love and duty as her favorite heroine.

"Good Sabbath, Master Newton. What are you reading today, may I ask?"

"Good Sabbath, Miss Emily, missing the Revival Meeting again?" His eyes twinkled. "Please call me Ben now. We've known each other for months, and I'm not a real *Master*, just a humble apprentice of your father charged to tutor you in rhetoric, though you hardly need my teaching. I'm reading *Ralph Waldo Emerson's Essays*: "Nature" and "The Poet." But, as you can see, I'm supposed to be reading this law book of your father's and have hidden Emerson's slim volume within. Reading is the only industry your father allows on the Sabbath. Thank goodness he lets me take my tea here in your kitchen. It's lonely in my bunk at the office. If I boil a kettle on the pot-bellied stove there, I roast with it."

"Speaking of the heat, Ben, please tell me more about what Mr. Emerson says of 'the white heat of the soul' while I stir Mother's pudding. She can't hear what we say as she bustles about preparing Father's lunch. You know that Father and Sue Gilbert were both saved this August at meeting, but they didn't seem in 'the white heat of the soul.' True, Father sank to his knees the only time I've known him to be humble, and Sue Gilbert quietly swooned in her pew, but they showed so little emotion compared to the girls at Mount Holyoke. I don't know what to think about it. What does Mr. Emerson say?" Emily had chosen the task of keeping the pudding from scalding to be near Newton at the hearth. Vinnie had gone away to attend Ipswich Female Seminary, and Austin was off teaching immigrant Irish boys in Boston to earn money for Harvard, while Sue Gilbert was in Baltimore teaching mathematics. With her father usually away, Ben was often the only company to join Emily at meals or converse with her about writers and books. She'd fallen in love with his sensibilities.

His eyes brightened to have someone share his fervent passion over Emerson's philosophy. "Let me recite to you a prose poem of Emerson's that I've put to heart. I know you love to walk in the woods, Miss Emily. Emerson called this piece a prose sonnet, and it's titled "Woods:"

*Wise are ye, O ancient woods! wiser than man. Who so goeth in your
paths or into your thickets where no paths are, readeth the same
cheerful lesson whether he be a young child or a hundred years old.
Comes he in good fortune or bad, ye say the same things, & from age
to age. Ever the needles of the pine grow & fall, the acorns on the
oak, the maples redden in autumn, & at all times of the year the ground
pine & the pyrola bud & root under foot. What is called fortune & what
is called Time by men, ye know them not. Men have not language to
describe one moment of your eternal life. This I would ask of you,
O sacred Woods, when ye shall next give me somewhat to say, give me
also the tune wherein to say it. Give me a tune of your own like your
winds or rains or brooks or birds; for the songs of men grow old when
they have been often repeated, but yours, though a man have heard them
for seventy years, are never the same, but always new, like time itself,
or like love.*

"Oh, Ben, how true! It's what I've always felt. I find Emerson
enthralling. I want to write poetry with a tune as new and fresh as the
wind and rain. Do you think you could lend me Emerson's essays to
read after you've finished them? Father will be away in Boston all next
week, and the woods are full of asters and autumn plumage. Warblers
are flitting about and singing their little tunes. Perhaps, you'll have
a good ramble with me? I saw an essay by Emerson in a copy of *The
Atlantic Monthly* The editor, Thomas Wentworth Higginson praised
it fully. Austin took the magazine back to Cambridgeport with him.
I'd be so grateful to borrow your copy of Emerson's essays. I'd be ever
so careful. "

"Indeed, you can keep this little copy in your apron pocket, Miss
Emily, and share it with Austin, but please don't let your father see it.
I've read it many times. I practically have it by heart, now. It's quite
dog-eared. You've served me enough porridge and pudding to pay for
it many times over."

"Thank you, Ben. That's kind of you. Austin when he's home will
love it, too. Father shall never be the wiser." The twenty-year-old
Emily looked at the frail-bodied young man with his beatific gaze

and sensitive face. Ben was ten years her senior, but she felt him to be her soul mate. He'd encouraged Emily to write her own poems of emotional verity.

"If I happen to leave Emerson's essays on my chair as I get up to have the lunch at your mother's kitchen table, and you happen to find them here, and keep them to read, you'll not have to lie to your father as to where you acquired them. You can say you found them. Austin tells me your father's often repentant after being harsh, and I've noticed it's true. Your brother also says: 'What Father doesn't know can't rile him.' "

Emily grinned with Ben who enjoyed her smile. He'd sensed the sadness in her youthful spirit, longing to blossom free of her father's dictates, and her not knowing how to manage her own sensitivity or loathing of hypocrisy. He continued: "Austin says that he rarely debates his Father's beliefs, but just keeps his to himself in the interest of peace. Your Father has bid me tutor you only in mathematics, accounting, and rhetoric, but your vocabulary and grammar need no help. I think you're destined to be a poet, Miss Emily. Emerson offers excellent examples of good writing. If your father discovers I tutored you in them, then we can simply say it's a matter of good rhetoric. Emerson's so popular on the Lyceum circuit, in any case that I hear an essay of his will appear in the Amherst College *Indicator*."

Emily was lost in Ben's pronouncement of her dream. "Do you *really* think I could be a poet like Emerson, Ben? It's my desire, but father has decided there should be little poetry in this house. He's appalled when I read anything but scripture or household finance. God save me from what women call *households*! I'd so rather have the freedom that Austin has. Father feels the romantic novels that I enjoy joggle the mind. I barely get away with reading Shakespeare when he's about. He tolerates us reading *The Springfield Republican* so that we can keep up with the news and make conversation with his guests and associates, but it pains him to allow it. Yet, Vinnie, Austin, and I have learned his bark's bigger than his bite. He kindly brought me some novels from Boston—but they're all chaste and boring: no moonlit walks, or passionate reveries. I sent them to my friend, Sue Gilbert , who enjoyed them. She's more in tune with Father's religious beliefs. She's too busy teaching mathematics in Baltimore to share poetry with me these days. With Austin away, I feel quite lonely. I'm very glad you're here to tutor me. I learn much from you, Ben, of the world of thought beyond Amherst. The novels that Father brings me are about good little wives, and hardworking husbands, making their way in sweet rural villages, because of the virtues of their labors. They seem like fairytales for Puritan wives."

"Well, there's nothing wrong with the virtues of labor, Emily. Yet, there's the worship of creation, itself, and the vast learning of natural science, which when combined with the rich imaginative powers of a quizzical spirit, brings deeply felt awe of all that's wondrous on the Earth! Emerson believes we find truth through releasing feelings. He finds the *feeling* of awe for Nature a subject for good poetry. To be preached at is one thing, but to know the feeling of truth swelling in one's breast is most certainly another." Newton's eyes welled as he spoke. "Emerson says we know moral truths through feeling and empathy for our fellow humans. He says that the deep man does not bury his head in dark churches taking scriptures literally, thinking only of salvation from Jesus. But rather, 'the deep man believes the evil eye can wither. The heart's blessing can heal, and love can overcome all odds.' He's seen souls in the white heat of truth and believes in the power of love over Puritanical punishments. 'God as the power of Love itself,' is the essence of his transcendent message. We know God through emotions and feelings that intuit moral truths."

"Yes, Ben, and Shakespeare's Prospero says at last, when all is said and done, that "The rarer action is in virtue than in vengeance" giving us an *aesthetic* reason for kindness and forgiveness rather than a fear of Hell fires. Such beauty of behavior touches my soul." Emily's nose twitched and her lips quivered as she spoke. It's simply more beautiful to be kind." Emily was enraptured with her tutor who understood her convictions. "We don't need the threat of eternal damnation."

"Emerson feels the same. He says that we must look at The Sermon on the Mount, rather than the Crucifixion, to find The Prophet's truth. Love is a force that overcomes evil! Not dark literal beliefs in the mythology and superstition of scripture, or the fear of damnation, but the study of Nature, herself, brings enlightenment?"

"I hold these thoughts close, Ben. I've seen love overcome evil. I've seen a soul at the white heat."

"Of course you have, Miss Emily!" 'Nature is a language, and every new fact that we learn is a new word; but rightly seen, taken all together, it is not merely a language, but language put together into the most significant and universal book.' That's what Emerson writes. We need to study Nature to find the meaning of Creation."

"I've watched how blue birds and robins nurture and protect their family of siblings, all help the parents rear the young—just as the beaver's family does. If one blue bird falls from a nest and is lost, another family of blue birds shelters it and cares for it. Sun and rain make vegetation flourish for our tables. God's creation nourishes man's belly and his soul. These are the teachings of Nature that echo Christ's Sermon on the Mount. There is too much fire, brimstone, and punishment in cruel, old Puritanical ways." Emily was happy to uncork her cherished beliefs to Ben.

"Yes, Emily. Too much damnation and Armageddon, rather than care for the living as God gave life for the living of it. Yet, there's vulturism, too, on land, and in the sea and air. Nature can be fierce, too, and we must respect her forces and conquer negative greed and selfishness in humankind to make a better life on earth. Civilization, for the most part, has at least learned to rise above cannibalism. There's hope." Ben laughed. "If there's a God. Emily, surely he means most of all to teach us to be kind. "The rarer action *is* in virtue, than in vengeance," as you've quoted Shakespeare.

"Yes, Ben. When a teacher at the academy threatens a student with punishment, they only stutter more, just as the fear of damnation seems to make beasts of some people. But if a kind preceptor offers gentle and loving encouragement, the student flourishes from the empathy given. I love Father all the more when he's kind, and can't help disliking him when he's cruel to the horses. The horses obey Austin's kindly rearing better than Father's whip! Students at the academy thrive on positive encouragement better than at the switch that humiliates and stings their flesh and pride. The novel *Jane Eyre* teaches this precept well. 'Love is the only human force of emotion that saves us with nurturance and understanding in a world of labor and tribal enmity." Emily concluded. "That love is all there is, is all we know of love."

"Dear Emily! You speak with a poet's tongue. There's much sentimental verse afoot with ladies writing mere effusions with no true feeling—fashionable sentiments pressed into rhyme and meter. As if the poetic form preceded the thought, instead of springing from it. Such poetry does not reach the healing depths of which Mr. Emerson speaks. It is more word play than feeling." Ben opened his little book. "Here's what Emerson wrote in 1841 in The Poet:"

It is not meters, but a meter-making argument that makes a poem—a thought so passionate and alive, that, like the spirit of a plant or an animal, it has an architecture all it's own, and adorns nature with a new thing. The thought and the form are equal in the order of time, but in the order of genius the thought is prior to the form.

"It's the *only* way we shall forge a great new American literature, a national literature not imitative of England!"

"Yes, Ben, a national literature, an *American* literature," Emily agreed. That's what Austin spoke of in his graduation speech. He agrees with you, Ben! Austin said that after the Revolution, the wealthiest Tories here in the colonies took their education and riches back to Europe rather than concede American victory over the King's cruel colonialism. Only we pioneers of true *American* Republicanism and Jeffersonian ideals of democracy were left here to realize the dream of justice and equality in our new country. It's our duty as the educated ones of our new land to forge a literature that espouses truth and justice for all out of our own American tongue. We must not imitate English aristocracy, but create a literature wholly American with our *own* ideals out of the beauty of our *own* spirit and our *own* land!"

Mrs. Dickinson called from the other side of the kitchen: "Emily, come! Isn't the pudding long done? It's time to serve the reverend his lunch and join your Father at table." Mrs. Dickinson emerged from the sink room and busied herself slicing meat and bread. "Stir the soup and fill the tureen, too, Dear! Dish some out for Mr. Newton here in the kitchen. Pour the pudding to cool in the pudding cups, and leave one for Mr. Newton's dessert. Please hurry."

"I shall, Mother!" Emily called back dutifully.

"Your mother makes up in Christian charity for your father's Puritan severity, Miss Emily." Newton whispered and stood, winking at Emily, as he left his worn copy of Emerson's essays on the rocker. "You are very like your mother in looks and demeanor. She is a kind and humble woman, and a fine gardener!"

Emily was glad to hear her mother's virtue praised, as her father was more often the center of all attention and compliments. It made her feel that Ben's kindness was sincere and that he understood well what Jesus said when he spoke of how "the meek shall inherit the earth" and how "we are our brother's keeper." Though Emily regretted her mother's lack of interest in books and thinking, she admired her Christian sincerity, her generosity with food and flowers for neighbors in need of solace, her duty to her family. She empathized with her feminine position in the household and felt sad about the way her spirit seemed crushed by her husband's will.

Emily tucked the little volume of Emerson into her big apron pocket. "Oh, thank you, Ben." She whispered. You are a kind inspiration to me! If it were up to Father, I'd never gain a new idea."

"Think nothing of it, Emily. Your Mother's good pudding is payment enough! Do give her my compliments and thanks."

"I shall, Ben, and oh please, let's have a ramble in the *wise* woods as soon as you can get away from duties at the office! I know a path through the pines that opens out into an oak glen where we can find great peace and solace, a place where I found yellow lady-slippers and white Indian pipes nearby last spring. We need to visit Nature for the sake of our suffering souls."

"Indeed, we do, Miss Emily! The great pines are our true cathedrals."

"Yes, Ben, yes. Their aroma makes me glad of life! Good Sabbath, Master Ben!" Emily curtsied and hurried to her mother's bidding. She paused only long enough to tuck her "found" volume of Emerson's essays deeply into her big apron pocket under a tea towel.

November 1850: Austin's Thanksgiving Turkey

One day is there of the series
  Termed Thanksgiving day,
Celebrated part at table,
  Part in memory.

Neither patriarch nor pussy,
  I dissect the play;
Seems it, to my hooded thinking,
  Reflex holiday.

Had there been no sharp subtraction
  From the early sum,
Not an acre or a caption
  Where was once a room,

Not a mention, whose small pebble
  Wrinkled any bay, —
Unto such, were such assembly,
  'T were Thanksgiving day.

"Austin, wait! " Emily her auburn hair covered with her brother's grey, woolen hat, called after her robust sibling as he trooped ahead of her through trees and brush iced with the first snow of late autumn. All was glistening at the edge of their grove. The field beyond was blinding white in the sun. "You walk too fast. It's so cold, I can't keep up!"

"I don't walk too fast, Little Sister! I just have longer legs! It's not my fault you're no bigger than a wren!"

"Well, is it mine that you're as strong-legged as a horse? Slow down, please! I was up earlier making your breakfast, after all. Your big breeches are falling down on me and holding me back."

"Mother and Father are always telling you to eat more, Em, and you should, if you want to wear my breeches."

"I'd have time to eat more, if you'd eat less, the way I'm always serving you! I made you a grand breakfast. So pause a bit and wait for me!"

"Rest here a little then." Austin motioned for his sister to sit on the fallen log beside him from which he brushed the snow for her.

Emily sat close to Austin to collect his warmth. "Did you really like my Thanksgiving poem, Austin?"

"I did, indeed. Thanksgiving has become a reflexive, rather than reflective, holiday. It needs emotional meaning, deeper than feasting, restored to it. All the same, I enjoy the feasting."

"Yes, at Mother's and my expense of labor. Vinnie dusts China and polishes silver while Mother and I bake for days. Then you and Father gobble our lovely dinner in an hour!"

"Ah, but we men appreciate your womanly labors. Father brags about your baking everywhere. It's the only thing he boasts about, since he feigns humility in all else! Emmy, you've got to help me convince Father to let me go to Harvard for law. He thinks I should go to Calvinist Yale as he did. I want to move away from this Puritan life to a big city someday, perhaps Chicago or New York, maybe go West to practice law. I don't want to be stuck here in this little village forever. There's a wide world to explore out there."

"But, Austin, there's no place as wonderful as our Amherst with the multicolored Pelham hills framing it in autumn. I love this Pioneer Valley, made of our family's earliest American dreams. Father hopes you'll take over his practice as he did his father's. Amherst is Father's life, Vinnie, and I could never bear your going away without us. We'd die missing you and all the fun you bring into the house with your manly society and brilliant wit. Who will appreciate you more than we, your sisters, who love you so dearly?"

"Oh, you just fancy my friends, like George Gould! You don't need to flatter me to flirt with him."

"Austin, you know I *never* merely flatter!"

"Very well, Em, but Father is no fool like Grandfather Samuel was. He does well for himself. He won't need me as Grandfather needed him to restore our family fortunes and dignity. I want to see the world as Will Clark is doing in Germany. I've got at least to get to Harvard in Cambridgeport, to live near Boston. Help me persuade Father that it would be good for the family fortunes to have a son with a *Harvard Law Degree*. It will bring us respect from modern-minded men."

"I hope father does go off to Washington to represent our region in Congress! Think of the dancing parties, *Poetry in Motion*, we could have when he's away, but not unless he takes Mother with him. She'd be shocked to see us dancing!"

"That's my point! One has to get out of this Puritan village to enjoy life."

"We have fun here, together, Austin, and Father is away plenty of the time. If you promise me you'll come back to live in Amherst, I'll get Vinnie and Mother to help persuade Father, to let you go to Harvard instead of his Yale Alma Mater. If you tell him you'll live at Uncle Joel's in Cambridgeport to save money, he'll probably agree. Anything to save money! Mother will help as she trusts you'll be safer living with her kin. Vinnie and I can visit you in Boston. It'll be such fun to have you show us about and introduce us to your chums! But, I'd miss you terribly if you go so far as Chicago or New York. I'd never see you, and that would be so horrible for me! The decadence of those huge cities would be awful for your health. You always suffer neuralgia, sniffles, and coughing in grubby cities! Besides, New York approves slavery, and we Dickinsons of Massachusetts are Free Soilers!"

"Remember Sister, the Massachusetts Bay Colony was the first to legalize the holding of slaves in these United States, so we'd damn well better work at freeing them! Old England has made slavery unlawful since 1834. We New Englanders should be ashamed of ourselves, lagging behind with our talk of democracy and equality! That's what Clark declares as he sounds off on the college green and on the commons. You should have heard his stirring speech on the subject at Williston Academy. Sam Williston got up and said how his button factories could not have existed and brought him wealth enough to subsidize the academy had it not been for an intelligent black man who taught him how to develop the equipment." Austin enjoyed oratory.

"But, Frederick Douglass and Sojourner Truth have spoken in Nantucket, now, and in Boston! Our valley is not as evil as the South."

"True, but California's admitted to the Union this year as a free state. That's why I want to go there, prospect for gold and stake a claim to my own land like a red-blooded American pioneer!"

Austin's talk of going west frightened Emily to the core, not only for his welfare, but for her own and her Father's. "Sue said that Frederick Douglass returned from England, a freed man and started his own newspaper, *Northstar*, in Rochester. Sue has read so many exciting books while studying in Geneva, New York. She heard Sojourner Truth speak and says that the woman is every bit as stirring as Douglass. Sue lent me Douglass's narrative in '45 when it came out and was in a *fifth* printing. Imagine, Aussie! Such a stirring book published here in Massachusetts! Why I dare say there's not a single book ever published in California as yet! Wouldn't you love to write a book as powerful as Douglass's that many would read and hold in their hearts? Oh, Aussie, I'd die if you left our valley. You are the only one in this family I can really talk with, even if you tease me so. Think of Mother and Vinnie and how much we need our great Austin! If you leave New England, we'll surely perish without his manly presence."

Emily's face grew sad. Then she thought for a moment and brightened. "Sue was such a wonderfully smart girl when she attended the academy with me, Austin! Have you seen Susan Huntington Gilbert these days since she returned from studying in Geneva, New York? She's so lovely and so's her sister, Mattie. I adore them."

"Their sister, Harriet, married Cutler, didn't she?

"Yes, while you were away in Boston. They all work in his Main Street store. Poor Sue, she's an orphan, and her older sister, Mary, has died, too. Sue would be just right for you, Austin. She's so very clever. President Hitchcock's son at the college is courting her, you know. Her talk is so brilliant and learned. You thought her very pretty, too. Do you think you could win her hand over President Hitchcock's son?"

"If I wanted to, I dare say I could, but stop your matchmaking, Little Sister. It's risky business. Sue's pretty, and so are many others, but I rather fancy Martha as the sweeter Gilbert sister." Austin rose to resume the hunt. "Let's search the other end of the meadow near the woods. I've seen turkey there recently."

Emily scrambled to follow, pulling up her borrowed breeches as she went. "Oh well, you probably couldn't win Sue away from Edward Hitchcock, in any case." Emily wanted to irk Austin to action.

"Huh, if I wanted to, I easily could." Austin stomped off through the snow. "You know very well I'm the better man."

"Of course you are. That's why you deserve Susie over Hitchcock's son." Emily leapt forward to follow him. "Father admires Sue very much you know. She's been so helpful at church."

"It's me who has to like her if I'm going to court her! Look, a turkey!" Austin whispered as he raised his musket and fired.

"Did you get it?' Emily covered her ringing ears.

"No, I missed. It went that way. Come along!" Austin loaded his musket for another shot as he hurried ahead.

Emily followed quickly, keeping up her persuasion as she went. "Well, we can't have Amherst's most eligible bachelor wasted on a dull woman, just because she's pretty. Sue's a brilliant mind to match yours. Father would love the fact that he could take an orphaned daughter-in-law into our family. He'd have another daughter, and not lose you to a father-in-law. Just think, Austin, you'd have no father-in-law or mother-in-law to contend with! Isn't that a blessing? Sue's eloquent. It would take some pressure from me not to have to be the leading lady of father's trustee dinners, with mother always ill with her neuralgia. Sue knows how to entertain well, having been raised by a once prosperous innkeeper. She'd be such a good and graceful housewife. Mother, Lavinia, and I have asked her to Thanksgiving dinner with her sister Martha. Father approved the invitation. Their brothers continue to do well in Michigan."

"I know. I'd like to follow them!"

"They say life is hard on women out west. Her brothers have pledged a lovely dowry should Sue marry and settle in New England. Sue staves off all the young men. She's not anxious to marry."

"Emily, hush, you're scaring away any possibility of game for Mother's table with your chattering. Besides, I fancy Martha more than her sister, Sue. She's not as witty or clever, but so sweet and subdued. She reminds me of our Dear Sweet Mother."

"That's because Mother dotes on you and dreams of a grand paradise in which Austins have no end. Mother would die if you went west. I like Mattie, too, but Sue has an independent mind. She's not happy being beholden to her brother-in-law and sister, Harriet, who has to work so hard at Cutler's store! She plans to be a teacher of mathematics. Fancy that for a woman! I so admire her. If I were a man, I'd propose to her myself! She'd be good at household management. She'd not have to read that book *The Frugal Housewife*, that Father pressed upon mother to make her into a fit wife for him. He's always urging me to read it, too, but it's so boring. I'd rather read Emily Bronte. Sue likes romantic novels, too."

"No doubt Father's correct in saying they joggle the mind of young women. Hush! I think I heard a gobble."

Emily crouched behind her brother and whispered. "Still, he brought me three chaste novels when he came back from Northampton last week. He's such a contradiction; *Father, can I go out to swim? Yes my darling daughter. Hang your clothes on the mulberry bush, but don't go near the water.*" Emily sang the nursery rhyme to illustrate her point.

"That rhyme's Father for sure, he'd like to keep us in a nursery forever." Austin thrashed through the snow with Emily struggling behind him, hanging on his coat to scamper over the drifts. "He does the same to me. Encouraging me to understand the wide world, but wanting me always to stay next door at Amherst College to do it!"

"He's even worse with Vinnie and me, Austin!"

"That's because you're girls, and he should be to keep you out of trouble! He did seem to encourage you towards my good friend, Leonard Humphrey, at dinner the other night!"

"That's because he knows good friends don't get nice girls in any trouble by demanding kisses of their friend's sisters. Besides, Leonard is teaching at the Academy and he respects that. I wrote a splendidly naughty Valentine for Bowdoin to tease him. One for George Gould, too!"

"I'm afraid Father doesn't like my good chum, George, hanging about you Emmy. He says George is too poor and sickly. You'd better watch what Valentines you send around this gossipy town! We Dickinson's can't stir a twig without the whole town quaking. I've learned that the hard way."

"George is a fine lad, Austin, and I so admire him, but not as attractive as Cousin William Smith Clark. I understand from the

Sweetsers that Clark's studies in Göettingen are going splendidly. He wrote home about the custom of kissing in greeting and having Christmas Trees! Clark is the most dashing man I've ever met! Next to you, of course, Austin, the most eligible bachelor of all Amherst!

"Leonard's more the man for you, Em. Father might approve him. He's to be offered the head master position at Amherst Academy. Clark's too ambitious and poor. He won't stay put. I wish Father would allow me to go to Europe, but he'll never do it. I'll have to settle for Boston. I'm being kept here to help Father spy on the professors and trustees. He's so worried that they're not frugal, and he wants them to be good Puritan teachers who follow every rule strictly with the students. The college is doing fine, but he'll never get over Grandfather Sam's nearly bankrupting it. He harps on how he has to retrieve our Dickinson honor if he's to succeed in going to Washington as a Massachusetts representative. He's planning on joining the Temperance Society, too. All those Town Meetings he led have gone to his head."

"No, Aussie, that's not it. He wants to go to Congress so that he can get the railroad to come to Amherst for the good of the seminary and town."

"Exactly. All he cares about is the success of Amherst over Northampton. The success of Amherst College, the financial good of the town, bringing the railroad here."

"Yes. He works himself to death, and expects us to take care of mother and the household. As a result, he's hardly home and with mother often in bed with her headaches, we do as we please much of the time."

"Well, why can't he just leave the house to you girls and Mother and let me be my own man?"

"Oh, Austin, sometimes you're as restrictive as father! It's as if Vinnie and I and Mother were meant to do nothing but serve you both for the rest of our lives. In any event, Father will be home for Thanksgiving."

"Good Puritan wives and sisters serve their men, Emily, because the men must make careers in the world to feed women and their babies in order to proliferate our stock. We're your protectors. You should not have to go off into the grubby world and work on your own as Sue Gilbert did. It's not ladylike!

"Well, if you married pretty, smart Sue, she'd not need to go off and teach to earn a living to get away from Mr. Cutler and his dusty store. She's spent her whole youth doing chores in her father's inn, and now it's her brother-in-law's store. She's too smart, clever, witty, and beautiful for that. She and I so enjoy reading books together. Her observations are always brilliant. She'd be such a fine wife for you and a wonderful sister for me!"

"I see your scheme. You want me to keep your school chum in Amherst for *you*!"

"Austin, really, it's *not* just that! I think Sue fancies you over all the men of Amherst, and they all fancy her more than *any* other. She's the most charming. President Hitchcock's son fancies her most, but Sue says you are the handsomest and smartest of all—like our father whom she admires so. She feels she could help a man be a congressman, because she knows how to keep a house and entertain. She pities mother's shy ineptitude, as much as I do. Fancy that! Yet, she loves Mother for her true Christian piety. They get on well at The Bible Society together. Sue is always helping Mother at church."

"All right, Em, I concede that Sue is interesting and pretty. Now, stop chattering like a busy wren! Your matchmaking is spoiling my turkey shoot. If you keep prattling in my ear, I'll never catch our Thanksgiving turkey!"

"All right then, I'll hush, but don't say I never told you! Sue's turned down some eligible Amherst suitors to go off and teach school. You'd make a good match. Father says it's good that I invited an orphaned young lady like her, because she's such a good presence at church. I promise to help convince father you should go to Harvard, not Yale, for your law degree if you are especially cordial to Dear Sue. Imagine: 'William Austin Dickinson, Esquire, Harvard University, hanging his shingle in Amherst! I can see it now, and with lovely, brilliant Sue Gilbert Dickinson, teacher of mathematics, as his wife. Sue will be back from her apprenticeship, just when you've finished Harvard, come to think of it!

"Hush, Emmy, I see our Thanksgiving bird scratching through the leaves yonder. Marry Sue off to Leonard Humphrey, now that he'll be head master of the academy."

"Austin, how can you tease me? You know I'm hoping Leonard might be my beau."

"Then do send him a Valentine. He sent you one last year. I think he fancies your wit and likes to read your compositions on botany."

Emily whispered gleefully. "Austin, should I? Do you really think Leonard fancies me?"

"George Gould fancies you even more, and he's become quite a Transcendentalist like Emerson. He has a wit to match yours, if only he had money. Write a Valentine for him, and he'll love it. It will have to be very clever. He's a smart lad. Almost as clever as me."

"Yes, indeed. I've heard your conversations at the kitchen hearth. He's deeply sincere and sensitive." Emily holding up her breeches struggled to keep up with her hearty brother as he strode through the deep snow of the meadow.

"Do you think I'd pick a dullard for my best friend? Now, let me hunt, girl! I see the turkey we shall have for Thanksgiving dinner." Austin whispered as he raised his musket. "There's our Tom turkey at the edge of the meadow. Be still as a toadstool." Austin whispered.

"Must you kill it, Austin?" Emily spoke softly, stopping still in her tracks. "Its beautiful iridescence gives me the palsy—just to behold such color refracted in the sun." Emily thought how Benjamin Franklin wanted the turkey as national emblem more than the bald eagle, proclaiming it more intelligent and familial. "Look, Austin, it's so peaceful in that patch of sun. We can have carrots and turnips for our dinner. I'll bake a great walnut and cranberry bread for Father. Don't shoot!"

"Hush, Em!" Austin whispered back. "I've promised mother a Thanksgiving turkey for her table. Stop shivering at my elbow while I take aim."

Emily fell to her knees in the snowy grass and covered her heart, silently praying for the bird. "What a beautiful and sad creation we live in!" she thought as she covered her ears with her mittens and Austin fired. Her brother's musket rang through the November woods as the sun began to rise higher, 'a ribbon at a time.'

The turkey, stung by Austin's bullet, fell dead in a quivering flash of iridescent feathers that brought tears to Emily's eyes!

"I've got it!" Austin raced ahead triumphant to bag his game.

February 1850: "Such Transcendental Prospect"

A deep man believes…the heart's blessing can heal,
and love can overcome all odds.

—Ralph Waldo Emerson

Sitting in the family parlor, reading the Amherst College Newsletter, *The Indicator*—

Emily could not believe her eyes. There it was for all to see. Her Valentine letter for George Gould, and it mentioned her dog, Carlo, named for the dog in *Jane Eyre*. Had her father seen the Valentine letter and known it was hers? She read it again to see which phrases he might object to. She wanted to be ready with an argument, like a lawyer, to defend herself:

Magnum bonum, "harum scarum," zounds et zounds, et war alarum, man reformam, life perfectum, mundum changum, all things flarum?

Sir, I desire an interview; meet me at sunrise, or sunset, or the new moon—the place is immaterial. In gold, or in purple, or sackcloth—I look not upon the raiment . With sword, or with pen, or with plough— the weapons are less than wielder. In coach, or in wagon, or walking, the equipage far from the man. With soul, or spirit, or body, they are all alike to me. With hose or alone, in sunshine or storm, in heaven or earth, some how or no how—I propose, sir, to see you.

And not to see merely, but a chat, Sir, or a tete-a-tete, a confab, a mingling of opposite minds is what I propose to have. I feel sir that we shall agree. We will be David and Jonathan, or Damon and Pythias, or what is better than either, the United States of America. We will talk over what we have learned in our geographies, and listened to from the pulpit, the press and the Sabbath School.

This is strong language, Sir, but none the less true. So hurrah for North Carolina, since we are on this point.

Our friendship Sir, shall endure till sun and moon shall wane no more, till stars shall set, and victims rise to grace the final sacrifice. We'll be instant, in season, out of season, minister, take care of, cherish, sooth, watch, wait, doubt, refrain, reform, elevate, instruct. All choice spirits however distant are ours, ours theirs; there is a thrill of sympathy—a circulation of mutuality—cognationem inter nos! I am Judith the heroine of the Apocrypha, and you the orator of Ephesus.

That's what they call a metaphor in our country. Don't be afraid of it, sir, it won't bite. If it was my Carlo now! The Dog is the noblest work of Art, sir. I may safely say the noblest—his mistress's rights he doth defend—although it bring him to his end—although to death it doth him send!

But the world is sleeping in ignorance and error, sir, and we must be crowing cocks, and singing larks, and rising sun to awake her; or else we'll pull society up to the roots, and plant it in a different place. We'll build Alms-houses, and transcendental State prisons, and scaffolds—we will blow out the sun, and the moon, and encourage invention. Alpha shall kiss Omega—we will ride up the hill of glory— Hallelujah, all hail!

Yours truly, C.

It was clear that the mention of Carlo, so known about the town as Emily's constant companion, would disclose to all that the daughter of the eminent townsman and important member of the board of Amherst College had written the scandalous Valentine. As soon as Emily finished rereading the last line, she heard the front door bang. Her father pounded into his study and slammed his library door just hard enough to make Emily aware that he'd likely read *The Indicator* before coming home from his treasurer's office at the college.

She hurried to the back hall, grabbed her shawl from a hook in her "Northwest Passage" and ran out into the barn where she met up with Carlo, her black Newfoundlander given her by her father to protect her on her rambles through the woods and countryside. Carlo was dependable watchdog for the homestead, and a loyal protector of Emily when Squire Dickinson and Austin were absent.

Carlo's tail wagged happily as Emily opened the back door of the barn and ran with him towards the woods behind the house. She decided the best strategy would be to avoid her father until he'd had some time to calm down from seeing her Valentine in the college newspaper. She hoped he hadn't seen it, but something in the stride and the firmness with which he slammed his library door told her he had. She found a stump in the woods and sat down to look at her published valentine again.

"Oh, no, Carlo! I'm sure this is the skullduggery of Henry Shipley who edits *The Indicator* with George. It is just like that beautiful tempter, Shipley, to pull such a prank on George and me. She remembered the Valentine poem that had been sent to Bowdoin, her father's apprentice, the year prior. It had been published in *The Springfield Republican* and signed with the initials Q.E.D. It had made her father furious, even though it was less obvious it was hers. It ran through her mind as she sat with Carlo peering at *The Indicator*.

"Sic transit gloria mundi,"
"How doth the busy bee,"
"Dum vivimus vivamus,"
I stay mine enemy!

Oh "veni, vidi, vici!"
Oh caput cap-a-pie!
And oh "memento mori"
When I am far from thee!....

Put down the apple, Adam,
And come away with me,
So shalt thou have a pippin
From off my father's tree!

I climb the "Hill of Science,"
I "view the landscape o'er;"
Such transcendental prospect,
I ne'er beheld before!....

During my education,
It was announced to me

That gravitation, stumbling,
Fell from an apple tree!

The earth upon an axis
Was once supposed to turn,
By way of a gymnastic
In honor of the sun!

It was the brave Columbus,
A sailing o'er the tide,
Who notified the nations
Of where I would reside!

Mortality is fatal—
Gentility is fine,
Rascality, heroic,
Insolvency, sublime!

Our Fathers being weary,
Laid down on Bunker Hill;
And tho' full many a morning,
Yet they are sleeping still,—

The trumpet, sir, shall wake them,
In dreams I see them rise,
Each with a solemn musket
A marching to the skies!

A coward will remain, Sir,
Until the fight is done;
But an immortal hero
Will take his hat, and run!....

In token of our friendship
Accept this "Bonnie Doon,"
And when the hand that plucked it
Hath passed beyond the moon,

The memory of my ashes
Will consolation be;
Then, farewell, Tuscarora,
And farewell, Sir, to thee!

Her father's wrath would surely be upon her for such brazen publication so close to home, and his disapproval was very hard for her to bear. He was both so nurturing and authoritarian that there was no dealing with his criticism, always couched in terms of the reputation and financial well being of the family. Because he was an important lawyer of the village, and a trustee of the university, as well as a statesman, he had justification for believing that Dickinsons must set a proper example of behavior, and he never strayed from that dictate. With such noble reason, he pressed his brood into submission. Her valentine would surely offend his sense of propriety and family dignity.

"The part about Transcendental prisons surely infuriated him, Carlo!" She had a habit of talking to her big black dog as if he were a human companion. Though she did not expect Carlo to understand her words, she knew he always felt her emotions. He gave a whine and laid his head in her lap so she could pet and scratch behind his ears. "What shall I do? Father was so angry at the Valentine poem published in *The Springfield Republican*. Though it was an anonymous prank to tease Bowdoin, he called it obscene for a lady to write such suggestive things, spoiling her character, let alone publish it to the world! There is going to be hell to pay, Carlo! Perhaps, we'd better go fall in the river and catch a chill so severe that he won't dare scold us?" She rested her head on Carlo's, and thought of her predicament. Then she heard her mother's dinner bell clanging. "Well, we might just as well get it over with, Carlo! Perhaps, he will simmer into a hotter fury if we're late for dinner."

Emily, with her canine guardian following close at her heels, made her way back through the path towards the back of the house. The woods were frozen, but the evergreen hemlocks gave off their piney scent as she brushed past them. The sugar maples swelled with sap and threatened to burst their branches toward the sky. "Now, Father will forbid me to go sugaring this Saturday with my friends. He thinks it's a sin to eat too much maple syrup, in any case. 'Too many sweets will spoil your mind and make you decadent, Emily, and there is evidence it ruins the teeth. Beware excess!' says he, all the while being *excessively* austere." She tramped across the lawn growing angrier at every step with her confinement in her father's house and her dependency on his financial support.

"Damn! If only I was as hardy in body as Susie, Carlo! I'd run away and be independent as she!" In privacy, Emily swore in imitation of Austin. "I don't give a damn what Father says. I'm going sugaring this Saturday with our crowd if I have to climb out my bedroom window on a rope! Amherst is alive with fun this winter and I plan to have my share of it! Come, Good Boy, let's face the tyrant. Damn that tempter, Shipley! That handsome devil's made me pay sorely for trusting him to give George my Valentine. Poor George is doubtless mortified."

Emily entered the warm kitchen where her mother, dressed in her usual dark mourning dress with white muslin apron over it, was lighting oil lamps. An aromatic stew was cooking on the hearth. The smell of fresh baked rye met her nostrils.

"Um, Mother, your bread smells so good. Let me help you!"

" Emily. I'm glad you're on time for dinner. I'm afraid your father has something urgent to discuss with you. Prepare yourself for his sharp disapproval. He hasn't told me what it is, but he has that big frown on his face and came into the kitchen and smashed a copy of the college newsletter down on the sideboard, asking me where was his wayward daughter, the authoress! Dish a lovely plate of stew for him, Dear, and cut him a hearty piece of warm rye. Butter it well as you butter your tongue. Set it before him with a kind curtsy and a smile. Tell him you baked it especially for him. A man's heart is often reached through his stomach."

After donning her apron, Emily did as her mother advised. She prepared her father's plate while Carlo obediently took his place by the kitchen fire where his food and water bowl were ready. Emily with trepidation entered the dining room where Squire Dickinson sat waiting to be fed. As she carried his plate to him, she spoke mellifluously. "Good evening, Dear Father. I hope you've had a pleasant day. Here's your favorite beef stew, piping hot, with lovely carrots and potatoes I grew and harvested, chosen carefully from our root cellar. I helped Mother bake your favorite rye bread, and slathered it with butter that I spent all afternoon churning."

Squire Dickinson did not say "thank you" as he usually did. He knew why Emily was being unctuous, but waited for his family to assemble themselves at table. Lavinia came in to pour her father a glass of berry wine, and then take her place beside Emily. Mrs. Dickinson entered, wiping her hands on her apron. Squire Dickinson began to recite Grace as his wife and daughters bowed their heads. With Austin away at school, only the four of them were dining together. Maggie, the maid, had been allowed home early to spend supper with her family near the railroad station where she lived in the Irish ghetto also inhabited by Tom Kelly, the handy man of the Dickinson homestead. Emily regretted that Maggie would not return until morning as her father was always more private with his talk in front of the day servants. Maggie's presence, serving dinner, might have softened his reprimand, and she'd have had Maggie to comfort her distress afterward as they washed and dried dinner dishes together.

"Dear Lord in Heaven, we thank thee for this good repast, this fine food that thou givest us, and we are grateful for the health you have bestowed upon us all of late. We pray forgiveness for our many sins, and ask that you bless this good food prepared by our good wife and our daughter Lavinia. We pray for their health and well being and thank thee God for thy goodness, the ample fortunes which you have bestowed upon us, allowing us to live in our good home, in our blessed parish, devoted to Our Lord—spreading the word of his teachings from our village Church throughout the countryside of Amherst. Most of all, Lord, we pray tonight for the salvation of the soul of our wayward daughter, Emily Elizabeth, who embarrasses our household and our name by once again, daring to have published, before the eyes of the world, another of her bold and audacious Valentine greetings. We pray she will see how she hurts the reputation of her loving family by publishing such shameless blasphemy for all to see! We pray that she will, at last, learn to be a lady of delicate sensibility and feminine demeanor, like her Dear Mother, with the well being of her family and her church, topmost in her heart!"

Lavinia and Mrs. Dickinson looked sidewise at Emily from their bowed heads. They pitied her plight. She felt their gaze, but kept her eyes fixed on the table.

"We pray in the name of our Lord Jesus Christ. Amen." Squire Dickinson finished his impeachment, and raised his spoon, which signaled that all could begin supping. Lavinia was happy to dive wholeheartedly into her plate to satisfy her hearty appetite. She thought it best to say nothing and ignore her father's reprimand of Emily.

Mrs. Dickinson looked at Emily as if to command, "Say nothing in reply, Dear." She gently picked up her spoon and began to sip at her stew in a ladylike fashion nodding for Emily to do the same.

Emily decided that it would be best not to answer her father's prayer with a rebuttal. She followed her mother's suit. No one looked at anyone as they silently ate. When her father had finished his last morsel, Lavinia leapt up to fetch the tea tray from the kitchen. Mrs. Dickinson hurried after her to bring her husband cake for his dessert.

Squire Dickinson and Emily were left sitting alone. Emily kept her head down looking at her plate. "Emily Elizabeth," Squire Dickinson began, "did I not distinctly tell you never to allow publication of anything you write, ever again, since your Valentine to Mr. Bowdoin was published in *The Springfield Republican*? Did I not tell you never again to cause our family to endure such embarrassment? Do you not understand that a public advocate cannot have a daughter who publishes her writing, let alone writing of such a radical order? You know how unlady like it is, and, with your dog's name, Carlo, so prominently there to let everyone know who you are? Did you not swear to me, you would never publish another word again, especially not one espousing ideas of Transcendental nonsense that flies in the face of our blessed faith?"

"Yes, Father, but truly I did not allow nor seek publication. Henry Shipley is to blame. The star student of your college and Austin's fraternity brother tricked me. Shipley drinks too much to realize what harm he's doing with the mischief he loves to perpetrate!"

"Your friend, Mr. Gould, the editor of *The Indicator* is likely behind this embarrassment! That is what I shall tell the trustees should they bring up the discussion. Meantime, confine yourself to the house. No going to audit any lectures at the college, and no having Mr. Gould here in the parlor. I shall tell Austin to reprimand Gould and never allow him to darken my door again for this affront! If you did not put such Valentines into the hands of reckless boys, this would not have happened!"

"But Father, it wasn't George who published it. It was Henry Shipley. I know that Shipley's father donates much to the college, and so he feels he has a license to do as he pleases. It's not George's fault at all. Besides, Father, Valentine's Day is our only holiday here in the valley and everyone writes outlandish Valentines. No one takes them seriously. It's the one time of the year when everyone's allowed to let thoughts ramble uncensored by reason. Please, Father. You know that Austin and I enjoy Mr. Gould's conversation and learning. He's a devout young man studying for the priesthood. It was all Shipley's doing."

"Yes, Shipley's father donates a goodly sum of money to the college every year. Gould is poor as a church mouse. Unfortunately, I shall have to find some way to deal with Shipley, but Gould is a flagrant upstart, above his station, and no longer welcome in this house."

"Please, do not banish him for Austin's sake, if not mine. He's Austin's good friend and schoolmate. He's a gentle soul who has great respect for you, Father. My name was not on the valentine. Perhaps, most will not know it's mine nor care."

"Don't condescend the intelligence of the gossips of this village, nor of the trustees of the college. I did not say you could not write and send Valentines. I said you must not *publish* them. A state senator's daughter whose father is a trustee of the college must have a feminine decorum for the good of her family's reputation and the fortunes of her father's district. Haven't I made it quite clear to you that our family's financial wellbeing, including yours, Emily Elizabeth *Dickinson*, depends upon my reputation as an advocate and the good behavior of this family?"

"Yes, Father, you have made it very clear, but…"

"Then that is enough upon the subject. You will not go to the college for a fortnight and you will be confined to these quarters for as long, and Mr. Gould is banished from my parlors and kitchen hearth for good. Do you understand my wishes, Emily Elizabeth?"

"But, Father, you know how I love to audit the lectures at the college. It's my only education since I returned from Holyoke. Please, Father. George Gould meant us no harm as there is nothing too terrible in my Valentine. Many students are interested in Emerson's Transcendentalism. Why, there is an essay by Emerson titled 'Self Reliance' in the same issue of *The Indicator*, and much writing on women's right to education and to publication. These ideas are afoot among all of Austin's friends at the college!"

"I do not care what the other students are thinking. I know what my children should be doing. I've told you that a woman's place is at her hearth, laboring for the health and spiritual good of her family. Publication by a lady of your position in our parish is unseemly. Enough! I have spoken. Here comes Mother and Lavinia with our tea. There is no need to spoil any further this repast that Mother has labored over. I shall pray that my heart will soon forgive your trespasses against your family's reputation. I suggest you pray that forgiveness come soon, My Dear Daughter, and save your wit for conversation, as lady's should, not for publication. It's the auction of the soul, and thoroughly unladylike for a woman of your social station!"

'Yes, Father." Emily said with a lump of injustice forming in her throat like a ball of sticky bread also caught there. Her food was hardly touched.

"Now, finish your good supper. Waste not; want not! You need more flesh on your bones to keep well. I cannot send you to your room without supper, so do as Mother would have you! Enjoy her stew, and then go to the scullery to help with the washing up, as Maggie is off tonight! Oh, Emily Elizabeth, you have disappointed me thoroughly with these brash valentines of yours on public view."

"Yes, Father. I'm sorry." Emily repeated as she forced food down her constricting throat, tight with the anger she didn't dare speak. "But please know I never meant to disappoint you, only to write cleverly and have some fun. It was Shipley, George's co-editor who published…" But, Squire Dickinson exited without turning around to acknowledge her plea.

"Goodnight, Emily Elizabeth." He said flatly as he disappeared into his library and closed the door behind him. Emily knew he would be working long into the night and that she had best not disturb him, as he did look tired, and he did want the best for his family. He gave them all he could of a good life at home, and he worried so about their health.

Emily remembered the nights he'd sat at the end of her bed keeping watch over her when she was ill: feeding her medicine to quell her coughing; watching over her, sometimes sitting up all night by her bed to be sure she drank her Chamomile tea and took her cod liver oil; soothing her fever with cool compresses to her forehead, holding steaming bowls of camphor oil to her nostrils to clear her breathing. She knew he was proud of her prowess at writing. She'd been highly praised for her compositions at Amherst Academy and he'd awarded her with a gold watch on a bob to keep in her pocket. She carried it with her to and fro and to Holyoke Seminary. When she'd been homesick, she'd held it to her ear all night and listened to it tick to remind her of her protective father and the home she loved that he so securely provided.

Yet, she was angry at his attitude toward her having any fun outside their home. She felt he was wrong to be so scandalized by her playful valentines. Nearly all the young people wrote outlandish valentines in annual Amherst custom, some far more scandalous than hers. "Why, Vinnie even asks for kisses in her valentines—but hers were not published in newspapers, and that made all the difference." Emily realized.

August 1852: George Gould "Poetry In Motion"

Parting is all we know of Heaven—
and all we need of Hell

Emily dressed in her simple white house frock, carrying a book and a long-stem red rose, walked with Carlo through the sunset orchard of her father's estate. Most women wore such white housedresses only at home, but Emily dared wear hers through the woods and meadows. She dreamed of the white frocked women in Austin's picture books bought in Boston of pre-Raphaelite paintings and Turner landscapes. She'd read too, in *The Springfield Republican*, of Bronson Alcott's boycott of dyed clothes as a condemnation of abusive labor conditions in dye factories. The simplicity of white clothing was a way of worshipping Nature. "Silks, satins, and brocades were dyed garments produced in boiling hot factories under dangerous conditions, by underpaid workers for the decadent rich." Emily agreed with Alcott, a leading Transcendental thinker who always wore white.

Her Irish maid told her, "Women workers in starched-collar, factory laundries are beginnin' ta organize into unions ta protest their killin' labors fer poor wages. A brave Irish laundress, Kate Mullaney, in Troy, New York, is agitatin' fer workers' rights. She makes me proud ta be an Irish woman!" Maggie affirmed to Emily. "Kate's joinin' with the Iron Workers Union strikin' to end the brutish, fourteen-hour day!"

Emily felt less like dressing up in fancy clothes and avoided them as much as possible. The summer wind blew her hair in disarray as she wept and walked with emotional agitation and self-dramatization. Her dog, Carlo, strode beside her against the wind as earnestly as she. She felt like Catherine in *Wuthering Heights* on her way over the English Moors in search of her Heathcliff. To Emily's sniffles, Carlo offered a whimper. "It's too sad, Carlo, that we must say goodbye to our good friend, George—especially with Ben Newton gone to Worcester, too. Father must never know we've come to meet George in our secret place. Carlo, you're the best of companions. You know all, but never tell."

As Emily and Carlo reached the far slope of the orchard that went down into a wooded area to spy the tall slim figure of George Gould clad in his worn, dark jacket and white shirt sitting on a rock of the dry wall, waiting. "There's my Heathcliff!" Emily whispered. "He looks as despondent as me."

As Emily approached, her white frock blowing against her legs in the wind, George sprang from his seat. "Emily, you've come?"

"Yes, George. Thank goodness Father is off campaigning for federal funds to support his railroad or I'd not be able to say goodbye. I couldn't let you go without seeing you and wishing you well. Here's your copy of *Uncle Tom's Cabin*. I can understand why Harriet Beecher Stowe sold five thousand copies in two days! Father says an anti-slavery bill will soon be introduced in Congress."

"God willing, the Whigs will soon join the New Republican Anti-slavery Party." George nervously continued on the subject of politics to delay their goodbyes.

Emily followed his lead: "The Whigs will always be the staid Whigs, I'm afraid, Free-soilers, but not abolitionists."

The Springfield Republican says the new party will take the lead against slavery over the Free-soil Whigs." George always kept up with the news.

"Reverend Beecher, son of Father's old friend, has a parish in Brooklyn Heights where he's founded an underground movement to bring slaves from New York to Massachusetts now that we're a Free State. A piece of our Massachusett's Plymouth Rock is in Beecher's church, and he's had Sojourner Truth and Frederick Douglass to speak in his pulpit!"

"Reverend Beecher and Samuel Bowles are part of a group funding John Brown's militant movement, as I understand it. I shall join them in my preaching against slavery now that I'm graduated. Frederick Douglass's speech at the college was as moving as ever I've heard. His words ring in my mind still."

"Austin and I heard Sojourner Truth in North Hampton. She was just as moving. Even Father agreed, despite her being a woman."

"Your father is a good and God fearing legislator. I do have great respect for him. I only wish he had some for me."

"He does George. He knows you are a fine student of the Seminary.

He just disapproves of your courting me. He disapproves of all the men I like best."

"'Emily, I will miss you awfully. Here's your copy of *Wuthering Heights*. Bronte is as *unbearably* moving as you said."

"Did you really feel that, George? Father says I shouldn't be reading such Romantic drivel. Bronte had, at first, to write under the name of Curer Bell and pretend to be a man, but I always suspected that the author of this book was a passionate woman. Father decries passions. He says they should be kept in check for the good of the soul. Sue feels the Brontes' books will be read for all time. I'm sure of it! They will forever move thousands of people whose hearts are broken by love." Emily looked at George who sat sulking. "George, I'm so sad we must part. I didn't sleep all night. I've soaked my pillow with crying. I must look a fright."

"No, Emily, you look sweeter than ever —even with your eyes a bit red. Especially as you say your tears were for me. Can we sit awhile? The sun is setting beautifully over the Pelham Hills." George dusted a flat rock for Emily with his shabby handkerchief.

Emily sat beside him and handed him the rose she carried.. "This is for you, George. The best American Beauty of my garden! I've written you a poem to go with it. But, it's sad."

"This rose is so red in the sunset's glow, Emily. Its aroma intoxicates. Thank you. Please read me the poem so that I can remember it in your sweet tone."

Emily took a small folded paper from her dress pocket and read:

> *Nobody knows this little Rose—*
> *It might a pilgrim be*
> *Did I not take it from the ways*
> *And lift it up to thee.*
> *Only a Bee will miss it—*
> *Only a Butterfly,*
> *Hastening from far journey—*
> *On it's breast to lie—*
> *Only a Bird will wonder—*

Only a Breeze will sigh….

"Dear Emily, the beauty of our friendship will live forever in my soul. We have shared such fine thoughts together. I'll always remember sitting here at the edge of your orchard on many sweet afternoons while you read me the poetry of Emerson given to you by Ben Newton."

"I'll always remember, too, our times together, George. Please remember I will always love you, George,

"Emily, we think so alike.!" George drew a white rose from behind the rock where he'd been sitting. "Forgive me, that I dared pick this rose from the college garden for you."

"George, how gallant! And, it's white."

"Yes, like your simple frock, white and pure as a country bride's."

We've always been of one mind, George. It breaks my heart that Father stands so utterly against our engagement."

George's face fell. "So, you have come with his absolutely final answer?"

"Yes, Austin and I importuned him once again, as we promised, but he refuses to allow me to be betrothed to anyone who does not own land. He says he can't bear the thought of me working hard and having no secure where-with-all. I treasure your proposal, but he says we're too frail to make a go of marriage without financial support. He thinks of you as a man of good intelligence and character, but not yet able to sustain a wife and family. Susan has accepted Austin's proposal and Father will finance their marriage with a fine new house next door to ours. I want so for Susie to be my sister, and for Austin to stay in Amherst and not go West to new lands in search of gold. I've been sending Susie in Baltimore letters of my undying love. She is a good companion for the mind, like you have been to me. The only thought that keeps me from despair in losing you, is the dream of Susie being my sister forever more."

"Yes, Sue is very bright and witty." George held back tears. "She'll make Austin a good match for his clever and cultured mind. Ah, that we were as lucky as they. To be betrothed in joy instead of parting in sorrow, Emily. I wish I were a better man for you."

"Father says that in order to keep Susan and Austin here in

Amherst, he must build them a fine new home, and can't afford to finance our marriage with a good dowry. He feels I'm too young and should wait awhile, too. Father stands tall at table and explains firmly: 'In order to support you, your mother and Lavinia, Austin must come first to carry on my treasury duties at the college and to keep the firm going as I grow older. You must understand, Emily, that the Dickinson estate is at risk if Austin does not stay to carry on when I'm old, infirm, or dead!" Emily tried to imitate her father's tone as Vinnie might, to make George laugh.

Despite her attempt, for George it was no laughing matter. "There's wisdom in what your Father says, Emily. I have nothing to offer you except prospects of a learned mind and sincere heart. George's thin face was pale and wan. He coughed into his handkerchief. Emily could see he was not well, and though she loved him, she had no way to care for him. "Your father has made my last term at the seminary difficult. Your brother Austin has tried to help, but your father had all the trustees snubbing me for publishing your Valentine without your permission in *The Indicator*. Yet, the better side of his heart has managed to have President Hitchcock and his colleagues find me a position in Worcester—a small parish where I can serve as Assistant Minister. I hope to make enough money one day to return and beg your father for your hand. For now, I can only thank you for this rose, and your sweet poem, and your kindness to me. Thank Austin, too, and Mrs. Dickinson for all her good stews, breads, and sweet puddings. What fun we had talking at your kitchen hearth when your father was away!"

"Dear George, if only I had some money of my own. I'd care for you. I have nothing but what father supplies. And now he's off to Washington, and I haven't even any paper. He's become guarded with my writing supplies since my Valentines were published. That's why I've given you this poem on the back of a cocoa label. I can't persuade him that it was not you, but Henry Shipley, who inserted my Valentine before delivering *The Indicator* to the printer. It didn't help that the entire issue was dedicated to the theme of women's writings and also carried an essay by Ralph Waldo Emerson. Father had written columns, himself, when young under the title *Colebs*. His writings decried women's publication and work outside the home."

"Austin says he considers Emerson a dangerous radical."

"He has always been set against women having any occupation outside the home. He has insisted that Sue give up teaching once she marries Austin. She has demurred and promised to be a dutiful homemaker, as long as she can be an intellectually stimulating hostess. Sue is a peerless conversationalist."

George ruminated. "Henry Shipley was drunk, as usual, when he put your Valentine with the printer to squelch my reputation with your father. Yet, because he comes of well bred stock, and his father contributes much to the seminary, he's not punished for his waywardness."

He's so rich, handsome, and clever, the manikin professors never cross him. It's not fair! Not fair at all, George!"

"Our stars are crossed, Emily. If I had money, and a horse and carriage of my own, I'd carry you away to live with me this very minute!"

"I'm so sorry that Father stands against us. I know he thinks he wants what's best for me, but I wish I were a *son*. Sons always come first in their father's eyes. If a man I like is not of Pioneer Valley stock with landed wealth, Father wants none of him. I wish I had the courage to run away with you!" Emily took George's hand. She began crying again. "I stole away with Carlo. Mother doesn't know I'm here. She thinks I'm rambling in search of wildflowers. Only Vinnie knows where I've gone. She's sworn not to tell. She knows that we're the closest of friends and broken hearted to part."

"Though I've been graduated from the college with a good record of grades, I wasn't invited to the Graduation Celebration at your Father's house this year, but Shipley, the true scoundrel, was invited to attend."

"It 's so unfair, George. So utterly unfair, and it was no fun without you there, George. Austin and I missed you awfully. I can assure you we snubbed Mr. Shipley and gave him the evil eye. Both Austin and me! Vinnie was too busy flirting with Mr. Lyman to notice who wasn't there. But, she and Lyman must part now, too, as he's going South, but he promises to write. They are secretly betrothed."

George fell silent and looked so sad. Emily wanted to make him laugh. "Remember, the time when Mother and Father were away in Munson and Austin and I rolled up the parlor carpet and gave a dance?

"You called it *Poetry in Motion.*" George tried to perk up. Carlo put his head in George's lap to nudge for a pat on the head. George patted his head and scratched his ears.

You whirled me around the room as if you were the earth traveling around the sun and I, your little moon in centrifugal force!"

"You were light as a feather! Easy to whirl! Everyone cleared the floor for us." The memory made George smile.

"You are so tall and I so short, my feet barely touched the ground! We were a jubilant and comic sight, mind you!" Emily laughed to cheer him.

They began to laugh together "It was so much joy to dance with you, Emily."

"Lavinia pounded the piano all out of tune, but it didn't matter. Her rhythm kept us going. You were such a good leader, George!"

"You made me dance better than I ever have." George tried to keep laughing, knowing Emily was attempting to cheer. "And you were the greatest taffy-pulling partner a man could want."

"We won that taffy pull, pulling together in perfect unison."

"We did, indeed."

"I ate so much taffy my teeth ached. Of course, I had to hide it from Father and Vinnie. Father says too many sweets spoil the soul. Vinnie would have gobbled it all and been caught chewing." Emily tried to keep the laughter going.

There was another awkward silence. George gazed into the distance.

"When Mother and Father returned from Munson, Austin and I had put the carpet back upside down after our *Poetry in Motion* —with the lion emblem the wrong way." Emily kept laughing. "Mother found it so and asked what on earth had happened. I was petrified, and Mother so appalled, when I confessed to her what we had done, she could not bear to tell Father. She kept our secret rather than have the rafters of the house fall upon us."

Emily's laughter waned as George's had until their faces grew serious. There sad eyes met. "Austin was very unhappy that you weren't at our celebration and would be leaving Amherst. He's excited, though, about going off to Harvard. He promises to write to you. I shall, too."

"I think your father saw to it that his colleagues found me a job far from Amherst. At least, they found me work, though I'd rather stay near you, Emily."

"Remember, wherever you go, Dearest George, you carry my love, and Austin's, too. I'll write to you. Austin says he'll address the envelopes and put my notes in with his, and you can put yours to me in his, too. Austin leaves next week for Cambridgeport. Write him at Uncle Joel's. You have the address on Amity Street. It's here in your book, too. I put it in the front leaf, with my poem for you. You're so brilliant and amusing, George. You'll do very well."

"I don't feel so brilliant, today, Emily. I feel like a dunce."

"I have confidence you'll do well wherever you go. I know you will. I must leave now, or I'll cry my eyes out. Mother's dinner bell is ringing."

Impulsively, George took Emily in his arms and kissed her roundly on the mouth. She was shocked, but did not pull away from his kiss. It was their first lingering kiss and a new and exciting experience that dumbfounded her. As their faces parted, they stared into each others' eyes with new carnal realization. George caught his breath. "Before God, Emily Elizabeth Dickinson, forgive me! It's just that I love you so."

Emily composed herself by looking down at the white rose George had brought her. "I'll always love you as my very own true friend, George. Remember that a part of my heart goes with you forever."

"Emily, I will remember you as my first love. Keep our dream with Austin and Sue of a great, new *American* literature of spiritual transcendence and nature's beauty. You'll be a great poet one day. I feel sure it's so."

Again, Emily heard her mother ringing the dinner bell back at the house.

"You'll be a fine reverend and a spiritual leader of our Transcendental Movement, George Gould, just as Austin and I said you'd be. Goodbye, my dearest George."

"Goodbye, my dearest, dearest Emily." The two kissed once again, but Emily felt such a passion well up that it frightened her. She pulled away, but George did not immediately release her. The feeling of his body so close against hers was a revelation. His kiss both soothed her and made her ache.

"Parting is all we know of Heaven and all we need of Hell, George."

"Yes. It's sweet, sweet sorrow, my Juliet." George held her hands tightly to him.

"Let's hope to meet again some morrow! God go with you, George." Emily tore her hands away and turned to run.

"Goodbye, Dearest Emily, God be with you always." George patted Emily's familiar companion. "Goodbye, Carlo. Keep our little Miss Emily safe on her rambles."

Carlo whimpered and followed after his mistress, pausing only long enough to lick her salty tears from George's hand. Emily, crying blindly, stumbled over stumps and stones. She did not dare look back. George Gould's sad eyes took a part of her life into them that she'd never retrieve.

When at last she reached the house, Lavinia was inside the back door to the kitchen filling saucers of milk for her many cats, each of which had its own dish. She was excited to greet her sister. "Emily, you're crying. Mother was beginning to wonder where you'd gone. Dry your eyes on my tea towel and listen. I have some nice news for you. Guess who is going to be coming back to Amherst to teach botany and chemistry at the college next term?"

"Oh, Vinnie, what will it matter to us with George and Lyman both gone so far?"

"Well, Lyman and I are definitely bethrothed and will write to each other. Father has not objected to our writing and promising ourselves to each other. But, I'm not so sure that the site of William Smith Clark, Ph.D. from Göettingen, will not provide a bit of cheer to cure your missing George Gould."

"What are you saying, Lavinia?" Emily sniffled and patted her face dry on Lavinia's tea towel, but her eyes would not stop running.

"I'm saying, Dear Sister, that Dr. William Smith Clark has finished his doctoral studies and is returning to Amherst College to teach next term."

"Will Clark?"

"Yes, Will Clark, horse trainer *extraordinaire*, and doctor of chemistry and horticultural science, will be offering lectures and wild flower walks and women are invited to attend. Imagine? Here's an announcement that Luke Sweetser gave to Lyman and myself this afternoon."

Emily took the handbill and read it through wet eyes. It clearly said that Dr. William Smith Clark would be returning from Europe and would be appointed as the first Ph.D. scholar of Amherst College to teach chemistry in the fall term, and in the spring term, botany. It also said that Dr. Clark would be encouraging women of Amherst to audit his lectures and wildflower walks, as well as his spring gardening classes on the college lawn.

"Good thing that Father will be busy at Congress fighting for his railroad funds and the Kansas-Nebraska Act. Luke Sweetser said that Father's railroad is destined to open for sure. Father will be far too busy with that venture to be concerned about your attending Professor Clark's lectures, Em. You can have fun."

Emily stared at the announcement through her teary vision. Lavinia took the tea towel and dabbed at the corners of her sister's eyes. "Dry your tears, Em. There's much to look forward to this year."

"I thought Will Clark planned to be a doctor in East Hampton like his father, but he's taken up teaching my favorite of all subjects, botany, and chemistry!"

"Perhaps, his lectures and classes will help you forget your sorrows over George, and losing your tutor, Ben, and with Father away nearly all the time, and Mother nursing her headaches in her room most all days, you'll be able to attend Clark's lectures without Father nosing in. Besides, Mother will be glad to have you learn some new gardening care considering she can no longer do much for her plants, herself."

"It will be good for Mother to be entertained with new gardening ideas. Austin, too, loves horticulture, though he has little time for it these days. He and Sue will want to plant gardens around their new house when it's finished, and we'll soon be moving back to the Mansion and need to repair the gardens there." Emily tried to compose herself.

"Father has said you can have a Conservatory for exotic plants off the study."

"I know he offers it to distract me from my sorrow over George."

"Mother says when we're closer to our old meadow and possess our orchard again we will need to refurbish them. If Father doesn't approve your writing, he will certainly approve your learning more horticultural science for the good of his estate and the village, and to make up for forcing you to refuse George's hand!"

"This is, at least, something to look forward to. Thank you, Vinnie. Please tell Mother I don't feel well. I'll go up to my room and lie down to gather my wits. My head aches from crying. It was too painful to say goodbye to George."

"I'll make excuses for you Emmy, and bring you a tray of soup and bread, later."

"Vinnie, you're the dearest sister I could have." Emily gave Lavinia a long hug since there was no one to see such an uncustomary display of affection in the Dickinson house.

"I knew the thought of Will Clark returning would cheer you, Em! Heaven knows how obvious his interest in a certain Miss Emily was before he left for Europe!"

The thought of Will Clark being interested in her made Emily almost forget George for a moment as she climbed the backstairs to her room, seeking privacy with her disappointment. With her love for George Gould and her fascination with Will Clark mixed in her mind, she sat at her table and wrote:

> *I have a Bird in spring*
> *Which for myself doth sing—*
> *The spring decoys.*
> *And as the summer nears—*
> *And as the Rose appears,*
> *Robin is gone.*
>
> *Yet do I not repine*
> *Knowing that Bird of mine*
> *Though flown—*
> *Learneth beyond the sea*

Melody new for me
And will return....

Then will I not repine,
Knowing that Bird of mine
Though flown
Shall in a distant tree
Bright melody for me
Return.

Autumn 1852: A New American Literature

To: William Austin Dickinson, Cambridgeport, Boston

My Dear Brother,

Mr. Sweetser will be delivering this letter with box of Mother's goodies to you. It's Sunday, and they're all at church. I've begged to stay away in order to write you. Behold! Father's now completely saved, and so is Vinnie! Sue was saved with Father when The Great Revival penetrated our church. You'll remember that Vinnie said, Father fell to his knees, weeping, and came to Christ, and now he's been ceremoniously reborn and inducted into the church again. I cannot imagine Father in such a heat of emotion. I'm sorry I didn't witness the event. I'm still not moved and cannot believe such public displays are real. I'm stunned to think that Father has conceded to be "Reborn" as if Nature had not born him forth already. It astounds and confounds me. Such faith in Hell's fires frightens me, too. I need you here for comfort. Sue coming to Christ with Father has bonded him all the more to her as your future wife. Sue and Father wish that you and I would fall weeping to our knees and be born again to Christ, but I cannot believe in Calvinist pre-determination. I prefer the imaginative imagery of Revelation and the study of Nature, as Mr. Emerson preaches, and as My dear deceased preceptor, Ben Newton, taught me. The volume of Emerson's beautiful poetry he sent me remains my most treasured book. I cannot abdicate the wisdom of Emerson's Transcendentalism anymore than you can, Dear Austin.

I've been reading Elizabeth Barrett Browning's poetry and discussing Emerson's writings, particularly, "Nature," with dearest Susie. She enjoys Emerson's writings, but adheres to Calvinism. Somehow, she's accepted the two enough to satisfy herself. I don't understand that schism in her thinking and we debate it sometimes. Perhaps, you can, Dear Brother.

Elizabeth Barrett Browning's Aurora Leigh is a great book, Austin. It makes me feel exactly like the top of my head has been taken off. How finely she writes in subtle meter and rhyme, so that one is not distracted by any sing-song sounds in the mind. Barrett Browning is a master to emulate, and our Dearest Susie is so stimulating. She will stir your mind the longer you know her, and you will come to love her as much I do. I cannot help but adore her. She is so endowed with wisdom and knowledge! That she will be your wife and our sister makes Vinnie and me very happy. Since she and father are of the same mind, Father plans to be generous to the bride and groom, knowing their offspring will be born of his faith in his Calvinist Christ. For the sake of Sue's and Father's happiness, you could join the Church and be converted, but I have no heart to do so. I've read that George Eliot, one of my idols among writers, has refused, like me, to attend church, because she cannot bear insincerity. She's an independent woman of strong character. I aspire to be like her.

Home is a Holy Thing. Here, indeed, is a bit of Eden. I hope your time in Boston will not impair your health. I don't wonder if it makes you sober to leave this blessed air. If it were in my power, I'd waft it to you, as it comes to me this morning on a thousand little zephyrs. We're having such lovely weather—the air is sweet with the smell of ripe apples. Now and then a bright leaf falls. Crickets sing all day long. High in a crimson tree a belated warbler is singing. A thousand little painters are tinting hill and dale. I understand now, Austin, that autumn is most beautiful, and spring is the lesser. They "differ as stars" in their distinctive glories. How happy if you were here to share these pleasures with us. Fruit would be more sweet, and the dying day more golden. I drank to your health with sweet cider made from our orchard apples.

I thank you for the vial of Belladona and the one of glycerin. They've helped my cough and my dreaming. My eyes are big and shining from the Belladona, but I'm warned to use only the tiniest drop a day, as it can poison the body's system I've heard.

Ah, Dear Brother, I find life not so bright without Sue and you in town. Now that Susie has returned to teaching in Baltimore and is so busy with correcting her mathematics papers, she hardly has time to write to me, but when she does, I treasure the stimulation in her letters. How glad I was to know that you hadn't forgotten us, and think of us daily, and look forward to home, "the rustic seat," with so much happiness. You wonder if we think of you as much as you of us: it's a great deal, Dear Austin. To look at the empty chairs in the kitchen almost obscures my sight with tears. I dream of your and

Dearest Susie's return. I'm so glad you are cheerful at Cambridge, for cheerful indeed one must be to write such a comic affair as your last letter. It had Father and me and Vinnie and Mother in stitches. I've never seen Father laugh so. He believes you are every bit as good as Shakespeare, and that we shall bind your letters for the Library shelf. Your letter so raised me up.

I'm a useless poet like Ik Marvel of Longfellow's Cavanaugh, which you gave me, but your words will make things happen in the world. Your graduation speech at the college about "a New American Literature of our own landscape" was so inspiring. Martha and all the girls of our Sewing Circle still talk of it at every meeting. Your Dear Friend, George Gould, quoted it to me on the day of our parting, so inspired was he. Susie wrote of it in her last letter. No one has forgotten it, or you, my handsome bright brother, not for one minute.

Your very affectionate sister,

Emily, who misses you awfully.

Part 2

Master Clark Returns To Amherst

Wild Nights! Wild Nights!
Were I with Thee,
Wild nights should be
Our luxury!

… Rowing in Eden!
Ah! the sea!
Might I but moor
To-night in thee!

— Emily Dickinson, circa 1861

Early Autumn 1852: "Love Is Its Own Rescue"

It seems to me that dogmatic faith compels the best minds
and hearts to narrowness and insolence.

—Harriet Martineau

"Ah, Miss Emily, how good to see you!" Will Clark went quickly to Emily as she stepped hesitantly over the threshold of his classroom. She was among the very first students to arrive, and the *only* female who had chosen to audit his lectures in chemistry except for Professor Hitchcock's widowed niece, the dowdy Mrs. Howe, dressed in black mourning, who sat examining her textbook through thick spectacles.

Taking Emily by her small shoulders, Professor Clark gave her a kiss on both cheeks, then hugged her to him like a long lost friend. Though Widow Howe's eyebrows rose up above her spectacles, Emily was both pleased and astonished by Clark's affectionate embrace.

Will Clark knowing he'd deliberately surprised her laughed. "Forgive me. Kissing and hugging is an Italian and Spanish way of greeting, and you're a stoical Yankee lady."

Emily, not the least displeased, collected herself to reply. "I hope you've been welcomed back to Amherst with as much fondness as you offer, Master Clark. We're all so happy you'll be teaching here, our very *first* professor to attain a European Ph.D. We Yankees may not display our emotions, but I hope we feel them as much as any." Emily was trained to behave as her trustee father would have her do, with formal cordiality toward Amherst professors, though in Master Clark's case, the sincerity of her welcome was deeply felt. "Congratulations on the successful completion of your doctorate!" She found herself transfixed by Professor Clark's unusually bright blue eyes. He smiled broadly, aware of her intense interest in him.

"Here, Miss Emily, sit in the first row next to the wise Mrs. Howe. I always like the ladies to audit in the front row!" Professor Clark was charming old Mrs. Howe into better judgment of him. "The sight of their appealing faces helps me lecture more happily."

Clark whispered to Emily as he escorted her to a front row seat: "The sight of *yours*, Miss Emily, makes me feel I am really home again at last. Allow me to lend you my text to follow along. I'm pleased to see you're a women brave enough to wrap your mind around chemistry." With his Ph.D. giving him new status, he felt inspired to try courting her again.

"Thank you very much, Professor Clark." Emily answered softly. "I've studied some chemistry at Holyoke Seminary. I hope your course won't be wholly beyond my comprehension, and the loan of your text will certainly help me."

The room filled with students as Clark whispered back. "I'm sure my course will be easily understood by you, Miss Emily. You may well find it easier than many young men. Too many are smothered in scriptural recitation and wrought dogma. They have no room in their minds for the study of natural wonders. I have not found this to be true of you, though it is unfortunately so of most Yankee women, too."

Emily realized that Master Clark was well aware of a continental world beyond her provincial village, one she, Susan, and Austin, knew only from books. She hoped he was referring to the likes of a missionary daughter like Harriet Richardson Williston in his criticism of Yankee ladies. More intrigued by him than ever, she envied his cosmopolitan experience.

Clark took his place in front of the class as the campus clock clanged the hour. "Well, students, let us begin. I welcome you to the new science department of Amherst College where we shall have a state-of-the-art laboratory in the ground floor of Williston Hall, soon to be completed by the sponsorship of Trustee Samuel Williston who has generously endowed it. For now, we'll study in this rudimentary laboratory. Good lads and ladies, please turn to page seven of your texts and look at the diagram there of hydrogen and oxygen!"

Emily thought of how she'd heard from their common relatives, her neighbors, the Sweetsers, that Clark had taken very well to European ways. He'd written home that not only was he taken with the way Italians kiss and hug in greeting, but he'd decided to bring the charming custom of German Christmas trees back to the penitent Pioneer Valley where the holiday was spent in fasting and praying, affording no celebration or gift giving. He'd written: "I now prefer to celebrate with joyful gift giving, feasting, ornamented Christmas trees, and glorious music, the story of the Christ Child, born of the Holy Mother in poverty and innocence, to preach against injustice and offer salvation. The classical concerts I've heard in Austria, Bach's *Magnificat* and Beethoven's *Ninth Symphony* among them, have excited and exalted my spirit to a desire for reforming my fellow New Englanders to a greater joy in their Christianity."

Emily had no idea how much he considered her to be an old friend, and she was thrilled by his warmth—if embarrassed by his public demonstration. Calming herself with a deep breath, she opened the text he'd leant and studied the diagram.

"This morning, good lads and ladies," he said, bowing to Emily and Mrs. Howe, "We will consider the beginning of all beginnings. How earth has bloomed from a matter of two-parts hydrogen and one-part oxygen." He dramatically unveiled an apparatus that sat on a table at the front of the room. "Regard this new machine I've acquired for the college laboratory, an electric apparatus I learned of in Germany. Note that it's attached to a battery generator that produces electric heat. This machine will proceed to decompose water into separate elements of hydrogen and oxygen. Watch carefully as I take this glass of ordinary well water and pour it into this beaker. In a few minutes, as I speak, gases will form around each electrode in the beaker. Around one will form oxygen; around the other, twice as much hydrogen. You see?" He pointed to the thick glass beaker with its two electrodes.

Indeed, lads and ladies, be aware, the earth and we, ourselves, are composed nearly all of water, which is to be exact, two parts hydrogen and one part oxygen: H_2O as we call it in chemistry! These two gases when combined, in proper measure, create liquid. Watch as I take these two gases and produce a spark over this piece of platinum in the bottom of the reactor. *Voila!* A small explosion and the gases have disappeared. In their place are these droplets of water that I now pour from this platinum container back into my beaker. Note, lads and ladies, *water!* "

With great bravado, Clark proceeded to drink the water he produced. "Ah, H_2O! The substance of which you, yourself, are chiefly composed and without which our food does not grow and we cannot live! So, do stay out of my electrode machine or you might become nothing more than gasses, like a some stodgy people who already seem so!" Clark's eyes twinkled with laughter as the students responded with amazement. "*And*, I shall have great trouble putting you back together again with all the other subtle components: minerals, metals, and elements of which you are composed."

The students regarded the professor as if he were a magician. Their eyes grew large. They seemed to draw back from his machine with its platinum reactor while Emily leaned forward to examine it more closely. The entire process fascinated her as much as the handsome professor who noted her keen interest.

"Indeed, ladies and gentlemen, this is no alchemy, but chemistry! Science is miraculous. My German professors believe that God hath given man the ability to create, within the chemical laboratory, all the elements, gases, albumens, sugars, and chemical substances of which we are composed. If there were a God who forbade scientific inquiry, would he make us capable of understanding such elemental glories of *natural* creation? Therefore, I dare say, that all creation is to be studied and appreciated by man, using his God-given faculties of analysis! Thus, this morning, you have come to see that water is two parts hydrogen gas and one part oxygen gas, H20, and we have proven it before your very eyes.

If you doubt the precepts of our chemistry, just think what we know today that we did not know yesterday about the science of earth and the farming of the land! Or, for one example, remember, lads and ladies, Galileo of Italy, the Father of Science, was imprisoned by The Catholic Church for claiming our planet Earth travels around the sun, as we now know it *surely* does since the advent of our modern day telescopes. My cousin in Ashfield has produced a very fine telescopic lens in his laboratory. One clear night, I shall invite you all to the roof to sample its powers! We shall view the stars, the very dust of which we, ourselves, are made!

So, my dear students, develop a fond respect for what is proven by science to be so, rather than what is unproven, and mere conjecture or superstition. It is not blasphemy, in my eyes, or in the eyes of my great European teachers, to question *literal* scripture. One might rather view scripture as a kind of *poetry*: a *metaphor* for the reality by which we live our spiritual lives. Our faith need not be in opposition to our scientific inquiries."

Emily was enthralled with Clark as he crystallized her own beliefs as well as what Ben Newton, inspired by Ralph Waldo Emerson, had taught her. Moreover, Professor Clark seemed to smile particularly at her when he lectured.

Knowing Dr. Clark's penchant for wild flowers, she decided to bring him some, since he'd kindly lent her his chemistry text. She wrote a little poem to go with them. Coming early to his class the next session, before he arrived, she set upon his desk a nosegay of late summer wildflowers fashioned of purple New England asters, with one lone wild white rose in the middle trimmed around with calico asters. She'd arranged the flowers in a vial of water, wrapping the vial in an auburn ribbon, the color of her hair. Wearing her good chestnut-brown dress, with an auburn ribbon around her throat to match the one with which she tied the nosegay, she was careful not to sign the note with her signature. She imagined Clark would know the flowers were from her because of her auburn ribbon, and he would understand her pun, on the gardens of Auburn Cemetery in Boston's Cambridge.

When the lecture ended and the students departed, Emily rose to leave the classroom, as Clark read the note that accompanied the flowers left on his desk.

> *When roses cease to bloom, Sir,*
> *And violets are done—*
> *When bumblebees in solemn flight*
> *Have passed beyond the sun—*
>
> *The hand that paused to gather*
> *Upon this summer's day*
> *Will idle lie—in Auburn, —*
> *Then take my flowers, pray!*

Sincerely thanking you, Dr. Clark—as my nosegay tries to, and like we, lives by H_2O—for showing me how we are nearly all made of such ephemeral gasses, and live by the grace of water, and had best enjoy our little

*stay on earth, so full of natural beauty such as these, before we dehydrate
and return again to star dust.*

After quickly reading the poem with its prose notation, Clark
caught up with Emily as she made her way down the hall toward the
exit. "Miss Emily, how sweet to leave me these wildflowers with such
a charming poem and note of truth signified by the one white rose in
the center. They are from you with your auburn hair and ribbon."

"Yes, Sir, to thank you for making me feel so welcome in your class,
though I'm the only woman auditing aside from old Widow Howe.
And, to thank you, Sir, for lending me your text. Father would not
have purchased it for me, as he feels I should study only scripture and
household frugality. I find all you offer, utterly fascinating."

"You know how I believe in a woman's right to a full education and
a profession. I have encouraged my sister to study and teach. Are you
thinking of teaching, Miss Emily?"

"I wish I could. Father would not allow it. My friend, Sue Gilbert, is
in Baltimore teaching mathematics, and I so envy her independence.
Austin, too, taught in Boston to earn his way at Harvard Law School
where he is presently. I would like to teach rhetoric and grammar,
lexicography, and composition, even *poetry* as my dear, recently
deceased tutor, Benjamin Newton, suggested. He was my tutor and
father's law apprentice when I returned from Holyoke. He gave me
Emerson's essays and poems to read, but died soon after he returned
to Worcester. I treasure all I learned from him. He thoroughly agreed
with your scientific attitude towards the study of nature. He, too,
warned that scripture should not be taken literally, and he despised the
religious dogma that holds back the study of truth. He was a disciple
of Ralph Waldo Emerson, Bronson Alcott, and Margaret Fuller.

"Well, then you understand completely my feelings about a woman's
right to an education and a profession."

"Indeed, I do, Sir, but Father would never allow me a profession,
though he grants I'd be good at it. He says a woman's place is in
the home tending to her family's needs, as Mother does despite her
education. He feels my verbal skills are best used to correspond for
social grace or converse in entertaining his guests and associates."

"I'm sure you would be a marvelous teacher. I've an idea! Do you think you'd like to help me with reading through students' compositions? I have no assistant and am not good at finding errors of grammar and lexicography. President Hitchcock wants us to correct such matters across the curriculum. I'm better at oral than written presentation. Would it be of interest to you to read student chemistry papers for the course, since the ladies who audit are not required to write such? You say you're recently bereft of your tutor, and perhaps, I could give you special lessons or loan you my books to read in return for your assistance."

"It would be interesting to read and help correct your students' papers, Sir."

"Wonderful. I hope you'll be auditing my botany class in the spring term, Miss Emily."

"Indeed, I plan *especially* to attend your horticultural walks and botany classes Dr. Clark. Plants are my passion!"

"I could help you in assembling a sophisticated herbarium in the manner of the Linnaeus Society. I expect more ladies will attend the horticultural walks, and you won't feel so out of place, that is *if* you do feel out of place in my chemistry seminar."

"No, Sir, remember, I attended Amherst Academy with boys when still a 'boy' myself in short skirts and bloomers. My brother, Austin, has accustomed me to having lads in my home. Remember, when you were one? You've dined at our table and met with students in our parlor."

"How could I forget seeing you there? I'm glad that you recall my presence among so many others. You were known for your wit and compositions. When your brother, Austin, attended Williston Academy, and I was his tutor, he read us some of your fine compositions written at Amherst Academy in order to prove Amherst equally as literate as East Hampton. We were impressed with your masterful description of nature's floral bounties, your knowledge of ornithology, and your imaginative metaphors."

"Ah, you've a good memory, Master Clark. Actually, Father's more likely to approve my study of horticulture than chemistry. He encourages my gardening with Mother, and likes me to send flowers around to the parishioners when they're ill, or celebrating births or marriages, or mourning deaths. It helps Reverend Colton and Mother's Bible Society."

"I remember sorely all your father's sentiments, Miss Emily. Some things are *unforgettable*." Clark stopped and turned to look deeply into Emily's eyes. "I've never forgotten our talks."

"I'm so pleased, you've not forgotten them. I've remembered them well, and all you've espoused, particularly your gentle horse training, and your talk on Alchemy as the precursor of Modern Chemistry. I was in the front row with Father for your final student lecture upon your graduation from Amherst."

"I remember seeing you there. Your approving smile gave me heart, next to your Father's grim face. It outshined his for sure." Clark laughed.

"I know that you, unlike Father—whose face seems grim whether he is or not—have no problem wedding modern science with ancient scripture."

"Indeed, and neither does Doctor Hitchcock, our esteemed president of this seminary. Nor does our fine geologist, Professor Shepard, who so encouraged me to go to Germany for my Ph.D. Forgive me if I say that your father's behind the times with his Calvinist dogma."

"Austin and myself find him so, despite our respect for his decency. To tell the truth, I loathe all doctrines, if you will not find it shocking to hear me say so."

Clark was charmed by Emily's empathetic and passionate pronouncements and sensed in her a keen soul mate for his own convictions. "I hoped very much that you'd not forgotten me, Miss Emily, so in remembering you, I kept that hope. Thank you, again, for the poem and the nosegay. You know that wildflowers are my own passion. Hybrids are grand—but, what nature pushes out from her warm naked bosom is *more* enchanting."

Emily blushed at the words "warm naked bosom," as she felt hers aching with warmth for the deeper meanings the young professor conveyed. She noted that though he'd taken to wearing a beard and mustaches, in the style of a European gentleman, and seemed more mature, he maintained the enthusiasm of a boy.

"The plants I saw in Covent Garden were fascinating. I saw a water lily in a Japanese garden display that would hold a small child aloft in

the water, so huge was its pod, as much as six feet in circumference!"
He stretched his arms wide and his blue eyes sparked with liveliness
above his dark blond beard and mustaches.

Emily was equally enthusiastic. "How I wish I could see it! Do you
think we might acquire seeds for such here in New England?"

"I am attempting to propagate some since Japan has a similar
climate to ours. I could show you how to make a water lily pond
for your garden. I know of none in Amherst." Clark went on with
excitement at finding a keen ear for his passion: "I saw specimens in
various botanical museums of wondrous tropical plants that we've not
dreamed of here in New England. The cabinets of exotic specimens of
The Linnaeus Society in Europe are astounding. The best part of the
collection was purchased by Sir James Smith for $4,500 from Linne's
widow. The Linneus Society subsequently paid $7,500 to Smith's
widow for his collections. A tidy sum!"

"Indeed!" Emily realized that Clark was as much impressed with
scientific pursuit as the money to be made from it. He was the sort of
man she dreamed of—adventuresome and captivated with the beauty
of nature, but practical, too. "I've read of the famed Father of Botany,
but can find none of his books for purchase here in Amherst."

"I bought the horticultural diary of Carl von Lenne in London. I
have both his *Life* and *Correspondence*, and other valuable European
works of botany you could borrow. A horticultural museum is intended
for Smith College, soon, and I would like to create a state-of-the-art
garden here on our campus and begin to fill a greenhouse with rare
specimens to rival Northampton's botanical gardens. As treasurer on
the board, your father will have to agree with my plan, but I know
that Amherst is his passion, and he competes with what develops
in Northampton. I need the majority vote of the entire board for
me to forge ahead with my plans. Since you yourself have such an
interest in horticulture, perhaps you could help convince Treasurer
Dickinson."

"I shall certainly do my best to talk with Father about how
important your plan is for the college. Since Mother loves gardening
and it relaxes her neuralgia, he encourages it."

"You know that my mother's father was a fine statesmen, like your
father, and that it was a Smith who founded the Linnaeus Society. I

take more pride in my maternal surname in knowing that. My father, Dr. Atherton Clark, may be a poor country physician who gives medicine away too freely for his own good, but my mother's father was a statesman every bit as good as your father. Squire Dickinson need not look down upon the likes of me."

Emily realized that her father had hurt Clark's pride when he'd attempted to court her. "Master Clark, please don't let Father upset you with his stiff manner. He is just old fashioned and focused on Austin. He can't understand a *self*-made man, though he's that in many ways himself. He worries too much about his daughters' welfare."

Clark avoided admitting feeling snubbed by Squire Dickinson. "I look forward to your attending my horticultural walks in spring, Miss Emily. With Mr. Williston's patronage, I hope to create wonderful greenhouses and garden gazebos at our fairgrounds such as I saw in Covent Gardens and other places in Europe. Though I've invited all the ladies of the village to attend my seminars in botany, I especially look forward to your attendance. I know you to be among the most learned and astute ladies of the village.

"Father promises to build me a small conservatory before long, when we return to Grandfather Samuel's brick house on Main Street. I'll be able to garden with some greenhouse plants through our New England winters. He wants me to help Mother refurbish the grounds of our old home which he will soon buy back from Dr. Mack." Emily was hoping to compete in Clark's eyes with Harriet Richards Williston. Emily knew that Samuel Williston had much to offer Clark, and she wanted him to know that her father was becoming more prosperous, too. "I don't want to move from North Pleasant Street where life has been good. But, Father wants that big old brick house that his father built. He plans to put a cupola on top, and build an Italianate house next door for Austin who's now betrothed to Susan Huntington Gilbert. Dr. Hitchcock's son courted Susie, but she chose Austin." Emily hoped her news of village life would interest Clark. Impressed with his adventurous learning in Europe, she feared he found her provincial. "I look forward to your horticultural walks, Professor Clark, so that I might choose the proper plants for my conservatory."

Clark guided Emily across a more deserted route of the college grounds toward her home. "Let's take the short cut through the back trees of your property, Miss Dickinson. Please, call me, 'Will,' as you used to, if you *will*. Shall I call you 'Emily,' as I'd like?

As they walked farther away from students strolling the campus, Emily became more intimate in conversation. "If you wish, *Will*. I remember how you used to stop by our garden, sit upon our fence, and talk of all you'd seen in the woods. Vinnie and I used to call you 'The Whippoor*will*' when you'd stop to sing on our fence post." Emily teased Clark, resuming their long lost flirtation which both had once relished."

"I recall the afternoon I helped you pick daisies in your meadow?"

"I've never forgotten it, Will." Feeling shy at having disclosed her unabashed delight in him, she changed the subject. "Do you still hunt and excavate for beryl in the hills?"

"Ah, yes, and gemstones, too! I made myself a pretty penny to put myself through college with such enterprise."

" It was the talk of the town and the *Hampshire Gazette* that you found the largest of beryl ever in our hills. How I envied your adventurous expeditions! I remember an evening tea at President Hitchcock's when we women of the village were invited to socialize with the seminarians. Everyone surrounded you when Dr. Hitchcock and Professor Shepard praised your astonishing finds. I was so impressed with your discoveries in Acworth and Connecticut. "

"Would you like to go exploring with me? Your father would not allow it, but if he would, you could come with me to Orient Point or Mount Sugarloaf one lovely day. We can explore the caves there, and have a picnic European style. I'll bring the wine and cheese if you'll bring the bread. I recall what a good baker you are."

Emily tried to hide her thrill. "There are wonders to be found in our Pelham Hills and Connecticut River Valley."

"And vistas every bit as good as the Alps! The views from Mount Sugarloaf or Mount Toby are astounding! I know of caves we could explore. Perhaps, your brother would chaperon you? I always found him a congenial fellow, bright and witty, like you. Ah, but unfortunately, he's at Harvard now."

"Father, as you probably know, is off to Congress. He won the vote of our district and is now an official United States Congressman for the State of Massachusetts!'

"That must keep him away from home a great deal!"

"We're so proud of Father." Emily blushed trying to hide the excitement welling up in her from Clark's innuendo. Her heart pounded as she answered. "I would be very interested, *Will*, to explore with you. Father has bought me a Newfoundlander, a big diligent dog. I've named him Carlo after the dog in Bronte's *Jane Eyre*. Carlo's my chaperon in the woods. You know what Margaret Fuller said that Indians say of dogs?"

"What did she say?" Clark was amused by Emily's eager sincerity and spunk. He knew of Margaret Fuller as a noted American proponent of women's rights. He'd written reviews of women's writing and sent them home to Massachusetts newspapers to be published under a pseudonym.

"She wrote, 'The dog according to Indians was once a spirit; he has fallen for his sin, and was given by the Great Spirit in this shape to man as his most intelligent companion.' Carlo escorts me everywhere. His large teeth and big bark make him an excellent protector for a woman alone in the woods. Carlo *always* watches over us while Father and Austin are away. Vinnie loves her cats more, so Carlo has bonded with me. He has accompanied me on many a ramble when I've lost my slipper in the mud looking for Lady Slippers." Emily laughed.

"I like your spirit, Emily! You're a *Cinderella* fit for a Prince who seeks the Lady of the Lost Slipper." Will teased. "Do you know that Italian fairytale? I bought it for my niece and sent a copy from Italy to the Sweetsers, your neighbors.

I do, indeed know *Cinderella*. Vinnie and I often feel like her with our household duties tying us to the hearth while beloved brother, Austin, runs free. I heard of your travels in Germany at table with our Sweetser cousins. I love to read European novels by the Bronte sisters and George Eliot in particular, and the works of Elizabeth Barrett Browning, but I don't share such reading with Father. He would not approve."

"He would not approve your quoting Margaret Fuller, Emerson's and Alcott's associate, I'm sure! Her book, *Women in the Nineteenth Century* would rile your father's sensibilities.'

"Indeed, I have to hide Fuller's writings along with Alcott's speeches and Emerson's essays under my mattress—to say nothing of Madame De Stael's *Corinne of Italy*!" Emily laughed with Will at her outwitting her father's stuffiness. "Austin saw Fuller in the library at Harvard, once when he visited a friend in 1840—when she was the *first* woman ever to be allowed to do research there. I wish I could have seen her. Father thought it a bad idea to allow women in the Harvard library. That's one reason he wanted Austin to attend Yale instead."

"You've been reading even more widely than I'd imagined!

"Sue Gilbert, and my cousins, Fanny and Lou in Cambridgeport, help me acquire books Father would censor. I read them at night in my room, or hide in the cellar with a candle when the others go to church." Emily delighted in her naughty confession that she hoped made her seem more daring and continental in Clark's view. I have a portrait of George Eliot hanging on my bedroom wall. And, I've one of Elizabeth Barrett Browning's hands my cousins sent from Boston's Peabody Book Shop where Fuller held her 'Conversations with Women.' "

The Brownings were involved with the *Risorgimento* in Italy, and much respected there. Margaret Fuller, as well as George Sand, were Elizabeth's Barrett Browning's friends as you might know. Fuller's death at sea was such a tragic loss to American sensibilities. Emerson sent Thoreau to comb the beaches of Fire Island for her trunk with her account of the Risorgimento."

"I read that in *The Springfield Republican* in a tribute by Samuel Bowles. I wept for her and her child and husband, all drowned at the peak of their lives. Such a tragedy."

"She should have stayed in Europe with her husband, Ossili, and remained a foreign correspondent for *The New York Daily Tribune*." Clark wanted to intrigue Emily with all he learned firsthand in Europe's drawing rooms. As he still had hope of courting her, he wanted to bring out her determination in defiance of her father, feeling that if he married her, her father might come around to accepting him.

Truly, the prospect of marrying Harriet Williston did not excite him in the least. He'd written home to his sister that he "loved Harriet some," but his marriage to Harriet was his father's and Williston's idea, far more than his own. Harriet's father had already offered funding for the new chemistry laboratory needed at the college, but he feared being beholden to anyone. He'd prefer that the whole board, including Treasurer Dickinson, approve his plan. "So you ramble alone in the woods with Carlo, do you?"

"I search for wildflowers and birds, often, Sir. 'Wise are ye, old woods,' wrote Emerson. It's inspiring to sit alone in the forest and listen to the wood thrush sing. The tranquility of the trees, their aromas, the majesty of pines and oaks like natural cathedrals, the songs of birds move me to poetry."

"I imagine your poems are wonderful, Emily. I'd like to read them." Emily realized that Will had walked her almost all the way home.

"Would you? Father won't allow me to publish any, and since they're the snow of my soul, I have no desire to turn them into commerce. Publication is the commerce of the soul, I think. I used to share poetry with Henry Emmons, an Amherst student who courted me, but he had to leave town and has been engaged to another. I shared poetry with George Gould, but Father's had him banished from our home, and finally from Amherst, for an unabashed valentine I wrote for George which that charming scoundrel, Shipley, published in the college *Indicator*. I used to share my poems with my deceased tutor, Benjamin Newton, but he went home to Worcester, fell ill of consumption, and died." Emily lowered her head.

Professor Clark took her hand as if at a funeral and looked sincerely into her eyes. "I'm so sorry for the loss of your beloved tutor, Miss Emily. Do you think of him often?

"Every day." Emily grew serious and dared recite with feeling a poem she'd written regarding Benjamin Newton:

> *To know just how he suffered would be dear;*
> *To know if any human eyes were near*
> *To whom he could entrust his wavering gaze,*
> *Until it settled firm on Paradise.*

To know if he was patient, part content,
Was dying as He thought, or different;
Was it a pleasant day to die,
And did the sunshine face his way?

What was his furthest mind, of home, or God,
Or what the distant say
At news that he ceased human nature
On such a day?

And wishes had he any?
Just his sigh, accented,
Had been legible to me.
And was he confident until
All fluttered out in everlasting well?

And if he spoke, what name was best,
What first
What one broke off with
At the drowsiest?

Was he afraid or tranquil?
Might He know
How conscious consciousness could grow,
Till Love that was, and Love too blest to be,
Meet—and the junction be Eternity?

"How lovingly expressed, Miss Emily. You bring tears to my eyes with your words. I'd be glad to have my student feel so for me!"

Emily was embarrassed that she'd dare recite her poem for Newton to Clark. His sincerity had prompted her to share her feelings with him. His accessible nature was so different from her father's. Yet, he had all the dignity and authority of her father. It was enlightening to realize that a man could have such confidant authority and be emotionally sensitive.

"George Gould: do you remember him?"

"Yes, an excellent seminarian who did a wonderful job editing *The Indicator*."

"George thought my poems good, but he has been graduated and gone to work at a parish in Worcester. Sue Gilbert used to read my poems, but she is busy now teaching in Baltimore and hardly has time to write me letters. Vinnie and mother do not care much for poetry and are too busy with the blessed *household*. God save me from households."

Emily embarrassed herself by enumerating her losses, loneliness, and her loathing for feminine duties of the home. She changed the subject to a lighter one. "I used to dress in my brother's clothes and hunt with him. I confess I do not *always* behave as a Yankee lady, but have a rustic soul. You've become a European gentleman; learned and of fancy mustaches and finery!"

"Why should you always behave as a Yankee lady, Emily, when you're an adventuresome woman with a mind for science and poetic appreciation for our rural glories?"

Assured of Will's affinity for her, Emily began to relax into intimate talk. "I'm afraid you see me as a bumpkin, Will!"

"Nonsense, Emily. I met many sophisticated women in Europe where persons of your sex are freer. To be candid, I find your rustic ways *more* charming. Yet, if I dare speak my mind, I've always felt your father holds you too harshly to his dogma to allow you to bloom fully."

"Well, if I leave the house with Carlo, my guardian Newfoundlander, Mother doesn't worry where I've gone. Father's often far away in Boston or Washington these days. Vinnie's too busy with Mr. Lyman and her cats to care where I go. So, as Austin often says, 'What Father doesn't know won't rile him!'"

They laughed as Will offered his arm in a gentlemanly fashion, and they walked on. Emily took it, feeling a sensation through her whole body simply in touching his arm as they walked on.

"I have wanted to accompany you on your hunting expeditions in search of beryl and gemstones ever since I heard of the big beryl you discovered in your sophomore year. Your rock of Arkansite and association with William Byrd Powell of Kansas is still the talk of our students when they gather around the specimen case at the college.

"Powell, is famous for the many skulls and thousands of rocks in his vast collection. He's an eccentric geologist, if ever there was one."

"Even Father thought your discoveries a credit to the college and praised your initiative."

"Biblical scholars and lawyers interest him more. He is still attempting to fight on the side of the churches as an antidisestablishmentarian, I hear. He wants to keep our taxes going to local parishes rather than state and federal coffers. That's a sure way to deter the advancement of science education in this Puritanical valley."

"I, myself, am secretly a great believer in the *separation* of church and state, as my first real friend and tutor Benjamin Newton was. He leant me a lecture by the Free Thinker, Frances Wright, which is much in agreement with Emerson. My tutor, Ben Newton, was an avid disciple of Emerson's, you know." With Will Clark, Emily was proud of her progressive views. "But, Will, Father is a decent man of honor with good intentions, and …"

"The road to Hell is paved with good intentions, Emily, but I'd better not complain of your father, as he's come between us enough, and he has fathered a smart daughter."

Emily silently looked down at the ground, not knowing how to reply.

Clark took Emily's hand as they reached the back gate of her grounds. "You'd adore Italy where Elizabeth Barrett Browning and Margaret Fuller are so accepted."

Her hand trembled in his and he held it tighter for assurance. "Ah, Italy, my blue peninsula. I go there in my dreams," She dared recite a verse she'd written to hint at her repressed feelings:

> *Our lives are Swiss, —*
> *So still, so cool,*
> *Till, some odd afternoon,*
> *The Alps neglect their curtains*
> *And we look farther on!*

> *Italy stands the other side,*
> *While like a guard between,*
> *The Solemn Alps,*
> *Forever intervene!*

"I wish you could have come to Italy with me, Miss Emily. Your poetry would flourish there where passion and art are freer to express themselves."

"Yes, Will. I remember what Margaret Fuller wrote when she lived in Italy: 'Once I was almost all intellect; now I am almost all feeling. Nature vindicates her rights, and I feel all Italy glowing beneath the Saxon crust. This cannot last long: I shall burn to ashes if all this smolders here much longer. I must die if I do not burst forth in heroism or genius.'"

"Exactly recalled. I felt the same. Is that how you feel, Emily?"

Emily boldly led Clark to a bench where they could talk unseen at the back of her garden. As they sat secluded, she brimmed with feeling. "Oh, Will, I don't dare feel exactly as I do, but you've had such a chance to know the world. I envy you. Father hardly allows Lavinia and me out of Amherst, unless it be for a trip to Boston to visit our little cousins or Austin, or a trip to Washington with him which he proposes. We'll see the Capitol and meet congressmen and senators. We'll see George Washington's Tomb and we we'll stop in Philadelphia, too, on our way home." Emily wanted Will Clark to know that though she couldn't offer a dowry as rich as Harriet Williston's, she'd something of interest and prestige to offer.

"Emily, when you're there, you must hear a popular preacher I heard in Philadelphia where I traveled for my chemistry supplies—one Reverend Charles Wadsworth. He preaches Presbyterian beliefs very compellingly. I feel that I prefer Presbyterianism to Calvinism, though I can trust you to understand that I dare not declare such thoughts at *this* seminary. The Presbyterian philosophy of atonement and redemption seems more in tune with the Sermon on the Mount and our Lord's belief that only those without sin, as there are none among us, should cast stones."

"It's ironic that Calvinism sometimes seems devoid of Christianity in its truest sense."

"My patron, Mr. Williston, like your father, adheres to Calvin's old Trinitarian doctrines of predestination, if not as strictly as your father."

"I understand very well your feelings, Will. Please don't imagine I'm a complete country bumpkin. I've read more than most women of this village."

"Emily, would I tell you my innermost thoughts if I didn't see that? Harriet Williston reads nothing but scripture and Calvinist doctrine. I can't share my enthusiasm for science and Presbyterianism with her. She'd be aghast and squeal to her father."

"Poor Harriet. She's a Puritan missionary's daughter. It can't be helped."

"You're exciting to converse with, Emily. Come prospecting with me this very weekend—early Sunday morning when the rest are at church? The woods will be still and quiet. We'll see many fine specimens of ornithology, too, as they awaken to the dawn. The birds in Linnaeus European cabinets are spectacular. I know you love birds as part of Heaven on earth."

"Indeed, I've learned many of their calls and songs. I hear Mr. Cardinal calling Mrs. Cardinal right now. Do you see him there in the bush?"

"Yes, and her little *tick tick* answer there in yonder bush lets him know she's near!" Will smiled broadly at Emily's answering grin.

"Do you still hope to find gold or silver to be mined in the area? That might assure Austin's staying in Amherst, too, along with my dear Susie."

"I still have hopes."

"I envy the freedom of boys!"

"Why wouldn't you, Emily—with your fine mind shackled by the oppression of women in the provincial mores of this village."

"You understand my deepest desires, Master." She was as excited as a child. "Do you think we might find some dinosaur fossils as President Hitchcock did?"

"It's possible we might!" Clark smiled, thrilled with more ideas than prospecting in mind. He enjoyed helping Emily defy the domineering father who had rejected his courtship of her. Subconscious vengeance, as well as sexual attraction, motivated his desires. He felt assured enough of Trustee Williston's patronage at the college, not to worry inordinately about Squire Dickinson's disapproval.

They stood up. "Next Sunday morning then. Wouldn't it be marvelous if we found more fossils, or valuable beryl, or even gold or silver in our hills?" The petite, five-foot Emily smiled innocently up at her taller, worldly professor.

He penetrated her Belladonna enlarged eyes with his shining blue ones, and kissed her on the forehead. "Where shall we meet?"

"In the oak grove at the huge rock above the cemetery behind my house, southwest of cousin Sweetser's house, at 5 o'clock Sunday morning."

Clark was as boyishly excited as Emily. "Excellent idea. I know that rock well." Clark lifted Emily by the waist, whirled her once around and set her down in front of him. "With you light as a feather, Othello, my stallion, will easily carry us both to Montague and onto Sugarloaf Mountain with your dog, Carlo, running behind, if he will!"

Emily felt her exhilaration rise towards his exuberance. "If I bid him, Carlo will follow me to the ends of the earth with you."

Autumn 1852: Duty Is Dull. Home Is Bright

Dear Austin. Are you lonely in Boston?

I'd be so please if some lovely morning, you'd lock the schoolroom door on those Irish boys and run to sunshine here at home. Boston's dingy corridors cannot be good for your cough, Dear Brother. Don't waste too much health teaching those ruffians. Oh Austin, it's wrong to tantalize you so while you are bravely fulfilling your duty. Duty is dull, and home is bright and shining, and the spirit and the bride say come for all things are ready! I had a long letter from Sue, exhausted by teaching mathematics in Baltimore. Her sister, Martha came over to read it with me and we had a lovely time reading about our Susie. I dream of our future family: Susie your wife, and Susie, our sister. Martha and I spend time together often. We fill every minute with thoughts of you and Sue. Sue says in her letter she has had a "brief letter from you." Won't you write her a longer more romantic one. Shall I have to do all the courting of dearest Susie for you? Should I have been the boy student of this family and you the maid stuck in the kitchen baking Father's favorite gingerbread?

Father says you were wearing a white hat, cocked up at the sides when he saw you. I shall like it for sure. I read in The Springfield Republican that Bronson Alcott has started the trend of wearing white in Concord to boycott the dye factories where workers faint of the heat and are paid so purely. Some have even perished of the hot steam vats where the dyes are boiled and the fabrics immersed. I want so much to see your white hat, even if Father disdains such a romantic style.

Father says you ate little dinner when you dined with him during his surprise visit. He didn't know whether you were not hungry, or whether it was astonishment at seeing him there. You must be healthy again soon! We'll have a busy day for you at the Cattle Show. I'm entering my Indian Rye Bread in the baking contest. The whole town is in an uproar over Professor Clark's planning to introduce a racetrack at the Fair Grounds, and of course, Father, in his Puritan way despising gambling, is on the side against Clark, as usual. Mother came home yesterday from a pleasant visit to Monson. Her family all send their love to you. Vinnie sends much of hers. Days, fly away! I write while they've all gone to meeting and I steal my Sunday morning solitude, as usual. Though father attempts to drag me to church, I disappear, retiring to the root cellar with a candle and a book, and he can't find me and gives up rather than be late for the sermon.

Lovely spring days will come again, Austin, for Susie and you and me to ramble all dressed in white through the vistas of the Pelham Hills and have romantic picnics of berry wine at Orient Point. We shall disobey Father's Temperance Society. I've hidden a few bottles deep in my closet behind my dresses where Father never goes, though many of the fellow's of his society do not count homemade wine as a fury in the brain, so much as whiskey and sour mash. Mother has not missed the bottles, so we need not fear Father's zeal for his Temperance Society. The students of the college have been making much trouble and vandalism when drunk in their fraternity meetings, I must admit. They are not as sober as the former crop of students, like you and Clark, George and Lyman, who knew better how to behave as gentleman, even when tipsy. Oh Dear Austin, if wishing could bring you home, you'd be here already. Maggie is addressing and mailing this scandalous letter for me, so the gossips at the post office won't read it from my hand.

Thanks many times for sending me the poems of Robert Burns. I've read them over, and over and sent them onto Susie. I like them very much, but not so much as those of Mrs. Browning.

Your very affectionate sister, Emily

Fall 1853: Sugarloaf Mountain, "Love Is All There Is"

> *That Love is all there is—*
> *Is all we know of Love....*

After more than a hard hour's ride, Professor Clark gestured toward an outcropping of rocks near the top of Mount Sugarloaf a few miles from Amherst.

"Emily, that's where I once found a large amethyst geode. I sold half for a goodly sum after I cracked it in two. I kept the other half for Professor Tyler's cabinets at the college. That amethyst paid for my books and tuition my final semester at the college."

Emily had clung to Clark's waist as they rode with her mounted behind him on his black stallion, Othello. Carlo, who had run along behind them, now stood panting beside them as they gazed out over the Connecticut River Valley at a spectacular panoramic vista. The morning air was fresh with invigorating piney aroma and the sun lit all in view with vibrant color. They beheld the many hues of evergreens amidst deciduous fall foliage bright with rust, orange, yellow, and crimson leaves ornamenting the hills and dales of the valley spread out before them. A dark-blue, glassy bend of the meandering river lay in view below, snaking towards ghostly purple hills on the distant horizon framing multicolored mountains.

Holding Clark by the shoulders, Emily leaned forward in her seat behind him on his horse. Enjoying pressing her body to his back, she surveyed the dazzling New England autumn laid out before her. "I've never seen such a magnificent view of our valley before, Master!" Emily, stunned by the beauty of the mountain vista, was utterly satisfied that, at last, she was on an expedition with the man she'd admired beyond all others. Not large and brawny, but taller and bigger than his small and eager student, he felt more at home outdoors than in. His hiking and riding had made him muscular, sinewy, and more agile than most men of his class. He felt manly with Emily leaning close upon him, glad her light-weight did not tax his horse, and delighted to share with her the vistas he knew and the places he'd explored so well.

Earlier that morning, Emily, covered by her long black cape, and accompanied by Carlo, had noiselessly left home by the back kitchen door. She carried bread and apples wrapped in a tea towel. "I'm going rambling for wildflowers. I'll be back before sundown to help with supper," read the note she left on the kitchen sideboard for her mother and sister. "I've taken lunch with me. Never fear, Carlo is near."

Seated in the front row of Clark's chemistry class, she'd exchanged many fond glances with the handsome professor all through the week, since they'd first planned their expedition. That past Friday morning, she'd delivered to him some carefully corrected, student chemistry papers he'd given her.

Now at last, after much anticipation, they reveled in the pleasures of their journey. "Shall we dismount and explore, Emily? I want to show you a cave just over there."

"Whatever you say, Master." They'd become comfortable with each other on the long route, through the deserted woods and up Sugarloaf Mountain. As they traveled, Clark imbued Emily with his superior knowledge of wildlife and geology. A cave at the top of Sugarloaf Mountain had become Clark's hideaway from the world. He was eager to show it. Clark dismounted and lifted Emily by the waist from his stallion. He set her down gently directly in front of him and smiled at her. "What a lovely morning ride we've had."

Emily smiled back: "We've gathered fine specimens of autumn wildflowers for my herbarium. Fall warblers serenaded us with morning vespers."

Clark opened his saddlebag where they'd stashed their picnic lunch. "Now, I'm hungry." He poured water from a canteen into tins he'd brought for Carlo and Othello while Emily surveyed the scenic panorama through binoculars he supplied to her.

"Look, Will! A cluster of petrified Indian Pipes at the edge of that hemlock grove. I need a good specimen for my herbarium. Oh, and I can see a pine warbler pecking among the cones up there." Emily surveyed the vista through the binoculars. "This is the most wondrous morning I've ever spent. I've never witnessed this breathtaking view of our valley. I've only come to Mount Sugarloaf on hay rides in autumn, and we never journey this high." They began walking toward the grove of hemlocks where Emily had spotted Indian pipes.

"A wagon could never come this high. It takes a strong stallion like Othello. Next time, he'll carry us to Mount Toby in Sunderland. On a clear day, you'll see Mount Monadnock in New Hampshire, Ascutney Mountain in Vermont, and Greylock in the Berkshires from Mount Toby. There are interesting botanicals up there for your herbarium."

"Dr. Hitchcock leads excursions from the college there, but they're for men *only*. I've never had the pleasure to go. Austin's raved about it," Emily pouted.

Clark put his arm around her shoulder as they walked. "Don't fret. I'll take you up on Othello. I know the back horse trails where no one will see us. We'll be alone in the observatory if we go very early on a Sunday when most are at church! It's a spiritual experience, better than any sermon to see New England from Mount Toby."

Emily was elated with the prospect, "I'm sure it is, Master."

"Here's the Indian Pipes you spotted. Let's take specimens for the class, too."

Their hands met as they bent and reached for the same stem. Emily returned Will's gaze. He stood and pulled her to him, kissing her firmly on the mouth.

The day was warm and dressed in her white, pique housedress, her black cape left draped on Othello's back, Emily felt Will's body pressed firmly to hers as they kissed. Before she could utter a word, Clark lifted her, still clutching Indian pipes, and carried her to the nearby entrance of a cave he'd hoped to show her. Just inside the entrance was a bed of evergreen branches of pine and hemlock he'd made there two weeks earlier. He'd made it to take refuge and wait out a rainstorm during one of his solitary excursions.

He laid Emily on the evergreen branches and kissed her again. "Aren't you hungry for lunch, Will?" was all she could awkwardly manage by way of resistance. He fetched their lunch bundles. She unpacked them and held the buttered bread up to him. He sat facing her and nibbled it from her hand. When she held an apple out to him, he took a big bite staring her in the eyes, and then began to unbutton her dress.

"My little Eve," he whispered with a smile. She found the courage to say nothing. He kissed her again in the French style he'd learned. She was the only woman he'd ever brought to his mountain lair, though he'd dreamed often of bringing a lover there. Thrilled by his kiss and touch, she fell back upon the pine boughs. He began to press into her, but she pulled away and rose to her feet.

"Will, we're not married. I mustn't! What will become of me?" Frightened, she went to the cave entrance to look at the view. She lowered her head and buttoned her dress, wondering if he'd lured her to his cave simply to have his way with her.

Will came up behind her and put his hands on her small shoulders. "Emily, you know I would have asked for your hand, and gladly married you, but your father will never consent to me. I have nothing to offer but the salary of a professor, and my position is very dependent upon the good graces of Trustee Williston. He's building me a new laboratory at the college, and you know Williston's been pushing his adopted, Harriet, at me for years. Your father's been discouraging me away from you for as long."

"Yes, Will." Emily felt assured by his words. "What can we do?"

"Clark paused and thought, then spoke softly as he pressed his mouth to Emily's ear. "I could marry you secretly in our own natural ceremony here on the top of Mount Sugarloaf." He turned her to him. "Emily, I know that I'll always want to be with you more than Harriet."

Emily found sincerity in Will's eyes. After deliberating, she answered: "I've always wanted you more than any other. Teach me how to be your true lover, Master."

"I will, Emily, with Nature as our witness!"

"I read of a pagan ceremony in a novel by Fullerton. The master in the story called his student mistress, Daisy"

"I've wanted to make love to you since the day we picked daisies in your meadow. I could feel your desire matched mine."

"But, Will, I'm afraid…"

Clark led Emily back to his bed of pine and their picnic lunch. That sat down facing each other . "Emily, I know what you're thinking, but forgive my candidly saying that German scientists and doctors have their means for preventing pregnancy. I've learned how to take good care. You've nothing to fear." Clark opened the wine he'd brought for their lunch and took a long drink, then passed it to Emily. "Will you trust me?"

"I want to trust you, Master." Emily drank from the wine bottle.

"Can you meet me again next Sunday morning at five while the rest are at church?"

"Yes. Father will still be away. Mother and Vinnie won't rise until seven when Father's not home."

"I'll bring you a gold wedding band from my grandmother. She gave it to me to give to my wife someday. Never tell anyone of its source. Grandmother Smith had it engraved with the name 'Philip' inside the band, because I've loved horses since I was a small boy. I want you to be sure, Emily. Take the whole week ahead to consider our union."

That Will would give her his grandmother's ring and time to think about their secret union, made Emily feel surer of his love. "I fell in love with you the day you trained our horse so gently against all precepts of punishment. I myself called you *Philip*, Lover of Horses in Greek. You said you named Romeo, because I loved Shakespeare's plays. I watched your hands pet him so softly and longed for your touch."

"I was attempting to court you that day, Juliet, but your father firmly discouraged me."

Emily took Will's hands in her small ones and examined them closely. "I wanted your beautiful hands to pet me as you gently stroked Romeo that day. You're not like any other man in Amherst, Master Clark." Emily kissed Will's palms one by one, then held one to each side of her face.

He gently smoothed her hair back from her temples and kissed her forehead. Clark raised the bottle in salute to Emily and drank again, passing it to her. "You're like no other woman, Daisy."

"You remind me of my first, true friend and preceptor Ben Newton, though you're younger and handsomer. You've taken his place in my heart." Emily drank again and passed the bottle back to Will.

"You and I have the same philosophy, the same poetry of natural science in our souls, Daisy. We're meant to be lovers." Will drank again, and passed the bottle back to Emily.

"I adore your sensibility and your teaching, Master."

"I confess I've wanted you for a long time, Daisy."

"Happily, next Sunday, I'll be your secret wife by Nature's decree, Master."

"I'll bring my grandmother's ring. She always wanted my happiness above all other considerations. I could never give her ring to Harriet. Harriet doesn't like horse riding, and will only travel by carriage. You'll be my soul mate, and I yours, despite your father." Will drank from the wine bottle again."

"Come dressed in white, as I shall. We'll seal our own bond without priest." Emily, growing heady with wine raised the bottle and drank again. Some keep the Sabbath going to church, I keep it staying at home, with a bobolink for a chorister and an orchard for a dome." She laughed. "We'll be husband and wife in the white heat of truth. Reverend Edwards A. Park has sermonized on a theology of *emotions*, just as Emerson has." Will kissed and fondled her again, and Emily spoke breathlessly to keep from submitting too soon. "Reverend Park the boldest of New England's preachers. I believe as he does, that feeling is what makes truth."

"I love and want you, Emily. That's my true feeling," Clark whispered in her ear.

She followed, whispering into his. "I love you and desire you with my whole self, Will. That's my truth." This time, she boldly kissed him first. "I'll never love another as much. All we share in spirit can't be duplicated. I'll die for beauty, and you for truth, and we'll inhabit earth."

Will answered with kisses, running his hands over her shoulders and breasts.

Emily resisted him with sincere words. "Bushnell, too, says that revivalism is spent and a new kind of spiritual life is dawning that will require no priests, but only aesthetic truth."

"Let's drink to the full communion of aesthetic spirits, My Little Daisy." Clark declared downing nearly all the remaining wine and handing the last to Emily.

Emily drank, thinking to herself: "I cannot let Father spoil my happiness again, as he has too often. He kept me from George Gould. Henry Emmons was frightened away by his sternness. I couldn't visit Ben Newton in Worcester, because he'd never allow it. He'll not keep me from Will Clark, whom I want more than any other. She held the bottle aloft in a toast:

"To the Dionysian gods of the trees, hills, birds, and flowers of Mount Sugarloaf, I announce that I, Emily Elizabeth Dickinson, am betrothed to you, William Smith Clark. We'll be naturally married, and nothing will break our union made of the beauty that's truth."

"Resolved," answered Will. Emily quickly wrapped the remaining apples in her tea towel to stand and exit the cave, before Will could kiss her again and dissolve her resistance. Hand in hand, they regarded again the splendid autumn view, before feeding their trusted dog and horse the remaining apples, and riding home with Carlo following.

Later that night at her writing table, Emily's feelings welled in poetry:

> *My Life had stood—a Loaded Gun—*
> *In Corners—till a Day*
> *The Owner passed—identified—*
> *And carried Me away—*
>
> *And now We roam in Sovereign Woods—*
> *And now We hunt the Doe—*
> *And every time I speak for Him—*
> *The Mountains straight reply—*
>
> *And do I smile, such cordial light*
> *Upon the Valley glow—*
> *It is as a Vesuvian face*
> *Had let its pleasure through—*
>
> *And when at Night—Our good Day done—*
> *I guard My Master's Head—*
> *'Tis better than the Eider-Duck's*
> *Deep Pillow—to have shared—*

> *To foe of His—I'm deadly foe—*
> *None stir the second time—*
> *On whom I lay a Yellow Eye—*
> *Or an emphatic Thumb—*
>
> *Though I than He—may longer live*
> *He longer must—than I—*
> *For I have but the power to kill,*
> *Without—the power to die—*

Then, she wrote to Austin in Cambridge, feeling she had to speak to someone about the attributes of Clark whom she now adored with steady determination. She knew that Austin appreciated Clark's knowledge and daring, even envied him in many ways. She wished she could enlist Austin's advice, but she dared not tell him the whole truth of her rendezvous with Clark—or time alone in the cave on Mount Sugarloaf. She knew that Austin would only fear for her welfare. Vinnie would simply not be able to keep a secret. She might slip in teasing her in front of Austin, or worse. Susie was away. A letter to Austin, even if a partial telling, would comfort.

Dear Austin

I send this daring letter through the help of Luke Sweetser's servant. Our Dear Maid, Maggie, who is smitten with Sweetser's handyman, has addressed it for me so that no one at the post office will see my writing on the envelope when Sweetser's man drops it to post. Inside, I've hidden a brief letter to our friend, George Gould, which you can send onto Worcester. It tells him that it's best he find a wife in Worcester, and give up all hope of our meeting again. Dear George must be free to find another. I wish him well most fondly.

And, I tell you with abandon, Austin, I would burst with joy should Will Clark have me for his wife. I'd be his for eternity. He is the man of men about this town these days—except for my dear absent Brother, of course. Clark is so full of the white heat, the truth of Nature, I cannot help but admire him as I loved dear buried Newton, my first true Master who set me free of the Dark Age of Puritan Iron, as Emerson has called it in his essays, given me by Newton. As Hawthorne writes in The Maypole of Merry Mount in Twice Told Tales, "Jollity and gloom are contending for an empire," everywhere in our valley this autumn, but with Father gone from the household, jollity is winning. Clark's classes have helped me comfort my grief over Newton's death.

Vinnie flirted upon evenings in the parlor with her beau, Lyman. Even sitting on his lap and wrapping her long curls around his neck, but don't dare say I told you. Not a word. She's happy and innocent, content with Lyman's letters. As for me, I flirt with the newly returned Professor Clark as I sit auditing in the front row of his chemistry class. He gives ladies the front seats, because he says our pretty faces inspire his lectures, and lads can see over us. Despite Williston's attempts to claim him as his son-in-law, I feel he fancies me more than Harriet. Can you please, please, Dearest Austin, help me persuade Father that he'd make a good son-in-law?

I never told you that Newton showed me the writings and lectures of Frances Wright and Margaret Fuller, as well as Harriet Martineau. They all had their influence on Mr. Emerson. They're deep thinkers and daring women, indeed. Rebels from the domination of men, as Susie and I wish to be. I am after the truth and Clark wears it on his sleeve. He is so brazen a champion of science as the true study of God's Creation, so full of lively affection for all the beauties of the world that blossom around us. He adores flowers, birds, rocks, the wise woods as I do. I could gather baskets of wild roses with him forever and never have the basket full enough. He is a bird that has flown from beyond the sea to bring us news of better worlds, where affections rain warmly and Nature and Science are one with God. He has met many German Pantheists in Europe, he says.

Clark's so Cosmopolitan, now, and very affectionate toward his students. His lectures enthrall us with knowledge and laughter. My herbarium grows richer every day from my rambles on walks with his devoted students. We found Indian pipes, perfectly preserved, hiding in the mulch in the shaded woods when I strayed a bit from the others, and he was thrilled that I pointed it out for his lecture. Did you know that lichen are actually a fungus and algae living in symbiotic relationship, as men and women should? Not a woman the servant of a man, but his equal! Susie and I feel that a woman can be every bit the equal of a man in thought and mind and should be the compliment of a man in marriage, not his slave or servant doing only his bidding. Sue misses you. Please write a truly romantic letter to her soon. Don't lose your own true love, as your poor sister may.

Do you think Father would ever consent to Clark as my suitor if he were to desire to court me? Can I have a tiny hope? Will you help me convince Father? I know that Father would not approve as Clark has no money except his salary, and what Williston offers as patronage, and Harriet Williston has her eyes fixed on him. You will be so lucky to land Susie on the shore of your heart, as I seem to lose the men I admire most, like Ben Newton, George Gould, Henry Emmons, and, now, perhaps, Will Clark. I have so little hope that I shall ever marry a man I can tolerate well. A true soul mate as Susie is yours! You're so fortunate to have such a thinking companion to excite your days. Mother and Father make little conversation beyond household matters. It's sad to see how little they share of their souls beyond the household. Mother sees herself as Father's humble servant and little more. We miss you Austin. Write to Susie. She is wanting for a long letter from you. Shall I have to woo her myself for you to teach you how proper romantic courting is done? Write to right all wrongs, Dear Brother!

Your affectionate and adventurous kin, Emily

When she finished Austin's letter and addressed it to Cambridgeport, she couldn't help but write of her planned adventure with Clark.

> *A Wife—at daybreak I shall be—*
> *Sunrise—Hast thou a Flag for me?*
> *At Midnight, I am but a Maid,*
> *How short it takes to make a Bride—*
> *Then—Midnight, I have passed from thee*
> *Unto the East, and Victory—*

Autumn: 1853: "Sue Forever More!"

… She did not sing as we did,
It was a different tune,
Herself to her a music—
As Bumble-bee of June.

Today is far from Childhood,
But up and down the hills
I held her hand the tighter,
Which shortened all the miles.

And still her hum the years among,
Deceives the Butterfly,
Still in her eye the Violets lie
Mouldered this many May.

I split the dew but took the morn,
I chose this single star
From out the wide night's numbers,
Sue—forevermore!

"My Darling Susie, I love you so!" Emily cooed with her head on Sue's shoulder in her parents' big bed, and snuggled closer to her former school chum for warmth. Mrs. Dickinson and Lavinia were away, visiting Squire Dickinson in Washington. Emily had feigned not feeling well to be allowed to stay at home with Susan Huntington Gilbert as her nurse and companion. The room was dark, the house, cold and silent, except for the far off snoring of cousin John Graves, the girls guardian for the week, who was asleep in Austin's room. Carlo slept at the foot of the bed on top of the quilt warming the girls' feet. The Franklin stove had burned its coals to cinders, and neither girl wanted to get out from under the quilts to scoop more coal from the bucket. Emily wanted to confess her feelings for Clark to Sue, but she feared what Sue would say.

"Emily, we've talked through the night. I see the dark blue light of dawn at the window. We should sleep a little. Aren't you weary?" Sue tried to turn away, but Emily hugged tighter."

"Susie Dearest, there is something I still haven't told you. Something I want to secretly confess to only you. I yielded to beautiful tempters. There is one golden thread in what I've been trying to tell you."

"Well, what is it then? We must have some sleep."

"I'm deeply in love."

"Now, how new a confession is that?' Susan laughed softly. "Who is it this time? I thought it would be Ben Newton forever. Then, George Gould forever more. But, there was Henry Emmons after him. And somewhere before those, there was dear, departed Leonard Humphrey."

"Oh, how I mourned the death of Leonard Humphrey, Susie. He was probably the only one of all that Father would've accepted, after Leonard became the headmaster of Amherst Academy. But, please, don't mock my feelings, Susie. You know I love you and covet your opinion more than any man's. My life closed twice with the deaths of Ben Newton and Leonard Humphrey. I truly loved them both as dear friends and mentors. You know I'd have married George, but Father would have none of him. And Henry, whom I rather fancied, escaped me because of Father's unwelcoming ways. When Henry went off to be betrothed to Miss Phelps, I was heart broken again. You know my heart's been broken by death and loss too often, not of my own accord. How can you laugh at me, Susie?" Emily turned away weeping in sorrow.

Sue turned to hug against Emily's back. "My poor Emily, forgive me. I was only teasing to cheer you as Austin does. Tell me, who holds your heart now?"

"You will never tell a soul. Honor is its own virtue."

"Of course. You know you can trust me!"

"It's Professor William Smith Clark."

"You two were always a bit smitten with each other, so what's new in that?"

"What's new is since he's back in Amherst, and I've been auditing his chemistry class, and he's been attempting to court me while Father's been at the Capitol. Listen to what I wrote about him.

He fumbles at your spirit
As players at the keys
Before they drop full music on;
   He stuns you by degrees,

Prepares your brittle substance
   For the ethereal blow,
By fainter hammers, further heard,
   Then nearer, then so slow

Your breath has time to straighten,
   Your brain to bubble cool—
Deals one imperial thunderbolt
   That scalps your naked soul.

"Hmmm, you're certainly impressed with him. Why has Clark been attempting to court you? He's destined for Harriet Richards Williston, the last I heard."

"He is, but, oh Susie, he confessed he finds me far more interesting. You know Father will have none of him, and would never want to cross Sam Williston who wants Clark for a son-in-law." Emily sobbed, her shoulders shaking.

"Well, then, why love Clark, Dear Emily? There's no use investing your heart in the improbable. It only leads to pain." Sue petted and rubbed Emily's back to comfort her.

"But Susie, he makes me feel like Kathy in *Wuthering Heights*, introduced to Nature and all its glories by Heathcliff. I feel free and wild like a gypsy on our walks in the woods. He thrills me with his knowledge!"

"I know you've been auditing Clark's chemistry classes, and planned to attend his botany walks, but I hope you haven't been going alone with him into the woods Emily. I don't think he's entirely trustworthy. He's adventuresome and cosmopolitan. I imagine he's had affairs with freer European women while studying abroad."

With Sue's pronouncement, Emily could not bring herself to confess her private marriage and rendezvous with Clark—not even to her closest friend, and soon to be sister-in-law. "Carlo is always with us, and other students of his classes go rambling with us, too." Emily kept her back to Sue and lied.

"Clark's too adventuresome, Emily. Be careful. He's become a sophisticated European gentleman. He goes about town kissing and hugging everyone in greeting and on *both* cheeks like an Italian. He celebrates Christmas like a German. He put a Christmas Tree in his laboratory at the college I've heard. The trustees were aghast at such holiday cheer though I see no harm in it myself. I plan to hang Christmas wreaths at my home to cheer my guests. Clark gave candies to his students while the trustees bid all to fast as usual before our Puritan Christmas! He makes a spectacle of his behavior and engenders resentment. He shows too much bravado for his own good. Because Williston is his patron, he feels he can dare all! That makes me distrust him a bit. He feels he's beyond reproach. For example, that naked nymph sculpture named Sabrina, very Druid like, he purchased for the college garden pool. The students went wild over it, and stole it, I hear. The trustees were aghast, though Austin was highly amused and loved it!"

"Clarks's just very playful and loves to make the students laugh. He loves to tease the elders and amuse the boys. After all, Austin, too, admires European art and sculpture."

"Yes, Austin is, indeed, enamored of erotic European art and plans to order some for our home, but a private home is different than a college lawn."

Emily turned in bed again to Sue and hugged her close. "Are you so careful with Austin, Susie? Pray tell? You two are alone often it seems."

"Austin is more of a true gentleman at heart, like your dignified father who is a man of honor. He would not take advantage of a woman alone no matter what liberty he felt his social power afforded."

"Austin has so much in common with you, Susie. You're such a dignified couple, the most eligible and handsome people in town. Austin appreciates your learning, and your fine elocution. But, Clark, well, he's daring. He thrills and frightens me at the same time! He makes me want to gallop away with him on his horse, like Kathy with Heathcliff, over the meadows, and leave staid Amherst behind!"

"You? Leave your beloved Amherst? That will be the day! Did you know that Clark and Austin have been talking about someday redoing the common and planting more European trees? Austin has grand schemes for inviting Olmstead to design the common. He has such an eye for taste, your brother. I do admire his artistic temperament—just as suave as Clark's. He is forever showing me European art books he buys in Boston filled with nudes of Venus and Aphrodite."

"Well, you've been courting for three years now, Susie. You're practically man and wife. I know Austin has been envious to hear of Clark's adventures in Europe—touring all the museums and botanical gardens."

"Yes, all full of naked statuary of women. It's sad your brother had to go to Harvard for his law degree instead of study in Europe." Sue had aspiring tastes and would have preferred a European gentleman for her husband.

"Well, American law is *American* law and there is no use studying it in Europe, Father says! Austin will be living at home again soon, Susie, once he's passed the bar. I know how much both Austin and Father fancy you. Father talks of how helpful you are at church. He's so pleased to have come to Christ with you at the same revival meeting. Vinnie and I are happy beyond ourselves now that you're back home with us in Amherst. So is Mother. She says you're the most learned woman in her Bible Studies Circle. Father says he'll parade to church with you on his arm to announce your engagement when you're ready. We will be so pleased to have you as our sister, darling Susie." Emily again hugged Susie, kissing her firmly on the cheek as when they were children at the academy.

Susan, recently returned from Baltimore where she'd taught mathematics, was again living at Cutler's store in Amherst with her sister Harriet. She did not want Emily to think she was too anxious for Austin's attentions. "I have a feeling that Charles Hitchcock wants to propose before Austin officially does, Emily. Don't you think Charles a pleasant chap? He came to dinner at Cutler's last week."

"But, Susie, Austin so appreciates your elegant talk and intelligent reading more than Charley. You could share that with him. Charley's adhered to his father's professions of geology and paleontology and has no mind for poetry as Austin does. Charley would never share novels with you as Austin and I do. Austin is much handsomer and a better horseman, too. Wouldn't it be awful to have to play second-fiddle to President Hitchcock's daughter in that house. She is so precious to her illustrious father. We think you're prettier than she!"

Emily again kissed Susie, hugging her close. Sue drew away knowing she had power over Emily. Emily had abject admiration for Sue's independent demeanor and a tendency to want to possess her friends, body and soul. Susan allowed possession by no one. Sue, though she loved Emily and fancied becoming a prominent Dickinson, enjoyed taunting her a little: "I'm not so sure that Charles is not the better match for me, Emily. I hope Austin realizes I have my choices. I feel that President Hitchcock might be glad to have me as a daughter-in-law. Certainly Charles has shown considerable interest." Sue turned away again. She rarely returned Emily's affection as readily as it was offered. Emily snuggled to Sue's back to continue her persuasion.

"Mother and Vinnie and I, love you so much, Susie, more than the Hitchcock women ever could. I appreciate your poetic aspirations and literary endeavors, much more than they could. You'd be the shining star of Austin's household. Vinnie and I can't hold a candle to your charm. Father says he shall gift you and Austin with an elegant and grand house of your own design to live in as soon as you're formally engaged."

"But Austin talks of wanting to go West like my brothers who've made a success in Michigan." Sue turned back toward Emily.

Emily laid her head on Susan's ample bosom and breathed deep of her feminine smell. "You smell so good, Susie. "You'd never be happy in the uncultured West." Sue used lavender water or rose water in generous quantity, samples of French *toilette* waters acquired at Cutler's store where she was still forced to work for her sister Harriet's husband for her sustenance.

Sue enjoyed Emily's worshipful flattery, but saw no need to reciprocate. Snuggling in bed with Emily made Sue think of her lost sister, Mary who had died painfully in childbirth. Her heart had been numbed by the loss of her mother, then her father, and her most beloved older sister. Mary's baby died soon after Mary, making her suffering and death useless. Sue still wore her mourning in heavy eyes.

"Emily what happened to the lavender water I gave you? Smuggling it out of ole Cutler's sight for you was no easy task. He's such a penny pincher, even as he earns well from mine and my sisters' labors. He has the damper on his stoves open so wide we suffocate all winter. He's so proud of affording more coal than anyone in town, but that's the only lavish spending he does. He's such an insufferable fool who feels that young women should be nothing but servants. Why he even made Charles Hitchcock serve the adults at dinner the other night. I was utterly abashed that he sat all the young people at a separate table and made them serve the elders."

"Oh, Susie, don't upset yourself over Cutler. If you marry Austin, you'll be free of him. Emily played with Susan's hair as she lay beside her, her head up on one elbow, looking into Susan's moonlit face. "Susie, you smell as lovely as you look in the moonlight."

"Oh, Em, go to sleep. It's dawn!"

Emily could not resist the urge to snuggle her head deeper into Susan's ample breasts. She was subconsciously acting out her feelings for Clark, while, at the same time playing Austin to Sue. Diminutive, compared to others, she longed to be the one in control, but found herself always in the submissive role. She could feel Susan's firm, round bosom through her linen nightdress, and envied her plumpness. She felt Sue's nipple rise as she rubbed her check against it through her flannel nightgown. Impulsively, she kissed Susan on the lips as Clark had kissed her. Emily had tasted fully of Clark's desire for her and it thrilled her. She thought of their secret union of body and soul. The bond with Master Clark had made her beg her way out of another visit to Washington with her mother and sister to see their father at Congress. Sue would be at Church and then at Cutler's store the morning of Emily's next rendezvous with Clark.

Emily's touch excited the sleepy Susan. She had played at sexual encounter with other girls while at boarding school in Utica Female Seminary. She slid her palm up Emily's nightdress and pressed her hand between Emily's slender, firm thighs. The two women were sexually naïve, but instinctively they knew that caressing felt good and neither had any affection from a mother or father. Orphaned Sue was an anxious and depressed orphan whose older deceased sister, Mary, had been her only mother. Susan feared marriage with its dangers of pregnancy and the controlling demeanor of a husband. Emily was a great comfort to her during her grief over the death of Mary. Emily had played doctor with Susan when they were pubescent girls alone in Emily's room. They had explored their bodies out of sheer curiosity, but the feeling Sue aroused tonight was a new and more powerful one.

"Let me touch you Emily." Susan wanted to be in control the way a man was. It was less frightening to be the maker of feeling in another.

Emily opened her thighs wider as she experienced an irresistible thrill from Susan's soft fingers sliding into her vaginal folds and pressing against her clitoris. Emily had been touched so little in her life that a shiver, like the one Clark produced with his touch, went instantly through her. Susan knew how to stroke Emily to make her moan more. Emily felt her body go weak and her vagina ache with a flow of moisture. It was akin to the feeling she experienced when Clark kissed her and laid her on his pine bower.

"Pretend I'm your husband, Emily. This is how he would touch you before he tries to give you a baby to kill you, but I can give you only pleasure, little Em."

"My Darling Susie, I adore you. If I were a man, I'd court you grandly and marry you straight away! Here's how I'd kiss you!" Emily pressed her wet mouth firmly to Susan's. "I hope Austin pleases you well with his kisses. Can our New England boys court with the ardor of European men?"

"And how would you know of the ardor of European men, Emily?"

"Well, William Smith Clark has taught me a thing or two about European men. He's become so affectionate in greeting. I could faint at his manliness!"

"Emily. Be careful with Clark. Austin says he wouldn't trust him with his women."

"Oh, are we Austin's women then?"

"You know how it is. We belong to the men of our families. My brothers have gone West, so I have to listen to my horrible brother-in-law! Harriet, Martha, and I all have to abide Cutler's will. We have to suffer his foolery, even though we're all much smarter than he! He's the one with the money. I tried going away to teach, and earn my own to be free of him, but I was miserable in Baltimore, both socially and financially. The salary of a teacher is was not enough to live on without boarding in a little room in someone else's ugly house."

"Well, I fancy I am even smarter than Austin, who's awfully intelligent, and if I were he I'd never let you out of my sight, Darling Susie. I'd kiss and kiss you like this, long and hard, and beg you to marry me and swear to make you happy forever." Emily held Susan's breasts and stroked her nipples through her gown. You would be my eternal love!" I'd pet you like this, and make you all mine forever more!" Emily put her hand up Susan's nightgown and slid her fingers up between her plump thighs so their pleasure would be mutual.

"Emily. Don't stop," Susan whispered breathlessly. "Pretend you're Austin, and we're married.

Emily rolled over on top of Susan and firmly pleasured her until Susan sighed and moaned, muffling the sounds with her hand over her mouth. "Ah, Austin, make love to me, but give me no babies. Touch me, soothe me all over."

Emily caressed Susan everywhere she could. The smooth roundness of her warm flesh gave Emily sensual pleasure. Finally, the young women, relaxed and released from anxiety, began to fall asleep in each other's arms as dawn broke fully in the windows.

As they fell into sleep, Emily heard Sue murmur, "We are ready for husbands, Emily. You'll find your fiancée soon. That was a lovely, sisterly poem you gave me this morning."

"I like your praise because I know it knows. If I could make you and Austin proud some day a long way off, it would give me taller feet, Emily whispered back as she fell asleep."

Emily dreamed of her meeting with Clark, their secret marriage, their love making that had followed, their wondrous walks through the woods, picnics on his bed of pine in the mouth of his cave at Mt. Sugarloaf, ramblings in the plush woods, his kisses that warmed her body. In her sleep, hugging Susan, she imagined that Susan was Clark, her secret husband.

Later the next day, Emily sat at her writing desk and read the poem she'd composed for Clark for their secret wedding day. She'd give it to him to consummate their love in secret. She'd written it as her vows to her beloved Master.

> *That I did always love,*
> *I bring thee proof:*
> *That till I loved*
> *I did not love enough.*
>
> *That I shall love always,*
> *I offer thee*
> *That love is life,*
> *And life hath immortality.*
>
> *This, dost thou doubt, sweet?*
> *Then have I*
> *Nothing to show*
> *But Calvary.*

Tired from being up all night talking and making love with Sue, she fell asleep across her bed, dreaming of the day she'd marry William Smith Clark in their own ceremony on Mount Sugarloaf. It remained a secret she could share with no one, but Carlo and her memory.

Summer 1853: "I'm Woman Now"

> *I'm "wife;" I've finished that,*
> *That other state;*
> *I'm Czar, I'm "Woman" now:*
> *It's safer so.*
>
> *How odd the Girl's life looks*
> *Behind this soft Eclipse!*
> *I think that earth feels so*
> *To folks in heaven now.*
>
> *This being comfort, then*
> *That other kind was pain;*
> *But why compare?*
> *I'm "wife!" stop there!*

They had ridden with the wind at their back and Carlo close behind, until they reached the mouth of their hidden cave at the top of Mount Sugarloaf. It was a warm autumn day. The sun was still low in the sky, rising slowly to light the hillsides and the river's bend below. The water sparkled with the turbulence of wind as birds sang their morning songs. Branches swayed flipping leaves this way and that, making them dance light in the sunshine.

"I hear the chickadees' mating calls and the cardinals' duets. They're singing of our love." Will told Emily as he lifted her down from the back of his horse. They stood looking over the valley, and then into each other's eyes. They smiled with anticipation. Emily felt her spirit float above her body as Will kissed her fully on the mouth and held her close. He moved his hands over her shoulders, bosom, waist, and hips. She wore again her simple white pique housedress, unencumbered by petticoats or corset, for which her slim frame had no need. A wreath of daisies she'd fashioned crowned her head, just as she'd read of in the pastoral wedding of Hawthorne's May-pole of Mary Mount. Will wore his white cotton shirt unlaced at the throat. He reached into his pant's pocket and pulled out a white linen handkerchief in which he'd wrapped a gold wedding band. They knelt at the summit of the mountain on a bed of grasses and faced each other. "This is my beloved grandmother's wedding ring. I give it Thee, Emily Elizabeth Dickinson to wear always. I declare my love for you before Nature, and say my vows to the valley and sky and to the *chemistry* of *earth* that I worship. Creation is God's glory, and we are his joined within it. You shall be my soul mate and I yours, until death do us part."

"William Smith Clark, I take Thee for my wedded husband before Nature—under the blue sky of Heaven's dome. My gold crucifix is very like yours, plain and small. No one will know if we exchange our crosses." Emily took hers off and fastened it around Will's neck. He readily followed suit. With his ring placed on her finger, they soul-kissed so deeply they felt electricity throughout their being. "What Nature, truth, and beauty have joined, let no man put asunder."

"By the power invested in us to choose, I pronounce us man and wife." Will whispered into Emily's eyes, exciting her. She gazed into his, and then, taking a folded paper from her dress pocket, she read to him verses she'd written for him.

> *I'm ceded, I've stopped being theirs;*
> *The name they dropped upon my face*
> *With water, in the country church,*
> *Is finished using now,*
> *And they can put it with my dolls,*
> *My childhood, and the string of spools*
> *I've finished threading too.*
>
> *Baptized before without the choice,*
> *But his time consciously, of grace*
> *Unto supremest name,*
> *Called to my full, the crescent dropped,*
> *Existence whole arc filled up*
> *With one small diadem.*

> *My second rank, too small the first,*
> *Crowned, crowing on my father's breast,*
> *A half unconscious queen;*
> *But this time adequate, erect,*
> *With will to choose or to reject,*
> *I choose—just your throne.*

With her words, Will lifted her in his arms and set her on his throne of pine. He took a leaf full of dew and sprinkled it over her forehead, then kissed her again and slid his hand up between her thighs. He touched her firmly, and she moistened to his fingers. "Don't be afraid, Daisy, I'll be gentle and protect you."

Carlo, feeling the bliss in Emily's spirit, sat guarding the entrance to their cave, and from their bower Emily could see the blue sky and green mountain trees framing the cave's mouth as she gave herself, body and spirit, to Master Clark's desire.

"I'll always love you, Emily, no matter what else I do. We'll forever have our secret love, My Little Daisy." He whispered huskily.

His assurances helped her relax into him, and after much kissing and petting, and "rowing in Eden" as Emily called it, the lovers shared simultaneous release. Emily felt she died to be born into life for the first time in intense ecstasy.

That night, at home in her room, Emily's body ached with passion spent. She rose from her bed and sat, as usual, at her lamp-lit writing table. The house was still. Vinnie slept across the hall breathing softly. Mother lay, snoring lightly, as always now frail and ill, confined to her chamber. Father was in Washington, and Austin in Cambridgeport. Emily expressed, as usual, the feelings welling by penning a poem sent from her spirit to where Will slept alone in his faculty dormitory at the nearby college.

> *There came a day at summer's full*
> *Entirely for me;*
> *I thought that such were for the saints,*
> *Where revelations be.*

The sun, as common, went abroad,
The flowers accustomed, blew,
As if no soul the solstice passed
That maketh all things new.

The time was scarce profaned by speech;
Was needless, as at sacrament.
The wardrobe of our Lord.

Each was to each the sealed church,
Permitted to commune this time,
Lest we too awkward show
At supper of the Lamb.

The hours slid fast, as hours will,
Clutched tight by greedy hands;
So faces on two decks look back,
Bound to opposing lands.

And so, when all the time had failed,
Without external sound,
Each bound the other's crucifix,
We gave no other bond.

Sufficient troth that we shall rise—
Deposed, at length, the grave—
To that new marriage, justified
Through Calvaries of Love!

April 1854: "The Wife Without the Sign"

Title Divine Is Mine.
The Wife Without the Sign

Since the day Emily had given herself to Will and they had exchanged secret vows, she lived for the messages he would send via Luke Sweetser's handyman and Maggie, her trusted maid. Maggie would knock upon Emily's door three times to signify that a letter had arrived. Emily would open the door smiling, so excited to have a message from Will that she wrote a poem about such moments to send to him.

> *The way I read a letter's this:*
> *'Tis first I lock the door,*
> *And push it with my fingers, next,*
> *For transport it be sure.*
>
> *And then I go the furthest off*
> *To counteract a knock;*
> *Then draw my little letter forth*
> *And softly pick its lock.*
>
> *Than glancing narrow at the wall,*
> *And narrow at the floor,*
> *For firm conviction of a mouse*
> *Not exorcised before,*
>
> *Peruse how infinite I am*
> *To—no one that you know!*
> *And sigh for lack of heaven, —but not*
> *The heaven the creeds bestow.*

They kept each rendezvous secret via this clandestine method of communication, and met as often as possible in the woods early mornings, with Carlo as their watch to bark with warning if anyone approached. Few frequented the back roads or forest trails. If Emily's father was far away and not expected home, they met late nights in the Northwest Passage when the house was dark and Will could creep over the back lawn. Carlo knew not to bark at Will's scent, as Emily had trained him well, and Clark, affectionate with animals, often brought treats to Carlo. Her trustworthy dog was thoroughly obedient to Emily's every gesture. So much did the animal feel her love, and she his, they were one being alive in emotional unison. Carlo's guardianship enabled Emily's and Will's love affair, not only because of his devotion to his mistress, but because he cushioned Emily's loneliness when Will couldn't be with her.

When the weather was cold or rainy, they met in the barn at midnight behind the haystacks with Carlo on watch. There was a front and back door to the barn and Emily would leave the back one unlocked, so that Will could come through the oak grove adjacent to the Sweetser's house where he often supped. He'd sneak in where Emily waited with her lantern burning very low or only the moonlight streaming in the barn's hay loft to guide him.

Some early mornings, the couple hunted wildflower specimens for Emily's herbarium, and rock samples for Clark's cabinets at the college. Often, Clark met Emily and her Carlo secretly in the oak grove on the hill behind her house, a stand of trees hidden from the public streets of Amherst. He'd scoop her up behind him onto the back of his stallion, and they'd gallop into the Pelham Hills. Emily pressed herself to Clark's back, ducking branches with him. Her diminutive height made such maneuvers easy, and her slight frame never taxed Will's horse. Carlo ran eagerly along glad of freedom from his barnyard, and happy for the lovers' company.

Emily always wore her long black cloak covering her white pique dress. The cloak's hood concealed her hair and profile from passers they might meet, but few were seen so early on the back woods trails Clark knew well. If the professor saw a horseman approaching, as rarely he did, he ducked into the woods before they could be seen, and rode between the trees. Master Clark knew the surrounding woods well, having explored them for precious rock specimens all through his years at Amherst College.

Emily felt as if she were Catherine in *Wuthering Heights*, a country lass riding on the back of Heathcliff's horse. Clark was her exotic gypsy wanderer, introducing her to new sensuous glories of nature along with sensual thrills. Her father was often far off in Washington or Boston, obsessed with his Amherst to Belchertown Railroad and other legislative matters.

After they'd lunched on wine and cheese supplied by Clark, and bread and apples brought by Emily, they'd make love, hidden inside one cave or another that the "Master" had discovered. Caves had become homes away from home for them. Clark had taken his "Daisy," "where the sun don't shine," as they became fond of joking, to explore geological wonders that led to erotic ones on several occasions. They'd become familiar intimates, fond of calling each other by affectionate names: as in the Fullerton novel Emily had read. They shared their secret with absolutely no one and managed to remain undetected by even Vinnie, whom Emily considered too casual and giddy in her conversation, especially if relaxed on berry wine, to keep a secret well.

Sometimes the lovers undressed together to wade and swim in sequestered brooks and ponds to bathe themselves of the sweat and dust of hiking, climbing, and hard riding. They'd read Thoreau's *Walden Pond* and dreamed of building a cabin in the woods to enjoy their pleasures daily and retire from the decadent world.

Emily blossomed into a rosy woman in her Master's arms. Her life was transformed by his loving attention. "That love is all there is, is all we know of love!" She often declared in Will's arms. She'd more confidence in her poetry than ever as he read and praised poems she wrote for him and sewed into little booklets, or fascicles, as gifts to him. She learned of Europe and a wider world from Professor Clark, expanding her knowledge of botany. Her developing herbarium was kept beautifully to please him as much as herself, and her mother, with whom she shared her botanical discoveries, to cover for her time spent in the woods. Her father was content that her walks in the woods with Carlo seemed to be safe adventures that made her stronger, well, and content. He noticed that her coughing had subsided completely. Her face was rugged with health. She gardened well and amused her mother with new horticultural discoveries. The lovers had found deep companionship in their mutual interests, and inspired each other to new productivity

Soon, Squire Dickinson planned to take Emily and Lavinia to Washington with him. Emily planned to stop in Philadelphia on the way home to hear the popular Presbyterian preacher, Charles Wadsworth, whom Will had so highly recommended. During his trips to Philadelphia to acquire chemical supplies and apparatus for his new laboratory built with Williston's funding, Will had been affected by the Wadsworth's emphasis on redemption when he'd heard the preacher's moving and inspiring sermons.

One day, as they rested in sun in the Pelhem Hills on a slope of grass at Orient Point, Clark unusually down trodden, hesitantly relinquished his dreaded news to Emily. It was news she'd known to be inevitable, but had tried to deny would ever come.

She had coaxed the source of his sadness out of him, only to be stunned by it. "Will, how can you marry Harriet, now, after all we've meant to each other?" Emily whimpered. "I've given you all of myself, my heart and my soul, Master; am I betrayed by my love?"

Will had delivered his predicament as gently as he could. "I'm far more remorseful than I can impart to you, Emily." Clark's face was filled with the pain of his conscience. "You've known all along this would happen, Emily. I've confessed often Williston's plan for me. For the good of the science program at the college which he finances, I can't stave him off any longer."

"Even so, how can you marry her?" Her master would now be betrothed to the woman dubbed "The Queen" of Easthampton, Cousin Harriet Richards Williston, adopted daughter of her lover's wealthy patron.

"I can't put off the engagement to continue my half-hearted courting of her any longer." Will's guilt was overwhelming him. "I love Harriet some, but not as I adore you, Daisy." Tears escaped the corners of his eyes. "Emily, you're my beloved student and my soul mate. I want you to continue with your poetry. I want to help you publish it, even as you insist, anonymously, so that you can share your craft with the world. You have declared your disrespect of doctrine over feeling. Please don't wholly condemn me. Your father and Williston will never understand our fervor for the brighter truth preached by Reverend

Park, Margaret Fuller, and Bronson Alcott. Your father thinks of them as blasphemers. By Nature's glory, please promise me you'll not allow this coarse, financial necessity of our lives to break your great spirit—your marvelous talent for poetic thought so succinct with the truth of Emerson's ideal of feeling."

Emily, too bewildered to answer, kept her face averted.

"Look at me Emily." Will took her by the shoulders and made her face him. Their eyes were wet. "You've become a fine poet, just as your beloved preceptor, Benjamin Newton, said you'd be! I've read much poetry from Goethe to Shakespeare, Wordsworth to Emerson or Thoreau. I believe in your gift. We are soul mates bound forever, but Williston has pressed me to the wall regarding marriage to the Queen. I've run out of excuses for delay, and can feel him on the verge of fury. The good of the college and the advancement of science in our valley are at stake, Emily. What else can I do?"

"I don't know, Master." Emily began to sob. She broke free and walked away from Will to stare into the stream that ran past their promontory.

Will followed, and again turned her to him. "Your father will not have me as his son-in-law. I've tried to greet him warmly on many occasions at the college, but he snubs me coolly with minimal courtesy, unless I be in the company of Trustee Williston. He supports the importance of my pleasing Williston as patron and fears encouraging me toward you. He senses something. He's as shrewd as Williston, but would never speak his fear of our attraction even if he were aware of it. I've tempted him by speaking of your virtues as my student auditor, but he firms his lips and ignores my compliments of you, making it clear he will have none of an association between us. I've felt these powerful men of our region out, and they've made themselves clear in their unspoken actions!"

"What will become of me, Will? I want no one but you, and shall never want another so? You've made me your prisoner, forever." Emily's eyes beseeched Will's even as they streamed with tears and salted her lips, which he kissed gently to comfort her. Her small voice was barely audible through her sorrow. "I belong to you. We have married ourselves before Nature! Though I've known it was coming, your news strikes me like an arrow in my heart, a Tomahawk in my side....I can't bear it, I ..." She shook her head violently.

"Emily, you must be resigned and calm yourself. I regret beyond words causing you pain." Clark took her by the shoulders to shake her a little. "I'm a cad. Accept it!"

"Shall I return your ring, "Philip?" She began to furiously pry the gold band from her finger grown plumper with health since he'd placed it there. She knew his grandmother had intended it for his bride one day.

Will grabbed her hands and placed his over the ring. "No Emily! Please. Now, he was sobbing, too. Keep and wear it for me. I'll always be your bridegroom at heart. You shall go on living well in your Father's house. We shall fulfill our duties to our families and Amherst. Nothing has to change, but our outward selves. I'll never love you less than I did the day we gave ourselves to one another at Mount Sugarloaf and promised our souls beyond the grave. I love you, now, as then, with abandon, except for the pain I feel in telling you that I'm compelled to marry the Queen, even as my soul is yours unto death and for all eternity. Keep my ring!"

"Would I could take the Queen's place." Emily moaned.

"But, you are Emily Elizabeth Dickinson, the Queen of Amherst, and your family has the good of this parish at its heart, just as Williston has the good of Easthampton at his. You have been such a help to me, persuading your father to place his vote on the board in favor of allowing me wonderful gardens for my work at the college. You've helped me with student's papers and given me the time to expand my courses. You've taught me better grammar and lexicography, as I have shown you the Pelhem Hills and views from Mount Toby and taught you science, botany, geology, chemistry, and shared knowledge of my travels in Europe and all I learned there."

"You've made me feel I was there with you, Will. You are my golden guinea spent upon Covent Gardens, the Louvre, San Marco, my ride in a Venetian Gondola, my tear drop of India!"

"We've enriched each other, Dearest Emily, and will always be a part of each other. No one need ever know our secret."

"The church ladies gossip, Will. I fear we're suspected. We're often absent on the same Sundays. Sue senses what I'm up to. I stayed away last Sunday when you attended church with Williston to change their observation, but their dimity convictions pursue us. They'll never dare face up to you, Master. You have the stature of Mr. Williston's patronage, and your doctorate, but they condescend me with innuendo, cruel stares, mean whispers behind their hands."

"You have your father's stature to protect you. Their whispers can't affect you. They are mere trifling of jealous women, dried of passion. Ignore them."

"Austin is angry with me, because Mrs. Sweetser overheard Lavinia and I speak of his tryst with Susie in Boston at the Revere Hotel. Now the women gossip as Sue passes and she is aghast, so that Austin is furious with Lavinia and me. Sue and Austin will marry in Geneva to avoid a wedding here amidst the gossipers, and to spare Father the expense of having to invite the whole town. Father will use the funds for their new home instead."

"A wise move on their part, indeed. I wish Williston would give me for my college laboratory or gardens what he plans to spend on the Queen's wedding. It will be a grand affair and I shall have to play the happy bridegroom." Tears of sincerity continued to glide down the professor's cheeks. "I do not love Harriet as I do you. I tolerate her. She is decent and not uncomely, if boring compared to you, Daisy."

"Oh, my poor Whippoorwill." Emily kissed Will's eyes to comfort him. She knew how awful he always felt in not having the money he needed for his work. How he'd struggled for his education and had to be beholden to Williston for his doctoral studies in Europe. "Master, I've rowed in Eden with you. We've shared ecstasy. My body has flowered in your arms. You've made me stronger, Master, than I've ever been. Don't cry. You've told me that it's customary in Europe for men to have mistresses, and no one minds. Japanese men have Geishas who speak poetry to them, and it's a way of life."

"Yes, it's an accepted custom of that culture. Wives don't complain of it."

"Well, if the Japanese, and if the French and Italian Catholics condone it, then why not we Protestants?" Emily tried to laugh for Will's sake.

Glad to see her brighten, he joined in lamely "Catholics just go to church, confess everything, say novenas and are done with sin!

A convenient way to permit sinning!" He wanted to prolong her laughter.

"Will, let's become Presbyterians, secretly, and join The Church of Reverend Wadsworth, and pray for redemption!' Emily was sincere in her proposal. "Don't be sad, Sweet William!" Emily put her arms around Will's neck. "We'll survive on our secret love and be redeemed."

The professor felt better as his beloved seemed to recover her spirit. "I dream of someday studying oriental vegetation in Japan, where the *Geishas* speak poetry to their lovers who are their soul mates apart from their wives. The Geishas are gifted women, like you, who never have to risk childbearing. We've a higher purpose than a mere *household* between us, My Dearest Daisy. We've shared a love of science, poetry, the glories of nature. Nothing can take that shared enthusiasm from us."

The thought of giving up real marriage forever with Will made Emily desperate again. "Please, let me talk with Austin and get him to help me plead with Father, Will. He might allow our betrothal now that you're a Ph.D. professor...." She always feared pushing Will away from her with demands. She knew he was a glorious raptor unable to thrive in captivity. It was the regularity of marriage to Harriet Williston, as much as her pious personality, that frightened him, for he loved exploration, adventure, travel, the excitement of danger.

Emily intuited that it was partly the forbidden and furtive nature of their passion that thrilled Clark as much as any charm she had mustered to win his love. She remembered what George Eliot had written about the thrill of danger, and she knew that Eliot, really Mary Ann Evans, had declared her free union with a married man. She'd surreptitiously, sometimes with Susan, sometimes with her cousins of Boston, read many essays and lectures of women Free Thinkers. The words of Margaret Fuller, Frances Wright, Lydia Maria Child, Ernestine L. Rose, George Sand, Elizabeth Barrett Browning, were stored in her sensibility. They'd given her the courage to pursue her writing and reading and her desire for fulfillment against her father's wishes. She was not alone in her wish to be liberated from shallow conventions that bind the spirit. "Will, I want so much to be your wife and spend every night with you in a home that is ours. Dearest Master, my passion for you couldn't be tamed. I've kept guilt at bay with it. I must confront Austin with my secret and enlist him to talk to Father on our behalf. Please…"

Clark seized her by the shoulders and stared adamantly into her eyes: "No, Emily! Be rational! Your father will be furious with you and Mr. Williston with me. You'll destroy my friendship with Austin, too. No good can come of it. We must sacrifice our desires to the future of the college and the good of New England. Williston and your father are crucial to the advancement of science in this valley. If we speak of our love to them, your father will forbid you to attend my botany lectures and walks. He'll send you away to Boston to live with your cousins. Williston will cease patronizing my work, and our dream of greenhouses for Amherst. He'll disown me completely! Don't you think I've pondered this deeply? We'd become embittered with the grief we'd cause and our alienation from our families would alienate us. We'd be driven apart more than by my marriage to the Queen."

"Please, Master, let me try. Perhaps, Austin can persuade Father that…"

"Emily. I've lain awake many nights attempting to unravel our predicament, which was there from the start. I'd rather have you be my wife as you're already the wife of my soul, but no good can come of our defying Dickinson and Williston. We'd set them against each other, and you're well aware of their subtle rivalry to see which will bloom fuller, Williston Academy and Easthampton, or Amherst Academy and Amherst. Their only bond is in their trust in our Calvinist seminary. I've no money or land to offer you beyond my professor's salary. Neither have you, but by your father's graces. Your father has invested in a house for Austin with the plans underway. He hasn't enough riches to spare another son as Williston does. Our formal marriage was simply not meant to be, Emily."

" Yet, I want it so, Master. I want to be your wife. I want that divine title." Emily was abject. Perhaps, I'll burn in hell for eternity for my sins, my refusal to come to Jesus, with you, in the sacrament of marriage."

"Emily, I'm surprised at such thoughts! Are you weakening? You've just read me George Eliot's words on the hypocrisy of Evangelical preaching. I was born again to Jesus to please Dr. Hitchcock and my parents, when a young student, so that I could continue my explorations and learning, but after traveling the wide world, I feel differently. There is no one right way to worship God. God is all of Creation itself and we're a part of it. We've communed with Emerson and Thoreau. We've shared the most pleasurable part of natural bonding. The rest is mere domesticity and labor. You'll soon be moving back to your grandfather's brick mansion made new. I'll move into the house on the hill behind that Williston has bought for Harriet's dowry. Only the oak grove above Sweetser's will separate us. We can continue to meet for secret rambles with Carlo if you'll allow. No one need know we're lovers."

"We'll meet again beyond this life and our souls shall be intertwined forever, Will."

"I'll labor for the truth of science. Emily, you'll create the splendor of poetry, as you've quoted Keats to me: truth and beauty are one."

"Yes, we'll live and die for the beauty that's truth." Emily whispered, choking back tears, realizing she could keep Will only secretly.

"You've improved my writing. I've inspired yours, you've said. Your poetry's grown. My work's flourished. You've acquired the strength and daring you admire in *Jane Eyre*. We've shared our treasured books. I've given you knowledge of the life and work of Leanne." Will went on persuasively. "You're all you've wanted to become. Should you give it up to risk childbirth? I've taught you how to avoid childbearing."

Emily remembered the day Will brought a lemon and cut slices to show her how to insert one into her birth canal over the opening of her womb. He had drawn a diagram to show her *cervix* and *os*. Will had learned techniques from his physician father, who secretly taught frail housewives simple means of contraception to save their lives from too much dangerous childbearing.

"Listen to me, Emily. I must be candid to be kind. You're small and fragile. It doesn't make you less attractive, but it makes me fear you're bearing my children. I'd fear for your health if you tried to carry my child. I've heard the stories my father brings home of the agony of small women in childbirth. Harriet is hardier with wide hips. With her simple religious conviction, she'll make a good mother for bearing. You'll always be the comrade of my soul, free to write your poetry. I wouldn't have you risk childbirth through those little hips of yours for me. If I lost you to death, I would mourn beyond endurance. I feel guilty for taking your maidenhood, but no one knows. We've such *chemistry* between us. I couldn't assuage my hunger for you. Your desire propelled me. We were meant to make love.

"Love is it's own rescue."

" Yes, of course it is, as you've always said, and consider, too, Emily, how you've preached that we must be good Americans, furthering the culture and knowledge of our young and bountiful country—forging a new American literature and enlightenment as Emerson and your brother, Austin, say. I am committed to advancing knowledge of botany, chemistry, and agricultural science in this valley of our Yankee pioneers. Too many young Yankees are going West and deserting our blessed New England life. Amherst College educates them, but sends them to parishes far off. We can't keep them here unless there's a better future in agricultural gains in our valley. Williston can help to build your grandfather's seminary into a college where natural science flourishes over literal scripture and superstitious dogma. Your father's glad of it, despite his Calvinist sternness, and your brother is our mate in such ideals, too. Williston will provide all I need for my innovative work at the college, but he makes it clear that it all depends on my becoming his son-in-law."

"It's true Harriet's brother, Lyman, has deserted his Calvinist upbringing to become a radical Unitarian in Boston and Williston is bereft of any son."

"Yes, Williston sees me as the future heir to his fortunes—the one who will protect his women folk. He throws innuendo in that direction at every opportunity. 'The good of the college that we must keep in mind! If you wed my Harriet,' says he, 'You'll use my wealth toward the advancement of agricultural science in our Pioneer Valley, and one day, when I'm departed this earth, you'll be the man of my family.' Williston was a failed farmer before he made his fortunes in button manufacturing. Yet, he still sees farm life as the consecrated way of this valley, and wants to find the means to make it more lucrative for all."

Clark held Emily close. "I'll always love you Emily Elizabeth Dickinson, but I must marry Harriet Richards Williston. My poor parents are set on it, too. They hope to be freed of their financial struggles by me. My father is Williston's physician and he depends on the income he receives helping the people of Easthampton to medicine given by Williston. Sam Williston's a kind and charitable man who helps many. If I turn down his patronage, I'll have to seek my fortunes in the West. Will you forsake your brother Austin, and his wife to be, Susan, and your sister, Lavinia, and father and mother, and Amherst, and come with me to prospect for gold in California? We can stake a claim to land there!"

Emily thought hard. "You mean leave Amherst and go West with you, Will?"

"Yes, but I cannot promise I'll find gold or make a good life for you there. A pioneer woman's life is hard, and we can't be sure what our adventure West would bring. It's a gamble." There's no assurances if you come away with me; and the trustees of the college will be upset; your father embarrassed and wounded; and old Williston aghast and hurt. But, if you'll come with me, I'll go, Emily. It's our only other choice, as you and I are penniless without Squire Dickinson and Sam Williston."

Emily walked away from Clark and stood at the edge of a precipice with Carlo. She looked out over the valley. After a long pause, she returned again to Will. It was enough that he'd offered to elope with her. He'd proved his sincerity. She could go on loving him and believing in him. He'd placed the final decision into her hands. "I cannot leave Sue and Austin, Lavinia, Mother, and Father, and run away with you, Master. I'd break their hearts and Father would be distraught not only with my elopement, but with the breech it would cause with Mr. Williston and Amherst's Board of Trustees. We would be flying in the face of all the teaching you've received at the seminary. It would break Father's spirit, to say nothing of Sam Williston's. Amherst College is in our family tradition as deep as the roots of an American elm are in the soil. You're correct, Will, our love must remain undisclosed."

"Of course, Emily. I've thought long and hard about it."

"I've seen and heard often that small women like me have great difficulty with childbirth and die of it. I remember how Mother groaned and screamed and was ill for months after Lavinia was born. She never dared have a child again and hasn't been truly well since. Sue's sister, Mary, suffered and died, and lost her baby, too, dying to no avail."

"It's common my father tells me. Too many women die in childbirth. Why, half the children of the valley die, too, before they're grown. Typhoid, consumption, cholera, measles! Bearing babies is risk-ridden. Could you stand such strain with your sensitive spirit? I couldn't bear to kill you with love, my little Daisy. It'd be the end of my life to lose you, and destroy your poetry, too. You're a delicate little wren my sweet Daisy. I'll not let you wilt for me." Clark embraced Emily with decisiveness.

"There's no other way, then, Master?" Emily realized the wisdom of Will's arguments. Her father would be distraught beyond healing if she cost the college Williston's patronage. The fate of the seminary and the town had become his and Austin's life. Austin and Clark had planned to build a water works and replant The Common. Her father was bringing the railroad, at last, to help grow the student body of Amherst College. Clark, with Williston's patronage, was expanding the science program and furthering the reputation of the college in botany and agricultural studies.

"Think of it Emily!" Clark was openly relieved to have calmed her. He felt her body relax in his embrace. "You need never suffer precarious childbearing." He kissed her on the forehead. "You can live for poetry, for what you've called *possibility*! Your 'snow'—white and pure with the spirit of Horace Bushnell, Edwards A. Park, Ralph Waldo Emerson, Bronson Alcott, Margaret Fuller—admirable Americans of our new *Transcendentalism!*"

Late Spring 1854: "Philip, When Bewildered"

....Philip—when bewildered
Bore his riddle in!

Townsfolk were assembling at the Fair Grounds of Hampshire County on the morning of the Annual County Fair. Will Clark, who was on the board of directors and president of the agricultural society, dressed in his finest riding habit, came trotting on his black stallion, Othello, down the path toward the baking booth. He'd been asked to judge the breads baked by local women. The sun was shining and the glories of New England's early spring made the surrounding hills vibrant with fresh greenery. Clark was glad to be alive with a lilt in his well-groomed horse's step, and Emily's poem dancing in his head: "Inebriate of air am I and debauchee of dew…"

"Good morning Emily!" 'Sweet William' said as he met his clandestine lover whom he'd spotted from afar. His handsome face glowed tan and rugged in the sunlight. He leapt from his horse to take reigns in hand and walk beside Emily. "You're looking comely this morning in your blue dress and bonnet, with those fawn-like eyes of yours aglow, Miss Em! I hear your Indian bread loaves are up for judging."

"I've just dropped them at the baking booth, ready and labeled."

I'll try to be impartial, though I know your breads are the best in the county. Will you be with Austin and Sue, Saturday eve? I plan to come to their soiree as usual. Austin's invited Frederick Olmstead to meet us in hopes he'll redesign our Amherst Commons. May we sneak away alone afterwards if your father's still away at the statehouse?" Clark thirsted for Emily's intense passion. He need only stroke her, and she trembled, making him feel his manly prowess. His fiancée, Harriet, was wooden when he tried to kiss her.

Emily guiltily lowered her large sparkling eyes, but feeling how transient life could be, and loving the intensity of being alive in Will's arms, she lifted her gaze and smiled. "If you liked my poems as much, Sir, I'd have baked some into my bread for you to judge!"

"If the fair sported a poetry competition, you'd win first place without fear of gossipers, My Love." He whispered.

"Do give my bread mere second prize, if any, to avoid suspicion, Will. I'd rather you give my *poems* first prize if only in secret!" Emily glowered.

"My dear Daisy, you know I read them fervently. You're still angry with me because of my betrothal to Harriet."

"How couldn't I be? I both love and hate you, William Smith Clark!" She scowled.

"I don't blame you Miss Dickinson. I'm a cad. You should have none of me, but I adore the *snow* of your soul. I've sent your poem to Paul Bowles at *The Springfield Republican* with my agricultural column. I told him it's a student who wished not to be named and if he liked it, to publish it anonymously. I've changed two lines to 'Not all the vats along the Rhine/ yield such an alcohol' from 'Not all the Frankfort berries/ Yield such an alcohol...' It won't likely be detected as yours with a European metaphor rather than rustic one. Bowles liked it and will publish it for the pleasure of all!"

"As long as Father has no idea it's mine."

"I'll have my essay in folk dialect on agricultural advice to local farmers in the same issue of the paper. It will be published anonymously, too, under my initial "W." Bowles will pay the author of the poem through me, a sum that will buy much stationery for your secret cache. Though your father rations your paper since publication of your Valentines, you need not worry that your *snow* will have nowhere to land. Since I have many students, Bowles has no idea to whom the poem belongs. I hope his good opinion pleases you?"

"I suppose it does *some*, though your approaching marriage puts a pall on all." Emily frowned.

Come now, Daisy. Give me a smile, such as I find in your poem. Will tried to cheer her by reciting her poem by heart in total:

> *I taste a liquor never brewed,*
> *From tankards scooped in pearl;*
> *Not all the vats upon the Rhine*
> *Yield such an alcohol!*

Inebriate of air am I,
And debauchee of dew,
Reeling, through endless summer days,
From inns of molten blue.

When the landlords turn the drunken bee
Out of the foxglove's door,
When butterflies renounce their drams,
I shall but drink the more!

Till seraphs swing their snowy hats,
And saints to windows run,
To see the little tippler
Leaning against the sun!

It's charmed me so, I've memorized it easily. I can imagine you the 'little tippler leaning against the sun' in your garden! It gives me such delight to think of how you love flowers, birds, woods, and caves as I do. Scripture alone consumes Harriet…." Will frowned.

""Well, Professor Clark, let the Queen live in scripture, while I dwell in *possibility*." Emily looked around to be sure they were still quite alone on the path and isolated from all ears, then she wet her lips and smirked at her "Sweet William's" grin. "I'm sure you can sooner imagine me drunk beneath you in the haystack of my barn at night than in my sunlit garden?"

"If only I'd a fortune of my own, I'd sweep you away on my stallion this very minute." He looked her up and down and said, "You're a woman of many charms, Daisy."

"You flatter me, Master, in order to seal my lips against your indiscretions! I'll blush as crimson as the new exotic hibiscus you've just brought us at Austin's tea for the Agricultural Society at your flattery!"

"I never falsely flatter, but speak the truth. I know you, like your brother, see through insincerity and don't suffer fools gladly."

Emily stopped their little charade abruptly to whisper. "I must depart, Will. The Queen is coming some distance away down the path behind you!"

Will gave a little formal bow to Emily as she hurried away, and he turned toward his approaching wife-to-be, who came down the walk under her lace parasol.

"Will! There you are!" Harriet chortled as she sailed toward him.

Emily rushed toward the baking booth to be met by Lavinia. She'd suffered meeting Will formally in public too often. They kept a pact to speak with polite formality on such occasions to avoid suspicion.

"I feel immense anxiety to see Will greet his fiancée. I feel as if my heart is ripped from my breast and left pounding on the ground." Emily told herself as she walked toward Lavinia. "I'll be sick if I don't get a hold of myself. I must think of how he remembered my poem, and how Bowles of *The Springfield Republican* wants to publish it. I'll write another to please him, pleasing myself the more."

May 1854: Orient Point, Pelham

> *It's all I have to bring today—*
> *This and my heart beside…*

"Your wedding's in a few weeks, Will?"

"Yes, Emily, May 25th. Mr. Williston's purchased that fine Italiante dwelling with seven-and-a-half acres on the hill behind your grandfather's brick house. I'll not be living far off. Just two houses behind yours, and near The Sweetsers, beyond *our* oak grove."

"I've brought you a bouquet of daisies, like the ones we first picked together in the meadow long ago."

Professor Clark unfolded and read the poem that Emily presented nestled among the daisies she handed to him.

> *It's all I have to bring today—*
> *This and my heart beside—*
> *This, and my heart, and all the fields—*
> *And all the meadows wide—*
> *Be sure you count—sh'd I forget*
> *Some one the sum could tell—*
> *This, and my heart, and all the Bees*
> *Which in the Clover dwell.*

His eyes watered at her meaning. "It's a lovely verse, Daisy. Many bees will make more flowers bloom in future."

"Yes, Master, as you've taught us the vitality of pollination." Emily's eyes grew dim with worry. "May 25th is soon. You'll be my neighbor, and friend, and bridegroom."

Will lowered his head, knowing he'd soon have another bride. He couldn't speak as tears collected in the corners of his eyes.

Emily sensitive to his every mood, kissed his eyes as they sat on a familiar rock often used as their bench when resting from their search of wildflowers.

"Don't cry Master. You've given me your worldly eyes to see with, and I shall be your best student."

They sat despondently beside each other worried about what the future would bring. She picked up a handful of dry dirt and let it fall slowly from her palm through her fingers. In her hand remained the dusty carcasses of two honeybees. "I wonder if these bees were lovers when they died:

> *This quiet Dust was Gentlemen and Ladies,*
> > *And Lads and Girls;*
> *Was laughter and ability and sighing,*
> > *And frocks and curls.*
> *This passive place a Summer's nimble mansion,*
> > *Where Bloom and Bees*
> *Fulfilled their Oriental Circuit,*
> > *Then ceased like these.*

"You amaze me with the profound beauty that falls from your lips so easily, Emily, and with scientific truth in it, too." He held her to him. "Let's not be morose. Life and love are not over for us. We're Free Thinkers whose love can't be bound. All we're made of has always been here on earth. We're the chemistry of stars, and what's the use of stardust to worry over our small lives. Let's make the best of what we've had, my sweet Daisy, and not worry that necessity might part us for a time."

"We'll be of one dust in the grave." Emily held back tears.

"Meantime, my Daisy, you'll go on writing your wonderful poems and offer them to me to lift my spirit beyond the ordinary." He kissed her forehead, cheeks, eyes, and lips.

Emily slid down and rested her head on his knee, then looked up longingly into his face, but could say nothing even as her wet eyes beseeched him. She was memorizing his face.

"Oh, I almost forgot! Look what I've brought us to read today." Will drew a slim leather volume from his vest pocket. "Elizabeth Barrett Browning's *Sonnets from the Portugese*. I bought it when I traveled in Italy. I've saved it for my dearest love."

Emily looked through watery vision and accepted the book, bound in blue with gold lettering. She opened it. The title page offered a subtitle: "A Celebration of Love."

"Thank you, Will. I was borrowing Sue's copy."

"That's why I give you mine to keep forever as a celebration of our love, Daisy. Your own poetry would be treasured by many —just as Elizabeth Barrett Browning's is by you, if only you'd defy your father and publish."

Emily knew Will was compensating for hurting her. She wanted to believe him—that her only children should be her poems. "You've made a womanly poet out of girlish clay, Master."

"I've only fostered what was already there in you. Your mind was deep from the start."

June 1854: Lessey Street, Amherst

Neighbor—and friend—and Bridegroom....
Would I could take the Queen's place....

Emily stood pale and alone with Carlo at the edge of the oak grove behind Professor Clark and Mrs. Williston Clark's new home on Lessey Street on the hill behind Main Street where she would soon live again in her grandfather's house, the largest brick home in Amherst. With sunken eyes devoid of sparkle, she looked through the trees at the Clarks' grounds and felt a mixture of yawning sorrow and burning envy.

She knew that the newly married couple, who'd had a big wedding in Easthampton, were on their honeymoon in Niagara Falls, New York, and the house was empty. She imagined them in bed, at a luxurious hotel overlooking the falls, Clark kissing Harriet. She picked up a rock and shut the image from her mind as she tossed it hard and far toward the house. She moaned and slumped down onto a fallen log. Carlo, feeling her despair, licked her hand as she sat in sorrow. Finally, gathering her wits, she walked silently to the uninhabited house and tiptoed onto the front porch to gaze into the parlor through the partially draped windows that she wished were her own. She saw that it was finely arrayed. She stepped quietly onto the side porch and peered into the bedroom where a four-poster bed, hung with red velvet curtains, stood waiting for the couple's return. She imagined Harriet and Clark lying in it, and her stomach burned "Would I could take the Queen's place!" she sighed. Stanzas of a poem she had written by lamplight the night before spun in her mind:

> *I cannot live with you,*
> *It would be life ,*
> *And Life is over there*
> *Behind the shelf....*
>
> *I could not die with you,*

For one must wait
To shut the other's gaze down,
You could not.

And I, could I stand by
And see you freeze ,
Without my right of frost—
Death's privilege?

Nor could I rise with you ,
Because your face
Would put out Jesus',
That New Grace.

Glow plain and foreign
On my homesick eye,
Except that you than he
Shone closer by.

They'd judge Us—how?
For You—served Heaven, you know,
Or sought to;
I could not,

Because you saturated sight,
And I had no more Eyes
For sordid excellence
As Paradise

And were you lost, I would be,
Though my name
Rang loudest
On the heavenly fame …

Numb with dejection, she turned with resolve toward home on North Pleasant Street, but thought better of it and chose to visit the house where she'd soon live again in the Samuel Fowler Dickinson homestead. "Come, Carlo, let's look again at the house where I'll be doomed to live without husband, a spinster forever. Father is ecstatic to own it again, since Grandfather sacrificed all his fortunes to Amherst seminary. Father senses I'm sad and is solicitous about building me a greenhouse. He thinks I'm still sad because I lost Master Humphrey who died the same year as Ben Newton. He's heard that my old beau, Henry Emmons, picked another to betroth, and he's guilty for being stern with him, and with George Gould. If not for Father, I'd not have been free to fall under the spell of Master Clark. My stars are crossed, Carlo. An arrow of grief is lodged in my side forever."

She looked down from Clark's new home, purchased for the newlyweds by Williston, to the oak grove where she, cloaked in secret, had often met her master. Surrounded by seven and one-half acres of land with a carriage house at back where the wagon carried passengers from the village to the train station, the house was in the stylish Italianate manner that Austin and Susie were having built by Edward Dickinson for their home. Austin and Sue's house under construction rose new and nearly finished next door to the old Dickinson mansion. Emily knew that her father was hoping to outdo Clark's house for Austin's pride.

"Austin competes with Clark for stature in this town." Emily thought to herself. "They are friendly rivals. Sue's house will be equally grand and more modern, with central heating and gas lamps. Oh, that I could be as blessed as Sue and have a fine husband and home." Sue planned to call the house that Squire Dickinson was building for her and Austin next door to his, "The Evergreens," as it stood in a grove of tall pines and hemlocks. Sue and Austin would be only three minute's walk away from Emily's door. That thought sustained her. If she'd lost her heart to another woman's husband, at least she'd have Susie for her sister-in-law and Austin nearby to comfort her with companionship.

Emily had feigned physical illness for the past few weeks and did not attend Clark's wedding, though the rest of her family went to Easthampton for the gala affair. When she'd returned all abuzz, Vinnie had told Emily all the details of that late May day as Emily lay in her bed, drunk on sherry she had taken to help her sleep and to ease her mental anguish.

Vinnie had sat at the foot of Emily's bed and described the festivities. "The music was fine, Emmy, a string quartet. You'd have liked it. The feast Sam Williston served of roasted beef, puddings, and cakes accommodated over a hundred guests. The bride was dressed in a lacy white gown covered with tiny white satin rosettes. The groom escorted her to a waiting carriage that was festooned with garlands of flowers. I'm sorry you had to miss the spectacle. I know you admire Professor Clark's teaching. But, I noticed he only kissed Harriet politely with a little peck on her lips, not passionately as I've seen some grooms do when pronounced man and wife."

Vinnie in telling the story knew that Emily had fancied Clark, but she had no idea how intense their intimacy was. "If you ask me, Clark didn't seem ecstatic, but rather pensive whenever I caught him not under scrutiny. Other times, he seemed to wear a stiffened smile. He asked after, you, Emmy—at the reception, noticing your absence with a worried look."

" 'Where is your sister, Miss Lavinia? I hope she's well.' He asked after you, Emmy. I think he still fancies you. He regretted hearing you'd taken to your bed with illness. He told me to give you his warmest regards. He hoped you're able to enjoy writing your poems while confined. He said you had showed him some of your nature poems at the college and he thought them superb."

" 'Please do be sure to deliver my warm well wishes for Miss Emily's recovery, Miss Lavinia.' said he, bowing ever so politely to me. 'Do tell her I asked after her and hope she feels well again soon. She is among my brightest students, a beacon of enthusiastic learning, a talented young woman to be greatly admired. Do tell her I said so. We look forward to seeing her in botany and chemistry class when we return to the college to teach next semester. Tell her we'll miss her fine wit if she doesn't come to audit.' " Lavinia mimicked Clark to make her ill sister laugh, but Emily could do no more than offer a weak smile to satisfy her sister's antics.

"I shall, Professor Clark. I answered with a curtsy. 'I know she admires you greatly and will be glad you asked for her,' I told him."

Vinnie offered Emily a tray of tea and biscuits she brought upstairs with her. "Come, Emmy. Drink and eat, please."

Now, Emily carried a poem in her pocket as she walked through the oak grove that separated her homestead and Clark's new home. She'd scribbled the words on a cocoa wrapper she took from her dress pocket to remember what she'd written. Her verse writing relieved her intense emotions and helped her survive them.

> *My life closed twice*
> *Before it's close*
> *It yet remains to see*
> *If Immortality unveil*
> *a third event to me,*
>
> *So huge, so hopeless to conceive*
> *As these that twice befell....*

She had not dared show Clark the full measure of her distraught feeling over his marriage. She knew that if she'd become too hysterical, she'd risk never seeing him again. He'd be too worried about her to indulge her desire for him. She'd held back a great measure of her despair. Now, it was a leaden weight pulling her into deep depression. As she gazed back over her shoulder at Clark's new home, tears began, again, to escape her eyes, as on the last day she'd seen him. She wiped them away with fierce determination.

> *Behind the Hill—the House behind—*
> *There—Paradise—is found!*

She whispered to Carlo as the final streak of early June sunshine sank beyond the horizon. She drew in a breath of evening air. "Come, we must go home for Mother's dinner or she'll worry about us out beyond dusk, Carlo. My spirit is darker than it's been since Ben Newton died. My very ribs ache." she thought. "Carlo, your mistress is a fool to ever dream of taking the Queen's place!"

Carlo whimpered in return licking her hand as he followed beside her.

After supper, Emily went dejectedly to her room and sat at her writing table to pen:

> *The Face we choose to miss,*
> *Be it but for a day—*
> *As absent as a hundred years*
> *When it has rode away.*

Then, she dragged herself to bed and lay awake through half the night torturing herself with images of Clark and Harriet on their honeymoon in Niagara Falls. She tried softly singing old hymns to erase the thoughts. She recited passages from Revelations and monologues from Shakespeare to blank out thoughts of Clark. When she finally fell asleep, she dreamed she was drowning under the force of a white wall of Niagara Falls waters pouring down upon her with monumental force. She woke with a start to hear a heavy spring rain drumming at her windows.

Winter 1858: The Evergreens

"I had a guinea golden…"

When Emily had heard that Will's and Harriet's first child, William Richards Williston, had died late in the winter of 1857, and Will was grief stricken, she'd sent a small condolence note with a short verse and a bouquet of flowers from her conservatory to Will and his wife. She was charged, by her sickly mother, who could no longer tend to her Bible society duties for the parish, to write sympathy notes and send flowers or baked goods to families of the church who grieved or were ill. It was Emily's job to write a condolence from the Dickinson family to their neighbors on Lesey Street. She enclosed a short verse with her bouquet:

> *Could—I do more—for Thee—*
> *Wert Thou a Bumble Bee—*
> *Since for the Queen, have I—*
> *Nought but Bouquet?*

She heard nothing from Clark, but felt she had no right to expect his attention while he suffered the loss of his child. Still, her verse might remind him of the pollinating bee imagery of their erotic life together, and he would know she meant to offer him bodily comfort if she could. After sending the flowers to Will and his wife, she fell ill with consumptive coughing that left her weak in bed for many days.

The news that she was quite ill and unable to leave her bed reached Professor Clark's ears as news always spread easily about the town. She was pleased one day to have a small bouquet of violets delivered to her in a nosegay from Clark's greenhouse, delivered by Will's handyman. The message inside simply read:

Dear Student,

Thank you for the flowers for the Queen and I who grieve our dearly departed son. I wanted you to know, I shall be sailing to Italy from Boston. I am not well, and my father recommends a sea voyage to Italy for sunshine and rest. He hopes the sojourn will refresh me. I admit, my spirit is at low ebb. I hope you fare better, Miss Emily. Take these violets as a harbinger of spring and my desire to wish you well, even in grief, Dear Student."

Yours most fondly, Professor Clark

Emily realized that her longed for master was truly ill with grieving and wrote so that nothing in his message could compromise their secret relationship. It was the first time he'd written her since his marriage to Harriet. Feeling empathy for his pain, Emily, feeling she might not live to see him again, a few days later, wrote a letter from her sickbed in reply. She entrusted it to her day servant, Maggie, to be delivered to the Sweeter's handyman to mail it unopened to "Professor Clark" who had sailed from Cambridgeport a few days earlier. For decorum sake, offering in return nothing too compromising of their relationship beyond student and "master" it read:

Dear Master

I'm sick in bed, but more sorry that you are sick. I thought you were in Heaven, and when I heard from you again, it was so moving, and filled me with surprise. I pray that you will be better and in good spirits and health again very soon. I pray that everyone I love would always be well. The flowers you sent, lovely violets, are on my bed stand as a sign of spring. The robin is singing in my window. And spring is here though I hardly know her as she passes in breezes through my window, lifting the curtains ever so lightly, a zephyr's ghost I have not yet met this year. I hear the angels with their sweet songs as they play outside on the lawn. I wish I were a great painter who could send you a glorious picture, like Michelangelo's of Heaven's treasures. You seem not to understand the messages that my flowers brought to you. They disobey my wishes. I gave them meanings. They wanted to say what the West wind says as it kisses the new green grasses of the meadows. They wanted to bring you greetings like the colors of sunset and dawn. Please hear me, Dear Master. Today is the Sabbath and each Sabbath that passes with you far away on the ocean, will make me count the days until I, Will, see you again on the shore. I wonder whether the mountains of the south look as blue as the sailors say they do. I hope they are a glorious color for you. I can't write more today, as the pain stills my hand, but my heart beats toward yours. How strongly I remember when too weak to, and how easy it is to feel love even when far. Will, you tell me, please tell me as soon as you are well.

As ever, your devoted student

When she, herself, was well again, at last, Emily steeled herself against her loss of her master from the village. She would not even be able to listen to his lectures at the college—something she had continued to do, even though they had never met privately again since his wedding, and she retired to the back row of his classes. He always raced hurriedly from the room or busied himself conversing with matriculating students after classes.

She determined now to try to live with as much of a carefree spirit as possible. Five years had passed since their last rendezvous, and time had begun to heal her loss of intimacy with him, though she'd at first been very angry that he did not choose to meet her secretly, as he had promised he would when he told her of his impending marriage. She suspected that Clark, a religious man in some ways, felt that he was being punished with the death of his son, for his indiscretions, and would take a long time to heal his grief. He had wanted a son badly, she knew. She imagined him grieving in Italy, and waited patiently for him to write or return.

When days, weeks, then months passed, with no word from her beloved master, Emily, to cheer herself, began to attend Sue's and Austin's sumptuous soirees next door. Sue had decorated The Evergreens tastefully with a generous dowry sent her by her successful brother George of Michigan. Sue hosted gourmet dinners attended by local luminaries. To further divert herself from grieving the absence of her Master, Emily spent time reading in Sue's home library where subscriptions to all the important magazines of the day were housed with edifying texts, art books, and romantic novels. Sue bought books she and Emily were pleased to read and share as the subject of passionate discussion at The Evergreen's soirees.

At Sue's salon, Emily met a clever and well educated new friend called Anthon whose given name was Kate Turner. Anthon gave Emily a copy of Elizabeth Barrett Browning's *Aurora Leigh*, a novel in verse that had been published 1856, championing women's right to self-fulfillment. Sue, with Emily and Anthon, as well as Samuel Bowles, editor of *The Springfield Republican*, and his learned friend, Maria Whitney, along with Austin, who became fast friends with Bowles, had interesting debates around Sue's parlor fireplace all through fall and winter about women's rights.

Emily began to call Sue's and Austin's circle of friends "her crowd," and their presence added much solace to her solitary life. Elizabeth Barrett Browning and Margaret Fuller of New England had befriended each other in Europe in a feminist movement burgeoning there. Since The Seneca Falls Convention held in July of 1848, in upstate New York, Paul Bowles of *The Springfield Republican*, as well as Henry Wentworth Higginson of *The Atlantic Monthly* in Boston, had become champions of women's rights, they both editorialized with positive gusto on the subject. The issues of women's and negro rights, and John Brown's radical movement, afforded heady debates fueled by generous glasses of port wine at The Evergreens.

"The freer women are, the happier men should be to have them as companions and mates of the mind beyond the bedroom!" Bowles declared. "I agree with Margaret Fuller's views when she edited *The Dial* for the Transcendental Club. It's obscene to say that 'love is to a man a thing apart, to a woman's her whole existence.' Elizabeth Barrett Browning does not agree with her husband on that point. Women want fulfillment of their mental gifts as much as men do. How can I finance John Brown and fight for the rights of negro men to vote as I do, and leave out women's right to have a say in the governance of her country? The fruit of her womb is what populates the world. It makes no sense to leave her out of constitutional rights to be educated, own property, and vote her children's future." Bowles was adamant.

His companion and secretary, Maria Whitney and Emily's friend, Anthon, affirmed his pronouncement with theirs. "Women suffer to birth the race and raise it to fruition. They've a right to equality, and know well how to nurture civilization."

Austin and Sue had reservations on the issue of women's right to vote, as did George Sand whom all were reading. "Women are not yet generally educated enough to vote. Their influence should remain in the household where they can influence the men and children with their moral fortitude for what's good and proper." Ever since Squire Dickinson paraded Sue Gilbert to church on his arm to announce Austin's engagement, she attempted to please him with her views. She saw him as the father she'd lost and her rescuer. Since they'd been "saved" together in The Great Revival, Sue continued to engender her father-in-law's affection.

Though Anthon stood passionately with Bowles radical ideals for women's rights, Emily listened quietly, sure where she herself stood, but preferring to keep her views private, least they reach her father's ears or disgruntle Sue. She'd become less of a talker, more of a listener in debates, ever since Professor Clark had broken her heart by marrying Cousin Harriet. Emily was in constant mourning over the loss of her master's attentions and sexual passions. She buried her sorrows in the garden soil, loosed them from her skirts during rambles in the woods with Carlo, deluted them with wine, and quelled their bitterness with Sue's fancy desserts. Most often, she mitigated them by privately composing verse that she occasionally shared aloud with her crowd at Sue's soirees where she also enjoyed playing the piano to amuse. She did her best to forget Clark, though she found it impossible.

Into the night, at her lamp table, her door locked against all intruders, she wrote verse after verse to ease her anguish. She envied the very bedroom that held her master far off in the night and the huge ocean that brought him so far from her to Europe. Unable to withstand her longing in silence, she finally begged her dear friend, Elizabeth Holland, wife of the cultural editor for *The Springfield Republican*, Josiah Holland, to forward poems to Clark in Italy. The Hollands always knew Clark's whereabouts, because he wrote anonymous articles for the paper regarding his cultural observations of European art and women's writing, which he continued to champion. Emily read his pieces as if they were meant for her alone.

Emily's first brief poem to Clark in Italy read:

> *My river runs to thee:*
> *Blue sea, wilt welcome me?*
> *My river waits reply.*
> *Oh sea, look graciously!*
> *I'll fetch thee brooks*

From spotted nooks, —
Say sea,
Take me!

The verse ran through her mind like a song. She'd sung it to herself as Clark rode the sea to Europe. As a means of survival, she began again to sew her poems into booklets that she hoped to give Clark one day upon his return. He'd appreciated her poetry like no other friend since her beloved preceptor, Newton. Her second poem sent via Mrs. Holland said:

I envy seas, whereon he rides,
  I envy spokes of wheels
Of chariots, that him convey,
  I envy speechless hills

That gaze upon his journey;
  How easy all can see
What is forbidden utterly
  As heaven, unto me!

I envy nests of sparrows
  That dot his distant eaves,
The wealthy fly, upon his pane,
  The happy, happy leaves

That just abroad his window
  Have summer's leave to be,
The earrings of Pizarro
  Could not obtain for me.

I envy light that wakes him,
  And bells that boldly ring
To tell him it is noon, abroad, —
  Myself his noon could bring,

Yet interdict my blossom
And abrogate my bee,
Lest noon in everlasting night—
Drop Gabriel and me.

Again, no answer came, but as autumn turned to winter, Emily heard that Professor Clark was back in Amherst, and would resume teaching at the college. She heard nothing from him, and neither had he been seen about the town by anyone. All supposed he was still in mourning over the loss of his son.

One evening, Emily sat at Sue's piano in the parlor of The Evergreens glowing with gas lamps. The aroma of Sue's gourmet feast still wafted from the dining room, and guests languished about with glasses of port in their hands. Emily played a rendition of her wild composition titled, "The Devil." Her auburn curls tossed about, as drunk with her own music, she pounded a revelry of angry and gay notes offering a weirdly dissonant emotion. She furiously tapped her high-buttoned shoe on the floor to keep rhythm. Her audience made up of Susan and Austin seated near the fire as hosts, Samuel Bowles and Maria Whitney on the divan, Emily's new friend, Anthon, on the red velvet chair beside the piano, and several other guests, were highly amused by her deliberately exaggerated playing. Emily was now entertaining all with "The Devil" when suddenly William Smith Clark entered the room.

Susan, unknown to Emily, had invited Clark, recently back from Italy, to enliven her dinner table with stories of his travels. He'd said he'd try to come later, after his newly pregnant wife retired early for the night. Emily was shocked and pleased beyond her ability to believe she actually saw him there. Composing herself as best she could, she was relieved to realize that she was dressed in her finest blue gown, her hair newly arranged in French curls by Vinnie whose turn it was to sit with their ailing mother. A white lace collar surrounded Emily's face. Her cheeks were flushed with drinking.

As Professor Clark entered Sue and Austin's parlor from the front hall, he immediately took note of Emily and smiled and nodded in her direction. He was pleased to see her enjoying playing music with such gusto. He'd never wanted to hurt her. He still loved and wanted her more than Harriet who'd become pregnant just before he'd left for Italy. Harriet was confined to the house during another pregnancy, as was usual for women of her class when heavy with child. "I don't dare take a carriage ride, William!" She'd declared.

"But, my father says you must walk about the house, at least, for exercise, now that your father has provided you with a cook and a gardener to make life easy for you!"

"I'm tired, William. I'm going upstairs to pray and rest." Harriet's loss of her first child made her feel like a failure at mothering. Her morose disposition did not add anything to her lackluster demeanor. Clark felt he had to get out of their home in order not to suffocate. He enjoyed the company of people his equal in conversation, people like Susan and Austin, fast becoming the leading socialites of Amherst.

As Emily finished her dramatic composition, she stood and bowed with a mock flurry of a handkerchief she drew from her sleeve to wipe her brow mimicking an exhausted concert diva. "And thus dances the devil when he avails himself of the souls of all sinners, particularly those who indulge the flesh above the sincerity of the heart!" Emily announced grandly with a smirk in Clark's direction. Clark understood her veiled intent. Anthon peered in Clark's direction as if she knew the whole story of Emily's love and loss.

"Give us another poem, Emily!" Anthon, a little drunk implored raucously, taking Emily by the hand to keep her standing. Emily paused, thought, cleared her throat, and recited:

> *Of all the souls that stand create*
> *I have elected one.*
> *When sense from spirit files away,*
> *And subterfuge is done;*
>
> *When that which is and that which was*
> *Apart, intrinsic stand,*
> *And this brief tragedy of flesh*
> *Is shifted like a sand;*

When figures show their royal front
And mists are carved away, —
Behold the atom I preferred
To all the lists of clay.

"Another!" Anthon encouraged as the crowd joined in clinking and raising their glasses. "Yes, indeed, another, Miss Emily!" Professor Clark added his sober voice to the din.

Emily felt emboldened. This one is titled, "Consecration." I wrote it for all scorned lovers to send on Valentine's Day."

"That should suit many!" Paul Bowles interjected laughing with Maria Whitney.

Emily went on with her recitation:

> *Proud of my broken heart since thou didst' break it,*
> *Proud of the pain I did not feel till thee,*
> *Proud of my night since thou with moons dost slake it,*
> *Not to partake thy passion, my humility....*
> *Thou can'st not pierce tradition with the peerless puncture,*
> *See! I usurped thy crucifix to honor mine.*

Anthon applauded unable not to regard Clark as Emily spoke. The recitation made Susan an uncomfortable hostess. As applause subsided she beckoned to Clark: "Come sit near the fire, Professor Clark. I dare say we'd all like to hear of your travels in Italy, land of passion known to uncork artistic genius. Please avail us of your descriptions of what you've seen and heard. Did you meet the Brownings? "

Clark sat near Susan and Austin in front of the mantle and began to tell of his travels as the lamps burned low. Emily and the others listened with wrapped interest as more wine was poured late into the night. When Clark finished his description of Mrs. Browning's continuing interest in the quelled *Risorgimento*, and her disagreement with her husband regarding feminism, he began to describe with bravado, marvelous dishes he'd eaten and great works of art and architecture he'd seen in Florence, Venice, and Rome. He caught Emily looking at him with admiration in her gaze. When the evening finished, and all were leaving by the front hall, he took Emily by the elbow. "I'll cut across your property over the hill, Miss Dickinson. If you will tell your Carlo not to bark at me, let me escort you toward your door along my way."

Emily walked with Clark toward her homestead as the others dispersed or retired upstairs to bed at The Evergreens. Clark escorting her along the path between the shrubs and trees, whispered first. "This path is just wide enough for two lovers to walk side by side, Miss Emily."

"But we are not lovers, Mr. Clark." She retorted in an angry whisper. "Not for years."

When Clark saw that no one followed them through the darkness, he turned to Emily and drew her to him. "But I have wanted to be your lover again, My Little Daisy. I think of you often there in your house below the hill. Every time I pass on my way to the college, I wonder if you are in the window seeing me walk by. When I see the lamp in your window I know it means you're awake and writing poetry. I wonder if your poem is for me and if you're thinking of me."

Both Clark and Emily had drunk a considerable amount of alcohol and were excited by each other's closeness. Clark took Emily by the hand and dragged her behind a large tree near the edge of her driveway. He pressed his lips to hers and held her in a lingering kiss from which she could not free herself.

"Let me go, Will. I'm insulted that you think you can so easily resume our intimacy without explanation of your long silence. I've suffered horribly these past years as you neglected your promise to keep our bond despite your marriage."

"Emily, would you believe me if I said I've suffered miserably, too?

In answer, Emily drew away resisting as best she could his superior size and strength. "Emily, please don't pull away. I remember your touch and ache for it. The strength in your little hands." Clark held her hands and kissed them. " I read your poems and letters again and again and keep them hidden well where no one will find them."

"Then why no answers. You've doomed me to silence?"

"I felt I should resist writing, not to rekindle the flames of our desire.

I felt it was wrong of me to want to possess you when you should be free to find another to marry."

"But you suggested I *not* marry. That I be your *Geisha* forever more."

"That was selfish of me, to imagine you should be my *amore* while you were still young and capable of marriage to another who could give you all that I can't give.

Emily couldn't resist Clark, realizing he suffered pain of conscience. "But you gave me so much, Master. No other could match your gifts. I've starved without you."

"Emily, come with me now to explore the woods in the moonlight."

"You're drunk, Will. It's too cold. I'm freezing."

"We'll warm the woods as we used to." Clark kissed her again with breathless longing.

She could resist him no longer. She'd pined for this moment for years. "The house is asleep and Father's away. Come with me to the Northwest Passage, as you used to, Clark. I'll be your Lewis, again!" Emily felt brazen desire. She whispered laughing, tipsy with abandon. "It's warm and dark there."

The inebriated Clark followed the staggering Emily to her back door, and she took him to the hallway that had five means of escape to various parts of the mansion. She knew that Vinnie and her Mother would be fast asleep. When Squire Dickinson was away, Carlo always slept inside the back door guarding the house and only awakened to wag his tail at Emily's return and seek her affection.

Once inside the hall that Emily had dubbed her Northwest Passage, Clark pulled her to him again, running his hands over her small breasts as he kissed her. They sat at the bottom of the servant's stairwell and petted, kissing with desire. Clark took Emily onto his lap and stroked her thighs. She pulled away and he pulled her to him. They alternately gave into and resisted each other until at last their bodies merged quietly, Emily astride Clark's lap. They rowed to ecstasy, until Emily heard Vinnie's voice calling from the upper hall in a frightened whisper:

"Emily is that you?"

Clark stood and hurriedly buttoned his pants. He kissed Emily goodbye and left quietly and quickly by the back door, his heels tapping softly as he went. At the back door, he paused to whisper: "I'll send a note by Sweetser's handyman via Maggie. "We'll meet soon. I'll take you again 'where the sun don't shine,' Little Daisy. Bring me your poems."

"Yes, Master. Goodnight." Emily shut the door, turned and rushed back to the hall and up the back stairs, her skirts held high, her white color framing her face. Her curly hair tossled. She met Lavinia at the top of the stairs in the moonlight.

As Lavinia's eyes grew accustomed to the darkness, she saw the shadow of Emily appear climbing upward in her indigo gown with white lace collar. Emily's moonlit hair made a reddish aura of curls around her pale, but happy, face.

"Go to sleep, Lavinia!" Emily came breathlessly up the stairs, holding her white crinoline and blue satin skirts high. "I've been late next door at Sue's and Austin's soiree," she whispered. "Do go back to sleep, now, Dear Vinnie! Never mind me. I'm on my way to bed, with a bit too much wine in my head!"

Emily didn't want to wake her mother, asleep down the hall in her sick room. Their father was away on business. She hurried into her own bedroom across from Lavinia's. "Goodnight, Sister! Sleep well." She silently shut her door with a sigh of exasperation. Safely inside, she lit the oil lamp on her writing table and sat down in front of the window facing Main Street. She drew paper, pen, and inkwell from a drawer in the front of her small table. With glee, she wrote:

> *Did the harebell loose her girdle*
>   *To the lover bee,*
> *Would the bee the harebell hallow*
> *Much as formerly?*
>
> *Did the paradise, persuaded,*
> *Yield her moat of pearl,*
> *Would the Eden be an Eden*
> *Or the earl an earl?*

Early August 1861: The Civil War

> *The red upon the hill*
> *Taketh away my Will…*
> *I tend my garden for thee,*
> *Bright absentee…*

Again, Emily and Will Clark met in their oak grove to ride through the woods to one of their caves in the Pelham Hills. Emily brought poems to Will at every meeting. She'd brought him a short verse which she just finished reading to him:

> *I have no life but this,*
> *To lead it here,*
> *Nor any death, but lest*
> *Dispelled from there;*
>
> *Nor tie the earth to come,*
> *Nor action new,*
> *Except through this extent*
> *The realm of you.*

"Ah, Emily, that rivals Mrs. Brownings Portugese Sonnets. I'm not worthy of it." Since their tryst in the Northwest Passage when Lavinia had again nearly discovered them, they'd found many opportunities to meet secretly, on their way home from one of Austin's and Sue's gatherings at the Evergreens, sometimes, guarded by faithful Carlo, in the barn behind the homestead. Clark's wife, Harriet, "The Queen," as everyone still called her, was yet again pregnant and confined to home. She never came to the evenings of poetry, music, and intellectual camaraderie, sometimes attended by Samuel Bowles of *The Springfield Republican.* Bowles and Thomas Wentworth Higginson of *The Atlantic Monthly* had helped to finance John Brown's militant actions against slavery at Harper's Ferry. Since Sumner had been attacked in the Senate House, Amherst had been astir with news of the war's progress and Abraham Lincoln's insistence that the country remain undivided.

Clark's tone changed abruptly as he declared. "I have to tell you something very important, Emily. You won't like it, and I don't know how to say it, so I'll simply blurt it out: "I've volunteered to serve in the Union Army. It's the only honorable thing to do, and Sam Williston expects it of me. He's offered to give a rifle to any able-bodied student of the Easthampton Academy who wants to fight for the Union Army, and he needs me to set a good example."

"No, no, Will, no!" was all Emily could gasp.

"Even your admired Emerson has said, 'Sometimes the smell of gunfire is sweet!' "

"But, Master!" Emily's spirit sank. "No, no, you can't go. You're needed here in Amherst to teach chemistry and agricultural science. You've been appointed by the governor to further the science of agriculture here in our Pioneer Valley. That's no small thing! You're our first Ph.D. scholar—too valuable to lose to war. Why must you go? I'll die if you're lost. Father insists that Austin not go. Father's financed a volunteer in Austin's place, because he's the only able-bodied man of our family. Father says we can't bear to lose him as Mother, Lavinia, and I will have no one to care for us and his estate when Father's old and gone. Can't you pay for another to go in your place? It's customary for vitally needed men to do so. You're the only able man of Williston's family."

"No, there is Lyman, Harriet's brother, who has gone off to Boston to be a Unitarian preacher, and Mrs. Williston has able men in her family. Williston feels that I must volunteer as an example to others. He's correct. I must be a good example. I'll make a fine career of the military. I'll lead a cavalry on horseback. Good horsemen are needed, and Williston will help to finance a fine military horse for me, once I've made it to the front. I go to Worcester soon to command the 21st Regiment of Massachusetts Volunteers. I'd hope to drill enough volunteers from Amherst, but there aren't enough ready to go and I'm impatient to join the fray. I'll lead my regiment out of Worcester. It's an honor bestowed upon me."

"Is it because you're bored with your work at the college, Master, and tired of me?"

"Tired of you. Of course not! They 've dismissed me from teaching botany and leading wild flower walks. There were rumors that I was too flirtatious with the ladies who attended those walks. Ever since I put the statue of a naked nymph in the pond in the college gardens, and European paintings of voluptuous women in the hall outside my office the trustees are wary of me. There are some very inflexible trustees on the board, your father among the worst! Perhaps, he suspects us, the way he dragged you home from The Evergreens the night of the last snow with his lantern. "Emily, what is the meaning of this hour of revelry?" said he like an old coot, stopping you short at the piano in the midst of your playing, embarrassing you as if you were still a child instead of a woman of thirty-two years!"

"It's possible someone has seen us and tongues are wagging."

"That's why it's best I go away, now, to quell the gossip that may injure you more than me. I feel guilty for not loving my wife as I should, but her constant quoting of nothing but scripture, her relentless Evangelical zeal, is difficult to tolerate day and night. She was most surely raised as the daughter of missionaries. Her literal interpretations of scripture and lack of mind for science drive me mad."

"Please don't go, Master. Your intellect is needed here in this valley. I fear for your life. I'll miss you unbearably."

"Tend your garden for me while I'm away. Keep those rare specimens we've found alive in your conservatory. I may need cuttings when I return, in case my gardener fails me. You are the best of my horticultural students, Emily. Write to me. Send me poems and messages through Luke Sweetser's man and trusty Maggie, as usual."

"But you'll be far away, Master!"

"Perhaps, Sam Bowles will forward letters or poems. I'm to be a correspondent for his newspaper while in the field. I'll be writing news from the front for Higginson at *The Atlantic Monthly*, too. Perhaps, he'll forward some poems if you write to him and get to know him better. He's a good literary mind. He might publish your poems in *The Atlantic*. Then there's your friend, Mrs. Holland. She can forward through her husband's knowledge of my whereabouts. As assistant editor at Bowle's paper, Josiah Holland will also know where to write to me. There are ways you can write to me undetected by your father and this provincial town's gossips. Daisy, I will look forward to your letters and poems."

"This is our second awful parting, Master. We've renewed our love, only to lose it again."

"No Daisy, it's temporary parting only until the war is won. I need you to be strong."

"But how long will it take, Master?"

"Emily, your father and other trustees who are free soilers criticize me for talking too adamantly against the heinous practice of slavery, but Sam Williston is an abolitionist glad to have me do so. Bowles's and Higginson's editorials jibe with my feelings. Williston does not agree with your father that slavery can be gotten rid over time with new laws in the new territories. The Kansas Nebraska Act hasn't gone far enough, and The Missouri Compromise has proven worthless."

"But, Master, Father is concerned, like Mr. Lincoln, with keeping the Union together. He feels it's a paramount concern. Slavery can be dealt with by instituting state's laws, bit by bit, without so much bloodshed, can't it?"

"It's too late for compromise. Emerson is correct, "Sometimes the smell of gunfire *is* sweet!" We must rid New England and the country of the monstrous institution of slavery, once and for all. You've heard Frederick Douglass and Sojourner Truth speak. You've heard how Reverend Beecher feels with his rifles called "Beecher's Bibles," shipped to the front. You've read his sermons from The Plymouth Church in Brooklyn Heights. President Lincoln, himself, visited Beecher's parish to speak against slavery. It's rumor that Beecher runs an underground railroad North to Cambridgeport from Brooklyn. I'm going with my father's and Williston's blessings. I want yours, too, Emily. I must have it to endure."

"Master, I bless everything you do, every hair of your head and beard. There is never a time when you go without my blessings. They are yours for eternity. You know that, but I'm afraid for it, for our love, for your spirit, for your life, for your body."

"Don't be, Daisy. I'll come back to you alive if you believe in me. I'm yours by the right of the white election!" Clark smiling, took Emily in his arms and kissed her firmly on the lips. "No matter what else happens, we'll meet, as you always say, in Eternity."

Emily held him tight and returned his kiss with all her heart. "Please be careful, Will. You're a dare devil, I fear! She sank dejected down upon their bower of pine branches and wept silently. Will sat beside her and held her tight.

Look, dearest Daisy! I've a gift for you in parting. One that will inspire you." He pressed a volume bound in green with gold lettering into her hands."

She looked at the cover. Thereon the cover in gold lettering were the words; "Leaves of Grass."

Is this the poetry of Walt Whitman of New York which I've been told is disgraceful? Though my cousins in Boston like it."

"It's not disgraceful, but true to the spirit of our American democracy. Only a prudish Calvinist would find it scandalous. It's true to the spirit of Emerson's Transcendentalism and the abolishment of slavery. It is wondrous poetry that teaches us to be unashamed of the glories of our blessed bodies. It's the voice of these American states. Will Clark took the volume of Whitman's poetry from Emily's hands and kissed her upon the eyes, a light kiss upon each. He looked into her face and smiled. Here, rest on my knee while I read to you. Drink some more wine to soothe your spirit as you listen to Whitman's words. They ring true as your brother's speech at his graduation, regarding a *New* American Literature:

They sing as Emerson would have a poet sing. Emerson has declared himself an admirer of Whitman, and so has Abraham Lincoln. Whitman has printed Emerson's estimation of his poetry in the front of this volume. Listen, please, and no more tears. Breathe deeply and calm yourself. You're a great poet, my dear Daisy. You'll send me your poems. Why your maid Maggie can give them to my man, over the back fence and he'll mail them on to me. I want you to begin to gather your poems together in final copies for me. Come Carlo, keep our little mistress warm. Carlo curled up beside Emily. Clark put his arm around her and she rested her head on his knee and listened as they sat on his saddle blanket.

Clark opened *Leaves of Grass*. Look Emily at this photograph, Walt Whitman dresses as a simple rural fellow, in rustic white shirt, like a natural laborer. He abhors fancy clothes as much as you do, and as

much as Alcott does. Listen to what he says in his preface. Clark began
to read to her from the preface of *Leaves of Grass*:

AMERICA *does not repel the past or what it has produced
under its forms or amid other politics or the idea of castes or the old
religions… literature has passed into the new life of the new forms…
The Americans of all nations at any time upon the earth have probably
the fullest poetical nature… Here is not merely a nation but a teeming
nation of nations… Here are the roughs and beards and space and
ruggedness and nonchalance that the soul loves… One sees it must
indeed own the riches of the summer and winter, and need never
be bankrupt while corn grows from the ground or the orchards drop
apples or the bays contain fish or men beget children upon women…
the genius of the United States is not best or most in its executives or
legislatures, nor in its ambassadors or authors or colleges or churches
or parlors, nor even in its newspapers or inventors… but always most
in the common people. Their manners speech dress friendships—the
freshness and candor of their physiognomy—the picturesque looseness
of their carriage… their deathless attachment to freedom…their delight
in music, the sure symptom of manly tenderness and native elegance
of soul… the terrible significance of their elections—the President's
taking off his hat to them not they to him—these, too, are unrhymed
poetry.*

*The largeness of nature or the nation were monstrous without a
corresponding largeness and generosity of the spirit of the citizen. Not
nature nor swarming states nor streets and steamships nor prosperous
business nor farms nor capital nor learning may suffice for the ideal
of man… nor suffice the poet… The American poets are to enclose
old and new for America is the race of races. Of them a bard is to
be commensurate with a people. His spirit responds to his country's
spirit… he incarnates its geography and natural life and rivers and
lakes…On him rise solid growths that offset the growths of pine and
cedar and hemlock and live oak and locust and chestnut and cypress
and hickory and lime tree and cottonwood and tulip tree and cactus
and wild vine and tamarind and persimmon… and tangles as tangled
as any canebrake or swamp… and forests coated with transparent
ice and icicles hanging from the boughs and crackling in the wind…
and sides and peaks of mountains… and pasturage sweet and free as
savannah or upland or prairie… with flights and songs and screams*

*that answer those of the wild pigeon and high hold and orchard-oriole
and coot and surf-duck and red shouldered-hawk and fish-hawk and
white-ibis and Indian-hen and cat-owl and water-pheasant and qua-
bird and pied-sheldrake and blackbird and mockingbird and buzzard
and condor and night-heron and eagle…*

Though Emily was still weeping silently, her heart heavy as the
great rocks of Pelham, she was moved by Whitman's words as Clark
read passionately to her. She sighed, leaned comfortably on Clark's
knee, and listened attentively, looking up at his face as if he were her
savior. She would never love him more than at that moment when she
realized he could never be completely hers. He belonged to science
and his country. He belonged to his worldly ambitions more than he
ever could to any woman. The Queen would never own his heart
anymore than she herself could.

"Isn't Whitman inspiring, Emily? Your calling is to be a poet, not
a housewife. You have an intellect to rival any man's. I've seen that
in the way you've discussed my student's papers with me. In the way
we've shared books and learning."

"Yes, Master. I've learned so much from you.

"And I from you, Emily. You'll be in my spirit wherever I go. Never
doubt it." Clark in sharing Whitman's book with Emily, helped her to
stop crying. "Listen to what Whitman says here, Emily!"

*Men and women perceive the beauty well enough… probably
as well as the poet. The passionate tenacity of hunters, woodmen,
early risers, cultivators of gardens and orchards and fields, the love
of healthy women for the manly form, sea-faring persons, drivers of
horses, the passion for light and the open air, all is an old varied sign
of the unfailing perception of beauty and of a residence of the poetic in
outdoor people… The profit of rhyme is that it drops seeds of a sweeter
and more luxuriant rhyme, and of uniformity that it conveys itself
into its own roots in the ground out of sight…Who troubles himself
about his ornaments or fluency is lost. This is what you shall do: Love
the earth and sun and the animals, despise riches, give alms to every
one that asks, stand up for the stupid and crazy, devote your income
and labor to others, hate tyrants, argue not concerning God, have
patience and indulgence toward the people, take off your hat to nothing*

known or unknown or to any man or number of men, go freely with powerful uneducated persons and with the young and with the mothers of families, read these leaves in the open air every season of every year of your life, re-examine all you have been told at school or church or in any book, dismiss whatever insults your own soul, and your very flesh shall be a great poem and have the richest fluency not only in its words but in the silent lines of its lips and face and between the lashes of your eyes and in every motion and joint of your body…

"Whitman's words remind me of yours, and of Emerson's, and Ben Newton's, Master."

"Yes, my dearest Daisy, and his thoughts are like yours, transcendent. You 're a poet whose love of nature and naturalness, and loathing of religious dogma are like Whitman's."

Clark was relieved that he'd succeeded in comforting Emily and distracting her with *Leaves of Grass*. Here Emily, this book is yours to keep. Let it be your Bible. Hide it well from your father. You see, it's not scandalous at all, but true to our beliefs."

Emily deposited *Leaves of Grass* under the napkins in her picnic basket and reached in to lift a daisy she'd packed in a vial of water for Will. "Here, Master. Press this perfect daisy from my meadow in your bible and carry it with you, please, to remember me and the beauty we've shared in the woods and meadows. The crowd will cheer you as you go, but remember your small Daisy. I feared a rumor I heard from Austin that you planned to go to war. Here's a verse with it for you:

> *Beguiling thus the wonder,*
> *The wondrous nearer drew;*
> *Hands butled at the moorings—*
> *The crowd respectful grew.*
> *Ascended from our vision*
> *To countenances new!*
> *A difference, a daisy,*
> *Is all the rest I knew.*

Send me letters via Elizabeth Holland, Master. I can trust her more than anyone. She's a sister to me, far more clever and understanding than my dearest Lavinia. Your letters cannot come to the Amherst post office, Master. None of those gossiping clerks can be trusted."

"How well I understand, Daisy. Never fear. Bowles in Springfield will be in touch. He suspects our affair. But, with his eyes on Maria Whitney all the time, rather than set on his wife, Mary, he makes no moral judgment of us. He approves liberated women, at any rate. He'll be the man to know what goes on at the front with me. Holland, his cultural assistant, will know where I am and what I'm up to. The Queen is too busy with the children and household to write much to me. Her letters will be all pious prayers. I'll look forward to yours to sustain me in the field."

"I'll write, Master, to keep our souls in touch." Emily looked deep into Will's eyes as she'd learned directness and intimacy from him.

"Come to my drill parade next Saturday on the Common. I want to see you cheering in the crowd. Wave your white handkerchief and red paisley shawl in unison at the bandstand. I'll view you among the throng. I'll be departing soon after. This will be our last meeting until my return."

Emily repressed her tears for Will's sake and kissed his eyes. "Bless you, Master. Come home safely to me. I *will* be *always* waiting for my *Will*. My life goes with yours. Guard it safely."

Later in the evening, Emily sat at her writing table and confessed her despair to her little Norcross cousins in Boston to whom she wrote regularly, especially since her beloved Aunt Lavinia, their sweet and poetic mother, an aunt who had inspired Emily, had died a year earlier. Their father lingered, ill and grieving for his wife and was not expected to live long. Emily, Lavinia, and Austin had sometimes visited with them where they boarded in a house owned by Mrs. Bang on Amity Street, near Harvard, in Cambridgeport. Emily had become very attached to her Norcross cousins, Louisa and Frances. Lovingly addressed as Lou and Fanny, they relished reading books and sharing reactions to them with their older, articulate Cousin, Emily, who was more like a nurturing aunt to them.

Dear Lou and Fanny, My Dearest Little Cousins,

I wish 'twas plainer, the anguish of the world. I wish one could be sure the anguish had a loving side. Sorrow seems to me to be everyone's estate since the war began. Now, it takes my Will away, and you know too well my secret heart and how this event is breaking and worrying it…

Later that night as Emily lay in her bed, weak from grieving Will's pending departure, unable to sleep, she rose and lit her oil lamp. Gathering her shawl about her, she extracted *Leaves of Grass* from her locked bureau drawer. She hid the key back in its secret hiding place in her closet behind a lose baseboard, and took the book to the lamp to continue reading. Carlo, curled up by the Franklin stove, came to her side to be petted. She fondled his ears and patted his big head as she read propped up on her pillow beside her oil lamp.

The poet shall not spend his time in unneeded work. He shall go directly to the creation… His trust shall master the trust of everything he touches… and shall master all attachment. The known universe has one complete lover and that is the greatest poet. He consumes an eternal passion and is indifferent which chance happens and which possible contingency of fortune or misfortune and persuades daily and hourly his delicious pay. What balks or breaks others is fuel for his burning progress to contact and amorous joy. Other proportions of the reception of pleasure dwindle to nothing to his proportions. All expected from heaven or from the highest he is rapport with in the sight of the daybreak or a scene of the winter woods or the presence of children playing or with his arm round the neck of a man or woman. His love above all love has leisure and expanse… he leaves room ahead of himself. He is no irresolute or suspicious lover… he is sure… he scorns intervals. His experience and the showers and thrills are not for nothing. Nothing can jar him… suffering and darkness cannot—death and fear cannot. To him complaint and jealousy and envy are corpses buried and rotten in the earth… he saw them buried. The sea is not surer of the shore or the shore of the sea than he is of the fruition of his love and of all perfection and beauty… Exact science and its practical movements are no checks on the greatest poet but always his encouragement and support. The outset and remembrance are there… there the arms that lifted him first and brace him best… there he returns after all his goings and comings. The sailor and traveler… the anatomist chemist astronomer geologist phrenologist spiritualist mathematician historian and lexicographer are not poets, but they are the lawgivers of poets and their construction underlies the structure of every perfect poem. No matter what rises or is uttered they sent the seed of the conception of it… of them and by them stand the visible proofs of souls… always of their father stuff must be begotten the sinewy races of bards. If there shall be love and content between the father and the son and if the greatness of the son is the exuding of the greatness of the father there shall be love between the poet and the man of demonstrable science. In the beauty of poems are the tuft and final applause of science…

"No wonder, Will Clark loves Whitman, Carlo. They are brothers, as Ben Newton was to Emerson. Emily finished reading the Preface to *Leaves of Grass*. "Whitman says what Austin tried to say in his graduation speech. He says what Ben Newton espoused. His voice is like Will's, Carlo." Emily whispered to her dog, feeling lonely for her Master to share her thoughts. She scratched Carlo's head and continued reading. Inspired by Whitman's words, which she heard in the voice of Master Clark in her head, despite her emotional suffering, she turned to the poems. The volume fell open on a line that read, "I sing the body electric…"

When she finished reading the entire volume of Leaves of Grass, she sat again at her writing table to finish her letter to her Little Cousins in Cambridgeport who had recommended she read Whitman as Emerson had recommended him to all.

Oh, Little Cousins, you are so correct about Walt Whitman's Leaves of Grass, it is bold and true and heralds our American democracy, just as Emerson said. He lacks the craft of brevity and is not succinctly lyrical, but his words are plain and true poetry. The sort that at times makes me feel as if the top of my head has been taken off! Professor Clark has given the book to me and I am astonished at its amazing and candid contents. It stirs my soul to new heights, even as

I must bid goodbye to my beloved Master who is off to war tomorrow. Yes, Little Cousins, my greatest love has volunteered for the Union Army. My heart is lead. Yet, I am inspired by Whitman if laid low by my Master's departure. I'll write to you more, soon, of Whitman's poems. Meantime, 'I Sing the Body Electric,' and 'Myself, I Sing!' " And your dear selves, I salute!

Ever, your faithful affectionate cousin, Emily

Late August 1861: "The Anguish of This World"

Austin helped Emily up onto a bench where she could stand and watch the Amherst regiment of volunteers, led by Professor Clark, parade across the commons to the fife and drum corps. The throbbing drums and shrill whistles excited the crowd who cheered wildly as their little regiment of volunteers, marched past with their rifles, supplied by Sam Williston, on their shoulders.

Clark would leave the next day for Worcester where he would lead the 21st Regiment of Massachusetts to the front. With his men, he'd sail from Norwich, and after their training at Annapolis, onto dangerous Southern shores. The little Amherst regiment Clark had assembled and drilled, not yet outfitted in Union Army uniforms, came to a halt to present arms, and then be called at ease. Clark went to the podium and introduced the men each by name. Frazar Stearns, one of the handsomest and brightest students of the college, the favorite of Professor Clark, stood beside him. The two had become inseparable and would leave together for the front. Emily felt a twinge of jealousy for Clark's pet student, Frazar. He'd be able to accompany Clark into battle where she could never go.

After preliminary proceedings, the professor read with passionate vigor from the Declaration of Independence composed by Thomas Jefferson at the bidding of Samuel Adams during the First Congress of the United States of America in 1776—less than a hundred years before. He wanted to indicate to his audience that the current entry into the Civil War was necessary to secure unalienable rights for all men. The townspeople knew that Clark's patron and father-in-law, Sam Williston, was willing to supply guns to any who volunteered for the Union Army. Clark read with passionate conviction:

> *When in the Course of human events, it becomes necessary for one people to dissolve the political bands which have connected them with another, and to assume among the powers of the earth, the separate and equal station to which the Laws of Nature and of Nature's God entitle them, a decent respect to the opinions of mankind requires that they should declare the causes which impel them to the separation.*

We hold these truths to be self-evident, that all men are created equal, that they are endowed, by their Creator, with certain unalienable Rights, that among these are Life, Liberty and the pursuit of Happiness. —That to secure these rights, Governments are instituted among Men, deriving their just powers from the consent of the governed, —That whenever any Form of Government becomes destructive of these ends, it is the Right of the People to alter or to abolish it, and to institute new Government, laying its foundation on such principles and organizing its powers in such form, as to them shall seem most likely to effect their Safety and Happiness…

As the professor finished his reading, the crowd cheered and Emily waved her red paisley shawl in unison with her white handkerchief as high as she could.

Clark nodded in her direction and raised his hand in a wave toward the crowd that she knew was very much for her as well. Her eyes watered with the realization that he would soon be far from Amherst. Too impatient to wait for enough soldiers for an Amherst Regimen, he'd go to Worcester to command the 21ˢᵗ Regiment.

Austin, standing beside his sister, cheered with the crowd as Emily waved, "Clark will go with Frazar and the Worcester regiment to Annapolis where they'll be bivouacked before being sent South." Austin informed Emily, not knowing she knew all.

"Oh Austin, I pray the war might end before their regiment goes to the front.

"Not at all likely, Em. How I wish I were going with Clark, but Father won't allow it."

"I agree with Father, Austin. You must not go and leave us women all alone. We need you here in Amherst. We need Professor Clark, too. He's our best and brightest young professor of science. No one knows chemistry, botany, zoology, geology like he. And no one teaches it with such fervor. It would be horrible to lose you, Austin, and unthinkable, too, to lose Professor Clark!" Emily shook with adamant feeling. "How could we stand it?"

"Emily, I see you're still enamored of Clark, even though he's married to Harriet."

"It isn't that!" Emily feared she was betraying her secret. "I was over Clark since he married, but we do need men like him to teach in Amherst. I adored his lectures."

"Clark's a fine woodsman and horseman. He's the sort of confident men needed as mounted officers to lead the cavalries. The Union army is depleted and has only a few aged generals of any experience left. Williston wanted Clark to go to set a brave example of leadership for our commonwealth. Father says, 'Better Clark than me!' He feels Clark will get Frazar killed in battle along with himself. Perhaps, since Clark is not Williston's real son, but a son-in-law, it's easier for him to sacrifice Clark to the cause." Austin reasoned as he and his sister walked homeward from the village common with the fife and drum corps leading a parade down Main Street. "Father's a stuffy old Whig, but maybe the free-soilers are more humane. Working with state laws might be better than civil strife and all the bloodshed."

"But the Republican Party was founded in Father's rooms in Washington, Austin. Give Father that credit."

"Well, the Republicans in Washington are not as staunch in their abolition of slavery as Williston or Bowles of *The Springfield Republican*. The Whigs are quite willing to compromise their Calvinist morals to keep the Union together, and the Republicans are not very different, but Samuel Bowles believed in John Brown's brigade. Bowles writes that John Brown was the only Calvinist who wasn't a hypocrite. Father took poorly to that pronouncement and Sam Bowles has had to hem and haw to apologize for his statement to Father and his ilk. He wrote me to say how much he respects Father and that I should let Father know that he understands his fears for the Union. After Bowles helped to finance Brown at Harper's Ferry in '59, he, like Clark and Williston, was furious when Brown was hanged.

"So was Thomas Wentworth Higginson of *The Atlantic Monthly*."

"Yes, and Father and some of the other stuffed-shirt trustees told Clark to tone down his abolitionist speeches at the college. So, Clark resigned his professorship and enlisted, and recommended that his friend, Manross, take it over for him, at least until the war is over."

"So Clark went off to war because the trustees at the college, including Father, are too reserved about abolishing slavery?"

"Exactly. Clark's quite fed up with the timidity of some of the old Calvinists at the college. They disagreed with him about many things."

"But Clark was talking of volunteering ever since Senator Sumner was blooded and beaten by Senator Brooks in congress." Emily realized she should cloak what she knew of Clark. "Or, so Cousin Luke Sweester said!"

Austin frowned. "Father and his old pal, Judge Otis Lord, called for moderation at the Statehouse, saying, 'violence begets violence.'" They stick to ending slavery by instituting laws in the new territories and compromises in the senate. Clark is more radical than they."

"Clark was actually a free-soiler, too, Luke says, but after he heard of the dreadful defeat of the Union Army at Bull Run, he determined to enter the war."

"I don't blame him one jot. I'd go too if Father would allow. The split of opinions on the board of trustees has grown wider ever since Emerson and Thoreau took the side of the radical reformists while Nathaniel Hawthorne sided with the free-soilers."

Emily smiled. "Thoreau in his 54' speech in Boston called the Fugitive Slave Act 'a venomous reptile.'"

"What a speech that was! I've read it in *The Springfield Republican*. He likened the press to 'a gurgling sewer clogged with slime' and exhorted his audience to follow a higher law than The Constitution. That ruffled Father's feathers as constitutional law is his second bible."

"Thoreau turned Sam Bowles to his radical beliefs and *The Springfield Republican* has been staunchly abolitionist every since. But, Austin, why does bloodshed have to be necessary? I mourn all the suffering and dying."

"So do I, Emily! If that fool Franklin Pierce had not signed the Kansas-Nebraska Act and effectively nullified the Missouri Compromise that Father worked so hard for, this war might have been avoided. It was Pierce's stupidity that turned Brown and others so militant. I don't see why Nathaniel Hawthorne didn't see the foolery of Pierce in all this?"

"I'm proud that The Republican Party was founded in Father's rooms at the Wellington in Washington, aren't you, Aussie? Father's certainly known to clearly oppose slavery as morally repugnant even if he is a moderate about the war."

"Yes, Em, Father *did* fight with all his heart for the Missouri Compromise, but he remains a Whig loyalist and too old-fashioned after all to succeed in Washington these days!"

"Perhaps, Austin, Father was correct to be moderate for the sake of the Union. The carnage is already horrible! War's an abomination that can be avoided with compromise."

"Maybe so, Em, but even your beloved Emerson has proclaimed that John Brown's execution made 'the gallows glorious as the cross'!"

"Much madness is divinest sense, I say!" Emily took Austin's arm as they walked toward home.

"Hawthorne has infuriated Bowles by saying that no one was more justly executed than John Brown for his murderous treason. Still, I'm with Bowles and Higginson for Brown's aggressive methods. Williston and Clark are, now, too, as there's no choice. The war's begun. Bull Run has proved The Union Army must fight aggressively, or we'll have the Mason Dixon line moved North, perhaps, even to our doorstep."

"I've sympathy for Father who remains with the good of The Union at heart and holds fast to the commandment: 'Thou shalt not kill.' "

"I think Bowles and Clark secretly feel we New Englanders wouldn't be bad off with our own country separate from Washington, D.C. They'd probably like to move the Mason-Dixon Line up as far as Jersey. Ha, ha! It's too late for diplomacy and legislation! The south has seceded. The battle was declared at Fort Sumter and The Commonwealth has entered the friction! So, there's no use to Father's Whigish moderation now, in any case?"

"I read that Reverend Henry Ward Beecher has acquired the chains that held John Brown, and he stomps on them at the end of his preaching to rouse the crowds that congregate at his Plymouth Church in Brooklyn Heights. It's become a popular haunt for radical Congregationalists in New York. Oh, Austin, won't you take me there? I'd love to hear him."

"If Father and Sue would allow, I'd gladly take you. Beecher secretly smuggles guns to the front in boxes of Bibles. His Plymouth Church harbors a piece of Plymouth Rock to make us proud back home in the valley!"

"It's hideous that many New Yorkers side with the South!"

" Because, Em, of the cotton trade that comes to New York Harbors. The textile industries flourish there. Profit *always* wins out over moral fiber!"

The fife and drum corps faded into the distance and Clark was out of sight, making Emily more pensive as she walked arm and arm with her brother. "Elizabeth Holland says it's becoming dangerous in New York streets around *Scribner's* to take a public stance for abolition! There are conspirators on the side of The South everywhere there. She's frightened for her husband who's been offered editorship of *Scribner's Magazine*. He might leave *The Springfield Republic* any time now for that post."

"It's a more prestigious post for Josiah Holland. Good for him. I'm stuck here in Massachusetts forever it seems! Em, it irks me so not to go off with Clark."

"Dearest Austin," Emily hugged her brother's arm. "Amherst, Mother, Vinnie, your little Ned, and I cannot spare you with Father so often away. And what if the battle reaches Amherst? We will need good horsemen and leaders like you here to protect our village. What would our dear Susie and your son do without you? You're needed *here*, Austin."

"True, Ned and Sue need me. It's what keeps me from defying Father. I've no choice."

"Ever since you had your rendezvous at the Hotel Revere in Boston to test if your marriage would do well—when you first became engaged—I've been glad that your family would keep you home, Austin, away from danger."

"Sister, you and Vinnie must watch what you say. You set the whole town wagging their tongues at us because of that unescorted meeting in Boston. Be careful never to mention it in front of Sue. She was exasperated with you, and so was I. It's still entirely confidential and a sore spot with Sue and with me."

"Of course, it is, Austin. I'm careful, but, oh, you're red in the face to talk of it. I hope you were satisfied that day."

"Hush, Emily! Sometimes you behave as badly as the gossipy town ladies whose 'dimity convictions' you so deplore. Let's hurry ourselves home to Sue's lunch."

"Yes, My Dear Brother." Emily took Austin's arm again and their pace quickened. "Forgive me. I'll not mention your secret again, but I want to emphasize how much we couldn't live without you, our *manly* protector here in the village! We will need you if the battle comes our way." Emily always knew how to bring her beloved brother around with flattery. Though he was aware of her technique, he always enjoyed it.

"Clark and the others are going off to the front to make sure the war doesn't come to New England. I admire their courage. Father's so hot to keep me home, he's already supplied the $500, for the Irish immigrant soldier to go in my stead, and you know how hard it is for Father to part with his almighty dollar!"

"Oh Austin, I am *so* relieved it's done!" Emily sighed. "At least I might continue to have my brother alive and safe at home!" She danced on Austin's arm even though her heart was heavy as granite with the loss of her Master to the war's zone.

September 1861: "I Tend My Garden for Thee"

I tend my garden for thee,
bright absentee…

My Dear Daisy,

How happy I was to receive your packet of poems, sewn into a little booklet for me to carry in my saddlebags. The beauty of your thoughts refreshes my spirit and your words are a balm to my soul. It was kind of Mrs. Holland to forward the fascicle. Poor Sam Bowles, with his persistent illnesses and cough, is, perhaps, jealous of my adventures. He does not want to betray your brother, Austin, so dear to him, or your Father for whom he harbors much respect. We shouldn't trouble Bowles to forward our mail. He might not be as trustworthy with our secret in any case, as he loves his alcohol and his talk.

The note you sent with your fascicle of poems was poignant. I miss you as much as you miss me. How lovely it would be to have you here with me tonight. Yes, 'were I with thee, wild nights would be our luxury.' Dasiy, now that I am soon off to battle, I am happier than ever that we broke the rules of propriety to savor each other as we have. We've shared joy and thoughts deep enough to last a lifetime, especially if my life should be brief. I've never shared with The Queen what I've felt with you. I am glad to have known such a love as ours before I might die. I know you feel the same, dear Daisy.

For now, I am delightfully situated and enjoying the very romance of war. Today, I'm in command of the post with some 1500 subjects, the Colonel being away. I am progressing rapidly in my knowledge of military matters and hope to become an accomplished officer. The prospect now is that unless the rebels take Washington, which is probable, the 21st Regiment of Massachusetts Volunteers will remain in charge of this important post for some time. As we have splendid houses for barracks and a magnificent parade ground of 50 acres surrounded by water on two sides and on the other two by a high brick wall we are not very anxious to move, at least until we become perfected in drill. There cannot be found in the whole United States a more admirable station for a regiment. I live in a splendid house in a beautiful garden with an abundant supply of perpetual roses and other

shrubbery and most delicious grapes just now ripe. But, still, I keep
your Amherst daisy pressed in my bible with your anonymous poem,
dearest Daisy.

Yours ever, rowing toward eternity, "Master"

Emily treasured Clark's letter and slept with it inside her pillowslip
each night. His next letter, which came via Luke Sweetser's handyman
and Maggie Maher, however, dismayed her in that it contained no
mention of the second batch of poems she had painstakingly sewn
into a little booklet and sent to him via Elizabeth Holland. It offered
only a war cry:

We are all ready to endure hardship as good soldiers. I have acquired
a magnificent and trustworthy steed named Victor. I'm happy to say
that he is fully up to my expectations. He can run faster than any horse
in these parts, and is confessedly the most beautiful, graceful, and
manageable charger that has appeared here. Secretary of War, Simon
Cameron, rode him at the Grand Parade on Sunday and pronounced
him superb. It would do you good to see him jump a ditch or a fence.
I hope he will survive the perils of war and return with his Master to
enjoy a green age in Massachusetts.

We are to be attached to the second brigade of General Burnside's
Division under command of General Reno who is said to be a thoroughly
educated and very efficient officer. The expedition is a magnificent one,
including sixteen regiments of infantry, two batteries of regular artillery,
and one regiment of cavalry, as well as a large number of gunboats and
vessels of war. 'Victory or death' will be the war cry and those who
hinder us in our course must be many and brave.

Emily was disappointed to find that Clark seemed to have forgotten
their love and spoke only of war and his desire to enter the battle.
The letter was without salutation or closing, perhaps to keep their
relationship undetected, she reasoned There was no tender phrase for
her. She felt as if he were sending her the same war correspondence
he sent to Mrs. Holland's husband, Josiah, or Samuel Bowles at *The*

Springfield Republican. Disheartened and frightened that Clark's zeal for battle would get him into deadly trouble, she sat down and penned a poem that began,

> *Success is counted sweetest*
> *By those who ne'er succeed.*
> *To comprehend a nectar*
> *Requires sorest need.*
>
> *Not one of all the purple host*
> *Who took the flag to-day*
> *Can tell the definition,*
> *So clear, of victory!*
>
> *As he defeated, dying,*
> *On whose forbidden ear*
> *The distant strains of triumph*
> *Burst agonized and clear!*

Emily sent the verse off via Mrs. Holland as a cautionary warning that Clark not be too cavalier in battle. She sent no loving salutations, as he had sent none. "Perhaps, he is just too busy to think of me and had an aid copy the same letter he wrote to his family and the newspaper. The handwriting is a bit different than his," she rationalized to herself. "I should not be alarmed or hurt. 'Patience is the greatest of virtues' as Da Vinci said, and, my beloved Master has so often reminded me of that."

January 1862: "Neighbor and Friend and Bridegroom"

Neighbor and Friend and Bridegroom
Spinning Upon the Shoals...

Weeks passed and Emily heard nothing from Clark, though in desperation she mailed a verse to Samuel Bowles asking him to forward it to Clark in the field inside of one of his own letters. It read:

I have a king who does not speak;
So wondering, thro' the hours meek
I trudge the day away, —
Half glad when it is night and sleep,
If, haply, thro' a dream, to peep
In parlors shut by day.

And if I do, when morning comes,
It is as if a hundred drums
Did round my pillow roll,
And shouts fill all my childish sky,
And Bells keep saying 'victory'
From steeples in my soul!

And if I don't, the little Bird
Within the Orchard, is not heard,
And I omit to pray,
'Father, they will be done' to-day
For my Will goes the other way,
And it were perjury!

Still, no answer came and then an article appeared in *The Springfield Republican* on January 26th, 1862, one evening that shocked her spirit icy cold and made her regret her cloaked reprimand sent through Bowles:

Several steamships transporting Massachusetts soldiers, The Northerner among them, carrying The 21ˢᵗ Regiment to Hatteras Inlet on the coast of North Carolina, from January 14ᵗʰ to the 25ᵗʰ, were in the midst of a severe storm, their plight complicated by the shallowness of the inlet and its shifting sandy bottom which caused many of the vessels to run aground. A terrible storm blew up toppling some of the vessels. Some men were reported drowned, though their names were yet unknown. The men were weakened by days at sea in cramped quarters with no sanitary facilities, widespread seasickness, poor and inadequate food and water, and damp and wintry cold, with no means for physical exercise, and living in constant anxiety. Major Clark has written home to his family: "We are so thoroughly disgusted with this miserable spot we are caught in that we shall be glad to be delighted to move even into the midst of the enemy," but he has not been heard from since January 19th.

Emily took to her room and could not eat. Lavinia, not knowing the cause of her illness, worried. Carrying a tray of soup, bread, and tea, she tapped on Emily's locked door.

"Emily, please, open your door! It's only me come to bring you food. Maggie said you ate nothing this afternoon. You must eat. You will turn to skin and bones. Please, eat something for Maggie and me, just to make us feel better, Em?"

"Emily still in her night dress opened the door to her now stuffy room for Lavinia. Her face was pale and drawn. Her hair had not been combed. She was in the same white flannel nightdress she'd worn all week. " Come in poor Vinnie. I don't want to worry you or Maggie. I'll eat something to please you. You mustn't worry. Has the newspaper come?"

"That's all you ask for every day, Em. Yes, but there is nothing new in it?"

"Nothing at all new?"

"No, just that the ships with Massachusetts volunteers have still not arrived at their destination."

"Not arrived…" Emily slumped at her table and placing her elbows thereon, held her head up with her hands. Vinnie set down the tray and waited for her to raise the soup spoon to her lips." Come now, Emmy. Eat while it's still good and hot."

Emily complied, and slowly finished her soup and bread. "I do feel better for eating, Vinnie Dear, thank you."

"Of course you do, Em. Now drink your tea."

The next morning, to please Vinnie and Maggie, Emily dressed in her white housedress and dragged herself about the homestead doing her household chores with them. Suddenly, a knock came at the kitchen door. It was Susan. She had run over in her housedress and apron without a cloak. "Emily, I have good news for you!" Susan, instinctive and wise, knew what was troubling Emily though they never spoke of her love of Clark since Clark had married Cousin Harriet. Sue had not wanted to pain her with any thoughts of her lost love, but the women, both disapproving of the uses of war, shared news of their Massachusetts volunteer soldiers without mentioning Clark. Sue held out the latest edition of *The Hampshire Gazette*.

So in despair was she, that Emily could not process the thought of *good* news. "What is it, Sue, that stirs you so?" Emily wiped her hands full of flour from the Indian rye loaves she was kneading for her father and took the newspaper in hand. Squire Dickinson was usually at home now from congress, having lost the last election because of his stubborn adherence to his old Whig party, defunct due to the new Republicanism led by Abraham Lincoln.

"Read this article, Em!" Sue said pointing to the upper corner of the page. "The ships have been recovered. Some ran aground. Our neighbor, Professor Clark, and his adjutant, Frazar Stearns, are still among the living though some were drowned!"

"Oh, Susie, thank you for bringing this blessed news. I felt such utter sorrow for poor Professor Stearns, so worried over his son, and our neighbor, Cousin Harriet, so anxious about her husband and the father of her children. "Emily used mild words to cover the fact that she'd snatched the paper from Susan's hands too eagerly and read the article that explained:

The flotilla of 125 ships which left for Hatteras Inlet, North Carolina, carrying General Abrose Burnside, leading his Northern regiments into battle down the coast, met with a tremendous winter gale. Some ships collided in heavy seas and sand. Others ran around on sandbars. One lost its propeller. The surviving warships could not enter the inlet for days and ran out of fresh water. Two soldiers perished from typhoid fever and were buried at sea bundled in canvas weighted by eighty-pound shot. Two Northampton men were drowned trying to reach their ship after going onshore. After two harrowing weeks of worry, The Northerner, carrying Major Clark of Amherst College, leader of the 21st Regiment, and his student and firsthand man, son of the President of the college, Frazar Stearns, are reported safe, but the death toll is large. Forty men have been lost at sea.

Emily threw her arms around Sue's neck and kissed her, surprising the more sedate woman with her zeal and her sudden grin of joy from ear to ear. "Thank you for this good news. The war is such a disheartening spectacle. It rends my mind and heart to think of our Amherst men dying. It relieves my soul to know most are safe."

"Yes, Emily. I imagined it would," Sue said, straight-faced, all the while thinking, "Poor. Emily is still hopelessly in love with Professor Clark. What a waste of her spirit and soul."

After Susan went home to the Evergreens next door leaving *The Hampshire Gazette* article with her sister-in-law, Emily finished her bread baking with a sensation of immense joy. When the happily risen loaves were set on the cooling rack, she hurried upstairs and locked her bedroom door behind her. Only then did she allow herself to cry sobs of relief that shook her small frame as she read the newspaper's good news of Clark over and over again, letting it sink as blessed reality into her cranium. She took a handkerchief from her bureau drawer and sat with enraptured relief at her writing table to let words of joy flow from her pen.

Glee the great storm is over!
Four have recovered the land;
Forty gone down together
Into the boiling sand.

Ring, for the scant salvation!
Toll, for the bonnie souls, —
Neighbor and friend and bridegroom,
Spinning upon the shoals!

How they will tell the shipwreck
When winter shakes the door,
Till the children ask, "But the forty?
Did they come back no more?

Then a silence suffuses the story,
And a softness the teller's eye;
And the children no further question,
And only the waves reply.

She sent it to Bowles asking him to forward it to Major Clark at the front in North Carolina and begging him not to mail her earlier reprimanding verse, if he hadn't already.

April 1862: " I Had a Terror Since September"

Mr. Higginson…Say If My Verse Is Live?

Emily was beginning to suffer nervous prostration ever since thinking Clark was lost at sea, and since he had gone off in September to the front. She needed to do something to focus her mind which strayed constantly to worry over her Master's well being. She missed him so thoroughly, she could hardly think of anything else. One day, she read a "Letter to a Young Contributor," written by the distinguished editor of *The Atlantic Monthly*, whose essays on nature she and Professor Clark had thoroughly enjoyed. Editor, Thomas Wentworth Higginson, was a freethinker and an activist in civil rights for all women and for men of African decent. Higginson had concluded his scathing attack on nineteenth-century chauvinistic attitudes with high praise for Elizabeth Barrett Browning, Emily Dickinson's favorite poet.

"If my own poetry is going to be acceptable to any member of America's literary establishment, it would be by this man, Thomas Wentworth Higginson," she thought. Higginson, like Bowles, had helped to fund John Brown's militant raid on Harper's Ferry a couple of years earlier. She determined to send some of her poems to Higginson for his opinion of their quality, as Clark had often urged her to. Higginson's "Letter to a Young Contributor" spurred her on.

"Perhaps, if an editor as fine as Mr. Higginson likes my poems, I'll be able to focus on writing instead of worry over Will. I feel I'm weakening at the seams. My hands tremble as I try to tend to mother, darn socks, bake bread, and garden. Vinnie worries I've contracted the palsy before my time. I must do something to occupy my mind and steel my nerves," she ruminated, "Or, I'll be of no use to myself or Will when he returns." She was still afraid of her father's wrath should she decide to publish, so she did not sign her letter of April 15, 1862, but merely enclosed her calling card and put four poems in the envelope with a brief note:

Mr Higginson,

    Are you too deeply occupied to say if my Verse is alive? The Mind is so near itself—it cannot see, distinctly—and I have none to ask—

Should you think it breathed—and had you the leisure to tell me, I should feel quick gratitude—

If I make the mistake—that you dared to tell me—would give me sincerer honor—

toward you—

I enclose my name-asking you, if you please—Sir—to tell me what is true?

That you will not betray me—it is needless to ask—since Honor is its own pawn.

Enclosed were four verses titled: "Safe in their Alabaster Chambers," which she'd shown to Sue for advice and about which she had some confidence, "The nearest Dream recedes unrealized," "We play at Paste," and "I'll tell you how the Sun rose."

In his response to her letter and the enclosed poems, Editor, Higginson, asked Emily to tell him about her background and to send more poems so that he could better judge of her talents. In reply, on April 1862, she wrote again a little more boldly.

Mr Higginson,

Your kindness claimed earlier gratitude—but I was ill-and write today, from my pillow.

Thank you for the surgery—it was not so painful as I supposed. I bring you others—as you ask—though they might not differ—

While my thought is undressed—I can make the distinction, but when I put them in the Gown—they look alike, and numb.

You asked how old I was? I made no verse—but one or two-until this winter—Sir—

I had a terror-since September—I could tell to none-and so I sing, as the Boy does by the Burying Ground—because I am afraid—You inquire my Books—For Poets—I have Keats-and Mr. and Mrs. Browning. For Prose—Mr. Ruskin—Sir Thomas Browne—and the Revelations. I went to school—but in your manner of the phrase—had no education. When a little Girl, I had a friend, who taught me Immortality—but venturing too near, himself—he never returned—Soon after, my Tutor, died—and for several years, my Lexicon—was my

*only companion—Then I found one more—but he was not contented
I be his scholar—so he left the Land.*

*You ask of my Companions Hills—Sir—and the Sundown—and
a Dog—large as myself, that my Father bought me—They are better
than Beings—because they know—but do not tell—and the noise in
the Pool, at Noon—excels my Piano. I have a Brother and Sister—
My Mother does not care for thought—and Father, too busy with his
Briefs—to notice what we do—He buys me many Books—but begs
me not to rcad thcm—because he fears they joggle the Mind. They are
religious—except me—and address an Eclipse, every morning—whom
they call their "Father." But I fear my story fatigues you—I would like
to learn—Could you tell me how to grow—or is it unconveyed—like
Melody—or Witchcraft?*

*You speak of Mr. Whitman—I never read his Book—but was told
that he was disgraceful—*

*I read Miss Prcscott's "Circumstance," but it followed me, in the
Dark—so I avoided her—*

*Two Editors of Journals came to my Father's House, this winter—
and asked me for my Mind—and when I asked them "Why," they said
I was—and they, would use it for the World—*

I could not weigh myself—Myself—

*My size felt small—to me—I read your Chapters in the Atlantic—
and experienced honor for you—I was sure you would not reject a
confiding question—*

Is this—Sir—what you asked me to tell you?

Your friend, E - Dickinson.

Higginson wrote back saying that though her poems were
unconventional in form and would not gain acceptance if published
in *The Atlantic Monthly*, he found them quite original and true.
He conceded that they showed poetic talent and wit. He made
recommendations for putting them into a more accepted form of
punctuation and meter, but Emily, feeling of independent mind, did
not do so. She was happy that he found them "original and true"
and she was thrilled that he had taken her seriously and admired her
talent.

She began to correspond with him just often enough not to tire him too much with her concerns, and he promised to visit her should he find himself in Amherst on the lecture circuit sometime. She wrote back that she was not really interested in publication so much as in his evaluation of her work, but that his advice and acceptance of her talent had given her impetus to write more each day. She wrote to him a third time, excited by his encouragement of her talents. He had even mentioned that he might read some of her poems anonymously at a meeting of a Women's Literary Society in Boston at which he was asked to speak. She was greatly encouraged and wrote to him a third time, in June, as he had offered his friendship as encouragement to her writing of poetry:

Dear Friend,

Your letter gave no drunkenness, because I tasted rum before. Domingo comes but once; yet I have had few pleasures so deep as your opinion, and if I tried to thank you, my tears would block my tongue.

My dying tutor told me that he would like to live till I had been a poet, but Death was much of mob as I could master, then. And when, far afterward, a sudden light on orchards, or a new fashion in the wind troubled my attention, I felt a palsy, here, the verses just relieve.

Your second letter surprised me, and for a moment, swung. I had not supposed it. Your first gave no dishonor, because the true are not ashamed. I thanked you for your justice, but could not drop the bells whose jingling cooled my tramp. Perhaps the balm seemed better, because you bled me first. I smile when you suggest that I delay "to publish," that being foreign to my thought as firmament to fin.

If fame belonged to me, I could not escape her; if she did not, the longest day would pass me on the chase, and the approbation of my dog would for-sake me then. My barefoot rank is better.

You think my gait "spasmodic." I am in danger, sir. You think me "un-controlled." I have no tribunal.

Would you have time to be the "friend" you should think I need? I have a little shape: it would not crowd your desk, nor make much racket as the mouse that dents your galleries. If I might bring you what I do—not so frequent to trouble you—and ask you if I told it clear, 't would be control to me. The sailor cannot see the North, but knows the needle can. The "hand you stretch me in the dark" I put mine in, and turn away. I have no Saxon now—

> *As if I asked a common alms,*
> *And in my wondering hand*
> *A stranger pressed a kingdom,*
> *And I, bewildered, stand;*
> *As if I asked the Orient*
> *Had it for me a morn,*
> *And it should lift its purple dikes*
> *And shatter me with dawn!*

But, will you be my preceptor, Mr. Higginson?

When Mr. Higginson answered that he would be glad to now and then critique a few poems for Emily, a correspondence began that gave her sustenance away from her obsession with Clark and his opinions. She realized that this was good for her and she needed someone else to look up to in literary matters, besides Susan, always busy now with her household and children, and Clark, often unreachable in his busy military life. Emily realized that she had spilled her heart out to Clark, and he had not answered in kind. She knew she would have to be patient and not expect too much of him if she were to have some of his attentions ever again in future. But to be disciplined in her obsessive longing was easier said than done.

Febraury 1862: After the Battle of Roanoke

My River Runs to Thee....

On February 20th, after the battle of Roanoke, Major Clark paced about his tent. He had seen action and it was grizzly. He knew his father and mother and sisters would be worried along with his wife and children and father-in-law. He wrote home to his father to comfort them as best he could, deliberately under-playing the horrors of battle and portraying a falsely chipper mood. He was now struck with the idea that he might easily die in battle. He sat at his make shift writing table and communicated.

My Dear Family,

It is a glorious sight to see a thousand men marching straight forward into the fire from a thousand muskets aided by a battery of canons, and men never feel more manly than when they are doing it. When you listen to the roar and rattle of the battle and see the fire and smoke and hear the music of the musket balls, you wonder that any should escape unhurt, and yet that is a terrible fight indeed in which one in ten of the combatants is wounded. Our regiment was in the battle where the firing was kept up without cessation for two hours and a half and yet only 55 were wounded out of 800 in the ranks. It is a mercy that a gun-shot wound produces no pain as all our wounded men testify. Even when a bone is shattered or a limb carried away the sensation is only that of numbness or dizziness. Moreover, their wounds are not generally painful for many hours and even days so that the hardest time for the wounded soldier is the day after the fight, when everything is in confusion and everybody so exhausted that no labor is done which can possibly be avoided. The surgeons of course are overwhelmed with business and must neglect many of the poor fellows whom they would gladly attend to, if possible. I am sorry also to say that but a few of those in our Division are as skillful and efficient as they ought to be. None are as good or compassionate a doctor as you are, Dear Father.

Ever yours with much affection, William

Will always enjoyed complimenting his father, Atherton Clark, for his father-in-law, Sam Williston, to see. As he finished his hurried epistle, a messenger appeared inside the flap of his tent to deliver to him a small packet with the hand of Sam Bowles on the envelope. Clark, as eager as any soldier for mail from home, opened the letter to find Sam Bowles's writing inside:

Dear Major,

I've told ED that this is the last letter I can mail onto the front for her. I shall be leaving for California, and possibly then for Europe, to rest and to attempt to effect a cure for the coughing that plagues me. I shall be seeing MW there, as well. She has consented to come and help me with copy editing for The Springfield Republican for which I will continue to editorialize from abroad. I am sure I will find Europe to be all you have told me it is. Mrs. Bowles is not sailing with me, but will stay at home with the children. Please continue to send any war correspondence to me about your adventures and observations on the front lines. Mary will forward my mail and also write and tell all how to reach me. Enclosed, as you well can imagine, is a packet from ED, my dear friend AD's quaint little sister. This "snow" of her delicate spirit will no doubt refresh yours. She always and ever asks me how things are really going at the front and if I've heard from the 21st Regiment of Massachusetts. She is Empress of Cavalry, or, the way she suffers your absence from New England, is it Empress of Calvary? Be careful, My Good Man! Have you seen the New York City papers about the big trouble our famous comrade in arms, Reverend Henry Ward Beecher of Brooklyn Heights is in—with his filandering with married parishioners. His sister, Harriet's Uncle Tom's Cabin, our friend, Higginson says in The Atlantic Monthly, continues to create sympathy for the slaves of The South at every turn and is still an all time best selling novel for this bleeding country of ours. But, the scandal created by the married Beecher's affairs with ladies has hurt our cause in that he was one of the chief financers, along with Higginson and myself, of John Brown's Army of Liberators. We must be careful that our private lives do not taint our vital cause. Whatever else we do, we are men of honor as far as abolition of slavery goes, and liberation of women is paramount to our aims for this our great American land. We shall always stand for democracy in the world, even if we betray our vows to be loyal to only one mate and take others to our bosom in the fashion of Catholic, French, and Italian men. I've told Mary to take her freedom if she likes, but she will have none of it and is bound to her home and children. ED is bound to her father and her home, but if you asked, it is obvious she would join you in Hell, or on Mars, I think."

Yours, with limited honor, Sam B.—which might stand for "bastard" if AD knew I forwarded his sister's letters, as much as I enjoy pleasing the Little Wren.

*Faithfully yours, SB which many believe
stands for "Son of a Bitch" I fear.*

It was clear to Clark that Bowles did not enjoy having to forward mail from Emily to him at the front, and he was annoyed that Emily had continued to do so against his advice. He did not realize that he hadn't answered some of her letters and verses that had gone astray. He knew that Bowles was sending a dig signifying that he did not approve of Clark's affair with his best friend, Austin's sister—despite the fact that all who attended soirees at The Evergreens could easily assume that Bowles was having an unspoken affair with his children's nanny and his secretary, the lovely and intellectually gifted, Maria Whitney.

Emily had taken to corresponding with Maria, who was a distant cousin of hers, with empathetic innuendo for their shared plight as the secretly liberated mistresses of eminent and married men. Neither ever dared boldly refer in detail to their situation, for fear their letter might be intercepted, but it was understood between them in an unspoken and nebulous repartee. Bowles ended his letter to Clark by saying that Emily was sending her poem "Some Keep the Sabbath Going to Church, I keep it staying at home…" to Brooklyn's *Drumbeat* for free use." Clark knew that *Drumbeat* was a newsletter devoted to raising money for hospital care for the Union Armies. "The poem is enclosed with these others Emily wanted you to have."

Clark opened his packet from Emily. Inside he found, as before, a sheaf of poems on folded paper sewn together with thread to make a little booklet. The poems Clark found and read with tears welling in his eyes began with the lines "Did the harebell lose her girdle to the lover bee… I keep My Garden for Thee bright absentee… Success is counted sweetest by those who ne'er succeed… Flags vex a dying face…Glee the great storm is over… Neighbor and friend and bridegroom spinning upon the shoals… and… if you should die and I should live…" He understood their messages. He wept with guilt and joy in hearing from his devoted lover.

He wrote back to Emily via Luke Sweetser's handyman who delivered the letter, secreted in his hat, to Emily's loyal Irish maid, Maggie, over the back fence of the Dickinson estate. Maggie came running with her skirts high and the epistle in her apron pocket. She knew how happy such letters made her loving Mistress.

Maggie tapped three times on Emily's door after she breathlessly reached the upper floor of the Dickinson Homestead. Emily knowing the signal opened the door smiling. She hugged Maggie and took the letter from Maggie's hand kissing her roundly on the cheek. "Thank you, Maggie," she whispered. Then shutting the door quietly and locking it, she scurried to her chair at the window to read the epistle. It contained Will's news that the 21st Regiment might be allowed to furlough at home in the fall for a spell. Emily was overjoyed and apprehensive. She sat at her writing table and wrote.

> *If you were coming in the fall,*
> *I'd brush the summer by*
> *With half a smile, and half a spurn,*
> *As housewives do, a fly.*
>
> *If I could see you in a year,*
> *I'd wind the months in balls,*
> *And put them each in separate drawers,*
> *For fear their time befalls.*
>
> *If only centuries delayed,*
> *I'd count them on my hand,*
> *Subtracting, till my fingers dropped*
> *Into Van Dieman's land.*

If certain, when this life was out,
That your's and mine, should be,
I'd toss it yonder, like a rind,
And take eternity—

But, now, all ignorant of the length
Of time's, uncertain wing,
It goads me, like the goblin bee—
That will not state its sting.

She enclosed verses she'd written a bit earlier for Will:

He showed me heights I never saw—
"Woulds't Climb" He said?
I said, "Not so"—
"With me—" He said—"With me" ?
He showed me secrets
Morning's nest—
The rope the Nights were put across—
"And now, Woulds't have me for a Guest" ?
I could not find my " Yes"—
And then, I brake my life—and Lo!
A light for him, did solemn glow,
The larger, as his face withdrew—
And I could, further, "No"?

And:

I have no life but his,
To lead it here;
Nor any death, but lest
Dispelled from there;

> *Nor tie to earths to come,*
> *Nor action new,*
> *Except through this extent,*
> *The realm of you.*

The last poem, when received, only served to arouse the guilt of the battle weary Major Clark more than comfort him in the field. He was growing a bit weary of so much adulation, and Emily's constant need for a loving assurance that he could not fulfill, so busy and far from home and rest. Yet, he tolerated her poems as they flattered his manliness with such worshipful passion. He knew his Emily was intense in her loving and dreaming, and he saw this as her poetic nature to be understood and taken with a grain of salt. He knew she missed him greatly and her intense need of him made him feel more alive as he faced new battles. She responded easily to his touch, shuddering with ecstasy at his movements within her—more quickly and fully than any woman he'd known. His wife, "the Queen," was stoic and disinterested in sexual activity. He felt his sexual power over Emily and realized she'd known little affection in girlhood. Yet, her adulation also made him guilty and weary, even as it flattered his ego. He wrote to reprimand her for continuing to forward mail through Bowles and for making him her whole life. He was more comfortable with religion than she, and insisted she find God more important than himself. He felt it blasphemy to exaggerate her adulation so. And, he knew it was not good for her to expect so much from him, busy in the battlefield. He wrote to say she mustn't expect much attention while he toiled in the field—as much as he appreciated her verses and their skillful words so wrought with feeling, he could not be expected to reply with equal frequency or intensity.

Emily, aghast, immediately sent a letter through Mrs. Holland, her close friend and confidant whose husband Dr. Holland, was Assistant Editor to Samuel Bowles at *The Springfield Republican.*

It did not address Clark by name and was not signed by her, for secrecy's sake. Both she and Clark had agreed not to use each other's names on any letters. Emily wrote an abject apology:

Did Daisy offend you, Master? Daisy, who bows her smaller life to yours. Daisy who grows more meek every day and only asks something she can do to cheer you? Something she can do for love of you? Some little thing she can do to make her Master happy?

The love Daisy feels for her Master frightens her with its big gushing in her little heart, leaving her faint and pale. Daisy who never lost her bravery through that painful parting? I would shelter you in my small breast if I could be big enough for such a large Guest. Perhaps, Daisy upset her Master's finer tastes and blunders like the country bumpkin that she is. Perhaps, she annoys her Lord, and her preceptor's grace. Then teach her finer ways, but do not let her upset her Master's better reason. Pardon her. Even a small wren dares more than Daisy does. Daisy kneels before the knee that supported once her silent rest. Daisy kneels to ask forgiveness. Tell her errors, Master so that she might erase them with her life. But, do not banish her, do not shut her out. Only say that you will forgive her offenses, sometime, before death and she'll not worry. Wondering if you are well stings her more than any bee could. Wondering wastes her, and you said she had no weight to spare. The tears run over the dams of Daisy's eyes. She has an arrow in her side. Master, open the door of your life and take her in. She'll never be tired or noisy when you want to be calm and quiet. She'll be your best child, your obedient girl, and noone else, but you, will ever see her. Heaven itself is not so dear to her as you.

> *I've got an arrow here;*
>   *Loving the hand that sent it,*
> *I the dart revere.*
>
> *Fell, they will say, in 'skirmish'!*
>   *Vanquished, my soul will know,*
> *By but a simple arrow*
> *Sped by an archer's bow.*
>
> *My worthiness is all my doubt,*
> *His merit all my fear,*

Contrasting which, my qualities
Do lowlier appear;
Lest I should insufficient prove
For his beloved need,
The chiefest apprehension
Within my loving creed.

So I, the undivine abode
Of his elect content,
Conform my soul as 't were a church
Unto her sacrament.

As you wish, Master, Your Daisy

Will responded with a cooler letter to Emily's teasing and abject apology sent through Emily's Norcross cousins:

Daisy, do not fret. I think often of Thee. Remember, if all should be lost, I have been understood and loved deeply by an intelligent and spirited woman who will not forget me, a fine poet of astute words who is no country bumpkin, no more than I am. Yet, she must be very careful with her demands for attention, and her epistles so long as I am in the field and busy with this loathsome war. Write your heart in verse, but do not send reprimands for attention to me, and do not expect replies, as I face death daily and the death of dear comrades at my side. Cheer me if you will with loving regard, but not with worship, as I am merely a man of frail disposition, if a fool-hardy combatant who risks all for truth. He tells his Daisy and himself, That 'Patience is the greatest Virtue' as DaVinci said, and she must remember that.

Your affectionate and loving "Master"

I shall return more loving words as soon as I have the time, he told himself, but he had none as he was set to enter battle again and felt the duty to communicate with many at home. Battle fatigue had dulled his erotic nature. He needed to confide in his longtime, boyhood school mate, Manross, his proxy at Amherst College now, the friend who had accompanied him to study in Germany, his fellow chemist who had taken his post at Amherst college at Clark's recommendation to the board, when Clark had gone off to battle. He wrote Manross on March 30th with more honesty than he had to his father, after having survived the Battles of Roanoke Island and Newbern.

Dear Manross, My Good Fellow,

You have doubtless heard how we came, the Julius Caesar upon the Rebels hereabouts on the 13th and 14th at Newbern. We came—saw—we conquered! And now we rejoice to march beneath the Star spangled banner which though faded, worn and pierced by bullets waves more proudly than ever above us bearing the memorable words "Roanoke" and "Newbern". Though more than 150 of my brave boys have been killed, wounded or sickened in the two severe battles of Feb 8th and March 14th we can still bring out a formidable array of rifles and bayonets. Of the 904 enlisted men now connected with the regiment, 115 are on the list of sick and wounded, and the rest are doing duty of some kind. In an army however there is a great deal to be done besides fighting so that if required tomorrow to take the field I should consider myself fortunate to bring out 500 rifles besides the file-closers who rarely do much firing. The 21st has been in the thickets of both battles and has had more killed than any other regiment, and, we flatter ourselves that we have won as much glory and damaged the enemy quite as much as any one. We deemed it no small compliment that the General should select the 21st under command of an unfledged Lieutenant Colonel with his commission as Colonel yet to come, to lead the advance of the Division when it was expected we should be constantly harassed by the Rebel cavalry and be obliged to take three batteries before reaching Newbern. At Roanoke you remember the 21st was ordered forward the first night and stood on guard in the swamp and a drenching rain through the dark, chilly hours, without fire and within hailing distance of the enemy. I had one man shot within a few rods of me and we were required to keep awake and be constantly ready for an attack though our eyes where heavy with sleeplessness.

It was clear Clark felt that his regiment of volunteers from the North was being overused and abused by the General who cared more for the enlisted men from his own vicinity of the country than for Clark's volunteers whom he saw as more expendable.

My Dear Monross, we then took most of the 2500 prisoners there captured. A large and dangerous task in itself! One never knows when one might pull out a knife or a pistol and fire at us. We had made the first charge at both places, and I ordered my men forward to the charge by command of the General while the Rebels were doing their best in the way of fighting, while the Hawkins' Souaves', and some other regiments did not start till the enemy had already ceased firing and fairly begun to retreat. As for crossing bayonets with them, we have not yet had the pleasure, and though the rascals carry tremendous "Yankee slayers" regular cleavers, some two feet long—they somehow don't like to take the position necessary in order to use them. They have changed their views about the cowardly Yankees somewhat in the last few weeks and begin to think that they can hardly whip ten apiece in a fair fight. When they themselves are behind fortifications with plenty of cannon, they know they can't keep out an equal number of Yankees who have no artillery at all. The death of my noble Adjutant Frazar Stearns has been the bitterest trial of my life, and I feel now almost alone though surrounded by friends. He was killed instantly in the battle of Newbern, after a narrow escape at the Battle of Roanoke. I grieve his loss every day. Frazar was a valuable officer, intelligent, faithful, and brave as the bravest. He was knocked down by a bullet which struck the visor of his cap and drew a considerable amount of blood whilst he was simultaneously hit in the back of the neck from another bullet. My sorrow is more intense than I can bear, and only the thought of vanquishing the foe that has taken his life keeps me going.

Frazar had fallen beside Clark and just after, Clark rode his horse, Victor, in a fury right up to enemy lines and a cannon being fired by the rebels. Clark in battle frenzy leapt upon the cannon from his horse and cut the rebel cannoneers to death with slashes from his sword. He was not in a mood to brag about this feat to his friend. Not with his beloved comrade and star student of Amherst college, dead. It was clear that the dangers of battle had become more real to him than ever with Frazar's death. On top of his sorrow and battle weary woes, he felt enormous chagrin at losing Adjutant Stearns, son of Amherst College President, to whom he felt beholden. He sent the conquered cannon home to be a memorial at the college to his beloved student whom he'd urged into battle with him and whose wounded body was transported home for burial to Amherst accompanied by the conquered field gun.

Clark was disillusioned with the way upper ranks were running the show and sacrificing the regiments below their direct command. He had survived the bloody and costly battle at Fredericksburg, one of the worst for Union casualties, to be made a Colonel, but the victory was hollow with the loss of Stearns. By December 17th, he was ready to be more honest with his father who he knew would share his letter with Sam Williston and the rest of the family, while Emily had to content herself with second hand news from newspapers and fellow citizens of her village.

Dear Father,

The papers will give you some idea of the dreadful fate of the rebel city of Fredericksburg and of the gallantry of our soldiers in assaulting the fortifications of the enemy. Alas! That so many thousands of our bravest and best should thus perish in vain. Nothing has been gained by all our fighting, but knowledge of the real strength and position of the foe. We have 165,000 troops with 600 pieces of artillery, and yet, it is doubtful whether we can conquer the rebels so long as they remain behind their earthworks and other defenses. Still, I am sure our cause is just and if we persevere to the end, we must prevail. At any rate, I am willing to spend the rest of my life vindicating the loss of my men, and dearest of friends, in the horrid work of war to put down the proslavery rebellion.

Your loving son, now, "Colonel Clark"

Emily, like most of the citizens, and nearly all the students, of Amherst, attended the processional and funeral for Frazar Stearns. She wrote in late March to her "Little Cousins," Frannie and Lou Norcross of Cambridgeport, about the sorrowful occasion. They had forwarded some poems and confidential letters to Clark from her using their bustling Boston post office where Emily's hand would not be detected by the busy-body postmaster of her gossipy village.

Emily knew that Clark was expected home on furlough, She had sent a letter to him full of heartfelt condolences for his loss of his pet student and dearest comrade in arms, Frazar. She hoped that he would choose to stay at home after his furlough, now that he had lost his dearest friend and a star student of Amherst College. She enclosed a playful, light-hearted verse, rather than a heavier love poem to give the impression of a blithe spirit that could counteract his depression and be of solace in the wake of his sorrow. It read:

> *Bee! I'm expecting you!*
> *Was saying Yesterday*
> *To Somebody you know*
> *That you were due—*
>
> *The Frogs got Home last Week—*
> *Are settled, and at work—*
> *Birds, mostly back—*
> *The Clover warm and thick—*
>
> *You'll get my Letter by*
> *The seventeenth; Reply*
> *Or better, be with me—*
> *Yours, Fly.*

On June 25th, Colonel Clark returned by train for a short furlough in Amherst. His arrival was met by a pouring rain that did not stop a crowd gathering for a hero's return—including Emily discretely in the background. The crowd greeted him with three times three rousing cheers. Mrs. Clark was, of course, present and the couple were taken to their former residence to be guests of the present occupants who were renting and looking over their home on the hill behind Emily's homestead. Mrs. Clark had gone to Easthampton with her children to live with her parents, The Williston's, but she'd returned to Amherst for this occasion. In two days, Clark was to be honored guest at a strawberry festival given for the benefit of the wounded from Amherst.

Without noticing Emily at the back of the crowd, Clark entered the carriage that took him and his wife to their home on the hill a short distance from the station. Emily, with tears welling, watched Mr. and Mrs. Clark ride off in their fancy buggy. With Carlo at her side, she walked home to arrive soaked to the skin and late for dinner."

"Emily, where on earth have you been? I'm afraid Father is beside himself. If Carlo were not gone off with you, he'd have called the constable to search you out about the village."

"I tried to say that I thought you might have gone picking wild strawberries, but Father said, "In this rain?""

"Why would he not think I was at the train station with the rest of the townspeople and students, welcoming home our local hero, Colonel Clark? Why did he not go himself?"

"You know Father felt that Clark would get Frazar killed, and he has. You know how Father feels about the war. He does not condone the bloodshed."

"Well, nether do I, but our village hero deserves a rousing welcome! Oh, Dear Vinnie, please just tell Father I am not feeling well and went to my room to change, dry off and rest. I want no supper, but if you must bring me tea and toast from the kitchen later, I shall be ever so grateful, and I'll do your darning tomorrow to make up for your facing Father again for me, please Dear Vinnie."

Without waiting for a reply and grabbing the local *Hampshire and Franklin Gazette* from the family parlor where it lay unread that evening, Emily hurried up the stairs and shut her bedroom door, and turned the skeleton key that gave her refuge from the household. After removing her wet clothes, hanging them up to dry, donning her white flannel night gown, and lighting her oil lamp, she sat down to read the paper in the dusk gathering at the windows. She read a piece by one of Clark's soldiers that had been sent ahead from where his troop was stationed in the South to the home county paper:

Colonel Clark left us a few days ago for Washington and doubtless will be with you long before you get this letter. We are very willing he should be with you a few days, but we could not spare him longer. You are aware, I presume, that a few weeks ago he was afflicted with the mumps. It was remarked to me by the Colonel of another Regiment that Colonel Clark was so popular that everybody would be having the mumps now. And so it is, there is not a more popular Colonel in these parts. And being so held at Head Quarters he can obtain everything he may ask for. May he be spared yet for valiant service for his country.

Emily went to the strawberry festival with Carlo at her side hoping to get another glimpse, and perhaps even a nod, from her Master. She wore her bonnet low over her face and stood again in the background of the crowd that awaited Colonel Clark's arrival. He arrived quite late, and leapt upon the stage of the gazebo dressed in his blue Union army uniform with stripes on his shoulder, his long sword at his side, and his blue visor cap on his head. After saluting the crowd that had decided he would not appear, but were very glad to greet and applaud him when he finally arrived, he spoke on the war, stating that his heart was still in it.

Emily listened to his speech, noting how his face had changed and hardened. His hair was cropped close and his mustache was longer in the style of a handlebar curled at the long side ends, like a Southern gentleman. She'd read that such mustaches keep insects from flying in the mouth or up the nose as horseman ride through the trees. She imagined Colonel Clark on his horse, Victor, riding through a Southern field swinging his sword as he advanced in battle.

"I shall, if my life is spared, stick to this war until rebellion is crushed out.' Clark spoke with his usual lively zeal. "I have every confidence in the way the war is developing and I feel the Union will be preserved. We Yankees shall win it for our American country!"

Emily again went home with tears choking her as she walked with Carlo through the meadow and the orchard to avoid Main Street and any villagers she might meet along that route. The sight of her Master, so near and so unattainable for communion or touch, made her miserable. She had heard no word from him during the three days he'd been home on furlough. She feared his battle weary face that did not notice her presence or search it out in the crowd. War had changed him. She could see.

"He has forgotten me because of this bloody war, Carlo. I fear I've lost him totally." She whispered to her faithful Carlo as they sat together in the scullery where Emily churned butter for tomorrow morning's baking. She was beside herself with longing and anxiety and late that night she rose from a sleepless bed to dare to pencil the draft of a letter that she hoped to send up the hill behind her home to Clark's house via Maggie and Sweetser's handyman in the morning.

> *The daisy follows soft the sun,*
> *And when his golden walk is done,*
> *Sits shyly at his feet.*
> *He, waking, finds the flower near.*
> *"Wherefore, marauder, art thou here?"*
> *"Because, Sir, love is sweet!"*
>
> *We are the flower, Thou the sun!*
> *Forgive us, if as days decline,*
> *We nearer steal to Thee, —*
> *Enamored of the parting west,*
> *The peace, the flight, the amethyst,*
> *Night's possibility!*

The letter in which the poem was to be enclosed read:

Master.

If you observed your bullet hit a bird—and that bird told you he was'nt hurt, you might be moved by his civility, but you would surely suspect his word.

Here's a drop of crimson from the wound that pains your Daisy's bosom. I don't know how I was made, but by and by my heart, filled with you, outgrew me. I've heard of something known as "Redemption" which can comfort sinners, both men and women. I've asked for it.

I haven't confessed, but you've changed me. I'm more mature, now, Master. But, my love for you is the same. If it were fate that I might live where you live, breathe where you breath, I'd find the place and be there, but that sadness and cold are nearer to you than I can be drives me to despair. If only I could take the Queen's place, I'd be in heaven on earth, I'd be a Presbyterian redeemed for all my sins. I want to be closer to you than the very coat your tailor made for you to wear, but being with you is forbidden me. I'm frightened that you may laugh at my bleeding heart, Sir, but haven't you a heart in your breast that feels as mine does? Does it tremble when it wakes in the night to its own rhythm? I tell you all. Daisy confesses and denies nothing. My want is like a bashful Pompeii trying to talk with Vesuvius. Pompeii, admitting her desire to be vanquished couldn't look her life in the face afterwards.

Daisy confesses that she's ashes, smoldering in Vesuvius' wake. Daisy's arms are small and yours have held the horizon, and the sea came so close to you, you danced in her. I don't know what you can do for Daisy, her petals wilting for want of wetness, but if she had a beard on her cheek as you do, she'd come and carry you away with her. What would become of her Master if he cared so for Daisy as she does for him? Has he forgotten her in fight or flight or foreign land? Couldn't Carlo and he walk with her in the meadows for an hour and no one but a bobolink be the wiser? Daisy used to think that if she died in a hurry, she could see you in Heaven, but the whole town is going to Heaven with you and you won't be sequestered there at all. Say that Daisy may wait for you and she will, but she's waited for a very long time. Thank you, Master. I'm not sure what you can do for her, but what would you do with her if she came all in white killed by the heat of her heart? Would you make a little coffin for the living? Daisy wants to see you more, Sir, than all she dreams of in the world reaching to the skies. Don't you want to come and be with your Daisy, Master? Daisy will not disappoint you. It would comfort her just to look at your face while you looked at hers. She'd play in the woods with you until dark, and you could take her again, "where the sun don't shine."

Will, will you tell her if you will? Her rose blooms for you. Her bird rides the air searching for you. Come to her, Master, come to her in white. Daisy waits open to her Master.

Emily felt afraid to send the letter via Maggie and Sweetser's handyman up the hill to her Will. She reasoned there was too much strain on him, home for only a few days, to visit his family. She pushed the penciled draft into her drawer with some unfinished poems and thought better than to send it. She would keep it for another day and try to be patient as her Master had bid. Just then, she heard a pebble strike her window. She wondered if she was mistaken, but no, there it was again. She opened her window that looked toward the Evergreens and there in the shadows, she detected the figure of her Master standing in the moonlight and motioning up to her to come down. She dawned her shawl over her white nightdress and sneaked, her heart beating as if it would leap from her chest, down the back hall stairs to the scullery and out the back door. She went to Will who stood in the shadows of a great Hemlock. He lifted her in his arms and kissed her mouth. She swooned with joy as he carried her to the barn, Carlo following closely behind them.

That wild and daring night, she would experience an ecstasy greater than any she'd ever known with Clark. He would release all the pent up emotions that had dogged him through the war and make love to her with greater passion and wild abandon than ever he had before, and she would respond thoroughly to his caresses, offering her own with complete abandon.

Emily lay in bed all the next morning feigning illness so that she could dream over and over again of her late night tryst with Colonel Clark. He had come to her in his uniform and that made their meeting all the more adventurous and exotic. Emily recalled again the poem she had sent Clark in the field:

> *Wild nights! Wild nights!*
> *Were I with thee*
> *Wild nights should be*
> *Our luxury!*
>
> *Futile the winds*
> *To a heart in port, —*

> *Done with the compass,*
> *Done with the chart*
>
> *Rowing in Eden!*
> *Ah! the sea!*
> *Might I but moor*
> *To-night in thee!*

She wanted to believe that her poem had affected his longing so that he had become a wilder and more excited lover for her than ever—one who could not resist seeing her again. She felt satisfied with their night of lovemaking and felt it would help her through the war.

Indeed, Clark told her he had carried her poem, "Wild Nights," folded inside his vest pocket and read it often on the battlefield to help his spirit make it home again to her. He told her it was a favorite of his of the many poems she had sent him. That it would make a lovely song to be set to music for all the lovers who were separated by the war.

September 1862: "Mine By the Right"

Mine By the Right of the White Election…

Emily sat in Susan and Austin's parlor. Austin sat in a far corner busily reading a brief regarding his defense of a client at the Northampton Courthouse in the morning. Sue was flirting with Sam Bowles over sherry, even though Maria Whitney had come on his arm to visit. The three women were arguing whether women should be free to publish and have careers and vote. Samuel Bowles and Maria Whitney were sure they should. Emily sat more quietly, demurely listening, remembering what Will Clark had said about such matters. Sue was not so completely convinced, saying that a good Christian woman's place was in the home and not making a spectacle of herself in print. Emily mused how Sue had changed since her marriage.

"My husband rather agrees with his father, that a woman's place is in the home and her education meant to enrich her family life." Sue gazed demurely at Bowles to goad him for she didn't really believe fully in what she was saying, but loved to raise the passionate ire in him.

"My husband, women say, stroking the melody…" Emily thought to herself.

"Every person, male or female, has a right to fulfill their potential, including their intellectual potential, to the highest degree possible." Sam Bowles bellowed, full of his favorite homemade berry wine that Emily always brought to him from her wine cellar.

"I agree with Sam," said Maria smirking in his direction flirtatiously. "But, then, I always agree with Sam to flatter his ego, and he falls for it completely. Actually, I shall always do exactly as I please, and it pleases me to be a working woman, especially for a clever editor like Sam. It keeps me in touch with the world and earns my own keep so that I don't have to answer to anyone in particular, unless I choose to do so." Maria sat beside Samuel Bowles and took his arm to distract his gaze from Susan.

"Susan, you surprise me! I took you for an independent woman." Sam enjoined.

"I am an independent, if married, woman. I dare say I have as much to say about what happens in this house as my husband. Austin does not constrict me in my views. He has his and I have mine. He feels that the Union should not be divided over the issue of slavery. I feel as his father does, that we should have worked things out with legislative actions and debates on the floors of the legislatures of the states, one by one, reforming them with moral persuasion. We should have slowly and surely swayed popular opinion with reason, and scripture, not guns. Nathaniel Hawthorne seems to think John Brown deserved being hanged to death for taking the law into his own hands."

"Well, I'm shocked at your timidity, My Dear Mrs. Dickinson! John Brown was a great American. I agree with Beecher and his guns as Bibles campaign. Slavery is heinous and must be stopped at once, and women deserve the vote as much as any human being. Sometimes war is necessary. Even Emerson has said so."

"Well, I agree with Susie. The war accomplishes only carnage and solves nothing. Too many have died and the war lingers on, bloodier each day. There has got to be a better way, by Heaven!" Emily finally spoke up.

Maria wearied by the the same old conversation picked up the evening paper from the tea table to which the Irish maid had just delivered it. "Look at this headline in *The Hampshire Gazette*, Sam! We had better get back to Springfield. You've been utterly scooped by *The Gazette* regarding a terrible tragedy. What a horror is this? Speaking of the carnage, our local hero and our dear acquaintance is lost. Prepare yourselves for shock and mourning and listen to this front page item which I must bring myself to share with you, despite the sorrow it costs us all:

Another Hero Gone

The 21ˢᵗ Regiment of Massachusetts volunteers was ambushed in the dark of night by confederate soldiers after the battle at Chantilly where the regiment suffered its severest losses. Finding it impossible to make a successful stand, the regiment retreated, at least some of the companies in reasonably good order.

Maria paused looked gravely at Emily, feeling it would be best for her to hear the news among her friends and family. She shared Emily's secret, but could not speak publicly of it. Then she continued reading as Emily braced herself for what she felt was to come.

In the general confusion of retreat, Colonel William Smith Clark and eight of his men were separated from the rest of the regiment and surrounded by the enemy. Faced with the imminent threat of capture, they bravely rushed through the ranks of confederate soldiers. It is believed that all were shot down and lost in the line of duty. Colonel Clark, formerly a professor and doctor of chemistry and botany at Amherst College, husband of Harriet Richards Williston, and son of Dr. and Mrs. Atherton Clark of Easthampton, was a man of heroic conduct at the battle of Roanoke. His gallant charge at the battle of Newborn will never be forgotten. He believed every man's duty was to give himself to the service of his country until this hateful rebellion of The South is crushed out. He had declared as much at the recent Strawberry Festival held not long ago in his honor at the fair grounds for benefit of the valley's Union wounded. Colonel Clark allowed no private claims to interfere with this duty. Cheerfully, he gave himself to the work and most gallantly he performed it. He has lived a noble man and died a hero. His heroic deed and his manly character will ever be remembered by a grateful and sorrowing public of this valley where he contributed much to education, first as a Master of chemistry and the natural sciences at Williston Academy, and later as the first Ph.D. of Amherst College to be educated abroad . While at Amherst he taught horticulture and chemistry and erected a glorious garden for the training and enjoyment of his students.

Emily's head swam as the lights of the room blurred in her vision. She was not sure whether she was still alive and breathing. She fell back in her chair in silence and could not speak. Maria took charge of the situation to cover for Emily as best she could. "Here, Sam, take the paper. Anthon and I will help Emily home to her room. Austin, bring some cold water, please. We know well how this terrible sort of news of our boys in battle upsets Emily's sensitive disposition. I'm afraid she is about to faint." Maria wanted to get Emily away where she could soothe her in private, knowing full well that the news would devastate her. Maria wanted to get it out while she and Emily's friend, Anthon, were around to help her.

Anthon grabbed Emily's shawl and wrapped it around her shoulders while she and Maria helped her to stand. They ushered her quickly to the hall where Austin appeared with a cold glass of water in hand and bid his sister to drink.

"Now, Emmy, take a good gulp of water to help you breathe. There now, take it easy, Em. There is nothing to be done for this horror of war. I can't believe our friend, Clark, is gone. It is too terrible. Frazar Stearns and now Will Clark, such wonderful men lost to this endless bloody Hell! It breaks all our hearts."

"We must get her home, Austin. We will see you later when we've got her to bed."

Austin rejoined Susan and their guest, Samuel Bowles in the parlor. Both sat looking quite sad and dejected. "What a pity! Colonel Clark gone! It's too terrible." Sue sighed.

'Terrible for your sister, Austin! She was very fond of Clark."

"Yes, we know. He had attempted to court her when he was a senior at the college, but Father would have none of it because Clark didn't have the where-with-all to suit Father as Em's suitor. Father scared him off with his cold demeanor. Emily was always sad about it, I'm afraid."

"I don't think she was ever fully over Clark, even when he married Harriet. This will be hard on her." Sue enjoined worriedly.

"Yes, Sue, but we mustn't talk too much of it, as she denies her feelings for him, and we must spare her some dignity." Austin insisted.

"Of course, the poor little Empress of Cavalry! I won't say a word to goad her feelings." Sam Bowles promised. Though he envied Clark's swashbuckling career, he was sad to see him fallen. "What a damnable pity for the Union army and Massachusetts to lose a man as forward thinking and valuable as Clark!"

"We must not talk of it, unless Emily does." Austin warned again.

"Well, at least, she is not now a widow with Clark's many children to raise alone, as poor Cousin Harriet must now do." Sue remarked sadly. "Thankfully, Harriet has The Williston's fortunes behind her to shore her up."

"She must be utterly devastated." Austin replied.

"Yes, I shall send flowers and a card in the morning. Emily usually performs such tasks for all us Dickinsons, but she will be in no mind for it." Sue conceded.

"I know she'll mourn the loss of Colonel Clark even more than Frazar Stearns. She adored his lectures and he so inspired her horticultural pursuits, especially the exotic species in her conservatory." Austin worried.

September 1862: "One Who Died For Truth"

....One Who Died for Truth
Was Lain in an adjoining room...

Some Days retired from the rest
In soft distinction lie,
The Day that a companion came—
Or was obliged to die.

After much comforting from friends, Anthon and Maria, Emily found herself alone in her bed, with only the moonlight at her window. She could not weep. She was determined to die so that she might meet her Master in eternity. Her sorrow was beyond tears. She felt angry that Will's body would not be hers to bury. After a full day in solitude, too sick at heart to move or eat, she climbed in the night from her disheveled bed to write at her lamp table of how she should have the right to bury Clark when his remains were returned North. She wanted to see his face, touch his hands, hold his body to hers, one last time before he would be interred. Holding him, even in death, was all she could think of. She wanted to share his grave with him and planned how she would. She could not think at all clearly. All day and the night before, she had relived their secret times together in her head. All day she had read and reread his letters and the poems she had sent him, particularly the last ones. Finally her pen scratched furiously across the paper she took from the drawer in her writing table. By the flickering lamp she wrote:

Mine by the right of the white election!
Mine by the Royal Seal!
Mine by the sign in the scarlet prison
Bars cannot conceal!

Mine here in vision and in veto!
Mine—by the grave's repeal

> *Tilted, confirmed, —delirious charter!*
> *Mine, while the ages steal!*

But there was no one to whom she could mail her poetic release. Finally, realizing that Clark was gone from her forever unto eternity, she wept herself to sleep. In the morning, she took Carlo with her and went for a walk to their old meeting place at the large rock in the oak grove that separated his house from hers, trying to realize that he would never come to Amherst again. His wife had rented their house and gone to live with her parents in Easthampton for the course of Will's tenure as a cavalry officer.

Emily walked with Carlo through the woods to the back of Will's house where a carriage house held a buggy that went to the railroad station. She wondered when and if his body would be returned to Amherst and what sort of memorial would be given him at the college.

As she looked at his house there on the hill, she thought of how happily he had gardened in his lavish greenhouse, and how many exotic varieties of peonies he had grown on his lawns. How thrilled he was to have his own race, trotting track around the house. How glad he had been when his children were born and survived. How cheerful and inspiring he had seemed with his students as he walked them through the meadows and fields at the edge of woods in search of rare specimens of wildflowers. What a gifted teacher he had been. She remembered the dignified figure he cut as he sat on his stallion, Othello, riding through the town. How thrilled she'd been when he would ride up to her and sweep her onto the back of his horse to take her galloping through the back roads and wooded trails to Orient Point in the Pelham Hills or Mount Sugarloaf or Mount Toby in Sunderland where the college had an outdoor botanical laboratory. She saw his smiling face before her. His cheer had always been contagious. It was that she yearned for most. He had made her feel alive. She saw in her mind's eye his clear blue gaze so full of passion and hope in the future of their American land. She remembered the way his face glowed when he gave his lectures on chemistry and botany. She could not stand. She sank to the ground and hugged Carlo's neck, fainting as he stood whimpering in empathy.

Emily planned to attend the memorial for Professor Clark that would be held at the college, and after that walk the whole way to and up Mt. Sugarloaf and sleep forever in their cave on their conjugal bower. She would wear her white dress and his gold ring, that simple band inscribed with the word "Philip," that he'd placed on her finger as his true soul mate and natural bride. "We'll sneak away, Carlo, all the miles up Mount Sugarloaf as our last pilgrimage to him."

> *A solemn thing it was, I said*
> *A woman white to be,*
> *And wear, if God should count me fit,*
> *Her hallowed mystery.*
>
> *A timid thing to drop a life*
> *Into the purple well,*
> *Too plummetless that it come back*
> *Eternity until.*

She dragged herself up from the ground behind Will's house, and with Carlo, circled around and back through the oak grove, and sat on the rock where she had so often waited for Clark. She dreamed of meeting her beloved Master in eternity. All she could do to survive the screaming pain in her heart was write as if talking with him:

> *I died for beauty, but was scarce*
> *Adjusted in the tomb*
> *When one who died for truth was lain*
> *In an adjoining room.*
>
> *He questioned softly why I failed?*
> *"For beauty," I replied—*
> *"And I for Truth—the two are one;*
> *We brethren, are," he said.*

> And so, as Kinsmen, met a-night
> We talked between the rooms,
> Until the moss had reached our lips,
> And covered up our names.

Carlo licked the salt from her palms that caught her silent tears as her hands lay like small dead birds helplessly upturned in her lap.

September 1862: Chantilly: "Another Hero Gone"

I had a terror since September I could tell to no one.

Beyond exhaustion, Colonel Clark, bruised and bleeding at the ankles, walked endlessly, hiding in ditches, rock caves, and corn fields. He had shed his Union jacket and cap for fear of being noticed, and wore only his white shirt, quite torn, and his trousers held up by their suspenders. His boots were wet and his feet ached. He was thirsty as he had not come upon drinkable water in awhile. He had eaten green apples and raw corn and they troubled his digestion. He leaned by a tree and felt he would vomit. His head throbbed. He had been walking for four days trying to find his way back through enemy territory attempting to meet up with his command in Alexandria. He had been scrambling through and hiding in the woods. He was beyond exhaustion.

When he slept at night under the stars, he was rudely awakened by visions of the hideous battle he had lived through, seeing his men shot down beside him. His regiment had suffered its worst loss of casualties since the war began. The battle of Chantilly had been a particularly brutal one for his men and a few, of them, eight to be exact, had been lost from the rest as they retreated. As they were about to be captured, he led a small charge through the enemy lines toward the hope of freedom, but all of the eight with whom he charged had been shot down, and he had only managed to survive by falling into a ditch at the edge of the field where he lay still and undetected. Then he crawled off into the woods and began to make his way back to his command.

Finally, after four days of a painful journey on foot, scratched, bruised, bitten by insects, jacketless and hatless, he had returned on foot to his command. When he hobbled into camp and fell upon the ground, his men were astounded and immediately rushed to his needs. They carried him to his tent, and soothed him with water and food, and cool compresses. He seemed to his battle weary soldiers like a ghost arisen from the dead, a magical survivor who had returned to give them heart to accomplish the impossible. Before long he was talking of his adventures and sorrows.

With eight others, I became separated from you, and all to a man have perished. I can't believe I am alive to tell of it. I fell into a ditch behind some rocks near the edge of a wood and lay still until the shooting stopped and the enemy began to set up camp. Then I crawled into the woods by dark and began to make my way back to you. I pinched myself every hour in order to be sure I was still among the living as I walked and hid, crawled and hiked, eating nothing but green corn and apples and drinking the water of running brooks. If not for my experience as a young geologist scouting the woods for precious rocks and ores, and if not for my trusty compass, I'd not be here now. I had to keep my ambition strong to reach you, as many times I thought to give up and die in some field, my stomach ached; my head swam so, but the moral of my story is, Boys, be ambitious!"

The men of Clark's regiment smiled with relief to have their popular Colonel back among them, leading them onward.

Months later as Clark sat outside his tent on the battlefield at Antietam, he read his obituary in the *The Hampshire Gazette*, he smirked sardonically, thinking. "I shall have to go home and pound upon my door and demand to see the 'Widow Clark.'" But his sardonic cheer was momentary for he was suffering another great loss. His dear friend, Manross, had joined the Union Army only to be killed at Antietam. Clark had offered him a position in the 21st Regiment, but Manross had decided to stay with his own unit. "Ah, if you had to die, old friend, perhaps it was best that you not do so under my command, as I'd never have forgiven myself. Frazar face haunts me daily, and now, you too, old friend are gone from me forever. This war is a miserable hell of useless losses. We have accomplished little with all this bloodshed. He wrote home:

> *I am disposed to continue in this army until discharged for better or for worse. I have been recommended by Major General Burnside of the 9th Army Corps who wrote from Antietam to Major General McClelland, commander of the Army of the Potomac, to request for me the rank of brigadier general. I have been commended for my role in the North Carolina campaign, especially Newbern, where my dearest Frazar fell, and the Virginia campaign, and the current campaign in Maryland, but I am weary of this war. Since I have lost*

so many men in battle, particularly my dear sweet, Frazar, and my hearty friend, Manross, I feel no glory in my military accomplishments. I have received a very complimentary letter from our Honorable Congressman Charles Delano, expressing hope that I will not resign while the war continues. He said that all the Senators and Congressmen would recommend me for Brigadeer General, but I am disheartened or dissatisfied with the government, because those in charge of affairs act neither wisely nor well. Yet, the principles for which we fight are right and honorable and must be maintained. President Lincoln's heart is in the right place and it is a large one, whatever may be said of his brain. Both Lincoln and Burnside are honorable men. We are under order to march tomorrow, but no one knows where. God grant that it may not be to new disasters and frightful butchery.

You have doubtless heard the slanderous report respecting my intemperance said to have originated with Major Hawkes of Templeton. I have sent to Mrs. Clark a certificate from the Major to the effect that he never saw me intoxicated nor had reason to believe I drank intemperately. I trust that will satisfy the minds of anxious friends. If any others wish to defame those who are laboring and battling for their welfare, they can do so.

And, please do publish the account of my survival sent earlier in The Hampshire Gazette, least my comrades at home in the valley should think me a ghost of the living dead when they set eyes upon me. I am recovered and ready to march again.

Most truly and hopefully, your native son, Colonel Clark

Emily had been beside herself with joy when she'd heard the news that Clark was returned to camp alive and recuperating well at Antietam, but she dismayed that he was ready to march again with the armies of the Potomac. His near deaths since his entry into the war had caused her to suffer bouts of nervous prostration, sleepless nights, loss of appetite, and shaking hands. She resolved that if she were to be well enough to greet her hero again, should he return home finally, she must focus her mind on other matters, particularly her writing and gardening, and the care of her mother. She did this with determination, taking many long walks with Carlo to calm her spirits.

She found that few people interested her now. Women seemed to gossip as she passed, and she began to feel they knew of her torrid affair with a married man. She kept more to herself, except for close friends, especially those out of town, and her family. She felt when she entered The Congregational Church and walked down the aisle to her family pew that whispers of women were all around her. She had never liked going to Sabbath services in any event, except for the sermons of Reverend Wadsworth of Philadelphia that Clark had recommended whenever he returned from that city where he sometimes shopped for chemical supplies for his laboratory. The sermon of Reverend Park had stirred her so regarding the poet's reverence for nature that she found most sermonizers, ever since, dull or duplicitous.

Whenever she walked in the woods, however, she felt a peace searching for wildflowers, listening to bird song. It made her think of Master Clark and the herbarium he had inspired her to keep which she hoped to perfect for his return. Any new find for it would mean little unless she could share its discovery with him. She missed his affection, his energetic encouragement that had stirred her to poetry and given her life new meaning. She missed their lovemaking as much as their talk. She would dream that he was with her walking through the woods. She would lie down on a grassy slope at a meadows edge and with Carlo keeping guard, close her eyes and dream that Clark was with her, touching her, kissing her with sensuous hunger, entering her, soothing and stroking her until she released herself to ecstasy. She imagined conversations with him and pictured their meeting, dreaming of what would transpire, what he would tell her, what she would say. She found it almost impossible to stop herself from thinking of him quite constantly and the longing made her ill, yet full of hope for his return.

> *Hope is a subtle glutton;*
> *He feeds upon the fair;*
> *And yet, inspected closely,*
> *What Abstinence is there !*
>
> *His is the halcyon table*
> *That never seats but one,*

> *And whatsoever is consumed*
> *The same amount remain.*

Her only peace came while she was writing her poems. As she wrote, she told herself that perhaps Thomas Wentworth Higginson might like the poem she composed. She began to try to make herself hope for a wider audience for her poetry than Clark, Sue, Elizabeth Holland, and her Norcross Cousins—despite her father's restraints. She had begun to send some of her poems to other friends, to Samuel Bowles, Maria Whitney, Anthon. She wrote many that were not specifically for Clark, but might be appreciated by anyone, philosophical poems about all manner of subjects that struck her fancy. As she wrote of hope, she found that though her poem might have to do with the hope of his return, it was about hope in general.

> *Hope is the thing with feathers*
> *That perches in the soul,*
> *And sings the tune without the words,*
> *And never stops at all,*
>
> *And sweetest in the gale is heard;*
> *And sore must be the storm*
> *That could abash the little bird*
> *That kept so many warm.*
>
> *I've heard it in the chillest land,*
> *And on the strangest sea;*
> *Yet, never, in extremity,*
> *It asked a crumb of me.*

Her Master was her Muse, but because of her familiarity with his wide and clever mind, his inspiration took her writing in all directions. He had before going off to war begun to review books he read for various newspapers, and he had encouraged his sisters, as he had encouraged Emily, to perfect their writing skills and their poetry so that they might become teachers one day—in case they might, because of circumstance, need to earn their own living. Emily dreamed that, someday, she might become a teacher and earn her own keep so that she could leave her father's home, which to her in some ways felt like prison. Yet, she had all she needed there, and her father was indulgent, and Vinnie loving. She began to suspect that because her mother was ill, off and on, since the birth of Lavinia, he feared her or Lavinia leaving his household. She felt he had unwittingly discouraged their marriage to anyone to keep them for himself. "Father wants us to be mistresses of his domain forever, Vinnie! He will never approve any suitor for either of us, and so, dearest sister, find love where you may!"

Lavinia was not sure of Emily's meaning, but she needed little encouragement to be sociable with men and so she left the homestead as often as possible to visit their cousins or go about the parish while Emily began to stay at home, more and more often, to care for their bedridden mother who suffered painful bouts of neuralgia and spent most of her days in her room, leaving Emily more and more to the overseeing of household chores with Maggie. Lavinia, who had no great desire to read or write, as did Emily, took over more of the household management so that Emily could have time to be alone in her room. In return, Emily wrote all messages of condolence or congratulations that needed to be sent around the town, often enclosing a little verse or poem to cheer or mourn or congratulate.

Emily could hardly stop herself from writing poems or letters to friends or family, nearly every night by her lamplight and the locked drawer of her bureau began to fill with bits of paper of all manner and sizes filled with poems, or fragments of poems, some finished and sewn into booklets to send onto Clark, and some unfinished within which she never truly decided which exact word from her large and growing vocabulary to use in crucial places. She corresponded frequently with others and their letters and hers began to fill her bureau as well. She kept those from, and drafts to, Clark tied together and hidden in Maggie's chest, a locked box where the maid kept a few personal items of her own for use when she was at work almost daily in service to the Dickinsons. Both Maggie and Emily shared a key to Maggie's trunk.

Though Maggie went home to her own quarters most nights, she occasionally stayed overnight at the homestead if a family member were particularly ill and needed special attention. She had become close to Emily, during Emily's illnesses. Emily shared her feelings about Clark with Maggie, even as she kept her love for him secret from Lavinia as best she could. It was Maggie who had run upstairs to deliver Clark's letters through Luke Sweetser or George Montague, neighbors of the Dickinsons and Clark's when he'd lived at home on the house on the hill behind.

Emily sent letters to her "Master" often, always calling herself "Daisy" and Clark, "Master" or disguising his name in a poem with the world "Will" or "Whipporwill" or "Sweet William" and having Maggie address the envelope in her hand, which she would enclose in a letter to Elizabeth Holland to forward onto Clark. She exercised as much caution as she could and waited patiently for reply. Finally, one day she had a letter from Clark through Mrs. Holland that did not mention her in any way, but was a copy of one sent to his men, which gave her news of his plans, and was reprinted in the local newspaper as well on June 12, 1863:

Officers and Soldiers fo the 21st Massachusetts Volunteers:

In the program of events the sad hour has come when I must bid you farewell. During twenty long months we have together borne the hardships, faced the dangers, and enjoyed the pleasures of military life. We have exulted together in victory, and have consoled each other in times of disaster. We have rejoiced over the deserved promotion of many of our brave comrades, and we have wept together over the lifeless forms of our numerous and loved companions who have died for their country. I regret exceedingly that the cruel fate of war has so reduced your ranks that I can no longer remain your Colonel, but having been with you on every battlefield, I know your merits, and will never cease to remember and admire; you. I have endeavored to be faithful and just in the discharge of every duty of my responsible office, and if I have inadvertently neglected or wronged any one, I pray you pardon me.

Go on, gallant soldiers, under your new command, as you have valiantly and obediently. Hoping this rebellion may soon be crushed and I may have the happiness of welcoming the 21st to dear old Massachusetts, I bid one and all, most affectionately, Farewell.

Colonel Clark

Though his words were not for her alone, Emily felt a great relief, but soon began to worry that she had not, herself, received any messages for arranging a tryst as when he had been home on furlough for The Strawberry Festival.

"Has his horrible experience of the war washed away all his feelings for me? Will he be changed and unapproachable? Will he no longer want me?" She lay away nights worrying over what would happen upon his return. Since no letters or messages came from him, Emily attempted to go about her daily chores and writing quelling her anxiety with the activity of her household duties.

Clark, meantime, had come to know that the remainder of his regiment would be split into other companies sent onto Kentucky from Ohio and he could not follow as his men would be under other commands. He had tried to argue that his regiment be refurbished, but in the bureaucracy and contingencies of war, his plea had fallen on deaf ears. Also, his promotion to brigadeer general had never come to him, and he did not know why. Perhaps, it was the mere confusions of war that had delayed it, or it had gone astray and not been instituted, and so, wearied and disgusted by the neglect he was tendered after his brave deeds and near deaths, he had written a simple letter of resignation to the officers in charge stating:

> *I hereby respectfully tender my resignation and ask to be honorably discharged from the service of the United States. My reasons are the reduced condition of my regiment and my belief that I can be more useful at home than in the arms under existing circumstances.*
>
> *I am respectfully*
> *your Obedient Servant,*
> *Colonel W.S. Clark*

Clark was homesick and his wife wanted him back to help with the children. She wanted to reside again in her own home in Amherst. She had persuaded her father, Sam Williston, to beg his son-in-law to return and concede that he had done enough for the cause at the front. Colonel Clark arrived home to Easthampton in May, rather subdued and dejected, but soon returned to live with his family in the house on the hill behind Emily's in Amherst by June, and to teach again at Amherst college. He made no attempt to contact Emily and she began to haunt their old meeting place in the oak grove on the hill in hopes of seeing him there. Finally, she sent the letter she had kept in a penciled draft locked in her bureau among her poems. She put it into a final draft, and with the idea that she would, at least, see some sort of outcome rather than waste away in doubt and wonder, and she mailed it in trepidation.

Time passed and no answer came. At the start of January, Abraham Lincoln passed the Emancipation Proclamation freeing slaves in the Confederate States and throughout the nation.

The retired Colonel Clark gave a stirring speech at the college which Emily attended. He nodded to her seated near the front row. Afterward, she formally shook his hand and complimented him on his passionate speech in celebration of the proclamation. He thanked her and said that she looked well, but nothing more passed between them in that public setting. It was announced from the podium that Colonel Clark had been asked to run for a seat on the State Senate by the Republican party. Emily realized that would take her Master away from Amherst to Boston's State House, should he be elected in November.

"I wish you well for your senate campaign Professor Clark, " she said with a curtsey, doing all she could to contain herself with propriety in the public setting.

"Thank you, Miss Dickinson." Will answered formally aloud, and then he added in a whisper out of earshot by others, *meet me by the back door of the barn tonight at midnight, Bring Carlo. It's so cold; no one will be out.*

Emily's heart leapt, even though she had been grieving the death of her Uncle Loring Norcross who had died recently, leaving her young Cousins Lou and Fannie orphaned in their boarding house in Cambridgeport.

Will resumed his formal tone. "I'm sorry to hear that your uncle passed, Miss Dickinson. I read it in the obituaries. My profound condolences. Perhaps, you will be visiting your cousins in Boston more often, and if I should be at the state house in fall, perhaps, we can all meet for tea in Cambridgeport. As you know, my brother-in-law, Lyman, lives near your cousins. One of your Norcross cousins attended his Unitarian school for girls."

"Yes, indeed she did, Professor Clark." Emily answered as more people gathered at the edge of the podium to speak with the professor and compliment his speech.

"Goodnight, Professor, Emily smiled, as they gave each other another little bow, smiling inwardly at what Clark seemed to be suggesting. Namely, that he and Emily could meet, not only later that night, but in Cambridgeport in fall far from Amherst's gossipy eyes and ears.

Emily sailed home through the snow, her skirts and spirits high as she knew that she would finally see her Master late that very night, and perhaps see much more of him in spring, if she could manage to get away to be with her orphaned cousins in Boston. As she trundled through the snow homeward in her high boots, she devised a scheme.

"If Will wins the state senate seat, I shall make the excuse to father that my eyes are troubling me, just as Sue did when she wanted to meet Austin secretly at the Revere Hotel in Boston. I'll say that I must go and stay with Fanny and Lou in Cambridgeport for ophthalmologic treatments. Father doesn't know that Sue used that rouse. He won't say 'no' to my need for eye treatments, and I'll also say I want to comfort my little cousins left alone by their parent's deaths. Vinnie will assume my household duties for a spell for such a reason. Oh, I am a wicked woman, but I must have time with my Master. I must grasp love while I can find it, or I shall die for lack of it. I am growing old without a husband, and Will shall be my only lover for all eternity. Don't I have a right to a bit of happiness? If I must die a spinster, it shall only be in the eyes of Amherst, but not in truth, not in my spirit, not in my body and soul. I shall always know that I have been desired and loved by a fine, noble, brilliant, and courageous man."

Lavinia had stayed home with their ailing mother as she cared little for speeches or lectures and the house was quiet as Emily entered. All were asleep except for Carlo who rose from the hearth to greet his adored mistress, his tail wagging at the feeling of her happiness and, as usual, at the sight of her.

She took off her gloves, wet boots, and heavy cloak, leaving them by the back door for later use, and swept up the stairs to her room, Carlo following her. She sat at her writing table and waited, with an eye to her pocket watch, dreaming of what would occur later that night when the village was completely dark and asleep. She would rendezvous with Clark at the back door of the barn at the stroke of midnight. She wrote a poem about snow and moonlight, then tucking it away in her drawer. She changed into her white flannel nightgown, leaving on her high boots and stockings. She snuffed out her lamp, and crept downstairs. At the back door, she covered her nightdress with a black wool cloak and dawned its enveloping hood. With Carlo following, she crept out into the night.

The moon was full making snow shadows everywhere across the garden and orchard as she crept silently through the cold night, soft new snow cushioning her footsteps. She found her Master, a shadowy figure near the edge of the woods at the back door of the barn. Carlo, accustomed to their rendezvous and the scent of Clark, led Emily to him, wagging his tail in greeting. Clark gave Carlo a biscuit from his pocket, as he often did upon greeting Emily's watchdog. They sneaked into the back door of the barn where a pile of fresh hay was kept for the horse and cow. The horse, too, was used to Clark's scent, and it received an apple, as usual, from the Master to keep it happy and quiet. Moonlight streamed in from the hayloft window.

Then Clark swept his Daisy up in his arms and laid her down in the hay. In the barn smelling of fresh hay and chicken feed, she felt as if she had achieved paradise. "My little Daisy. I've missed you and dreamt of having you. I've arisen from the dead to return to you."

"Oh, yes, Master, it has felt like the journey to eternity, but now that I reach Heaven again in your arms, the time behind us has vanished, and this moment is forever." The lovers behaved as if no time had past since they last held each other. They gave freely of themselves, Clark leading Emily into passionate embraces and she reciprocating with fervor. The cold night made their bodies seem silken and warm in contrast as they pressed themselves together; the moonlight gave their faces a ghostly perfection. The adventurous daring in their meeting intoxicated them as they shared a deeper ecstasy, having survived more than either thought they could endure. Emily whispered a verse to Clark as they lay, passion spent, in each other's arms.

> *A death-blow is a life-blow to some*
> *Who, till they died, did not alive become;*
> *Who, had they lived, had died, but when*
> *They died, vitality begun.*

April 1863: "We Here Highly Resolve"

We here highly resolve....
a new birth of freedom....

That final summer of the war, the Battle of Gettysburg in Pennsylvania saw the greatest number of Civil War casualties. That Colonel Clark was no longer on the battlefield contented Emily and made her glow with happiness. Clark, she knew, was touring Western Massachusetts seeking the state legislative seat. Having been nominated, as a popular war hero, by the new Republican Party as a Free-Soil candidate, he was, on November 3rd, elected to be the state representative from the Amherst region. Emily had prepared the family in advance with complaints about her eyes, saying that Fanny and Lou knew a fine ophthalmologist she could visit in Boston, and she could stay with them while she underwent examinations and treatments.

Edward immediately worried about his daughter's eyesight, and being always concerned with his children's health, consented for her to go. Vinnie was solicitous, making Emily feel quite guilty, so that she almost told the truth to her sister, but the thought of Vinnie unwittingly spilling her secret in conversation was too terrible to abide. Emily was steadfast and stuck to her story saying that her eyes were troubling her so that she could barely read at all. In April she was ready to set off for Cambridge in pursuit of State Representative Clark who would be housed at times down the street from her cousins in Harvard Square with his brother-in-law, Lyman Richards Williston. State Representative Clark would also have a room at The Revere Hotel in Roxbury where she might meet him in a more anonymous setting.

Lyman Williston, Clark's brother-in-law, was a noted Unitarian preacher and follower of Emerson, much to Squire Williston's Calvinist dismay. Fanny and Lou, her orphaned cousins, attended recitals at Lyman's school for girls. One of their Norcross cousins had also been schooled there. Emily was thoroughly excited about her forthcoming trip into liberal Transcendental territory. She could hardly contain herself. She felt as if she was to be let out of prison, and it was difficult to feign worry about her eyes.

"I wonder if folks let out of Chillon prison feel any more elated than I?" She asked herself as she came sailing down the stairs, her skirts flying, dressed in her best dark, auburn traveling gown and white lace collar. The dress was a rich color that enhanced her chestnut red hair and large brown eyes. Her curly hair, cut short, was carefully arranged under her brown bonnet with its satin auburn ribbon. Her cheeks were pink with the sun she soaked up hiking with Carlo through the meadow. She wore her mother's ivory broach on an auburn ribbon around her neck. Her dark red paisley shawl was over her shoulders and she wore matching brown, leather gloves and high button shoes for her trip. Maggie helped her bring her brown leather traveling trunk downstairs. It was not heavy, for she'd packed no books, knowing her cousins would have plenty available for her in their library, and also not wanting to arouse suspicion concerning her eyes which actually were fine, except for the strain of too much reading and writing by flickering lamplight late into the night when the rest of the house was asleep.

"There now, Miss Emily. Tom will be bringin' yer carriage around front for ye in a moment. Too bad Mr. Dickinson is not here to bid ye goodbye."

"He's busy with a case in Northampton, but I spoke with him last night, Maggie. He gave me an allowance for my trip without my having to ask."

"Well, that's nice, Mam. Now you be enjoying yerself good there in Cambridge. And don't let nothin' upset ye. Have yerself a good time no matter what; promise me! Relax and smile. Nothin' makes a woman prettier than a happy smile."

"I will, Maggie. I'll try to smile as often as possible. And here's for you. Thanks, Maggie for all your help packing!" Emily gave Maggie a kiss on the cheek as she pressed some money into her hand. "You have a good time while I'm away, too. Let the dishes air dry in the rack, since I won't be here to dry them for you."

"Oh, Emily, do take good care of yourself and rest your eyes well!" Vinnie entered the hall to bid her sister goodbye. "You look lovely and so sophisticated! I haven't seen you dressed so well since our trip to Washington. You look like a city lady already!"

"Vinnie, I'll miss you and you're so good to do my household chores while I'm away. I'll make it up to you when I return. You'll lie about and have a rest while I do your work. And I shall serve you cakes and tea in bed while you read novels." The sisters giggled in unison.

"Now, Em, don't worry about the house or Mother. I'll take care of everything here. You just rest your eyes and do as the doctor orders."

"I shall, Vinnie. Thank you. You're the best sister one could have."

Carlo followed Emily to her waiting buggy and whimpered with his tail waggy in anticipation. Emily patted her Carlo's large head. He stood almost as tall as she. "I'll miss you, Carlo. Be a good boy and stay. I'll miss you Vinnie. I'll miss you Maggie. Stay well. I'll write as soon as I get to Cambridgeport. Take good care of Carlo for me!"

"Goodbye Emmy!" Vinnie stood at the door and waved. "Be careful and stay safe and well and do write us immediately so we know you're safe. Tell Fannie and Lou I send my regards and affection, and Mother sends hers, too, of course. Promise not to try to read too much. Let Lou read to you. Go with God, Emily!" Vinnie waved as Tom put Emily's trunk on the back of the buggy and then helped her up into her seat. He clucked and jerked on the reigns to set the horse to trotting and the wagon rattled down the drive headed for the train station. It was one of the very few times that Emily had gone off alone to travel far from home. She was thrilled and anxious.

As she sat in the train that her father had worked so hard to bring to Amherst, she thought of how appalled he would be if he knew her real reason for traveling to Cambridgeport. She felt a surge of guilt at deceiving him, especially since she'd accepted a goodly allowance from him for the trip, he giving her funds he thought she would need for the eye doctor. She decided she could not allow anything to spoil her chance to be with her adored Master. The thought of seeing him and of spending time away from Amherst with him where no villagers could spy on them exhilarated her and pushed the guilt from her mind. "I have a right to a life of my own. I'll be thirty-five next year, an old maid, and I have a right to be loved as a woman, to enjoy some freedom, to see the world a bit and leave the gossips of this town behind."

Fannie and Lou were waiting for her when she arrived. They were excited to have their Cousin Emily staying with them for a long visit.

Fannie had moved in with Louise to give her room to Emily. Their apartment on the second floor was a modest one, but they'd fashioned Emily's room with books, paper, and pens ready at a writing table. They knew Cousin Emily's wit had always entertained them, and they expected she'd bring intrigue and excitement with her. "

How sweet and kind of you Cousin Fannie, to give up your room for me. But, you shouldn't have. I could sleep on the sofa in the living room.

"We won't have it otherwise. We're comfortable together. We've put Mama's coverlet, all newly washed on your bed. We know how you loved her, Emily." Fannie lowered her eyes in grief. Their father, Loring, had died a year ago and their mother a year or more before him, both of consumption. Aunt Lavinia Norcross, for whom her Sister, Vinnie was named, had been Emily's favorite aunt. Their connection was inherent in their interests. Lavinia had been a poet who loved to read and dabble in writing. Fannie and Lou had been inspired to appreciate reading fine literature because of their mother.

Aunt Lavinia Norcross had married her own first cousin, Emily's Uncle, Loring Norcross. The marriage had been frowned upon by many, but condoned by Emily who felt that true love should always triumph over convention, because emotional truth was paramount. Emily had confessed to her "Little Cousins" her love of her distant cousin, related to her through the Sweetsers, William Smith Clark. They knew many of the details of her struggling, star-crossed love affair. Emily had found relief in being able to discuss it with Lou and Fannie. They knew that Clark had loved Emily before he married Harriet Williston, and felt that he should have rightly been her husband.

"He's here in Harvard Square! Will Clark is here! We saw him walking only yesterday. He's staying with his brother-in-law, Lyman, just up the street!" Louisa was only too happy to convey the news. She was at an age when romance enthralled her and the idea of an illicit love affair intrigued her greatly. Yet, she was more realistic and mature than the girls of Amherst. She and her sister had read all the romantic tomes Emily loved, and they had been raised unconventionally, especially when compared to Emily's Puritan rearing.

"Oh Emily! Can you bare it? Clark's right up the street living with Lyman. " Fanny added her zest. "We like Lyman's Transcendental

Sermons very much. They're so like Emerson's. You'll love them, too. You must come to hear him.

First, before I do anything," Emily planned, "I must make an appointment with Dr. Henry Willard Williams at the corner of Arlington and Newbury Streets. There needs to be a bill for my eye exam sent to father soon, so that he will never suspect my real reason for coming to Boston.

"We passed by there yesterday and made the appointment for you for tomorrow afternoon, Emily. Uncle Edward will never suspect a thing?" The girls giggled with glee at the thought of their stuffy uncle being duped. They had fled Calvinist dogma to join a far more liberal transcendental group, one that believed in redemption of sin, and worship of Nature in Emerson's fashion.

"Oh, Lou! Oh, Fannie! I feel awful about fooling Father and making him spend money on an ophthalmologist that I do not *really* need."

"But, Cousin Emmy, you do use your eyes so much in reading and writing by lamplight at night! We're sure they are strained and should be examined. Dr. Williams is the very best eye doctor around. He helped Lou greatly when she suffered eyestrain. And, there is no way for Dr. Williams to tell that you see well when you read his charts. You must miss many of the letters. Say that an "o" is a "c" and an "f" is a "t." Say it all looks blurry, and how can he be the wiser!" Fannie prattled with mischievous joy. "Love is what matters in this world! More than anything! True emotion is what counts. Our parents felt that when they married, and they loved each other so to the very end. Father couldn't bear to stay alive without Mother; he had to join her beyond the veil."

"Yes, Fannie. That love is all there is, is all we know of love, and it is it's own rescue."

Emily felt pensive and sinful for deceiving her father, but she did not want to disappoint Fannie or Lou being morose about it. "Shall I rest a bit now? The journey was long and the carriage and train fairly rattled my brains to bits."

"Oh, yes, Emily, rest!" Lou was solicitous. "Feel free to take a good nap and unpack your things. We've made room in the closet for your dresses. We haven't told you that Clark and Lyman greeted us in the square. Lyman knows we have a cousin, Emily, in Amherst and he introduced us to Clark. When we said you were arriving by train today, Clark seemed to perk up. "Ah, says he. You must invite me for tea to see Miss Emily, a friend from Amherst, when you have the time," Lou reiterated. "I've shared horticulture projects with her brother. Miss Emily is a fine botanist," says he.

"Emily's face brightened. "He said that to you? Yesterday, in the square?"

"Indeed he did. He did.' Fannie bubbled. "And guess what?"

"What? What?" Emily was excited.

"He's coming to tea this *very* day at 5:30 o'clock on his way back from the State House. This very day, Emily!" Lou and Fanny chimed in together. "This very day!"

"Oh, so soon!" Emily was thrilled. "I must rest and freshen up to look my best!" Emily nearly flew into her room with Lou and Fannie toting her trunk, one on each end.

"Do freshen up and rest, Emily. We've poured clean water in the washstand pitcher. And, look, we put two red roses, leaning together, in a vase for you." Lou blushed, still shy and demure in her radical beliefs.

"And we've baked ginger cakes for tea using your recipe. We'll have jasmine tea, too! It will be a lovely teatime. We plan to excuse ourselves and say we've been invited to a recital after about an hour, so as leave you too alone." Fannie giggled.

"Oh, My Dear Little Cousins, you're too good to me. You're my salvation!"

April 1864: Cambridgeport, Little Cousins

That love is all there is, is all we know of love…

"Your cousins were sweet to leave us alone. Do they know?" Will took Emily's hand as she attempted to clear away the tea things. After an hour of making pleasant chatter with Representative Clark, and thrilled to have a Congressman in their parlor, Louisa and Frances Norcross had insisted they had a recital of a friend they must flee to. They departed, demanding he stay and finish tea with Emily. "This is Emily's home as much as ours, so stay, Congressman Clark, stay, please. You two Amherst cousins must have much to share regarding news of home. We must be off. We're so pleased to have made your acquaintance Congressman Clark." Louisa said as she and Fannie quickly dawned their bonnets by the door. "Good afternoon, Dear Emily." They said, their skirts sweeping out the door that they hurriedly shut firmly behind them before anything more could be said about their departure.

Emily turned to Clark as he took her hand. "Oh, Master, I can't believe I am here in Cambridge with you. Yes, Lou and Fannie know, but they are of liberal views. They feel we belonged together before you married The Queen. They feel we have a right to our love and our union. They are as discreet as we, however, and will never breathe a word or tell a soul.

"Good. I am pleased they've left us alone."

"Are you, Master?"

"As pleased as I can be." Will took Emily in his arms and kissed her lingeringly on the mouth. He gazed in her eyes with his old intensity.

She sighed with bliss. He carried her to her bed. Their reunion was filled with passionate hunger for each other. Emily knew that Fanny and Lou would not return until late that evening. She was relaxed in her Master's arms. They held each other close for hours after love making, without fear or anxiety of discovery, lying comfortably in Emily's bed together—the door to her room locked and closed. Though Emily would rather have heard about his interest in being with her in days to come, Will told her of how The Morrill Act would make it possible for him to fight for the new state agricultural college to be founded in Amherst. He was deeply involved in a struggle to bring it to their home region.

"Sam Bowles will be dismayed. He wants the agricultural college for West Springfield."

"He has already editorialized against Amherst as the location."

"As much as I love Sam and his friendship, I do believe he is jealous of you Will, and of your brave exploits and heroism in the war."

"I've sensed an anger in him, but he shouldn't make so much of my so called heroism. It was simply necessity that drove me, not bravery. The need to survive is strong in all of us."

"Yes, if we are happy and healthy it is, but Sam is ill and disgruntled."

"Do you feel happy and healthy, now, My Little Daisy."

"I'm happy in your arms, Master. But miserable when we're apart."

"You must have patience, Daisy. We can only be together occasionally. Even here in Cambridge much duty calls me to the legislature, and I am appointed as Secretary of the Electoral College now, too. I discovered this morning that I'm called to serve in that capacity as well. I shall be very busy, and you mustn't expect to see me as often as I would like to see you. It's the way it is, as duty calls me, or I'd not be here in this town. I can't see you often."

"Don't say that, Master. It spoils the glow of this diamond afternoon, spent in Heaven." To avoid further discussion of how few their reveries might be in Cambridge, Emily recited a verse to charm Will.

> *To make a prairie it takes a clover and one bee, —*
> *One clover, and a bee.*
> *And reverie.*
> *The reverie alone will do,*
> *If bees are few.*

Then she kissed him passionately touching him to a renewed excitement, as his lust for her had taught her to be bold in hers for him. They made love again as the light in the window began to fade. "You Master are my bee and I your clover who will always be waiting for you whenever you have time to hover in reverie, no matter how few minutes you can give me. Each second you give me is precious and fills me with glee. You know I kneel to no other."

"Emily, you should kneel to no one but God. I am only an *imperfect* man and I have been selfish in wanting your love. I wish you would publish your poetry to receive the praise you deserve for it from others. I am not a poet, but I know when I read your writing, it moves me and stirs my mind. Let me send some verses to Luke Sweester at *The Roundtable*, in New York and some more to *Drumbeat*, in Brooklyn, too. You'll will see how well others love your poetry."

"But, Master, You know Father would be furious to read my poems as he'd find them embarrassing and heretical, and he depends so on me to be a lady. Sue, too, feels it is not ladylike to publish my soul as if it were at auction.

"By God, Emily, how old fashioned! Your father loves you with a Calvinist strangle hold, and Sue has succumbed to his demands, taking the part of your mother for him, too. Nonsense! Modern women like Margaret Fuller, Louisa May Alcott, Frances Wright, and European ladies like Mrs. Elizabeth Barret Browning, your idol, or the Bronte sisters have no problem in publishing now!"

"Please, Will, Father's an honorable man. His heart would break, as he feels only poor women with no father's estate to protect them, publish."

"Yes, he is honorable, and I know it, but he holds his women back with the love and care of an iron chain. He has held you, your mother, your sister from blossoming out, and now he has Sue in his grip, too. It is he who kept us from courting and marrying in the first place!"

"Emily realized that Will was correct. She lowered her head in sorrow. "But, Sue and Father like each other, Will" was all she could say in return.

"Emily, you've a right to be a poet and publicly!" Will was a bit exasperated with his attempts to give Emily a wider meaning for her life than her father's domain. He feared her emotional dependence upon him, as he felt he could not adequately reciprocate or give her the time she wanted and the energy he no longer had to carry on their secret affair. He wanted to give her strength of purpose, should he need to stop seeing her. The war had broken his spirit for passionate intrigue. Yet, he'd missed his time with her, more than he'd missed his home and wife. "I love you dearly, Emily, but it's no use trying to give you the strength to defy your father."

"It's easy to speak of defiance, Will, but would you defy Mr. Williston, your father-in-law? I depend on father for everything from my daily bread to the clothes on my back, and he's good to me in all things except his desire that I keep my writing to my circle of friends and acquaintances. He simply does not want me to publish, and cause him embarrassment as a statesman. Surely you understand the difficult role of a statesman's daughter."

"Well, I am now a statesman, Emily, and I would never tell my daughter's not to fulfill their minds or have a career, or publish their writing. Why must you hide your poetry from the world?"

"But, even you, Master, have published many articles and essays *anonymously*. I'll give you some of my poems to publish anonymously. We'll see how they are received. Can you place: 'Some keep the Sabbath going to church/ I keep it staying at home/ With a Bobolink for a Chorister/ And an orchard for a dome…' I've perfected it with your suggestions.

"Very well, my greenhouse poet. I shall not press you more to blossom out of doors. I'll ask our mutual cousin from Amherst, Charles Sweester, to publish it in *The Roundtable*, his literary weekly in New York City….

"But, Father will find it especially scandalous!"

Will groaned. "*Anonymously!*" He conceded.

Emily was ever trying to appease him and reason with him. "Master, our love has blossomed *anonymously* out-of-doors under nature's glorious skies and trees! That is enough for me. Do you realize that this is the first time we've been together in a real bedroom, indoors alone, and safe from the small minded gossips of Amherst."

Clark laughed a little at the realization. "True, and I prefer our love out-of-doors." He was feeling more and more guilt at meeting clandestinely with Emily, especially now that he was actually with her in a bedroom belonging to her cousins. He feared that he was courting too much danger for his own good as a statesman.

"Emily read his mind. "Never fear, Master. Lou and Fanny are entirely discreet and they love me and would never do anything to hurt my happiness. You can trust them completely. They are free spirits who believe in love as natural." Emily kissed Will fervently.

"It's getting late, Emily. I must go and leave your cousins to their home."

"When will I see you again, Master?"

"I can't be sure, Daisy. I'm beleaguered with work. I'll post you a message."

"Please don't let it be long, Master."

"Goodbye for now, Daisy. Stay well and patient. And don't wilt in the Boston air." Will's heart was aching with his need to leave Emily and see her less. He was bent upon lobbying to have the new state agricultural college placed in Amherst instead of West Springfield, in order that he might help found a more liberal school of science and secure a teaching position that he could better enjoy than the one he held among some of the stuffed Puritan shirts of Amherst College. He wanted to earn his own way with less dependency upon his father-in-law. Samuel Bowles editorials in *The Springfield Republican* against his plan were quite convincing, and that worried him. With all the lobbying he was bound to do, his placement as secretary of the electoral college burdened him with additional duties.

"Remember, Emily, I'm as busy a man as your father, and be patient with me. Write your poems. Read your books. Enjoy Boston. See the Peabody Museum, but please don't expect too much time of me." Clark kissed Emily goodbye, but not without first warning her as he exited, nervously peering down the staircase to be sure no one saw him.

Emily quietly shut the door behind him and leaned against it wondering. Congressman Clark had left her with a feeling of foreboding that cast a pall upon their blissful afternoon.

July 1864: "The Whippowil That Sang"

Dear Vinnie, Do you remember the Whippowil
that sang on the Orchard Fence, and then drove to the South…?

Emily was so thrilled to have so many new and interesting books to read in the library of her Boston Little Cousins. Lou and Fanny spent their meager funds mostly on progressive books which were readily available in the Boston area. They were often out at play rehearsals for local theatre groups, leaving Emily alone in the evenings. Very occasionally, she was able to spend time alone with Clark if he wasn't too busy for her, though he told her he was frightened of someone seeing him enter or leave her boarding house.

Emily read so much to occupy her time that she did indeed strain her eyes, or perhaps, she strained them in an effort to have a real reason to visit Dr. Brown, and assuage her guilt over leaving Vinnie with the household work and care of their ailing mother.

Dear Vinnie

Many write that they do not write because that they have too much to say — I, that I have enough. Do you remember the Whippowil that sang one night on the Orchard fence, and then drove to the South, and we never heard of Him afterward?

He will go Home and I shall go Home, perhaps in the same Train.

It is a very sober thing not to have any Vinnie, and to keep my Summer in strange Towns—but I have found friends in the Wilderness. Fanny and Loo are solid Gold, Mrs. Bangs, the Landlady, and her Daughter very kind, and the Doctor enthusiastic about my getting well—I feel no gayness yet. I suppose I had been discouraged so long. You remember the Prisoner of Chillon did not know Liberty when it came, and asked to go back to Jail. Clara and Anna came to see me and brought beautiful flowers. I am glad of all the Roses you find, while your Primrose is gone. Emily wants to be well and with Vinnie—If any one alive wants to get well more, I would let Him first. I am glad it is me, not Vinnie. Long time might seem further to Her. Give my

love to Father and Mother, and Austin. Tell Margaret I remember
Her. Dear Vinnie, This is the longest letter I wrote since I was sick,
but who needed it most, if not my little Sister? I hope she is not very
tired, tonight. How I wish I could rest all those who are tired for me.
The doctor says I must tell you that I "cannot yet walk alone." Thank
you all for caring about me when I do no good. I will work with all
my might, always, as soon as I get well. Tell Mother to catch no more
cold, and lose her cough, so I cannot find it, when I get Home—Tell
Margaret I hope her finger is better—You must not miss Gray Pussy,
I'll try to fill her place—

Affectionately, your sister who misses you.

November 1864: Home To Amherst

To wait an Hour—is long—
If Love is just beyond—
To wait Eternity—is short—
If love reward the end—

Emily was despondent because she saw Clark so little despite having deceived her family in order to spend time in Cambridge and be near him. She waited patiently for his messages and visits, but they were few and far between. She missed her family and her home and Clark's term in the statehouse was coming to a close. He would soon return to Amherst to be with his wife and family for the winter. She begged to take the train with him so that they might talk on the ride home. He consented to meet her at the station and sit with her on the train. She wrote home, excited about the prospect of seeing Vinnie again, but warning Vinnie to meet her in Palmer, the station prior to Amherst.

Does Vinnie think of Emily?

Good news. Emily may not be as capable as she was, but will do all she can to help. I have been sick so long I've forgotten the sun. I hope my plants are all alive, for home would seem very strange without them, now that the world seems dead. I shall come home in two weeks. You will get me at Palmer, yourself. Let no one beside come as the Whipporwil may ride the same train as me. We want no gossip of our old romance of youthful days, before his marriage to The Queen, you'll understand. Say nothing of it to anyone, I beg you.

Love, Sister

Clark insisted he would only ride the train back to Amherst with Emily if she arrived at Palmer, as his family's carriage would meet him at Amherst Station—his wife seated with some of his younger children aboard and his handyman driving.

Emily acquiesced for his sake as well as her own. She didn't want to exit from the same train as Clark at Amherst Station. Someone had seen Emily in her veiled hat visiting Clark at The Revere Hotel.

In the hall on her way to his room, Emily was nearly recognized by a woman from Amherst who was visiting her husband in the state court. Despite the veil Emily wore to disguise herself, she heard a woman call after her as she scurried away. "Emily Dickinson of Amherst? Is that you?"

She had pretended not to hear the woman and had hurried into the stairwell, only to knock on Clark's hotel room door, after the woman had vanished from the hallway.

Regardless of gossip, Emily was somewhat relieved to be headed for a winter respite at home. She'd grown weary of waiting, always waiting, for Clark, always longing for his attentions, and she missed Carlo and Vinnie. The plan was for her to resume her time in Cambridge in April and stay again through spring and summer when Clark resumed service at the state house.

Though Vinnie was not privy to Emily's affair, she knew that Emily had once fancied Clark in her school days, and he had her. She simply assumed that they liked to talk and visit together on the train, and wanted to avoid gossip. It did not occur to Lavinia that Emily could possibly have been carrying on a passionate affair with Clark in Cambridge.

Winter 1864: "We Weigh the Time"

> *Before He comes*
> *We weigh the time,*
> *'Tis heavy, and 'tis light.*
> *When he departs,*
> *an emptiness*
> *Is the superior freight.*

Emily's writing helped to soothe the absence of Clark from her life. He was determined to spend the winter committed to his family and the prospects of the new state agricultural school for which he had spent much time lobbying the legislature. During their homeward train ride, he'd confessed to her:

"Emily, I am feeling a good measure of guilt, and I must devote my winter days in Amherst to my family as well as to the founding of the agricultural college of which your father is also on the board. We must be extremely careful not to jeopardize this important project. My children have had too little of their father while I was at war, and, now, while I have been in Cambridge serving at the state house. Daisy, we can't see each other this winter. In April when we return to Cambridge, we'll meet again. Be patient. I'll miss you, but you need to write your poems, tend your plants, and devote yourself to your family. Write many poems for me to see, but don't send them by Sweetser's man. I'll read them in spring!" Clark wanted to gently have Emily begin to get used to not seeing him.

Emily sensed that, and she began to write philosophical themes and avoid the longing for love that had often been her theme. Thomas Wentworth Higginson had written back to her about poems she'd sent him. Clark had placed four of her poems anonymously in *Drum Beat*, *The Round Table* and *The Springfield Republican*. They had received favorable reactions from some readers who had bothered to write in about them. Also, Higginson had written her with distinct praise for her talents. He'd also taken the time to present her with very specific editorial suggestions for rewriting her poems to make them more uniform in meter and conventional in punctuation. She returned his thoughts with enthusiasm, but kept her poems as she wanted them:

Dear Friend,

If fame belonged to me, I could not escape her; if she did not, the longest day would pass me on the chase, and the approbation of my dog would for-sake me then. My barefoot rank is better.

You think my gait "spasmodic." I am in danger, sir. You think me "un-controlled." I have no tribunal.

Would you have time to be the "friend" you should think I need? I have a little shape: it would not crowd your desk, nor make much racket as the mouse that dents your galleries. If I might bring you what I do—not so frequent to trouble you—and ask you if I told it clear, 'twould be control to me. The sailor cannot see the North, but knows the needle can. The "hand you stretch me in the dark" I put mine in, and turn away. I have no Saxon now:—

> *As if I asked a common alms,*
> *And in my wondering hand*
> *A stranger pressed a kingdom,*
> *And I, bewildered, stand;*
> *As if I asked the Orient*
> *Had it for me a morn,*
> *And it should lift its purple dikes*
> *And shatter me with dawn!*

But, will you be my preceptor, Mr. Higginson?

Mr. Higginson became a little fascinated with the author of such letters. He asked to see her photograph, wondering what sort of a woman she was. He was happily married and had no intention of pursuing any romance with his correspondence, but his curiosity was highly aroused. He was thinking of presenting some of Miss Dickinson's poems, anonymously, to The Women's Literary Society of Boston. Miss Dickinson responded.

Dear Mr. Higginson,

Could you believe me without? I had no portrait, now, but am small, like the wren; and my hair is bold, like the chestnut bur; and my eyes, like the sherry in the glass, that the guest leaves. Would this do just as well?

It often alarms father. He says death might occur, and he has moulds of all the rest, but has no mould of me; but I noticed the quick wore off those things, in a few days, and forestall the dishonor.

You will think no caprice of me. You said "Dark." I know the butterfly, and the lizard, and the orchis. Are not those your countrymen?

I am happy to be your scholar, and will deserve the kindness I cannot repay. If you truly consent, I recite now. Will you tell me my fault, frankly as to yourself, for I had rather wince than die. Men do not call the surgeon to commend the bone, but to set it, sir, and fracture within is more critical. And for this, preceptor, I shall bring you obedience, the blossom from my garden, and every gratitude I know.

Perhaps you smile at me. I could not stop for that. My business is circumference. An ignorance, not of customs, but if caught with the dawn, or the sunset see me, myself the only kangaroo among the beauty, sir, if you please, it afflicts me, and I thought that instruction would take it away. Because you have much business, beside the growth of me, you will appoint, yourself, how often I shall come, without your inconvenience.

And if at any time you regret you received me, or I prove a different fabric to that you supposed, you must banish me.

When I state myself, as the representative of the verse, it does not mean me, but a supposed person.

You are true about the "perfection." Today makes Yesterday mean.

You spoke of Pippa Passes. I never heard anybody speak of Pippa Passes before. You see my posture is benighted.

To thank you baffles me. Are you perfectly powerful? Had I a pleasure you had not, I could delight to bring it.

Your Scholar

Higginson replied again with ideas of how Emily should make her poems more acceptable in terms of even rhyme and meter and conventional publication. Again she enclosed a few poems for him to evaluate.

Dear Friend,

Are these more orderly? I thank you for the truth. I had no monarch in my life, and cannot rule myself; and when I try to organize, my little force explodes and leaves me bare and charred. I think you called me "wayward." Will you help me improve?

I suppose the pride that stops the breath, in the core of woods, is not of ourself. You say I confess the little mistake, and omit the large. Because I can see orthography; but the ignorance out of sight is my preceptor's charge.

Of "shunning men and women," they talk of hallowed things, aloud, and embarrass my dog. He and I don't object to them, if they'll exist their side. I think Carlo would please you. He is dumb, and brave. I think you would like the chestnut tree I met in my walk. It hit my notice suddenly, and I thought the skies were in blossom.

Then there's a noiseless noise in the orchard that I let persons hear.

You told me in one letter you could not come to see me "now," and I made no answer; not because I had none, but did not think myself the price that you should come so far.

I do not ask so large a pleasure, lest you might deny me.

You say, "Beyond your knowledge." You would not jest with me, because I believe you; but, preceptor, you cannot mean it?

All men say "What" to me, but I thought it a fashion.

When much in the woods, as a little girl, I was told that the snake would bite me, that I might pick a poisonous flower, or goblins kidnap me; but I went along and met no one but angels, who were far shyer of me than I could be of them, so I have n't that confidence in fraud which many exercise.

I shall observe your precept, though I don't understand it, always.

I marked a line in one verse, because I met it after I made it, and never consciously touch a paint mixed by another person. I do not let go it, because it is mine. Have you the portrait of Mrs. Browning?

Persons sent me three. If you had none, will you have mine?

Your Scholar

A month later, Mr. Higginson volunteered to lead the first regiment of freed slaves for the Union army. He traveled to the frontlines of the war where he was able to dash off a letter to Emily telling her his news from his encampment in South Carolina. Emily was amazed and saddened at his sudden departure from Boston so suddenly. She feared for Higginson's life and was afraid she'd lose their budding literary friendship. She wrote back to South Carolina with some immediacy and a heavy heart, but she attempted to keep her message as light and witty as possible, not to distress Higginson:

Dear Friend,

I did not deem that planetary forces annulled, but suffered an exchange of territory, or world. I should have liked to see you before you became improbable. War feels to me an oblique place. Should there be other summers, would you perhaps come?

I found you were gone, by accident, as I find systems are, or seasons of the year, and obtain no cause, but suppose it a treason of progress that dissolves as it goes. Carlo still remained, and I told him.

Best gains must have the losses' test,

To constitute them gains.

My shaggy ally assented.

Perhaps death gave me awe for friends, striking sharp and early, for I held them since in a brittle love, of more alarm than peace. I trust you may pass the limit of war; and though not reared to prayer, when service is had in church for our arms, I include yourself.... I was thinking to-day, as I noticed, that the "Supernatural" was only the Natural disclosed.

Not "Revelation" 'tis that waits,

But our unfurnished eyes.

But I fear I detain you. Should you, before this reaches you,

*experience immortality, who will inform me of the exchange? Could
you, with honor, avoid death, I entreat you, sir. It would bereave*

Your Gnome

Emily was sad that she would not now have Editor Thomas
Wentworth Higginson to help occupy her mind while Clark was
unavailable to her, so near, but far. She continued to occupy her days
with housework and writing now that she was home again from Boston
and completely without attention from her master. She cooked and
baked and cleaned as much as she could to alleviate the work she'd laid
at Lavinia's feet during her months in Boston. The hard work assuaged
her guilt, and she stayed up later than ever reading and straining her
eyes so that she could surely have an excuse to return to Boston and
Dr. Brown's care in the spring. Vinnie and her father worried that she
worked too hard with her compromised sight and should rest more.
She insisted she did not need excellent sight for housework, as much
as for sewing, reading, and writing. Her family was unaware of the late
night hours she kept reading by flickering lamplight. Nor did they in
the slightest imagine her heartache over Clark, or her real reason for
going to live with her Norcross cousins.

April 1865: "Lincoln Is Assassinated"

Emily returned to Boston in spring to follow State Representative William Smith Clark where he would again serve in the legislature, lobbying for an agricultural college to be established at Amherst. She found herself at the home of her Little Cousins in Cambridgeport on the April 14th, 1865, the day that President Abraham Lincoln was assassinated by John Wilkes Booth at Ford's Theatre in Washington, D.C. The news brought shocked crowds into the streets to read the extra newspapers issued hot from their presses.

Emily read the news aghast, standing in Harvard Square with Fanny and Lou, all of them feeling at a loss. The joy that the end of the war had brought was abruptly obliterated by the shroud cast over the country by Lincoln's assassination. Emily was aware that Clark would be occupied at the statehouse with the sorrows and worries of his Republican President's murder and probably have no time for her. She felt selfish in harboring the thought, but she'd come all the way to see him, and compromised the truth to do so, and she'd waited patiently all winter to renew their love. Lincoln's death had left her with a deep and dark foreboding. The world seemed to be spinning off its axis. She sat down to write home to Lavinia with the idea that thoughts of home as a final refuge would comfort her dark feeling of doom.

Dear Vinnie,

I write with deep sadness from Cambridge, knowing that Lincoln has been shot and the whole Union is plunged into despair. I know that all our friends in Amherst will be tolling the bells and mourning. He was a poet at heart and my heart bleeds for him. Frederick Douglass has recanted his criticism of Lincoln and said that whatever Lincoln's faults were, "in his heart of hearts he loathed and hated slavery." Douglass has admitted that Lincoln's firm wartime leadership saved the Union and freed the nation "from the great crime of slavery. Douglass said, "The hour and the man of our redemption had met in the person of Abraham Lincoln." We all gathered in Harvard Square to morn our murdered president at the tolling of the bells. His train will pass through Boston in its rounds of the people who loved him and who mourn him so profoundly. I feel a funeral in my brain, treading, treading...

Representative Clark from Amherst and all the assemblage of the State House mourn and now the legislative buildings are drapped in black and purple mourning flags. I'm sure that Austin is aghast. How suddenly the world has changed from spring to freezing winter in an instant. We were all so joyous just a few days ago when General Lee surrendered to General Grant at Appomattox, ending the bloodbath of the long, hideous war. Now, all are plunged into despair over Lincoln's death. We know that he hoped to rebuild the South and end animosity with generosity. Now that he is gone, hate will linger. Much of his cabinet wishes to pillage our Southern countrymen in revenge, as Father has no doubt told you. Sherman's march to the sea was cruel, indeed, and now Our Dear President, a man of poetry if ever a politician was one, is dead, and we are a Union distraught, bereft, and bereaved, examining our souls for reason, and our Union is drawn with hatred at the Mason Dixon line for longer eons to come.

Give Mother and Margaret a special kiss and tell them to be brave and remember that I always remember them, and, of course, you, Dearest Sister. Of course, you, Vinnie.

Your affectionate and saddened, Emily

Will did not come to Emily or contact her for many days. When finally he did it was with a curt message.

Dear Daisy,

As you might imagine, I have been deeply involved with Republican Party matters and have had no time to come to Harvard Square. I am staying nearer the State House at my hotel and working long hours. Stay well and be patient. I will contact you when I can.

Yours, Master

The note, cool and brusque, offered no Romantic solace to Emily's anxious spirit. It was the least loving and most abrupt note Emily had ever received from her beloved Will. Numbly, she lay on her bed, tears rolling from the corner of her eyes. Her patience was worn thinner than her oldest linen. "I can't wait to see him. I've been here for weeks and he hasn't called upon me once, or invited me to his room at the hotel."

She reasoned she could stand it no longer, and even his wrath would be better than his silence. She dressed in her best auburn gown, shawl and bonnet, wrapped some of the ginger cakes she had baked for Fran and Lou in a gingham napkin, and went out into the square to find a handsome cab. Pulling her veil down over her face and lowering her bonnet as far as she could over her eyes, she alighted from her hired carriage in front of the Revere Hotel. She walked briskly past the desk. It was late in the evening and she wanted to appear to be a guest returning home. Taking a back staircase, she found her way to Clark's room and tapped on the door three times, using their prearranged signal for prior meetings. A light came from under the crack below and through the glass of the closed transom at top.

"He must be in," she thought, her legs quaking in her boots, as she knew he would not want her to come uninvited. What if a colleague were visiting? She would use the excuse that she was in the neighborhood and dropping some of the gingerbread she knew her neighbor from Amherst, Representative Clark, had liked so at the Hampshire County Fair when he was judge of the baking contest there, and leave. She had her little speech prepared in case a stranger be present.

After a pause, Clark answered the door. He was disheveled and pale and obviously alone as she could see beyond him into the lamp lit room where papers were piled on a writing table. His face was not welcoming. "What are you doing here at this hour?" He was aghast.

She tried to be nonchalant. "I was in the neighborhood at the library, and brought you some ginger cakes. Are you alone. Sir? May I come in?"

"Oh, of course, but I was reading over some important legislation and not expecting anyone. My room and I are quite unkempt." Clark quickly motioned her in, then put his head out of the door to look up and down the hall and assure himself that no one saw or heard them.

"Oh, Will, the unkempt quality of your room means nothing to me. What matters to me is that I've been here for nearly two months and not seen you."

"Has it been that long?"

"An eternity to me. I've waited all winter, patiently, for our time together to dawn this spring. Spring was all I've dreamed of, Master. You, spring, and Boston again! Can you forgive me? Can I beg you for a little time. "

"Speak very softly, please."

"I am speaking softly. I always speak softly." Emily felt hushed.

"It's just that the walls of this hotel seem paper thin and many statesmen stay here now since Lincoln was shot." Will whispered. "We've all been working very hard. The party is in disarray. We're all behind in considering important pieces of legislation. None of us has any time for recreation."

"Oh, Master." Emily came closer and whispered softly engaging his eyes. "I hoped I was more than recreation to you. I hoped you'd have shared solace with me when our President was shot. I felt so alone and in despair without you. I was deeply concerned for your spirit, too. I know you admired him as I did, as a good soul, an honest soul, a moderate man committed to human decency who always loathed slavery. A poetic spirit who brought us through the war and kept the Union together." Emily was struck with the fact that Will had not taken her in his arms once he'd closed the door, as he'd always done when she'd visited upon his summoning." She tried to put her arms around him, but he moved away, making her feel rejected and anxious.

"Please have a seat," he said. I make a terrible host tonight. I've had no time to comfort my own spirit, let alone anyone else's. The state house is abuzz with discussion of various suspected plots of Lincoln's assassination. There are several theories about the assassins, and no one is sure that Booth acted alone. We have all been devouring the newspapers and listening to the telegraph and talking of what will become of the Union and what we must do. What must be investigated, prosecuted, and so forth. I'm afraid that all my lobbying for the State Agricultural College at Amherst will be lost in mourning and forgotten. Lincoln's death has an effect at every level. We must all re-examine our souls. Life is short and death is eminent at any moment for all of us. The war has taught me that lesson, and now the assassination of my president has secured that lesson deep within my spirit."

Will came to Emily where he motioned for her to sit and sat beside her, talking softly in an exhausted voice. "Understand, Emily. I have been feeling guilt about our secret relations, more than I've ever told you or felt before. That is why I've not tried to see you. Though being so busy has also been a problem. I cannot deceive your father and brother, and my family, my wife, my children, my father-in-law, any longer. I was hoping you might forget me…"

"Forget you? I'd as soon forget my right arm. Master, how could I ever…"

"The truth is my mother-in-law knows you're in Boston, Emily. She asked Sam Williston to ask me if I'd happened to see Miss Emily Dickinson in Harvard Square to say hello. She said she understands you are consulting an eye doctor here, and wonders if you would recommend him to her, because her eyes are bothering her, too. I think it is a cloaked warning from her, as she's never liked me and always been suspicious of my motives for marrying Harriet. Harriet has confessed that her mother suspected me as a 'gold digger' before we married. I fear she may be sending spies about Boston to check on me. It is not a good thing for you to come to my hotel so late in the evening alone and unescorted."

"But, it is late for me to go home now, Master, and you had not minded in past. How was I to know your feelings? Can't I stay the night and leave very early by the back stairs?"

"I suppose you will have to now. I don't dare go down to the lobby to summon you a carriage at this hour. We'll be easily observed and if the lobby is quite deserted with a stray congressman here and there, we'll stand out all the more."

"I can go by myself, Master, if you want me to." Emily looked down, feeling ashamed and reprimanded.

"No, no, it is too dangerous for a woman like you at this hour out in the streets. You'll have to stay." To Emily's dismay, his face was grim and unhappy about the prospect. He stood, went to the door and peeked up and down the hall, and then went to the window and nervously looked out at the street, pulling the drapes shut.

"I'm sorry, Master. I needed so to see you and know you're well." Emily felt foolish. She'd made a mistake in coming to him. He was not the man who had promised to resume their love when last she saw him in Harvard Square at their Little Cousins. "I'm very sorry. Daisy did not mean to trouble you. She only wanted to see you more than anything in the world. Emily lifted her veil, took off her bonnet and put it on a table. Then she went to Clark and put her arms around his neck and looked deeply into his eyes. She kissed him warmly on the lips. "Will, I've longed so for you."

Clark drew away from her slowly. Taking her hands from his neck, he let them drop from his as he moved away from her. "Emily, I must resist temptation. It's not fair to you or my family. I am a sinner who must repent."

Her heart sank into her shoes. She felt distraught standing there with her rejected hands clasped in front of her, her head lowered in the shame of rejection. "Master, please…" was all she could whisper. "My spirit is breaking."

"No, Emily. You must be strong and courageous for your family's sake, as I must be. We must repent. You must return to Amherst as soon as possible. I will arrange for my friend, The Reverend Wadsworth, to come to you to hear your confession and offer repentance. I have secretly converted to the Presbyterian faith. Sam Williston would be appalled if he knew. I will still attend our Congregational Church at home in the village, but while here in Boston, I've been attending a Presbyterian meetinghouse recommended by Wadsworth. I go incognito.

Wadsworth has told me that we can only be redeemed of our sins if we truly repent them. I'm sure it's so. We must repent, Emily. The world is changing. Lincoln is dead. The war is ended. There is much work to be done to shore up this Union. There is so much legislation to be enacted, so many bills to be pondered and read, so many plans to be made for the Massachusetts Agricultural College, so many proposals to be put forth, so much burden upon me, I am exhausted with it. I cannot feel carefree. I can no longer lead a double life. I must be sincere and honest with myself, my wife, my children, my growing daughters. My sons are coming into their manhood. I must set an example. Emily, I must set you free of me. For your own well being."

Emily appeased her hands with smoothing her skirt as she stood. "And is there no tiny bit of room for Daisy anywhere in the vessel of your life, Master?" Emily words came out choked through tears. Is this the last I shall see of you?"

Clark came to her. "Emily, sit down, and listen carefully, please. I want to try to be honest at last." Emily submitted to the chair to which he led her. He felt cruel. He felt confused with his feelings for her as he still held great affection for his little poet, so full of sensitive observation—so small and vulnerable to him, her big doe eyes welling with abject sorrow.

"Emily, Dear Sweet Emily, Emily. My Little Daisy..." He knelt before her and took her small hands with their long delicate, but hard-working fingers, in his. He knew she labored at home, strenuously weeding in her garden; potting in her conservatory; churning butter; baking and billowing at the oven; tending her ill mother. He knew she did not have great joy in her life and he felt a terrible guilt. "I've been so selfish to take advantage of you, a fine lady, full of spirit and sensitive of intelligence. It's been so wrong of me to want you for myself and want my life with the Williston family, too. I should have eloped with you to the West and risked a new and honest life with you, My Daisy. I should have taken you to a new horizon to bloom. Instead, I've been a Janus-faced coward, living in two worlds, trying to have too much for myself, keeping you for me, keeping you waiting, when I should have freed you to find another long before this. I disgust myself with selfishness. I confess how wrong I've been and I need to set you free to bloom unto yourself without the chains of me holding you from new horizons."

"No, Master. I've wanted no other. My spirit was lonely before you took me into your life. You taught me love when I was still a girl, and I want only your love and no other's for all time. And, I can wait a long time, Master, until my hair is silver and you walk with a cane. I can wait until eternity for you. I can wait until *sempiternity* for you! Please, Will, don't banish me. I can't live banished from your face, from the hope of ever seeing you alone again. I will be more patient. I promise." Emily looked down into Will's eyes as he knelt before her with their hands entwined in her lap. "Just leave me with a little hope that we will be together again."

Will bent and kissed Emily's hands where he saw his grandmother's gold ring still on her finger. He felt a sexual stirring for her, but restrained himself from giving her hope that could not come to fruition. Yet, there was something he felt he could try to give her. "Little Daisy, the poems of yours I sent to *The Springfield Republican, The Boston Post, Drum Beat* and *The Roundtable*, have all received good response. Many wrote to ask who is this anonymous poet who writes so vividly and wisely. You are a fine poet, Emily, and you need to go on with your writing. You are an American original, the poet Reverend Park and Professor Hitchcock predicted would be born of our valley's glories.

"What can poetry mean to me *without* you, Master. I write it for *you*, for *your* eyes, for *your* response, for *your* thought exchanged with mine." Emily could not stop weeping, though she was trying hard to hold her tears in. "I can never care for the commerce of my soul."

"Nonsense, Emily. You must keep writing to Higginson as you told me you have. Didn't you say he was going to reintroduce you to Helen Hunt Jackson, your old school chum at Amherst Academy. She's doing well with her literary ventures. She can be a great encouragement to you. I know she'll recognize your talents."

"Higginson said he would send her some of my poems, but he went off to the war, and I haven't heard from him lately, Master."

"I know he's well and will be returning. His regiment of blacks survived for the most part. They did well for themselves. I read it in a dispatch that will soon be in the news."

"I'm glad of that." Emily looked up at Will but her face revealed only abject sadness.

"You must understand Emily. Please understand and forgive me. I can't bear hurting you." Will's eyes watered and he kissed Emily's hands again. "I'm beside myself with guilt."

She bent down and kissed him on the lips. "Our love needs no redemption, Master. It was real and natural and good and it gave us Nature's pleasure. Our love is its own rescue. Others kept us from marriage, not ourselves. We married under the sky and before our creator. Our love was of the earth and natural. You said so."

"Yes, Emily, it was good and true in feeling, and it was mainly your father that kept us from it, but I don't want to pain you by reminding you of that yet again. Emily, our love must become all of the spirit now. We must give up the bodily element of it and keep only the memory and joy of it in our hearts. We shall always have what we learned from each other in our minds."

Emily realized that it would likely be the last time she would see her Master intimately and alone, and the thought chilled her. She began to shake with despair. "All I know is how much I love and want you and wish to be with you in body and spirit, Master."

"Will, held her hands and looked up into her distraught face from where he knelt in supplication before her. He felt the anxiety in her body. It frightened him. He wanted to comfort her. He stood and lifted her in his arms and carried her to the bed and lay beside her."

"Emily, Emily, My Poor Little Daisy. I have ruined your life."

"No Master, you have shown me great love. You have shown me how big my heart can grow and how full the well of it can grow. You've taught me the world that I could not see alone. My river runs to thee." Emily pulled Will's face to hers and kissed him again and this time his lips melted to hers as they used to. "I've needed you so. I've longed so to be with you." She whispered breathlessly through her grief. He could not resist her hands on his chest and sliding down to his groin. He could not hold back from her warm kiss and supplication. "Please, Master, I've waited all winter to see you again. Let me remember this night and hold it in my mind's eye for eternity. Our bodies united against the infinity of time." Emily spoke softly in Will's ear and he gave in. He made love to her, tenderly and sadly, and he wept when he reached his orgasm, and so did she. Then he lay beside her spent, sad, and remorseful, though anxiety was drained from him. Emily lay in her Master's arms, calmed, yet grieving that she would not be able to make love with him again. Their hands were clasped as they slept through the night, her head on his chest.

When she woke at dawn, Will was already dressing. "Come, Dear One, we must part. Our revels are ended and dawn is here. I must summon you a carriage and send you safely back to your Little Cousins. Try to forgive me. You must be strong now, Little Daisy, and promise me you will not wilt in waiting. I want to end your longing, your waiting, your sorrow over me. You will forget me with time. Yet, we will have our lovely memory for as long as we live."

Emily could no longer argue. She realized that Will was adamant and in pain, too. "I'll be ready in a few minutes," she said softly. Picking up her gown, stockings, and shoes, she hurried into a small adjoining dressing room, splashed water into the pitcher at the nightstand, washed her face and hands and dressed quickly. She had never needed to wear a corset. Her figure was slim and petite and her waist still as small as when she was a girl and had first met Master Clark as Austin's teacher at Williston Academy. She would forever have the size of a child and Will had found her small size enhancing of his manhood.

When she emerged having made herself as presentable as possible, Will brought her bonnet and veil to her and helped her don it. He pulled the veil over her face, after kissing her gently on the forehead and eyes. "There you are. You look fine as any lady." He wanted to be kind and encouraging. He truly loved her.

"I brought you ginger cakes." She whispered leaving her little gingham wrapped bundle of cakes on his table.

"You brought me love and worlds of delight. You were my aphrodisiac for the glories of our valley. You brought me spirit and inspiration, and you have brought me the best ginger cakes in Hampton County and in all of Boston." Will tried to smile. "Emily, Emily, I will always love you, My Little Daisy," he gasped. He stood before her holding her hands in his. "You will always be in my prayers. This must be our last conjugal union. You're still youthful and look well. Your skin is clear, your hair richly auburn. Thirty-five is not so old. You can still find an honest man to make you an honest woman. Forget me. I'm a scoundrel not good enough to kiss the hem of your skirt. Promise me you'll take good care of yourself, Daisy! Promise me you'll keep on with writing your poetry. Promise me you'll talk with Wadsworth when he visits and write again to Higginson. I think you have done well to write to them and make them your spiritual and poetic guides. Wadsworth is a good and decent reverend and a fine sermonizer. Go for a carriage ride with him so you can talk in privacy when he visits. I've sent him an honorarium for his church and asked him to come to you when he can. Let him talk of redemption. True repentance will save our souls. We will meet again, pure and white, in eternity."

"Yes, Master, pure and white in eternity." Emily held back her tears and smiled bravely for her beloved Will."

"Forget me, Emily Elizabeth Dickinson. Forget me, except as a specter of your past, but remember all we have taught each other, My Dearest Student. Keep tending your plants and let them bring joy and beauty for your own sake. Remember me kindly in your prayers when you can, and remember that I'll always love you from afar and respect your intelligent sensibility, your poetry, the snow of your spirit. Go with God and be well, My Little Daisy. Reverend Wadsworth will come to you to help you redeem your soul. He will bring good counsel from the Presbyteries. We are not predestined for Heaven or Hell, as our Calvinist fathers believed, but must earn our way in paradise, here on this bountiful earth, with true repentance."

Will lifted Emily's veil again, and again kissed her on the forehead and on each of her eyes in the sign of the cross. He held her to him for the last time. His eyes were welling. "I will go ahead to the lobby. You take the back stairs. I'll call a carriage to the side door of the hotel and give him the fare to Harvard Square and ask him to wait for a lady in reddish-brown dress and veiled bonnet. Get off in the square, but do not go to your cousins' door until he has departed. Take this." Will put money into Emily's hand. "The driver will expect this promised gratuity for waiting. You'll come out the side door veiled and climb into the carriage. Keep your face averted and go home safely. I'll watch from the lobby, reading behind a newspaper, to see that you go off safely." I will send a messenger to your door for your message that you are safely home later this morning. Be well, and go with God, Daisy."

Emily obeyed. "Goodbye, Master," was all she was able to emit as the door closed behind him. She was too exhausted to say more or argue otherwise. She knew that Fanny and Lou would be worried if they didn't find her in her bed when they awoke for breakfast. She waited a few minutes, peeked out the door to be sure the hall was empty, then followed Clark's instructions.

The livery drove her through the fog of early dawn at a steady pace. She sat as still as stone, her spirit numb in the early morning dank, her body jostled by the carriage wheels over the cobble stones of the city. Boston was not yet quite awake and neither was Emily. In her mind, the words of one of her poems played like a litany of loss.

> *So huge, so hopeless to conceive*
> *As these that twice befel.*
> *Parting is all we know of heaven,*
> *And all we need of hell.*

She felt half alive in a nightmare. Only the milkman's carriage crossed her path as her livery horses clip-clopped into Harvard Square.

January 1866: "Love Is Anterior To Life"

Emily had left Carlo alone a great deal in order to go to Boston. She'd stayed with Lou and Fanny until fall in order to heal her spirit and continue seeing Dr. Brown as was arranged. Her eyes now truly suffered strain. She had hoped that another message would come from Will asking her to meet with him, but it didn't come. She had not expected it would. She knew he meant what he said. She was weary of waiting and of begging and tried to enjoy the company of her cousins and their books, the sights of Boston and Cambridge, without thoughts of Will. Every time Will came into her mind, she forced herself to think of something else. Still, he came into her mind every few hours. The depression she felt in knowing she would not feel his warm body near hers, or share her intimate thoughts with him, or he with her again, caused her body to shiver with despair. She sat at the window of the little room where she stayed with her cousins and wrote:

> *Heart! We shall forget him!*
> *You and I, to-night!*
> *You may forget the warmth he gave,*
> *I will forget the light!*
>
> *When you have done, pray tell me*
> *That I my thoughts may dim;*
> *Haste! Lest while you're lagging,*
> *I may remember him!*

It was a poem she'd written years earlier after Will had married Harriet and she'd not heard from him for some time. She revived it in her own memory to give herself strength and to remember that Will Clark, her beloved Master, was married to another. She felt the same numbness she had felt then, the same despair, the same coldness at the center of her being. She considered suicide, but realized it would be a selfish act that would hurt Vinnie, Ausitn, and her father and mother, as well as Carlo, terribly. "You've no right to despair, Emily Dickinson, 'You've plenty of love of family to live for. Lou and Fanny would be devastated if you killed yourself. Will would feel unending remorse. You must be strong and find purpose beyond him."

Weeks passed in reading, walking through the city, and supping with her cousins at their boarding house. She tended to her eye doctor appointments and cooked for her Little Cousins. She helped them tidy the flat they rented. She took walks with them every evening in the square, and went to Transcendental lectures, half-hoping to bump into Will who might be visiting his brother-in-law, Lyman Williston. But, it seems he never came to Harvard Square. She thumbed through magazines. She walked, to and fro, aimlessly taking in the sites of the city, sometimes imagining she saw Will approaching, but it was never him. She sighed and walked, and walked and grieved, until the summer passed and it was time to venture home again.

This time she rode all the way to Amherst Station alone and alighted from the train to be met by Lavinia with Tom driving the family carriage and Carlo in the back wagging his tail in delight at seeing her. Carlo's greeting helped her survive her arrival. Tom let him loose in the barnyard upon return, as he was beside himself prancing with joy at the sight and smell of Emily. Lavinia was solicitous of Emily as they entered the back door. "You look tired, Emmy. Maggie will give you dinner." Lavinia's solicitations made Emily remorseful.

Maggie at the kitchen door greeted her warmly into the house. When at last they were alone and Lavinia, after having poured milk into her many cat's saucers, hurried upstairs to spoon Mother's dinner into her, Emily fell into Maggie's arms and wept softly. "It is over and done Maggie. My life is shattered. I shall never see him again."

"There now, Miss Emily. Yer life is yer own dear life. Isn't it for the best? Seein' how's his situation won't be changin', and yer still young lookin' and should be free ta meet another man… His bein' with ya', keeps ya' from lookin' about …"

"That's what he said, Maggie. He wants me to be free to find another, but I won't. I'll don my white housedress and never again leave my father's properties. I want no other. I shall belong to him forever." Emily wept having held in her tears for months to comfort her cousins.

There now, Miss Emily. There now! Yer conservatory has been missin' ya', surely. Yer orchids need ya' fully. Your Mother is waitin' fer ya' upstairs. And, yer Carlo is so happy ta see ya, he's about waggin' his tail off." Maggie went to the kitchen door to let Carlo come in. She heard him whimpering for his mistress at the door. "Carlo missed ya terribly n' brooded about the barnyard like a sick puppy while ya was gone, Miss Em."

Emily went to old Carlo and took his big head in her little hands and kissed him on his black, furry crown. She scratched him behind his ears and he seemed happy again. He whimpered with joy as dog's sometimes do making a slight, high-pitched, suppliant, noise in the back of his big throat. "Oh Carlo, my loyal Dear Carlo, we'll go walking in the meadow, you and I. I'll take you running in the orchard again, Dear Carlo. You'll have the best of the fallen apples this autumn." Emily sank to the floor and clung to Carlo's neck, petting him.

But, Emily's relief in seeing her loyal best friend was to be short lived. That January old Carlo succumbed to illness and lay before the hearth, hardly breathing or raising his head. Emily blamed herself for having left him alone too long to stay for so many months in Boston.

"Now, Miss Emily. Don't be blamin' yerself. He's a big tired, old doggy, that one. Sixteen makes him a hundred in human years. They can't live ferever n'ever. Ya know that. A dog lives twelve years at best. He's a good dog, but he's older than them kind can git! Don't be blamin' yerself. That dog's had hisself a very good life with ye lovin' him as ye did; better than some Irish children I be knowin', so don't be blamin' yerself, Missy Dearie." Maggie had found that comforting Emily had become a major part of her chores as Emily worried over Carlo.

One morning in late January, Emily came down to make the household breakfast porridge, and put the tea kettle on for the morning's meal as she had done all of her adult life at the homestead, only to find that Carlo lay still and lifeless on his bed of old blankets beside his bowl of water near the hearth. He had no longer been able to climb the stairs to her room. His eyes would not open and he did not rise to greet her as he had so often done. She knelt beside him. The warmth was gone from him. She laid her body over his and cried silently. She had expected it. There was nothing to be done. The veterinarian had said when her father had consented to calling him.

"I'm afraid his old heart is slowing down. It hardly pumps. Just let him lie here by the warmth of the hearth until he expires, Miss Dickinson. He's old and weary and it is time for him to rest in peace." The doctor had snapped his bag shut and left.

Emily sat leaning across Carlo's still and furry form for a long time, until Lavinia and Maggie made her go up to her room and lie down.

"Come Emmy. Tom will dig him a good grave in the orchard where he loved the fallen apples so. He'll rest peacefully in his favorite place. He had a good, long life. You loved him well. Come! Come upstairs and lie down. Maggie's bringing your tea and toast. Come, Emmy, please." As Lavinia had often done through the years, she half carried her older, more frail, and sensitive sister up the stairs to her room. Emily lay in her bed all the rest of the day mourning the passing of her feline friend and loyal companion of the woods and meadows. Carlo had given her security and freedom to explore the wonders of her beautiful valley, its hills and dales, autumn woods, brooks, and spring meadows. He'd facilitated her union with Clark and their meetings. Now he, too, was gone from her. Another companion in nature lost. When she finally rose from her bed, she took her pen in hand at her writing table and wrote.

> *Love is anterior to life,*
> *Posterior to death,*
> *Initial of creation, and*
> *The exponent of breath*

For the remainder of the winter, Emily moped about the house. She did her chores with regularity and tended her sick mother's bed dutifully, and baked breads and cakes for her father's dinners, and helped Maggie dry the dishes—but much of her spirit had gone out of her. Late at her writing table, she continued to compose occasional poems, but not at the pace she had when she'd sent them to Clark away in the war. Resigned to her fate, she wrote one afternoon at her dining room writing table:

There's a certain slant of light,
On winter afternoons,
That oppresses, like the weight
Of cathedral tunes.

Heavenly hurt it gives us ;
We can find no scar,
But internal difference,
Where the meanings are.

None may teach it anything
'T is the seal despair,—
An imperial affliction
Sent us of the air—

When it comes, the landscape listens,
Shadows hold their breath;
When it goes, 'tis like the distance
On the look of death.

Spring 1867: "I Shall Not Live In Vain"

One lovely May morning, Emily wrapped her blue shawl around the shoulders of her white, pique, housedress and went downstairs. Spring was calling her from the window. She could smell the West wind returned to a zephyr over the meadow grasses, stirring up scents from the sodden earth. She exited the back door of the homestead, and walked across the garden to the orchard where Tom had dug a grave in the icy earth for Carlo late in January. The snow had thawed from the earth now. A white washed, wooden-cross stood at the head of the mound Tom had made of stones over Carlo's grave when early spring thawed the earth. Birds were singing over Emily's head.

Titmice and chickadees sang their love calls as they came and went with blue jays qweedling their mating song, nuthatches honking their little nasal sounds, and goldfinches cheerily twittering their lyrical tune. They pecked at the sticky green buds and the dry seeds of budding apple blossoms that fell lightly around her and caught in her auburn hair. Still devoid of grey, it had grown long again and was looped over her ears and tied in a neat bun at the back of her neck, a style she'd learned long ago from pictures of Elizabeth Barrett Browning. Her cheeks were rosy again from walks in the meadow. Suddenly, she found a baby robin lying in the grass at her feet near Carlo's grave and heard its mother twittering her warning call in the tree above.

Emily looked up through the branches to where she could see the robin's nest nestled and the mother hopping from branch to branch in helpless alarm. The pinkish white blossoms made branches of lace against the clear, azure sky. Emily spied the orchard ladder leaning on a tree nearby where Tom had left it. She took the wooden ladder and leaned it against the tree where the robin's nest was hidden above. She gently picked up the baby bird, stroked its newly feathered, tiny head with one gentle finger and held its beak to her ear. It peeped softly. She gently covered its eyes with her hand to quiet it, nestled it in the breast of a fallen leaf, and put it in the pocket of her dress where the stub of a pencil and a small sheet of paper were always stashed at bottom. Then she climbed the ladder slowly and gently taking the baby robin from her pocket, she placed it carefully back into its nest next to its peeping siblings. She quickly descended as the mother alighted near her nest carrying a worm for her children. Emily smiled happily at the sight of her.

She sat on the large rock that Tom had placed at the foot of Carlo's grave, so that she could come and visit her old friend's spirit and pray. She breathed deeply of the thawed earth and surveyed the beauty of the orchard in spring. A light breeze full of the smell of apple blossoms and fresh green grass filled her with intoxication.

> *Let me not thirst with this Hock at my Lip,*
> *Nor beg, with Domains in my Pocket—*

She thought. I'm too old to marry, and father and Clark were right. Childbirth is dangerous for a woman small as myself—when heartier women, and so many, too, die every day to bring life forth. I'll live as a spinster married forever to My Master. I can no longer stand the perturbations of trying to love or be loved as a woman. My poetry did not win him, and that was really all I had to give him. To be loved as a sister and a daughter will be enough.

Then Emily sighed deeply with her face to the morning sun. She took the stub of pencil and a ginger can label from her pocket. She thought of the Dickinson family condolence message she had recently sent to a neighbor of her parish, with flowers from her conservatory, to comfort the loss of a loved one. Spring made poetry well up in her as it had often done. On the back of the ground ginger can label, she wrote:

> *If I can stop one heart from breaking*
> *I shall not live in vain;*
> *If I can ease one life the aching*
> *Or cool one pain*
> *Or help one fainting robin*
> *Unto his nest again,*
> *I shall not live in vain.*

May 19, 1886: "In My Own Grave I Breathe"

I Died for Beauty....
So give me back to death,
The death I never feared
Except that it deprived of thee;
And now by life deprived
In my own grave I breathe....

Laid out in the finest wooden coffin available in Amherst, and dressed in white, the corpse of a diminutive woman awaited her mourners. Tears wet Lavinia's cheeks and salt stuck in her lashes. She was grieving, as she daydreamed of a night in the distant past when she and her sister, Emily, were considered among the most eligible *belles* of Amherst. She slouched exhausted in her rocking chair, her cat in her lap. Her head ached from crying. She stood up and crossed the darkly draped library to her sister's coffin. A few mourners were soon to attend the Victorian homestead on Main Street—the largest brick house in the village of about 4,000 inhabitants. They were coming to pay their respects to the mythical woman enshrouded there.

Lavinia, still crying, bent over the body and slid a mysterious gold ring from the finger of her sister's corpse. She remembered that Emily had worn the gold band for nearly thirty years, but would never tell anyone where she acquired it or why she wore it. Lavinia looked inside the band for any clue to its meaning. She could barely read, for the first time, an inscription she found inside. Taking the worn gold ring to the window and drawing aside the Victorian drapery, she was able to discern the name "Philip" engraved inside. She clutched the ring to her heart and wept, wondering what it might mean.

"Why *Philip?*" she puzzled, then quickly tucked the ring into her bodice for safekeeping—just as her sister-in-law Susan, bearing funeral flowers, entered the room.

Lavinia knew her brother's wife was a proper lady and did not approve of some of her own or Emily's behavior. On one late evening, Susan had caught the unmarried Emily in the arms of a man in the parlor and complained to Mrs. Todd about it. Vinnie knew that Susan thought Emily and herself of loose morals. In their family home next door to Susan's, she and Emily had, of late, harbored trysts between Susan's husband—their older brother Austin Dickinson—and his pretty, young mistress, Mrs. Todd. For allowing this unspeakable trespass upon her marriage to Austin, Susan had been furious with her sisters-in-law, Emily and Lavinia.

Dry-eyed and grieving inwardly, Susan, dressed in her usual black mourning clothes, placed a fresh nosegay of violets and *cypridium* at the throat of the small, frail corpse. "These are for faithfulness." Susan whispered. She, herself, with the help of a neighbor, had prepared the body of her sister-in-law for viewing and burial. She'd lined the coffin, painted white, with white flannel, washed and wrapped Emily in a white woolen shroud, combed out Emily's thick auburn hair, and arranged it around her face, pale, and smooth as porcelain. She hadn't needed to close Emily's eyes, as they had been at rest when Emily died. A faint beatific smile of peace seemed to mark her visage giving it a spiritual aura. Susan had the servants cut pine boughs for the coffin's bier. The aroma of fresh pine permeated the room to cover the smell of death.

"Here Vinnie," Susan whispered, "You can give her these." She handed Vinnie two pale yellow heliotropes quickly fetched from Emily's plant conservatory just off the library.

Vinnie tucked them in Emily's hands folded over her lap: "Take these to Judge Otis Lord! Dear Emily!" she whimpered. Vinnie's eyes welled again, remembering how Emily and Otis hoped to marry in their later years, after the judge, an old family friend of their father's at the State House in Boston, was widowed. "If only Judge Lord hadn't died, Sue! He would have protected Emmy and me in our old age and given Em a new reason to live. She always wanted to care for someone. After mother died, and father was gone, there was no one who needed her care so much. I was always the healthier one." She turned to Sue whose face was dismal with despair. "It would have ended all the nasty gossip about Em, if she'd been at last a respectable wife to Judge Lord."

"Lord's envious niece besmirched Emily, calling her "a man-crazy hussy." I attempted to defend her, but now, I shall never have my complete peace with her except in heaven." Sue whispered as her voice caught in her throat with sorrow.

"Don't despair, Sue! Emily always loved you to the end, even though you disagreed about religious matters." Vinnie, feeling guilty, tried to cheer Susan. They had been sisters-in-law for so long: "Look, Sue, there are butterflies in the garden; bees are buzzing around Em's May flowers; birds are singing, just as she would have wanted. It's as if they've come to serenade her to Eden." Vinnie could not stop sniffling into her handkerchief. She'd soaked more than a dozen. "Emily told me herself: 'No one except Shakespeare ever taught me more about people than Susie!' And, you know how she adored her Shakespeare."

"Yes, Vinnie, she wrote that to me once, I recall." Sue wanted to comfort even though she harbored disappointment in Lavinia. "It is a lovely spring day just as Emily would have wanted. She was so intimate and passionate, in her love of nature, she seemed herself a part of the springtime sky—the summer day and bird call. May her spirit rest in peace. With the violets and lilies. Shrouded all in white, she looks like a relic of a saintly nun in the Romantic paintings of Austin's art books, Doesn't she, Vinnie? Her sensitive spirit shrank from the world."

"Yes, she was too sensitive for this world, Sue." Vinnie thought of all the men she and her sister had adored, or lost, throughout their lives, and how they'd whispered in their rooms upstairs to each other of their heart's passions and unrequited loves. Sue would not have approved of such amorous thoughts and desires. "Emmy was, oh, so spirited when young! Remember, Susie? How she loved to dance when Father and Mother were gone away? Her *Poetry in Motion*, she called it. How she'd make us laugh with her witty antics? Her Devilish composition on the piano was thrilling? Her clever lyrics?" Escaping into the past, Vinnie smiled.

Sue's mind flashed back to Emily in her youthful twenties playing the piano at The Evergreens, composing satiric songs in Sue's and Austin's elegant drawing room full of eminent guests, Samuel Bowles, Maria Whitney, William Smith Clark, Catherine Scott Turner, even Ralph Waldo Emerson once. She imagined Emily laughing, dressed in silk brocade, a satin ribbon at her throat, a white lace collar. Her delicate fingers tripped over the piano keys as she tossed her curly auburn hair about. Her foot tapped a rhythm. An assemblage of intellectual men and women were laughing and smiling in the light of the gas lamps in Susan's parlor. Delicate refreshments, *petits fours*, cream cakes, cinnamon custards arrayed the tables with sparkling glasses of port, sherry, berry wine, and in winter, mulled hard cider and rum eggnog.

Susan imagined the glee on the faces of her guests, the amusement on her own—her parlor soiree so full of life and joy and clever conversation. The assemblage was discussing the Italian *Risorgimento* or debating German pantheism; or the Kansas-Nebraska Act; Elizabeth Barrett Browning's *Aurora Leigh* and Robert Browning's latest books, and the falling out of the two famous lovers over the ideals of feminism; Nathaniel Hawthorne's latest book; Ralph Waldo Emerson's newest talk on Transcendentalism for the Lyceum; or Margaret Fuller's ideas of female liberation along with Bronson Alcott's lectures on liberal education. Sue's thought went to her husband, Austin, young and handsome, seated beside her before the sparkling fireplace when Sue was a happy hostess and a young bride long ago.

For momentary relief, both Lavinia and Susan escaped into the past with their separate memories of the once lively sister who now lay cold in her casket.

Finally, Susan broke the silence by softly quoting her own obituary for Emily that she'd begun to compose in her head. Needing to quell her grief with useful activity, she imagined how her words would look to Massachusetts's society. After all, they were Dickinsons, public aristocrats of their valley, and must uphold appearance and propriety. Sue sincerely wanted to redeem her sister-in-law's image for public consumption.

"'Emily Dickinson's wit was a Damascus blade gleaming and glancing in the sun. Her swift poetics like the long glistening note of a bird one hears in the woods in June at high noon, but never can see.' That's what I'll write for the *Springfield Republican* and *Amherst Record*, Lavinia! 'Emily Elizabeth Dickinson caught the shadowy apparitions of her brain and tossed them in startling word pictures like a magician to her friends. We were all charmed with their simplicity as well as profundity. She managed to make the tantalizing fancies which elude our bungling into verbal rapture.' "

Lavinia, impressed with Sue's words, forgot her grief for a moment. "Emily so admired your brilliant talk, Sue. She marveled at what a gracious and cultured hostess you are. She adored you so, Susie, when we were all young and filled with happy dreams of what we'd become. If she were a man, she'd have married you herself, but being a girl, she matched you with our Dear Austin. She wanted you so desperately to be our sister-in-law and Austin's wife. Oh, Sue, she was so utterly torn by her devotion to Austin and to you, as I am. He'd been so sick with the brain fever, himself, too, and we nearly lost him. Please try to understand how difficult it would be to deny him happiness after his near death from typhoid, and…"

"Let's not speak of that now, Lavinia! This is not the time or place."

Easily intimidated by Sue's intelligent authority, Lavinia anxiously changed the subject: "Emily's garden rivals nearly all others in Amherst. How shall I be able to tend Em's conservatory so full of exotic plants and blossoms from Europe and the Orient? And Professor Clark, her favorite horticultural teacher, not around to give advice—called back by Our Lord Jesus just a few weeks ago, too. Poor broken man! Em was so upset when she heard he'd died. She lost too many friends and loved ones these past few years. She never got out of bed again after she heard of Professor Clark's death."

"Don't fret, Lavinia. Maggie will help you. Maggie knows all about Emily's wants."

"Yes, Dear Maggie will help me with Em's conservatory, and Tom, too. Tom was always in the garden and orchard working with Em when she was too weak to dig. Thank God for giving us Yankees such good Irish immigrants to work for us!"

"Why she did not choose more eminent pall bearers instead of your Irish field hands is beyond me, but she must have her last wishes."

Lavinia was distressed by Sue's snobbery. "What would I do without Maggie Maher and Tom Kelly? Emily loved them so. Remember how she'd run to Tom's shoulder for comfort when awful things happened, and…."

"Now, Vinnie, President Seeyle of the college is coming, and President Emeritus Hitchcock will be here. I wish I could greet him. I could've married Hitchcock's son, Charles, instead of Austin. Remember?"

Lavinia spoke under her breath: "How could I forget, when you remind me daily…?"

"Reverend Jenkins is coming all the way from Portland. Pull yourself together for your distinguished guests. Have you arranged for the field hands to carry her bier to West Cemetery, as she desired?"

"Yes, through the meadows in view of the house and through the barn and out the back through the gardens and the orchard, to her rest in West Cemetery?" I've explained it all to Tom just as Emily wished. Tom is gathering the men from the fields right now." Vinnie began weeping anew with the thought of burying her sister with whom she'd spent her entire life. Vinnie's long, black, wavy hair, turning gray at the temples, swept into a bun at the back of her neck, was disheveled. Her black brocaded bodice was stained with tears. Her favorite orange-and-white-striped tomcat rubbed against her hem purring as if to comfort her.

"Look!" Susan uttered alarm as she gazed out the window up Main Street. "I think I see Thomas Wentworth Higginson's carriage coming! Remember, Lavinia, he's come all the way from Boston where he's editor of the *Atlantic Monthly*. Here's the poem by Bronte, Emily wished to have read. 'No coward soul is mine, / No trembler in the world's storm-troubled sphere; / I see Heaven's glories shine, / And faith shines equal, arming me from fear…' " Sue handed Lavinia a piece of paper, but recited the words from heart as much for herself as Emily. "Oh, I'd love to greet Higginson myself, but, no, give him this to read! Austin is coming up Main Street, too, with Mrs. Todd and her husband, David, beside him in our carriage. Sweet Jesus, help me! I'll depart through the back door. Tell them I'm too bereft to attend. Tell Austin I've prepared Emily for viewing. Let him know that I do my wifely duty for his kin despite the ignominy he causes me to suffer." Sue moved toward the hall of the back parlor.

"Yes, Sue, she looks so peaceful all in white as she'd want and with the violets at her throat, the heliotropes in her hands. Just like a Romantic painting of a white angel amid flowers and trees! I can't bear to look at her so still and lifeless, but you've done very well by her, Sue. Thank you so much." Vinnie whimpered into her handkerchief. Her eyes, usually bright with a mischievous twinkle, were red with crying and framed by purple rings. She sank into her rocking chair nearly fainting. She'd be alone now, with only the day servants and her many cats, in the big brick homestead built by her grandfather,

Samuel Fowler Dickinson, nearly a century ago. Her tomcat leapt into her lap and she snuggled him to her face, stroking his mane. "Please stay, Sue. Em would want you to be here." Vinnie rocked holding her big cat close as a baby.

"I pray for Emily's soul. She was never 'born again' unto Our Lord, Jesus, as I was, as you were, as your mother and father were, Vinnie!" Sue replied. "'Poets all!' she said to me. 'Poets light lamps, themselves go out....' Well, Emily did light lamps of passion and love, and now her light is out. Her words live in my memory." Sue withdrew toward the door. "Certainly, you cannot expect me to be civil to Mrs. Todd, Vinnie!" Sue glared at Vinnie to make her feel guilty for befriending Austin's mistress. "Haven't I borne enough deception and degradation before the eyes of this town, a wife scorned by her husband and his paramour? I cannot support a moment more, even for Dear Emily's funeral. Your Father, if alive, would understand my plight. He always approved me, ever since we were saved by Jesus in church together on the same Sabbath Day in 1850. I have paid my respects and prayed heartily for Emily's soul. I feel God will forgive the sins of such a sensitive and frail soul as Emily's. The Catholics believe in absolution. Let us hope they are correct."

Lavinia felt compelled to answer Sue's subtle insinuation. "Emily's favorite reverend of Philadelphia, William Wadsworth, believed in *redemption*, Sue. Em would have had him officiate were he alive and could. Our Puritan fathers preordained our souls, and what striving does that demand of those as *imperfect* as *we*. I think Emily preferred Presbyterianism?" Lavinia, despite her abject sorrow, felt compelled to take the role that Emily would have were she able to speak, giving Sue's veiled innuendo back to her. "I've never known a *perfect* soul, Sue. Not even Father had one. Perhaps, Mother did, but she was always ill in her bed with neuralgia, so what sinning could she do? Oh, Sue, we should all become Catholics so that we can be absolved."

Sue ignored what she always judged as Vinnie's simplistic impertinence, even though she was considering converting to Catholicism and planned to take a trip to Europe as soon as she could to explore The Church there. Vinnie, in Sue's estimation, was better suited to housekeeping than thinking.

"Now, they are coming up the drive, Vinnie. I must be gone. I cannot face them. I'll go back to the Evergreens, dwelling alone with my prayers, and fittingly memorializing Emily at my desk." Sue, kept a stern composure though she felt great sorrow over the loss of her oldest friend, especially since they'd not spoken much since Mrs. Todd had begun to frequent the Dickinson homestead to play the piano for the ailing Emily who never came down to receive the musician. Emily rested on the top stair, or stayed in the shadowy hall, not far from her bedroom to listen, but always sent a rose, a note of thanks, or a poem with a cup of tea and cakes on a tray to Mrs. Todd via her faithful servant Maggie who was Emily's closest confidant. Sue wanted to believe that Emily never received Mrs. Todd, face to face, in deference to Sue's role as Austin's *true* wife. It made it easier for Sue to forgive Emily as she lay still in her coffin. Sue sincerely wanted to appease Emily's spirit. They had heartily admired each other's intellect.

"It's so good of you Sue to write Em's Obituary." Vinnie tried to compose herself. "You know my handwriting is impossible. I could never be as articulate as you. I shall tell them you are busy with Emmy's obituary, and are too grief stricken to stay." Lavinia wanted to assuage her estranged sister-in-law for Emily's sake as well as her own. Sue had been painfully judgmental of late, and she quaked at Sue's fierce determination.

"'I shall report her cause aright to the unsatisfied.' After all, we loved each other very much when we were young." Sue came quickly back to the coffin, bent and kissed the cool forehead of her oldest friend: "And, flights of angels sing thee to thy rest!" She whispered into Emily's ear, sharing for the last time one of the many literary references they'd shared through their lives in speaking and writing to each other since their girlhood at Amherst Academy. Her chin quivering with tears held back, Sue swept from the room and out the back door of the house, her black, silk brocade rustling as she went.

Susan Gilbert Huntington Dickinson with great dignity glided quickly across the back walk through the trees to the Evergreens— where she had lived with Austin, since 1856 after Emily had introduced them and pressed for their union so many years before. She bustled up the walk of her lavish home and did not look back for fear her husband, with Mrs. Todd in tow, might have seen her. She wanted only to give them her departing back.

Alone in the library, Lavinia Dickinson let her orange-striped, house cat leave her lap. She rose shakily from her rocking chair and forced herself to look once again upon the still corpse of her older sister. Her gorge rose in her throat seeing how motionless Emily lay—all life gone from her small, waxen face.

"Oh, Emily Elizabeth Dickinson, who could fathom you?" She whispered to the corpse. "Who was Philip? Not even I really knew you?" She took the ring from her bodice and held it out to the corpse. "Why did you always wear this ring? Why did you have to die and leave me all alone in our old house? How will I go on without Father, Mother, or you? I've never known life without you by my side. Here," she said holding the ring up for her dead sister. "Emily Dickinson, rise up, step out of that coffin if you want to wear this ring again. Who was Philip?"

Vinnie waited, half expecting Emily to rise and answer. She could not accept that her sister was now out of her body and would never speak to her again. When Vinnie asked Emily why she never married, Emily had answered. "Because I never found anyone I loved better than you, Vinnie!" Lavinia had clung to that idea to comfort her in her aging spinsterhood. "At least, I have a smart sister who loves me and finds me indispensably worthy." She'd thought, "Even though I never found a proper husband that father would approve."

Faint with viewing the corpse, she collapsed back into her chair, as Emily had when she'd viewed their sweet, young, nephew, Gib, arrayed in his coffin at age eight, just three years earlier. "Well then, Emmy, I'll wear your ring until I die!" Lavinia put Emily's gold band on the ring finger of her left hand. We shall be sisters bonded forever, until we meet in Heaven." Lavinia felt as if she was losing her wits over Emily's departure. She resumed her helpless weeping.

Maggie Maher, their household maid, came hurriedly into the room with a tray of tea and toast! "Now, Miss Vinnie, ye must have yer tea. I've made ye some nice cinnamon toast just as ye like it, slathered with apple butter. Miss Emily made me promise to take good care of ye with nearly 'er last breath. So, ye mustn't thwart my attempt for Her Dearly Departed Sake. Ye dunna want ta be collapsin' as Miss Em did after

Gib's departure that terrible, cursed day of '83! Ye'll be havin;' yerself a fit of nervous prostration if ye dunna be eatin' somethin' Lord, please ye now, Miss Vinnie! A bit of toast and tea, before the memorial service will help ye through it. Come now! I put fresh Chamomile n' ginger, too, in yer tea. Take a bite, Dearie! I hear them back by the barn, givin' up the horses ta Tommy. They'll be a comin' in a minute."

Used to nursing the Dickinson family, Maggie all but poured the warm and soothing tea down her mistress's throat as Lavinia reclined in her rocker. Maggie fed her bits of toast between every draught. "I'll not take "no" for an answer, Dearie. And don't I know how ya feel with our Dear One gone? Cried all the night, myself, I did, but we must be strong for Miss Emily's Dear Sake." Maggie hurriedly smoothed Lavinia's hair back as best she could, blotted her eyes and mouth with a napkin, and hurried to the door as the bell jingled announcing the first mourners.

Since Gib's death in 1883, Emily had become an invalid subject to fainting spells and edema. Austin and Vinnie, with the help of Maggie, had tended her. Emily lived on belledona, quinine and digitalis. She had loved the precocious little blond boy, her nephew, as her own. Gib was the hope of the Dickinson family, as he rode about the town on his large tricycle, befriending everyone, young and old, with a polite enthusiasm, clear-eyed innocence, and social acumen that charmed all. Emily could not bear his death, as he seemed to take all future hope of the Dickinson family with him to his small grave.

Death had always surrounded Emily. She'd known the demise of several schoolmates to cholera, pneumonia, or typhoid fever, before she'd reached the age of fifteen. Indeed, over sixty percent of all deaths were those of children from typhoid. Emily, when young, had been particularly struck by the death of her closest friend, Sophia Holland, which had plunged her into a deep depression. Her parents had sent her for six weeks to Boston to live with her favorite Norcross Aunt to recover. Then the deaths of her cherished preceptors, young Master Humphrey and Benjamin Newton, had crushed her, too. Emily, herself, had been sick often enough throughout her life. Illness or early death was a constant factor of her Pioneer Valley. With the death of her much loved brother's son, Gib, from typhoid, Emily had entered a period of apprehension and collapse and rarely got out of bed to come downstairs. Maggie, her trusted servant, had to bring trays to her room to get her to drink or eat anything which she hardly did. She suffered from inflamed kidneys, diagnosed as Bright's disease, and finally died of heart failure as far as anyone, including her physician, could ascertain.

Gib's precocious and imaginative spirit had been a beacon of light to Emily. But, it was the death, just a few weeks prior to her own, of the man who had given Emily the gold band, the man she had secretly loved as "Master" that had ended her *will* to live. She'd not left her room since, but languished in her bed too weak to do anything but read a little. Books had always been her most constant companions. "There is no frigate like a book to take us lands away," she'd often told Lavinia.

Romeo and Juliet was what she'd been rereading in her final days. Sue did not tell Vinnie that she'd pried the volume from Emily's hand when she prepared her for her shroud. On the open page Emily had marked Juliet's words upon hearing of Romeo's death: "I do remember an apothecary, a dram of poison….at that the life weary taker may fall dead." She'd died only eight weeks after the secret "Master" of her mind and heart had perished. Lavinia and Austin had heard her mumbling in delirium that final day:

> *I died for beauty, but was scarce*
> *Adjusted in the tomb*
> *When one who died for truth was lain*
> *In an adjoining room.*
>
> *He questioned softly why I failed?*
> *"For beauty," I replied —*
> *"And I for Truth—the two are one;*
> *We brethren, are," he said.*
>
> *And so, as Kinsmen, met a-night*
> *We talked between the rooms,*
> *Until the moss had reached our lips,*
> *And covered up our names.*

Afterword By the Author

Lover Of Science and Scientist In Dark Days Of the Republic
Solving The Mystery of Emily Dickinson's "Master Figure"
"Neighbor and Friend and Bridegroom…"

> *I climb the "Hill of Science"*
> *I "view the Landscape o'er"*
> *Such transcendental prospect*
> *I ne'er beheld before!—*
> —*Emily Dickinson, The Indicator, Amherst College: 1852*

Because of the connection to her creativity during its most emergent period, the identity of the mysterious "Master Figure" of Emily Dickinson's poems and letters has been a matter of great speculation and pointed disagreement among Dickinson scholars for over a century. Connie Ann Kirk in her 2004 biography *Emily Dickinson*, Greenwood Press, wrote: "…a scholar or historian who could somehow prove 'Master's' true identity would solve one of the greatest mysteries in American literature." We know a good deal about the life of our other most singular icon of 19th Century American Poetry, Walt Whitman, but details of Dickinson's personal life have become so mythologized that we can't see as clearly the edifying connections between her biography and poetic output. One can contend, as the poet Susan Howe does in *My Emily Dickinson* (See bib.), that this circumstance leaves many of her poems elliptical or impenetrable. Of course, the most famous of her works—those anthologized, recited, remembered, and taught—are *not* among such texts. The poet left behind about 1,800 poems, only eleven were formally published, and those anonymously, in her lifetime. The rest, many unfinished, were posthumously collected in her complete works.

Many feel, and rightly so, that an artist's biography need only be explored if it enlightens the art produced, and not for gossip's sake or the pleasures of voyeurism. Yet, due to recent scholarship that has come to light about who the mysterious "Master Figure" of Dickinson's poems and letters was, we can manage a whole new reading of this important poet's work. Undoing the mythology surrounding Dickinson's overblown seclusion, the trauma that brought her to it, along with the inspiration for her writing, the wearing of her notorious white dress, and reasons for little publication in her lifetime, renders a clearer reading and greater appreciation of her many posthumously published texts.

Emily Dickinson's "Master Figure"

Among the voluminous letters of Emily Dickinson, an estimated mere third that survived accidental or deliberate destruction or expurgation, are drafts of three, now well-known, and much read letters addressed, between 1858 and 1863, to an unknown bearded, and intimate, recipient called "Master" and "Sir." Dickinson scholars basically agree that these so-called "Master Letters" were part of a larger correspondence and indicative of a deeply emotional relationship that defined the poet's output. They comprise the story of an intimate and frustrating love, marked by passionate anguish over a separation and a lack of response from the beloved. The vitality of these three "Master Letters," has to do with the poetic and emotional intensity with which they signal the beginning of Dickinson's most creative period as a poet, an era that generally coincides with the years of the Civil War and follows "The Great Revival" during which Dickinson, like Whitman, never converted to "born-again" fervor. Though in her case her entire family, and nearly all of her friends, "came to Jesus Christ" to be "washed of their sins and reborn," Dickinson resisted conversion to organized religion, and espoused deep concern with the natural sciences. She is one of the most scientifically aware poets America has ever produced.

Scholars and biographers all agree that it was an emotional trauma that ignited the poet's imagination and enormous creative powers, but that crisis has remained a mystery until now. A new, carefully researched thesis by Ruth Owen Jones, professional historian of Amherst, Dickinson scholar, and guide at the Dickinson Museum since 1979, may change our reading of the poet's work forever. Jones's thesis is revelatory, because she has espoused the most plausible idea for Emily Dickinson's "Master Figure" ever to emerge from research within both the poet's texts and times. In her article, titled "Neighbor—and friend—and Bridegroom—" published in *The Emily Dickinson Journal*, Volume XI, Number 2, Winter, 2002, Jones proposes that Emily Dickinson's Master, the person she loved when she was thirty, and for whom she wrote hundreds of poems and the three "Master Letters," was an Amherst College professor of chemistry, botany, and zoology, and a Civil War hero by the name of William Smith Clark, a prominent figure of Dickinson's village, particularly during the period of her greatest output and creativity. He lived from 1826 to 1886 and died just a few weeks before Dickinson. Jones first presented her idea to the Emily Dickinson International Society in Trondheim, Norway, in 2001.

Many of the poet's poems, particularly the love poems, yield greater clarity when professor of science, William Smith Clark, a Colonel of the Civil War, is known to have been their inspiration. Jones's research into the historicity of the poet's village, as a former chairperson of the Amherst Historical Commission, and Vice President of the Amherst Historical Society, led her to discover the identity of "The Master Figure," and his effect upon the poet's writing where literary scholars who have searched mainly in the texts have failed. Yet, Jones has offered much *textual* evidence as well. Jones's solution to the mystery that has plagued the many Dickinson biographers helps readers of the poet to understand why she wrote as she did, and how much she was affected, like Whitman, by the Civil War and The American enlightenment, known in literature as the Transcendental Movement which espoused the divinity of humankind and a communion with the realities of the natural world as the proper road to spiritual and moral growth. It praised emotional truths of humane conscience and the realities of scientific inquiry over the dogma of organized religion and literal interpretations of scripture, just as free thinkers and rational scientists do today. Many feel that this movement is still the best part of our American literary heritage.

The two most highly rated icons of American poetry, Whitman and Dickinson—still entirely relevant to poets and students of poetry in our time—lived and wrote through "Dark Days of the Republic" as scientific reason struggled to be born amidst fanatical religiosity. Many American poets and writers of today feel they are living through and dealing with similar "dark days." Because the poetic styles of these two great icons are so completely dissimilar, and the social classes that produced them quite different, we do not tend to see how much the same forces, The Civil War and 'The Great Revival" influenced their work or how alike they were in theme and content. So concerned with "schools" and "style" are we, that we do not see how similar our struggle to produce relevant poetry resembles Whitman's and Dickinson's—both of whom wrote in rebellion of the accepted styles of their day, both of whom espoused themes celebrating scientific enlightenment over religious and social dogma, just as poets do today.

Also, because these two giants of American poetry wrote in very divergent styles, they have left younger poets a legacy of freedom to choose their prosody in great variety, from tight and pithy lyricism to rambling narrative free verse, but, their content jibes similarly with the times through which they wrote—repulsed by hypocritical elements of fanatical religious fervor, and social class, and attracted to scientific truth and social equality as fostered in the Transcendental movement of their era. Both of these iconic poets were concerned with striving toward egalitarian ideals, as many contemporary poets are concerned with how "The War on Terror" and "Religious Fanaticism" are impeding humane progress and retarding our democracy.

Two big upheavals, The Great Revival and The Civil War, permeated the atmosphere of Emily Dickinson's village and motivated her poetry much more than is realized by many readers of her work. Evangelical Puritanism swept through her valley and threatened her spirit with its Calvinist doctrine of predestination. The Temperance Movement that her prominent father joined was much enhanced by its forces, as well. Dickinson's poems and letters are fraught with spiritual conflict over the evangelical fervor that gripped her New England valley. The horror of The Civil War, which took over 600,000 lives and shook the faith of many, garnered the most able-bodied men away from Dickinson's village. Then, too, the Westward movement and the Gold Rush took eligible men away from the New England region, when the poet was in the prime of her life. During her most marriageable years, there were five women of her social class for every one eligible male. This fact offers good reason as to why she remained unmarried, and why she might have had an affair with a married man like Professor Clark who was married to Dickinson's distant cousin, Harriet Richards Williston.

Ruth Owen Jones new thesis on the life of Dickinson is bound to change the way Dickinson scholars view the impact of the Civil War upon her poetry. The war may well have taken her cherished lover, a married man, away from her. His presumed death in combat, when he was reported in local papers in September of 1862 as missing in action, coincides exactly in time with the mysterious trauma that all of her biographers agree marked her life and work.

Before this revolutionary thesis concerning Professor Clark, first Ph.D. scientist of Amherst College—founded and fostered by Dickinson's grandfather and father—is doubted as solving the great mystery of the "Master Figure," the myriad of evidence supporting it should be examined. First, scholars generally agree that it was during the Civil War years that Dickinson produced her greatest poetic output. On the first page of his introduction to the definitive edition of Dickinson's poetry—published at the Belknap Press, Harvard, 1999—R.W. Franklin writes: "She was most active in 1862 (227 poems), 1863 (295), 1864 (98), and 1865 (229), much of the latter two years while—under the care of a Boston ophthalmologist —she was sharing living arrangements in Cambridgeport with her Norcross cousins, Louise and Frances." After those years, her output slowed considerably. Indeed, Franklin notes on page 639 of his complete volume of ED's poems, that in 1866 she wrote ten poems, and in 1867, only 12. Quite a notable drop-off in output!

Clark, when serving as state representative after the war, spent the same years and periods in Cambridgeport, sometimes at his brother-in-law's home a stone's throw away from where Emily boarded with her "Norcross cousins. Jones surmised that the affair was broken off after the assassination of Abraham Lincoln in 1865, when many were reassessing their lives and Clark was planning to move away from Dickinson's neighborhood, with his wife and family, to found The University of Massachusetts as a college of agricultural science.

Since Dickinson's greatest literary output occurred during the years just before and through the time that Clark was at the front in the Civil War—Jones proposes that the original hand-sewn booklets, or now famous *fascicles*, as scholars call them, were made for Clark and sent to him in the field, via Samuel Bowles, editor of *The Springfield Republican*, and later by Elizabeth Holland, wife of Josiah Holland, assistant cultural editor. Emily wrote to Mrs. Holland prior to the war, March 2, 1859, saying. "Sister, You did my will. And I thank you for it…" Was she thanking her for forwarding letters to William Smith Clark?

From the front lines, Clark mailed war correspondence to editors, Bowles and Holland, who were therefore in close touch with his movements. Professor Clark, like his father-in-law, Samuel Williston, had been an outspoken anti-slavery activist prior to the war. Samuel Bowles, Josiah Holland, and Thomas Wentworth Higginson, other editors of Dickinson's circle were financial supporters of John Brown's well-known 1860 rebellion at Harper's Ferry. These three editors, or households, with whom Emily corresponded, and to whom she sent poems, moved in the same intellectual and ideological circles as Professor, later Colonel, Clark, and all three might have well been aware of his whereabouts and exploits during the war.

By aligning the chronologies of Dickinson's and Clark's lives, Jones shows us the impetus that stirred Dickinson's poetry during the years 1857 to 1865. Her thesis leads us to a whole new reading of the poet's work, and helps us to understand the "trauma," referred to by all Dickinson scholars, which led the poet to a somewhat reclusive life *after* the age of thirty-five when her affair with Clark had no doubt ended.

As biographers all point out, Dickinson was quite social prior to the age of thirty-five and was considered one of the eligible belles of Amherst, a charming party attendee with friends and gentleman suitors, and far from reclusive. Edward Dickinson, Emily's father, was a prominent lawyer of the town who served as a state representative, then state senator, and on the governor's council through the late 1840's and then was elected to serve in 1853 as a representative in the 33rd Congress of the United States. Emily with her sister, Lavinia, visited him and toured the national Capitol in March and February of 1855. Emily is known to have charmed with her wit the Washington, D.C. society that she encountered during her stay at the famous Willard's Hotel, hub of the social and political scene there. She dressed in uncharacteristic, finery and felt, she said, "like an embarrassed peacock" out of her rural element. Clark's Grandfather

Smith had also been a statesman, as Clark was to become a state legislator after the Civil War. They shared common political concerns in their families.

Jones was writing an introduction for a book she was preparing on Dickinson's flower poems, when she began to look around Amherst for which contemporaries of Dickinson were avid gardeners. In researching the gardens of 19ᵗʰ century Amherst, Jones, also a gardener, stumbled upon Clark's eminence with horticulture in Dickinson's day and his influence upon the landscaping of her village where many trees brought back by Clark from Japan were planted, some still found on the grounds of the Emily Dickinson Homestead Museum. It is obvious that the Master of Dickinson's poems and letters was familiar with flowers and the meaning of flowers. As a chief botanist of the region, Clark helped Austin, Emily's brother, to plant many trees and shrubs around the poet's town. Clark traveled to Europe and the orient and brought back exotic plants. Both Emily and her brother Austin were greatly interested in horticulture and used exotic species as part of their landscaping. Emily cherished her year-round plant conservatory in the Dickinson homestead. It occupied her as much as her poetry.

Professor Clark, as Dickinson's nearby neighbor, had a professional greenhouse at his home as early 1856. His house, which he shared with his wife and children, was located on a hill just behind The Dickinson Homestead during the period of Dickinson's greatest poetic output. Note these Dickinson stanzas:

> *"Heaven" — is what I cannot reach!*
> *The Apple on the Tree —*
> *Provided it do hopeless — hang —*
> *That — "Heaven" is — to Me!*
>
> *The Color, on the Cruising Cloud —*
> *The interdicted Land —*
> *Behind the Hill — the House behind —*
> *There — Paradise — is found! . . . .*

Jones began to discover more information about Clark, i.e. that he taught chemistry and then *botany* at Amherst College adjacent to the Dickinson's homestead—and led horticultural walks to which women of the village were invited despite their inability to matriculate at the all male institution. Emily's father often held parties and dinners for trustees, students, and professors, like Clark, at the Dickinson home where Emily is known to have served his guests along with her mother and sister, Lavinia. Clark and Emily's brother, Austin, appeared together as speakers on a program at Amherst College, in 1849, when the poet returned from her one year of study at Mount Holyoke Female Seminary. Commencement parties were held annually at the Dickinson home.

There is plenty of historical evidence that Emily as a young woman was a needed hostess and conversationalist at her father's gatherings and that Professor Clark would have been present at some of them. Susan, Dickinson's sister-in-law, also held literary salons at her elegant Italianate home next door, "The Evergreens," attended by prominent intellectuals and writers from Samuel Bowles to Ralph Waldo Emerson, and no doubt Professor Clark, a most cosmopolitan neighbor. Clark no doubt found the lively, witty Emily a likely candidate for a flirtation. By all accounts Clark enjoyed women and was a daring risk taker by nature.

Dickinson is known to have recited her poems and played her lively compositions on the piano at Sue's soirees. One of her favorites, she titled "The Devil." Habegger, among other biographers, mentions the late night revelry that brought her father's reprimand. He quotes Catherine Scott Turner, Sue's friend and guest known as Anton, concerning her pleasure in spending visits, between 1859 and 1863, at the Evergreens: "Those celestial evenings in the Library—the blazing wood fire—Emily—Austin, —the music—the rampant fun—the inextinguishable laughter, the uproarious spirits of our chosen—our most congenial circle." Kate remembered "Emily with her dog & her lantern…" used by the poet to see her way across the side lawn from the Homestead at night to the Evergreens and back. Kate Turner, a favorite reveler of Emily's goes on to remember Emily "often at the piano playing weird & beautiful melodies, all from her own inspiration. Oh! she was a choice spirit!" Kate recollects the time Emily's father appeared grim faced with his lantern to summon his reckless daughter home because her revelry had gone on too long into the night. The lovers could easily have met on one of these evenings.

Clark may well have walked Dickinson home on "the path just wide enough for two lovers," mentioned in her writing. He could easily have had trysts with her late at night in what she dubbed her 'Northwest Passage," after walking her home from Sue and brother Austin's house next door. Dickinson's "Northwest Passage,' (Note the similar name of the famed explorers, Lewis and *Clark*.) was a secluded back hall with easy escape exits to five parts of the mansion where Dickinson liked to meet with friends and relatives to read them poems or converse privately. This is documented in sources cited by Jones.

Professor Clark believed deeply in a woman's right to an education and professional life in a time when many did not, and he read and reviewed books and art, often by women, for *The Springfield Republican*. In his letters found in the library of The University of Massachusetts, we know that he encouraged his sister to "improve her poetry" and have a profession as a teacher of writing. In later years, Dr. Clark lobbied for women's right to an education before the board of the Massachusetts Agricultural College. We also know from Jones and Clark's biographer, John Maki, plus from local newspapers, that Clark was involved with the poet's father and brother in business ventures and horticultural projects, i.e. the county fair, the replanting of the Amherst Commons. Jones searched for connections between the Clark and Dickinson families and found many, including the fact of many plantings of Asian species of trees on Dickinson properties.

Jones realized that the lack of *surviving* correspondence between the two families was very suspicious, given the way that Clark *does* appear in two of the poet's *surviving* epistles as a familiar neighbor. In Thomas Johnson's and Theodora Ward's volume of the poet's letters from The Belknap Press at Harvard, Clark is mentioned in Letter 158 to her cousin Louisa Norcross and in Letter 255 to her brother, Austin. It's clear that Dickinson and her family were thoroughly aware of this man of science and intimate with him as an important personage on the Amherst sociopolitical and intellectual panorama.

More important and prominent than Dickinson in Mid-19th century New England, William Smith Clark was the *first* Ph.D. professor of Amherst College to be trained in Europe and was a leading horseman and horse trainer of the area, who led the 21st Regiment of Massachusetts Volunteers to the front of the Civil War. He was among the founders and the first president of The University of Massachusetts to oversee students at the college for agricultural science—which the poet's father also helped to found—and he was married to the adopted daughter of Samuel Williston—one of the wealthiest men of Western Massachusetts who provided him with the goodly estate on the hill behind Dickinson's home. For further evidence, Clark's biographer, John Maki, on page 10 of his book, writes: "For about ten years the Clark and Dickinson families were near neighbors. Emily Dickinson was born four years after Clark and died just over two months after he did. Clark and William Austin Dickinson, (the poet's brother)… were well known to each other as leading citizens of the village…"

It is particularly important, one realizes, to emphasize that Professor Clark was a *leading* teacher of the scientific subjects *most* found in Dickinson's poetry: horticulture, botany, zoology, chemistry, and mineralogy. For example, in 1861, Dickinson wrote:

> *"Faith is a fine invention*
> *for Gentleman who see!*
> *But Microsopes are prudent*
> *In an Emergency.*

And note the second and last stanza of this poem written around 1865:

> *Fire exists the first in light*
> *And then consolidates*
> *Only the Chemist can disclose*
> *Into what Carbonates—*

Or, for just one more example of many, these stanzas written around 1859:

> *"Arcturus" is his other name —*
> *I'd rather call him "Star"!*
> *It's very mean of Science*
> *To go and interfere!*
>
> *I slew a worm the other day —*
> *A "Savant" passing by*
> *Murmured "Resurgam" — "Centipede"!*
> *"Oh Lord — how frail are we"!*
>
> *I pull a flower from the woods —*
> *A monster with a glass*
> *Computes the stamens in a breath —*
> *And has her in a "class"!*
>
> *Whereas I took the Butterfly*
> *Aforetime in my hat —*
> *He sits erect in "Cabinets" —*
> *The Clover bells forgot!*
>
> *What once was "Heaven"*
> *Is "Zenith" now !*
> *Where I proposed to go*
> *When Time's brief masquerade was done*
> *Is mapped and charted too!…*

There are many more poems too numerous to mention here that show Dickinson's interest in subjects taught by Clark who was instrumental in stocking the flora, fauna, and geological specimen cabinets of Amherst College. That college was then a Puritan Seminary developing into a viable institution of higher learning, including the study of various sciences, while her father, Edward Dickinson, and later her brother, Austin, served as treasurer on the Board of Trustees. At the same time, Samuel Williston, Clark's father-in-law, also a staunch Calvinist like Emily's father, was an important benefactor of the college, endowing two prestigious chairs in the 1840's and later financing "Williston Hall and Barrett Halls," including a large chemistry laboratory on its ground floor—especially for his son-in-law, Clark, to teach in. Given both Edward Dickinson's and Samuel Williston's positions as leading citizens of the developing region, with the well-being of the college in mind as leading trustees together on the board, neither family would have exposed the extra-marital love affair even if they had known of it.

In 1857, Clark was appointed by Governor Gardner to be the chemist on the State Board of Agriculture. Emily won her prize for "Indian and Rye Bread" at the country fair in 1857 when Clark was judge of the baking contest. In 1860, Clark oversaw the building of the first fairgrounds, and the Dickinson family was always involved with the cattle shows and country fairs that were held there. Clark became president of the "Hampshire Agricultural Society" from 1860 to 61 and later in 1870.

No doubt, as Jones explains, Clark would have walked past Emily's windows on his way to teach at Amherst College every day. An admired orator, he may well have been "the Whippowil that sang… on the Orchard fence," mentioned in a letter from Cambridge, July 1864 to her sister, Lavinia (L293.) Jones notes that Dickinson tells Lavinia to meet her at the train in Palmer, alone, because she may go home with "the Whippo*wil*… who drove to the South…and returned" and would be with her on the same train from Cambridge. The train came to the depot at Amherst near her Main Street home. Did she ask Lavinia to meet her with their carriage, alone, at Palmer so that she would not alight at Amherst Station from the same train as her secret lover, State Representative Clark, who had once gone South to the Civil War?

Indeed, it is *impossible* that Dickinson would not have met Clark on many occasions in both her brother's and father's homes and at various college socials. In 1880, brother Austin owned land with Clark at Orient Springs in the Pelham Hills (evidenced by a Deed 358:151 in the *Hampshire County Registry*) They founded the Amherst Water Company together. Dickinson would have known Clark far better than *any* other man who has been posed as the possible "Master figure" of her letters and poems, as an outstanding student of Amherst College, and subsequently, as one of its leading lecturers on the natural sciences that captivated her most.

We also know, from much textual evidence, that Emily loved to "go rambling" in search of wildflowers with her large Newfoundlander dog, Carlo, mentioned to her "Master" as a companion for their proposed meadow walk in the second "Master Letter." It is more than likely that Emily Dickinson, after her one-year education at Mount Holyoke Female Seminary, attended the charming and charismatic Professor's chemistry and botany lectures, held adjacent to her home in 1853. He planted a state-of-the-art garden on campus with his students, and installed the statue of a naked nymph, Sabrina, therein, an act that caused a scandal in the town. He was a bold man. Emily would have been witness to all his industry and admired him greatly for his warm style of inspirational teaching. Upon Colonel Clark's return from the Civil War, he served as a state representative for three terms, very coincidentally, during *the exact same period* that Emily visited and lived in Cambridge, ostensibly to visit ophthalmologist, Dr. Williams. Dickinson never wore glasses and the eye malady for which she lived away from home for long periods of time is unknown. Also, Jones explains:

In the second Master Letter (L248), Dickinson recalled not flinching "Thro that awful parting." In the third Master Letter (L233), Dickinson asked "Could you come to New England would you come to Amherst—Would you like to come, Master?" It has, therefore, long been thought that the Master figure was not from Amherst. However, when Clark was away in the war, he did not always come to Amherst when on furlough. He would go to Easthampton where his wife and children were staying with her parents. Emily mentioned her Master's beard [Clark wore a beard.] and asked him, "Could you forget me in fight, or flight—Or the foreign land?" and "I wish with a might I cannot repress—that mine were the Queen's place—." She longed to walk in the meadow with her Master and her dog, Carlo, with no witness other than the bobolink—who wouldn't tell.

[p. 63, Jones, "Neighbor—and friend—and Bridegroom—". See bib.]

Clark was known as "Master Clark" at Williston Academy, which her brother had attended when Clark had been a teacher there, prior to their attending Amherst College together. Clark's wife, Harriet Keopulani Richards Williston, was nicknamed "The Queen," because she had been named for Queen Keopoulani when her father was a Christian missionary in Hawaii. Much evidence points *clearly* to Master Clark, botanist and ornithologist, as the recipient of "The Master Letters."

Clark was a forceful and respected man of the poet's region, and full of initiative, a statesman, like her admired father, but without the Puritanical stuffiness, the sort of man who therefore, one can easily surmise, would have attracted her attention. Clark while serving in the state legislature, sometimes stayed with Lyman Williston, his Transcendentalist brother-in-law, a few blocks away from Emily's boarding house in Harvard Square. Lyman had been struck with German Pantheism while studying in Germany, as Clark had, and Emily's Norcross cousin had attended a school for girls founded by that very brother-in-law who was a Unitarian, like Emerson, in rebellion against Calvinism.

The orphaned Norcross cousins, with whom Dickinson boarded in Cambridge were the children of the poet's favorite, deceased Aunt Lavinia, a poet who had first inspired Emily early on. These cousins were also intellectual rebels escaping Calvinism. They were great readers of progressive books who often supplied Emily with the volumes she desired to read and could not purchase in Calvinist Amherst. It is hard to imagine that they would not have read with her Walt Whitman's, notorious *Leaves of Grass*, known to be admired by Dickinson's idol, Emerson, especially since they later became members of Emerson's Literary Salon in Concord.

Many American students and poets are mistakenly of the opinion that Emily disparaged Whitman when all she is ever actually quoted as saying is, "I hear he's disgraceful," when answering a query as to whether she had read his book. She would be compelled, because of her father's social position, to pretend not to have read Whitman. It's clear from all of the biographies about the poet that she was often forced into a "ladylike pose," because of her father's social and political position and her dependency upon him for sustenance.

Dickinson's orphaned Norcross cousins, whom she addressed as "Little Cousins," probably knew more about the poet's inner life than any others, but their correspondence with her was highly expurgated by them to spare the details of her personal life to which they were no doubt privy as chief confidants. Though we have a significant number of the letters of Dickinson, we have few to her closest intimates, her "Little Cousins" and Mrs. Holland.

One may reason that Dickinson bid her sister and life long house companion, Lavinia, to burn any letters to and from, or about Clark, that would have embarrassed Clark's wife and children—still living in the town and attending the Dickinson family church at the time of Clark's and Emily's death a few weeks apart in 1886. The Williston-Clarks and the Dickinsons both had prominent family pews in the First Congregational Church of Amherst. Most of Clark's correspondence is also oddly missing. The lost letters would undoubtedly have revealed that "The Master" was a married man, and were destroyed for the sake of the lovers' reputations as well as to avoid the public ignominy to which their families would have been exposed.

Keeping in mind that George Eliot (Marian Evans of Coventry)—one of Emily's favorite writers—spent her life "living in sin" with a married man, Henry Lewes, and the fact that Austin, Emily's married brother, took a married woman, Mabel Loomis Todd, as his mistress in 1882—it is not improbable to imagine Emily doing the same. Mrs. Todd was the wife of the astronomy professor at Amherst College. It was Mrs. Todd who edited and saw to publication of Dickinson's first volumes of poetry after her death. Mabel Todd's drawing of "Indian Pipes," one of Emily's favorite wild flowers, adorns the cover of the poet's first posthumous volume of poetry. The affair of Brother Austin and Mabel Loomis Todd is well known and the subject of non-fiction as well as a novel. (See bib.) It demonstrates that the Dickinson children were not above straying into clandestine affairs, in rebellion against the strictness of their Puritan forebears. Edward, the statesman, was often busy and away in Washington or Boston and "when the cat's away the mice will play." His law practice throughout his life kept him frequently away arguing cases in neighboring districts. Biographers know that Emily and Austin gave a forbidden dancing party, and probably more than one, when their parents were out of town.

Moreover, both Lavinia and Emily Dickinson condoned Austin's affair and facilitated it to the consternation of Susan Gilbert Dickinson who is known to have withheld sexual attentions from Austin. Austin turned to Mabel Loomis Todd for physical affection denied him by Susan's Puritanical stance and fear of childbirth. Many women, like Susan's older sister Mary, died in painful childbirth in Mid 19ᵗʰ Century America. Susan had good reason to fear pregnancy and plenty of motivation for using valued, Puritanical mores, usual in her day, to withhold conjugal bliss from her husband. There were Calvinist religious tracts advising women to do just that for the good of their husband's souls. Perhaps, Clark's wife did the same, daughter of zealous Puritan missionaries that she was.

The majority of Dickinson's surviving letters was preserved by recipients. These letters rarely deal with the intimate issues of Dickinson's adult life, with the exception of her letters to Judge Otis Lord, written late in the poet's life after the death of her father in the 1874. These letters show her to be far from prudish. They are the erotically suggestive writings of a woman aware of sexual desires and experienced in love, not the letters of a virginal spinster in tone or content. It's interesting that Lord's niece is reported to have called Emily, "a man-crazy hussy," hardly the extreme statement that even a vindictive or jealous person could easily get away with saying about a virginal recluse.

Most importantly, Jones refers to the many references to "Will" as *double entendre* in Dickinson's poems. "The Red upon the Hill, [the carnage of the Civil War] taketh away my Will." Dickinson poems often play on the word "Will" the way Shakespeare does in his sonnets. Colonel Will Clark nearly met death twice at the front. The famous period of trauma, referred to by Dickinson scholars, Johnson, Wolff, and Habegger, (See Bib.) and other analyzers of Dickinson's work, matches near death experiences in Colonel Clark's war years. Dickinson's famous lines to Higginson in her 1862 letter: "I had a terror since September—I could tell to none—and so I sing as the Boy does by the Burying Ground—because I am afraid," (L. 261)—coincide with a time when Colonel Clark missing on his way to the front and then reported dead at The Battle of Chantilly in September, 1862. Also note, the image Dickinson uses is very like a Civil War one, where boy soldiers sang beside the burying ground, in the field, where often there was no Chaplain available to lead them in prayers or hymns. "That awful parting" which Dickinson refers to in the second "Master Letters," cited earlier, was very likely her parting with Clark as he went off to the war front and her anxiety when he was reported dead at Chantilly. Jones's thesis solves the mystery of that famous trauma, or "terror" spoken of by all Dickinson scholars that inspired her writing, and fits into her letters and poems where textual evidence substantiates it well.

Also, "Mine by the right of the white election…!" a mysterious poem, was written soon after Clark was mistakenly reported dead at the battle front, very likely referring to the body of Clark and the poet's secret union with him. If found, his body would be returned to Massachusetts, and his wife, for ceremonial burial. That poem, when read with the idea that the poet claims the right to her lover's body for burial, as his true soul mate, yields its enigmatic meaning—emphasizing the importance of Jones's theory for readers of Dickinson's poetry.

There is more writing about the Civil War in Dickinson's poems than some scholars attest to. This is made clear by Shira Wolosky in her article "Public and Private in Dickinson's War Poetry," as well as in her earlier book, *Emily Dickinson: A Voice of War.* (See bib.) There is one poem that talks of her absent Master, written when Clark was at the front. "I tend my flowers for thee, bright Absentee…" There is another which refers to "Neighbor and friend and Bridegroom" spinning upon the shoals," when Clark was part of a stranded fleet of ships with other men of his 21st Massachusetts Regiment as ships sank on their way South and Massachusetts soldiers were drowned. The many examples of the poet's writings that have to do with the Civil War are beyond the scope of this essay. Only a few of those having to do with Clark are quoted herein.

Another telling fact is that William Smith Clark was an affectionate letter writer to his students and family. His letters are *very similar in tone* to Emily's warmly demonstrative ones, not emotionally detached like her father's or brother's prose. Clark was known to have adopted European styles of kissing and hugging and showing affection, demonstrations that were markedly missing—according to all biographical accounts—from Emily's Puritan home and family style. Biographers have quoted reputable sources who observed that the Dickinsons, though fiercely loyal to each other, never touched, hugged or kissed. One can imagine the more affectionate Clark introducing Emily to the subject of "Wild Nights" of ecstasy, or "Rowing in Eden," and the suggestive bee and flower pollination of her clearly erotic imagery. "Did the harebell loose her girdle/ To the lover bee?" Quoting and demonstrating the many poems that seem to be addressed to "Will" Clark, botanist, would comprise a long essay in itself.

Ruth Owen Jones also points out that there is a gold ring in the Dickinson Collection at Harvard that Dickinson is supposed to have worn most of her life. Inside the band is inscribed the word "Philip" which means "horseman or horse fancier" in Greek. Both Dickinson and Clark knew their Greek and Latin, and Clark was among the best horse trainers and riders of the area. Emily's father and brother would, no doubt, have bought their horses with Clark's advice. He trained Morgans which were ridden by the ladies of the era as the high-stepping carriers who gave a smooth ride to women—not jogging them out of their side-saddles or making their skirts fly high in the wind. Indeed Morgan horses are still trained at The University of Massachusetts, Then, too, there is a curiously enigmatic poem which mentions a "Philip" who "—when bewildered/ Bore his riddle in!" [Franklin, 20, p. 27. Dated 1858.]

As if forecasting Jones's discoveries, Cynthia Griffin Wolff is one, among other, skilled biographers who does not believe the theories of the Master figure as either Samuel Bowles, or, the often mentioned, Reverend Charles Wadsworth, as plausible. Wolff in 1986 speculates that some other party, unknown thus far to scholars of Dickinson, is more likely the "Master."[1] Cynthia Wolff writes in her Radcliffe Series biography *Emily Dickinson*:

> *Consistently, Dickinson's love poetry turns away from all of the usual strategies. She might have chosen to write about the fortunes of a typical courtship as the Elizabethan sonneteers did—the uncertainties and the rejections and the bliss of momentary understandings all providing a variety suitable for poetry inspection. She wrote a few such poems; however, by far the greatest part of the love poetry assumes that the difficulties that beset lovers come not from within, but from*

without. Moreover, tacit in most of Dickinson's work is the notion that some arrangement like marriage that allows for sustained intimacy and the uninterrupted possibility for passion is the ideal toward which poetry best addresses itself. There is no intrinsic reason why Dickinson could not have written love poetry celebrating the dynamics of a happy marriage or even examining the difficulties of achieving that perfect union. Nonetheless, for the most part, she did not. Or her decision to turn away from worldly rewards might have led her to postulate unconsummated fidelity to a distant beloved as a glorious end in itself; the poetry of this pure adulation could become its own kind of prayer, an alternative, perhaps, to those directed toward God. Other poets have celebrated a spiritual love, but Emily did not choose to do so. Finally, she might easily have elected not to write love poetry at all. However, she declined this path as well.

Instead, her poetry about love follows a peculiar, frustrating pattern. The same poetry that postulates marriage, as the ideal, also accepts as a given that this "marriage" can never take place. It is not that the lovers are joined only to discover that they are unhappy together; rather, two lovers, perfectly matched and deeply in love, are not permitted to remain together. Over and over again, this pattern is repeated. And it is this persistent pattern that may be partially illuminated by an examination of her real-world relationships. [pp.386-387]

Is it more than coincidence that Dickinson succumbed to death just a few weeks after Clark? Her last letter, written to her "Little Cousins," shortly after Clark's death, a few days before her own, says merely: "Called back." As Jones points out, the last book Emily Dickinson was re-reading, before she died in May 1886, was "Romeo and Juliet." She died just a few weeks after William Smith Clark who died in March of that year. Dickinson is known to have highlighted the phrase in her text: "I remember an apothecary…" spoken by Romeo who wishes to commit suicide after hearing of Juliet's death.

Jones's idea of Dickinson's "Master" makes others' older theories—concerning Samuel Bowles of Springfield; Reverend Charles Wadsworth of Philadelphia; or Susan Gilbert Dickinson, her sister-in-law next door—pale in the light of her historical discoveries and the supportive evidence she has cited within the texts of the letters and poems themselves.

Three Unlikely Persons Proposed As "Master"

If one truly considers the evidence, others traditionally proposed as the "Master Figure" are not likely candidates compared to Colonel Clark. Samuel Bowles, influential editor of *The Springfield Republican*, thought by some eminent biographers to have possibly been Emily's "Master," was a married man who lived farther off in Springfield, and, there is much evidence in his correspondence that he was attracted to Emily's sister-in-law, Susan Dickinson. He was not taken to gardening or rambling in search of wildflowers as Clark was and as the intended recipient in Dickinson's love letters certainly appears to have been. Samuel Bowles actually took a close associate, Maria Whitney, Dickinson's cousin, and Clark's wife's cousin, into his home as a sort of governess and secretary. Many scholars imagine from his correspondence that he had a love affair with Whitney. Bowles more than once arrived at Susan's and Austin's home next door to Emily's with Maria Whitney on his arm. Emily's cousin, Maria, was a scholar with whom Emily shared sympathies, perhaps because she was committed in a "secret marriage" (Title divine — is mine!/ The Wife—without the Sign! ....) to be the mistress of William Smith Clark, just as Maria Whitney was the confidante, literary secretary, and likely mistress, of Samuel Bowles whose wife, Mary, was incapacitated by childbirth, confinement, miscarriages and still born children, much as Clark's was.

These facts, along with a study of the extensive correspondence between Emily and Bowles in which she always addresses him as "Mr. Bowles"—never "Master"—and her empathetic correspondence with Maria Whitney, with whom Bowles was enamored, makes it *extremely* unlikely that Samuel Bowles could have been "The Master." Emily appears very incidentally in Bowles's correspondence with others, and he is far more concerned with Susan Dickinson's or Maria Whitney's attributes when he writes. Bowles in one of his letters to his friend, Austin, refers to Emily as "The Queen Recluse." Was he implying she was the reclusive "Queen" of Clark in contrast to his public wife who was called "The Queen," after the affair was known and Emily had retreated to a more exclusive society to avoid gossiping women?

Another usual candidate for the "Master" figure, Reverend Charles Wadsworth of Philadelphia, was a very happily married man who also lived far off. One surmises from the formal tone of his *only* surviving letter to the poet that he was more of a spiritual advisor to her than a lover. Emily knew so little of Wadsworth that she had to ask many questions about him of his surviving kin in letters written after his death. He did not wear a beard as the Master figure and Clark did, nor was he particularly involved with flowers as Emily and Clark and the recipient of the "Master Letters" was. He would have had to live in the town to be intimate with her dog, Carlo, and her walks in her meadow as the Master appears to have been. The only extant letter from Wadsworth is quite cool, addressing the poet as "Miss Dickenson," and even *misspelling her name*, something her intimate "Master" would not have done.

Wadsworth even forgets to sign his letter with a signature as if he were dashing off several letters to various parishioners who had asked for counsel. Not evidence of any great intimacy, the letter offers to give communion concerning her trauma about which he says he knows nothing, so how could he have been the cause of it? It's clear that Emily sought his advice and admired his sermons, which preached *redemption* in Presbyterian style—something absent from the sermons of the Calvinist ministers of her town. One imagines she asked Reverend Wadsworth for advisement on "redemption" for her sins, as Clark might have during his weeks spent in Philadelphia shopping for chemical laboratory supplies.

Wadsworth's interest in "Miss Dickenson," daughter of a federal politician, might well have been a desire to convert her to his Presbyterian sect because she was troubled over the dogma of her father's Calvinist theology. Presbyterianism was quite radical in Dickinson's Amherst circles, but it's likely that Clark, a world traveler who frequented Philadelphia, was familiar with its progressive ideals and attracted to it's doctrine of redemption. It was Wadsworth's mission to spread the ideas of his revolutionary sect wherever he could among influential people. The poet's final one of only two Amherst meetings with the reverend, when they went for their famous carriage ride together, more likely concerned her secret conversion to the Presbyterian sect, rather than a love affair.

Though respected Dickinson scholar, Martha Nell Smith, has expounded in *Open Me Carefully* upon the love relationship between Emily and her sister-in-law, Susan Gilbert Dickinson—there is much evidence that Emily had a falling out with the religious, born-again, Susan. Emily could never give in to the Puritan Revivalism that surrounded her. She'd been too thoroughly enthralled by her tutor, Benjamin Newton, who introduced her to Emerson's poems, and therefore to Emerson's essays on "Self-reliance," "The Poet," and "Nature," imbued with Transcendental philosophy. Many readers today seem unaware that Emerson ended as a non-theist and a Buddhist and was considered scandalously radical for his day. Though Susan and Emily were very close in their youth, prior to Susan's marriage to Emily's brother, and though Emily, no doubt, had a youthful crush, even homoerotic feelings for Susan—there is much evidence that she fancied male students and apprentices, i.e. Benjamin Newton, Leonard Humphrey, George Gould, Henry Vaughn Emmons, and very likely William Smith Clark, among the interesting young men living in the vicinity and on campus of Amherst College next door to her home.

Vivian R. Pollack and Marianne Noble state, in the Oxford University Press *Historical Guide to Emily Dickinson*; "Historians of sexuality, as Carroll Smith-Rosenberg and Lilian Faderman, have supplied further context for understanding the homoerotic and possible proto-lesbian elements of Dickinson's desire, as expressed in the letters to Sue. Romantic same-sex friendships were the norm during the antebellum era..." In any case, it is also speculated that Dickinson was helping her brother, Austin, with whom she closely identified, to court Sue with fervent letters, hoping to bring Sue into the intimacy of the family as a sister and confidant, as well as the intellectual companion, and independent, female role model, she needed. Neither her mother nor Lavinia were fond of reading, writing and thought in general, but were more concerned with household duties and church going than books.

At any rate, Susan and Emily had the sort of literary and intellectual camaraderie that is usually attributed only to male writers. Susan was not only intelligent, well read, and a gifted talker with a talent for writing, herself, but instrumental to Emily Dickinson's development as a poet and writer. Though Martha Nell Smith's research is vital, Clark is far more likely the major inspiration of the poems Emily sewed into fascicles or booklets, nearly all written while he was at war. Clark, as Dickinson's lover, would likely have encouraged her to write her poems, and interestingly, as Jones notes, five of her eleven anonymously published pieces appear in newspapers that *also* publish writing by Clark. Did Professor Clark assist in getting some of Dickinson's work published?

Also, "The Master letters" are addressed to "Master" not "Sue" or "Susie" as Dickinson's many surviving letters to Susan Gilbert are. Also, "Master" is sometimes called "Sir," and has a bearded face. (See bib. *The Master Letters*, Franklin.) Sue was an adventurous young woman early on compared to Emily, and she studied at a more sophisticated school in Geneva, New York. Dickinson definitely admired her independence and may have used the excuse of eye-trouble for coming to Cambridge to rendezvous with Clark—just as Sue, according to her letters, had done some years earlier in 1853, in order to travel to Boston unescorted to meet with Austin at the Revere Hotel prior to their marriage. Dickinson would have had to feign a vital reason for escaping her father's domain, and the dutiful care of her ill mother, in order to live in Cambridge during the same, extended periods that Clark served in the state legislature there, sometimes living a stone's throw from where Dickinson boarded with her "Little Cousins," and sometimes living at the Revere Hotel in Roxbury, where Austin had met with Susan. There is little doubt that Susan helped Dickinson to become her own person with the courage to pursue her literary creativity as well as to escape the confines of her father's home.

Ruth Owen Jones's theory of "the Master figure," better than any other, explains the extreme secrecy surrounding the poet's life and the elliptical quality of some of her poetry, as well as her relative seclusion, after age thirty-five, within her family compound and grounds.

The Poet In Pursuit Of Science and Truth

In summary, Dickinson's poetry shows her to be more involved with the pursuit of science and a belief in emotional truth as the Transcendentalists defined it. The German pantheists of her day influenced Ralph Waldo Emerson and William Smith Clark. Both worshipped Nature for practical and spiritual reasons. New England could not have thrived without such men at her intellectual helm. The extremes of the Puritan mind and the Evangelical Fundamentalist spirit would have held America back from growing into the prosperous and influential nation it became under the growing ideals of the transcendental enlightenment that espoused the importance of scientific pursuits. Ironically, Dickinson, a woman, is one of the most scientifically aware poets America produced during that period of the great rebellion of The Brahmins of New England who defied "The Great Revival" of Puritanical dogma which sought to repress both scientific knowledge and women's liberties.

As such, her poetry is a bastion of light for our own dark times when ideas of Creationism threaten to submerge the truths so painstakingly proven by many great scientists since Darwin first pioneered evolutionary biology. Needed progress in stem cell research that could cure so much suffering from various diseases, as well as vital environmental facts regarding global warming are again being repressed by misguided religious extremists. Yet, America has built her egalitarian hopes upon scientific truths, and the separation of church and state is so utterly vital to her democratic freedoms. When we reread Dickinson's poems with the ideals of Emerson and Clark and the pursuit of nature's chemistry and scientific truth in mind—even as we come to better understand the passions and disappointments that inspired her love poems of erotic joy, loss, and frustration —we can celebrate her intelligence and progressive mind as *a lover of science and scientist*, a thinker who heralded the acceptance of Darwinism to come, and who found spiritual solace in understanding the beauty and wonder of the ways of the natural world.

> *A science — so the Savants say,*
> *"Comparative Anatomy" —*
> *By which a single bone —*
> *Is made a secret to unfold*
> *Of some rare tenant of the mold,*

Else perished in the stone —

So to the eye prospective led,
This meekest flower of the mead
Upon a winter's day,
Stands representative in gold
Of Rose and Lily, manifold,
　　　　And countless Butterfly!
　　　　[Emily Dickinson, c.1860, F. 147, p. 73.]

Other Misleading Myths Undone

Many readers of Dickinson continue to blame Thomas Wentworth Higginson's estimation of the poet's work as her main reason for not gaining more publication of her poetry in her lifetime, but actually Higginson had little to do with her desire not to publish. Elizabeth A. Petrino *in Emily Dickinson and Her Contemporaries, Women's Verse in America, 1820-1885,* explains that women writers of Dickinson's day and social class were considered to have abandoned their roles as wives and mothers if they published. Women were supposed to write pleasant effusions to augment their roles as the moral upholders of Puritan society and the spiritual guardians of their households. Women of the educated classes of New England did not attempt to publish for remuneration. Only women who were struggling to make a living would do so, not the daughters of statesmen or well-to-do members of the community.

Thomas Wentworth Higginson's well known evaluation of the poet's work as too innovative and unconventional in form, probably had little to do with her *ultimate* refusal to publish under her own name. Dickinson herself wrote on many occasions that her poetry was meant for private spiritual enrichment. There's epistle evidence that she argued with Samuel Bowles, progressive editor of *The Springfield Republican,* on this point. Bowles believed in women having public careers, where Josiah Holland, cultural editor of same paper, and later of *Scribner's Magazine,* argued that a woman's place was in the home. This debate raged on in print all during the century of women's struggle for suffrage.

Like Holland, Edward Dickinson, along with other Calvinists, insisted that a woman's education was strictly for the spiritual enrichment of her family, not the commerce of literature for public consumption. Edward Dickinson, as an adamant Puritan gentleman and prominent statesman, greatly concerned with appearances, would have frowned severely upon his daughter writing for commercial publication. His own published writings speak of a woman's place as bound by the home. Dependent upon her respected father's fortunes, out of necessity, Dickinson sided with Josiah Holland's views. Mrs. Josiah Holland was Dickinson's closest and most valued friend throughout her life. Dickinson admired the peace and security of Elizabeth Holland's good marriage and her happiness as a wife and helpmate to Josiah, her intellectual husband. This is clear from Dickinson's correspondence. Mrs. Holland's contentment in the role of wife, rather than independent writer or professional woman, had its influence on Dickinson.

Susan Gilbert Dickinson, the poet's sister-in-law, girlhood friend, and close confidant through her youthful years, seems to have agreed with Edward Dickinson and Josiah Holland. After Emily's death, Susan wrote in a Dec. 1890 letter to Colonel Higginson, editor with Mrs. Todd, of Emily's first published volume of poems: "I sometimes shudder when I think of the world reading her [Emily's] thoughts minted in deep heartbroken convictions. In her own words (after all the intoxicating fascination of creation) she as deeply realized that for her, as for all of us women, not fame, but love and home and certainty are best." (p. 86, *Ancestor's Brocades*. See bib.) Note the word "heartbroken," which implies a lost love.

No doubt Susan Dickinson was pleasing her father-in-law, and his Puritan social class, with her proper behavior. She seems to have somewhat repressed any desire to be a published author and had ambiguous feelings about the independence of a wife, enjoying most of all her position as a captivating hostess and conversationalist. After all, Edward Dickinson's son, Austin, gave his wife, the orphaned Susan, the social standing which she appears to have craved, and her father-in-law, Edward, built a large, quite modern, and stylish Italianate home next door to the Dickinson family home, especially for Susan and Austin upon their marriage. Emily's biographers agree that Emily had much to do with matchmaking Austin's marriage to her school chum "Susie" from Amherst Academy. Edward was pleased with his son's choice, too. Emily was herself much enamored of Susan's charms as her letters show, as well as involved with the maintenance of the Dickinson home, reputation, and social affairs as Susan was.

Though both Bowles and Holland, important editors, were her friends, Emily clearly sided, at least outwardly, with Holland's beliefs, as well as Susan's and her eminent father's, in the societal debate over women publishing their writing. As her eminent biographers, including Alfred Habegger, point out, the impropriety of publication runs throughout her poems and letters. In the following lines, she might be speaking of both her love affair with a married man and her love affair with writing poetry:

> *Best Things dwell out of Sight*
> *The Pearl—the Just—Our Thought.*
> *Most shun the Public Air*
> *Legitimate, and Rare—*

Harriet Martineau and George Eliot were accused of being unnatural and *manly* because of their writing profession. Louisa May Alcott, for one example, published her work out of the necessity of earning a living and because her father, Bronson Alcott, was a very progressive educator who was, along with Margaret Fuller, in rebellion against Puritan restrictions of women and children. Emily herself wrote:

> *Publication—is the auction*
> *Of the Mind of Man—*
> *Poverty—be justifying*
> *For so foul a thing....*

Emily often sent versions of the same poems to various friends and neighbors, and possibly the same poems to Susan as to Clark, maybe testing them out on Susan for her editing advice prior to sending them onto Clark. Dickinson did have an important readership in her lifetime, if not much commercial publication. Nearly 600 poems were sent to forty readers who sometimes passed them to others to read, a form of publication in the scribal sense.

Poet Of the American Enlightenment

Dickinson is not the little rural recluse who blossomed, oddly, out of nothing, that the myths surrounding her imply. Sue's and Austin's library next door at The Evergreens held the most stimulating texts and periodicals of Dickinson's day and the poet spent much time there, reading and exchanging ideas with Susan and her worldly guests. Dickinson lived in the midst of literary people with whom she corresponded often. Though some 600 poems were circulated in letters among more than 40 known correspondents, there were probably many more unknown readers of her poetry as well.

Feminist writers are pleased to know that, Helen Hunt Jackson, a poet whose novel, *Ramona*, was a bestseller in Dickinson's day, was a former schoolmate, friend and correspondent who encouraged Dickinson writing with great praise. One of the best known of Emily's works, "Success is counted sweetest" was published anonymously by Jackson in her anthology of prominent poets: *A Masque of Poets* issued in 1878. Many readers imagined Emerson had written Dickinson's anonymous poem. Jackson, a very successful writer, wrote to Dickinson more than once, urging her to publish and even offering to serve as her literary executor. "You are a great poet," wrote Jackson to Dickinson, in 1876. "—and it is wrong to the day you live in, that you will not sing aloud. When you are what men call dead, you will be sorry you were so stingy!"

The idea that Dickinson was a recluse who had little encouragement for her writing is much overplayed. Stimulating people surrounded her far more than many poets of our time who have lived in much greater seclusion. Her talents were encouraged by literary minds like Austin Dickinson, Susan Gilbert Dickinson, Benjamin Newton, Henry Vaughn Emmons, George Gould, Samuel Bowles, Elizabeth and Josiah Holland, Helen Hunt Jackson, and Thomas Wentworth Higginson, who called her poetry "great" even though he thought it too ephemeral and unconventional for publication.

Isn't it wrong to allow young poets of today to think that they can really write well in a reclusive vacuum without "feedback" or encouragement or other minds around for intellectual stimulation because the great poet, Emily Dickinson, did?

The poet had two Irish immigrant servants daily in her home with whom she was emotionally close: Tom Kelly and Maggie Maher, along with her sister, Lavinia, a few feet across the hall. She had her highly intellectual sister-in-law, Sue, and learned brother, Austin, and their educated children a few yards away in the house next door. She had her invalid mother at home and six part-time field hands and handymen now and then working her grounds and barn at various seasons. She chose these earthy laborers to be her pallbearers over others of her class she could have elected. There were the students and professor friends of Austin at Amherst College coming and going in her home or at The Evergreens next door. For much of her life, she had her father traveling home from Boston and Washington, as well as Northampton and other towns, bringing news of the world to her along with the society of his professional associates. This was true during many of the years of her so-called seclusion in which she received visits from Thomas Wentworth Higginson and Samuel Bowles, two of the most influential editors of her time, and statesman, Judge Otis Lord, as well as the Reverend Charles Wadsworth, the popular Philadelphia sermonizer.

Also, Dickinson's trusty, canine companion on her walks about the town and rambles through the countryside, the large, black Newfoundlander, Carlo, had died, in January 1866, by the time the poet did not travel beyond her father's properties. Daniel Lombardo in *Hedge Away* regarding annals of the poet's village, (See bib.) describes a period in which it is known many rabid, stray dogs prowled the streets of Amherst causing havoc in the town. Emily was diminutive. Perhaps, part of her keeping to her father's grounds had to do with fear of these rabid strays from which big, loyal Carlo could no longer protect her. Biographers tell us, her sister, Lavinia, had once been bitten by a dog so fiercely on her hand when going visiting in the village, that she had never been able to write well again. Perhaps, at least, part of the poet's desire to keep to her father's property was simply a practical matter.

Jones points out that in Emily's day, women gossiped fiercely about other women's indiscretions, and always blamed the woman who dallied with a married man not the man. Men were accepted as animal in nature, but women were supposed to uphold propriety and have no sexual feelings. Dickinson may likely have been avoiding nasty, gossiping women who got wind of her affair. We know she abhorred the "dimity convictions" of gentlewomen.

> *What Soft— Cherubic Creatures —*
> *These Gentlewomen are—*
> *One would as soon assault a Plush—*
> *Or violate a Star—*
>
> *Such Dimity Convictions—*
> *A Horror so refined*
> *Of freckled Human Nature—*
> *Of Deity— ashamed—*
>
> *It's such a common— Glory—*
> *A Fisherman's— Degree—*
> *Redemption— Brittle Lady—*
>   *Be so— ashamed of Thee—*

In addition, the myth that Dickinson wore white as emblematic of being a virgin or nun-like creature married to Christ, needs much modification. Far too much has been made of the white dresses Dickinson seems to have favored from age thirty-five on. There were several reasons why she might have worn these undyed, pique housedresses. For one thing, such housedresses were commonly worn by *all* women at home in place of the heavier formal dyed fabrics, i.e. brocades, woolens, satins, or linens, they might wear for travel or visitations out of doors. White housedresses were easy to wash without dyes running or fading, and lightweight in summer, comfortable for gardening and baking, and relaxing at home. Also, there was a rebellion against dyed and starched clothing as labor unions were forming to protest textile sweat-shops and boiling, hot, laundry factories, where workers suffered horrid and dangerous conditions and little pay. Bronson Alcott, one of the leaders of the Transcendental

Movement, had started a boycott of dyed and manufactured clothing in solidarity with the working classes. He and his followers wore white, homespun, or washable type clothing, as did Dickinson after thirty-five, in protest of workers poor labor conditions in textile dying and laundering factories.

Then too, as Judith Farr has explained at length in her book, *The Passion of Emily Dickinson,* (See bib.) the poet, like her brother, was taken with the Pre-Raphaelite paintings commonly found in upper class halls and parlors of the period. These paintings often depict little white clad figures of women, or men, or angels, against huge and grandiose natural settings and are emblematic of the Romantic movement toward wonder in the natural landscape and awe of the vastness of nature and its superior powers over man. Such paintings were no doubt admired and viewed often by Dickinson, a great lover of Romantic novels like the Bronte's *Wuthering Heights* or *Jane Eyre* or *The Mill on the Floss* by George Eliot, as well as a reader of Keats and Elizabeth Barrett Browning's poetry, particularly Barrett Browning's novel in verse titled *Aurora Leigh,* not to mention again the writings of Ralph Waldo Emerson, Margaret Fuller, and Henry David Thoreau, so influenced by Bronson Alcott's oratory. One thinks, too, of Nathaniel Hawthorne's story, "The May-pole of Mary Mount" in which the bride and groom wear simple white clothing in their rural pagan celebration in contrast to the black clothing worn by the Puritan priest who disrupts the ceremony with his Age of Iron mentality and Calvinist dogma.

No doubt Dickinson read that story of her popular contemporary, too. Dickinson's white garments may have been a commitment to her Transcendentalism.

Dickinson's wearing of lightweight, washable, white pique housedresses might as well be a matter of practicality more than Romantic pose, especially for a woman who liked to ramble through the woods, meadows, and gardens of her father's properties and who spent much of her day in her conservatory planting pots, or in her scullery, baking ginger bread, or churning butter. Emily Elizabeth Dickinson was far more known for her baking skills and her gardening than her poetry in the village of her time.

Relevance Of the "Master" Mystery Solved

By painstakingly searching through old copies of *The Springfield Daily Republican* and *Hampshire Franklin Express*, as well as *Amherst Record* where Clark often appears on page one, as well as other primary sources—historian, Ruth Owen Jones has discovered what other Dickinson readers and scholars have missed. More than any other person on the poet's horizon —William Smith Clark, eminent scientist of Amherst, is a logical candidate for "The Master" of Dickinson's writings as carefully explained and footnoted in her thesis, "Neighbor—and friend—and Bridegroom—." Agricultural science was greatly promoted in Dickinson's day because many young men were deserting the Northeast to adventure to the expanding West. New England farmland, full of rocks and stumps, had a short growing season compared to the cheaper, better, farmlands men were leaving Massachusetts in droves to acquire in the West. Professor Clark, his father in law Williston, and Emily's father, Edward Dickinson attempted to encourage young farmers to work the lands of their Pioneer Valley rather than migrate West. They were comrades in a cause of their region. With many of the young men of the area killed in the Civil War, or gone off to Western ventures—it is no wonder that Emily Dickinson and her sister, Lavinia, never married. It is not surprising that the poet had an affair with a charming botanist, who was a Civil War hero, a captivating speaker, and a staunch anti-slavery advocate—as well as business associate of her brother and father? There is no doubt she would have known and respected Clark highly, as the "Master Letters" tell of admiration for a master teacher.

Readers might be empathetic, rather than judgmental, in realizing that if Dickinson and Clark had fallen in love when Clark was a young student, before he went to Germany and returned to marry Williston's daughter—they would have been *star-crossed lover*. Clark was the son of a poor country doctor, born in a little clapboard farmhouse in the hill town of Ashfield, and would not have been in any position to ask for Emily's hand. According to his surviving letters, he afforded his education at Amherst College with financial difficulty and almost left part way through his freshman year for lack of funds. Dickinson's father would likely have snubbed him because of his financial status. Biographers have pointed out that the poet's father opposed his daughters' suitors if they were not financially secure. His father, Samuel Fowler Dickinson, had bankrupted himself founding Amherst College and Edward was traumatized by monetary difficulties early on. As an oldest son, he'd had to rebuild his family fortunes from the ground up which he did with the help of his wife and children. Emily and her siblings were part of Edward Dickinson's industrious efforts to regain financial security, good reputation, and help his community to thrive. He would not have brought an impoverished young man, such as Clark was prior to his marriage, into his family to support when he had his own son, Austin, to encourage and finance. Once Clark returned to the town and married the adopted daughter of a wealthy man, taking up life in his goodly residence, possessed of several acres and a horse-trotting track, on a hill behind the poet's homestead—the star-crossed lovers could easily have met secretly, and Emily might well have envied "the Queen's place."

In summary, the scientific terms in Dickinson's poetry—dealing with botany, chemistry, mining, gemstones, zoology—all specialties of Professor Clark—can be found by a study of the concordance to her poetry. She was part of the American enlightenment that espoused the observation of nature as a spiritual pursuit. This was the philosophy that Clark shared with Emerson, and President Hitchcock of Amherst College, as well as in later in life, with his Japanese students in Haikkaido where he traveled to found a College of Agricultural Science in Sappora, and where he was dubbed "Master" in Japanese by his devoted students. There is still a shrine to Master Clark there. Transcendentalism blends well with, and is derivative of, Taoist and Buddhist traditions of the East where gardens and pine groves are sites for shrines of worship. Emily's greatest occupation, aside from her poetry, was her plant conservatory and gardening.

Clark was the embodiment of Emersonian ideals, so admired by Dickinson, as he strove to replace the darkness of Puritan dogma as a champion of science. Emerson, inspired by Bronson Alcott and Margaret Fuller, foresaw the work of Darwin and heralded scientific inquiry, disavowing scripture as literal. As writers and intellectuals of New England traveled to Europe, like Clark, Ph.D. of Gottingen, they were attracted to German pantheism. Meantime, a desire to foster an original American literature was burgeoning along with egalitarian ideals. Whitman and Dickinson deliberately broke the strictures of old European styles of prosody, rhyme, and meter to consciously create an *American* style of writing based on free thinking.

Austin Dickinson's graduation speech from Amherst College was on the theme of creating a new American culture out of the glories of the Connecticut River Valley. President Hitchcock of Amherst College, a geologist who had discovered dinosaur fossils in the valley, and Dickinson's favorite sermonizer, Reverend Parke, had earlier espoused the same, declaring that a great poet would arise from their valley's inordinate natural beauty. Were they not prophetic? And was not Dickinson attempting to quietly fulfill their prophecy—by her late night oil lamp, secretly writing her new American, Transcendental art, dreaming of her scientist lover with his deep knowledge of nature and cosmopolitan culture. Little did she know that she was that great dreamed of poet!

Yet, it's important for young poets to realize that she did not write in a vacuum, a recluse, or "mad woman in the attic." All of her life, she was surrounded, or in correspondence with, learned and worldly family and friends, scientists, writers, editors, intellectual confidantes and working class servants who gave her their point of view as well. She had more of a daily support group than most contemporary writers who often write in rooms all by themselves without local professors and worldly editors as a constant part of their society. It is wrong to mislead young poets into thinking they can write as a recluse as well as Dickinson did.

As was demonstrated, there are many myths about Dickinson that need undoing. Reading her poems with her lover and mentor, William Smith Clark in mind, deepens their meanings and opens some of their opaque qualities to better understanding. It is why Ruth Owen Jones's thesis about the "Master" of Dickinson's work is important to American writers and poets, not for the scandal it must have stirred, nor for the gossip it likely brought down upon the poet causing her to flee into a more socially exclusive society, not to add to the speculation about her love life—but *for a clearer reading of her poetry!*

Bibliography Of Selected References

Amherst Historical Commission, ed. *Lost Amherst*, The Amherst Historical Society, MA: Amherst. 1980. [A pictorial geography of the 19th Century Village of Amherst.]

Bingham, Millicent Todd, *Ancestors' Brocades; The Literary Debut of Emily Dickinson: The Editing and Publication of Her Letters and Poems*, New York: Harper & Brothers, 1945.

Erkila, Betsy."Emily Dickinson and Class." American Literary History 4.1(Sp. 1992): 1-27.

Farr, Judith. "Emily Dickinson's 'Engulfing' Play: *Anthony & Cleopatra. Tulsa Studies in Women's Literature*, no. 2 (Fall 1990): 231-250.
———. *The Passion of Emily Dickinson*. Cambridge, Mass: Harvard Univ. Press, 1992.

Franklin, R. W., Ed. *The Master Letters of Emily Dickinson* MA: Amherst College: 1986.
———. *The Editing of Emily Dickinson: A Reconsideration.* Madison: University of Wisconsin P 1967.
———. "The Emily Dickinson Fascicles." *Studies in Bibliography* 36 (1983): 1-20.
———, ed. & introd. *The Master Letters of Emily Dickinson.* Amherst, MA: Amherst College, 1998.
———, ed. *The Poems of Emily Dickinson: Variorum Edition.* Cambridge, MA, & London:Belknap P of Harvard UP, 1998. Poems in this edition cited by "FP" & the number assigned by Franklin.

Habegger, Alfred. *"My wars are laid away in books": The Life of Emily Dickinson*. New York: Modern Library Paperback edition, 2002.

Hart, Ellen Louise & Smith, Martha Nell, eds. *Open Me Carefully: Emily Dickinson's Intimate Letters to Susan Huntington Dickinson.* Ashfield, MA: Paris Press, 1998. Poems in this edition were cited by "OMC" & the number assigned by Hart & Smith.

Higginson, Thomas Wentworth. "An Open Portfolio," *The Recognition of Emily Dickinson*. Ed. Caesar R. Blake & Carlton F. Wells, pp. 3-10.

Ann Arbor: U of Michigan P, 1964. First published in *Christian Union* 42 (Sept. 25, 1890): 392-393.

Howe, Susan. *My Emily Dickinson*. Berkeley: North Atlantic Books, 1985.

Johnson, Thomas H. *Emily Dickinson: An Interpretive Biography*. Cambridge, Mass.: Harvard University, Belknap P 1955.
————— & Theodora Ward, eds. *The Letters of Emily Dickinson* Cambridge: Belknap P of Harvard UP 1958. References to this edition will use this initial & give the number assigned by Johnson.
—————,ed. *The Poems of Emily Dickinson*. Cambridge & London: Belknap Press of Harvard UP 1955.

Jones, Ruth Owen. "Neighbor—and friend—and Bridegroom—", *The Emily Dickinson Journal*, Vol. XI, 2, Winter, © 2002.

Lombardo, Daniel. *Hedge Away: The Other Side of Emily Dickinson's Amherst*. Northampton, MA: Daily Hampshire Gazette, 1997.

Longsworth, Polly. *Austin & Mabel: The Amherst Affair & Love Letters of Austin Dickinson & Mabel Loomis Todd*. New York: Holt, Rinehart, Winston, 1984.
—————————. *The World of Emily Dickinson*. New York: W.W. Norton, 1990.

Leyda, Jay. *The Years and Hours of Emily Dickinson*, 2 vols. New Haven: Yale UP, 1960.

Maki, John M. (John McGilvrey), *William Smith Clark : a Yankee in Hokkaido*, John M. Maki. Publisher Sapporo, Japan : Hokkaido University Press, c1996. Subject: Clark, William Smith, 1826-1886. Massachusetts, Agricultural College President. Hokkaido Daigaku President..Alt title: *Yankee in Hokkaido*

Murray, Aife. "Miss Margaret's Emily Dickinson." *Signs: Journal of Women in Culture and Society* 24.3 (Spring:1999): 697-732.

Petrino, Elizabeth A. *Emily Dickinson & Her Contemporaries: Women's Verse in America, 1820-1885*. Hanover, NH: Univ. Press of New England, 1998.

Pollak, Vivian R., ed. *A Historical Guide to Emily Dickinson*, Oxford University Press; NY, 2004. {Contains the essays of various prominent Dickinson scholars on many issues surrounding her time.]

Sewall, Richard. *The Life of Emily Dickinson.* NY: Farrar, Straus & Giroux, 1974.

Van Kirk, Connie, *Emily Dickinson: A Biography*, Greenwood: CT., 2004.

Wolff, Cynthia Griffin, *Emily Dickinson*, with a foreword by R.W.B. Lewis, Radcliffe Biographical Series, Perseus Books, MA: Reading, 1988. Reprinted by permission of Alfred A. Knopf: NY. 1986.

Wolosky, Shira, *Emily Dickinson: A Voice of War, Yale*, 1984.

Jones Library: Special Collections. Vertical files of various documents on William Smith Clark, Samuel Williston, Emily Dickinson's Amherst, etc.: Amherst: MA.

Daniela Gioseffi

About the Author: Daniela Gioseffi

Daniela Gioseffi, poet, novelist, playwright, literary critic, essayist, performer, professor of literature, has traveled widely, presenting her poetry throughout North America and Europe. She has read her work and lectured at universities, cultural centers and international book fairs, in Madrid, London, New York, California, Barcelona, and Venice, etc., and performed her works for National Public Radio and Pacifica Radio in the U.S., CBC, Canada, and the BBC at Oxford and London. Her *Women on War: International Writings* won an American Book Award, 1990, and was published in Vienna and London, and reissued in a new edition, 2003. Her novel, *The Great American Belly*, was optioned for a screenplay by Warner Bros. and published by Doubleday and Dell, NY, as well as New English Library, London. Her fiction, "Daffodil Dollars" from her collection of stories: *In Bed with the Exotic Enemy*, 1997 won a PEN, 1990 short fiction award and was aired on National Public Radio's "The Sound of Words," hosted by Alan Cheuse. In 1993, she published her world compendium, *On Prejudice: A Global Perspective.* It won a Ploughshares Fund, World Peace Foundation Award, and was presented at the United Nations. Poems contained in her first book, *Eggs in the Lake* won award grants from The New York State Council on the Arts of the National Endowment on the Arts. Her four subsequent collections of poetry are: *Word Wounds & Water Flowers*, 1995, *Going On: 2000, Symbiosis*, 2002, and *Blood Autumn (Autunno di sangue)* 2006. Daniela has taught world literature and creative writing at various universities throughout the Metropolitan area for several years. She is registered with The Emily Dickinson's Scholars' Registry, and has published many critical articles and book reviews in numerous venues. She is a member of PEN American Center, The Academy of American Poets, The Poetry Society of America, and The National Book Critics Circle, winning the Sydney Sulkin prize for poetry reviewing in 1994. Her verse has been etched in marble near that of Walt Whitman and William Carlos Williams on a wall of Penn Station's 7th Avenue Concourse, and she has been awarded a Lifetime Achievement Award in Education from the Association of American Educators, and a John Ciardi Award for Lifetime Achievement in Poetry, 2007. Daniela has been a featured poet at The Peoples' Poetry Gathering, Poets House, and The Geraldine R. Dodge National Poetry Festival, and read her work, or been a featured speaker, on numerous campuses and at cultural centers nationwide.